The Piano Mirror's Power

Tim Mullane

ACKNOWLEDGEMENTS

First, many thanks go to Hildur Schmidt. She encouraged me in the beginning when only fragments of narrative threads and vague characters were fomenting inside my mind that would go on to encompass two books. Special thanks go to Tracy L'Etoile, a supportive early reader. Her genuine interest and comments kept me going. She stayed with me until the end of both books. And thanks go out to all those other readers of all ages who were engaged by my story, especially two of my dearest friends, Ron Saunders, Larry Campbell; Eric Lehto, as well as my sister, Sharon, who both gave the novel a careful reading, and to Jeff Gross for his necessary expertise. Lastly, I am grateful how words have opened up the lives of Maya Virk and Kougar Phelps to me. Those lives taught me that love is the only instrument of survival.

The Creeping Past

The screaming... The SCREAMING!

Again, the horrible, soul-wrenching scream rang out; a scream that shattered his mind and body. He went into a rigid shock. He felt a dark alien hand reach through his small boy's chest and grip his heart in a relentless squeeze.

Despite the stinging smoke, his unblinking eyes remained open as he watched his sister's arms writhing in the air. Suddenly, her pajamas became a bursting torch. She then bent over oddly and the flames began to suffocate her screams. The image burned Kougar's mind. He tried to force his eyes shut, but *something* would not allow him to.

"Run, Michaela, run!" Kougar howled. "Run! Please Run! Ru—"

Through his panic, in another part of his mind that seemed strangely detached, a voice said to him: *You could have run through those flames and reached her. You could have saved her... you could have STOPPED that screaming!*

..."Gaius. Help me," Kougar's voice gasped out as the nightmare frantically scratched at his insides like a demon trying to get out. "Gaius... Please."

Kougar's muffled, terrified moans crept down the bed and onto the carpeted floor like a heavy opaque fog. The mewing sound drifted under the bedroom door and out into the consuming blackness of the hallway where it dispersed into the silence like the last gasp of a tortured spirit...

It was a little after four in the morning. No light filtered in through the bedroom window. The morning lingered weakly somewhere off in the darkness. Kougar's parents, Joe and Maria Phelps, lay next to one another under the rumpled covers of their bed, just down the hall

5

from Kougar's room. Even though they looked deep asleep, they both knew that they were wide-awake. Both were as unable to open their eyes, as their minds were unable to let them fall again into the comfort of sleep. They both waited for the other one to say something. They both knew that 'The Day' was very close. Even though they wanted to say their own 'I'm sorry' ahead of 'The Day,' they never could. Joe's sigh filled the quiet space between them. He drew the covers over to his neck in a protective manner. His slender body felt cold, untouchable. He ran a helpless hand through his blond crew cut while his open blue eyes blinked intermittently like a slow Morse code signaling an SOS. Finally, he worked his lips together and said... something.

"You know, I think Kougar likes Bend." Silence. "Of course, it's always up to him and what... might happen. *Something* always does. It's just a matter of time." Joe's voice tailed off into the morning's emptiness that suddenly became as rigid as the pin of a grenade.

The pause gaping between them was abrupt as it was raw. They felt the room and their world start to close up upon them; it was closing with a sickening momentum that they tried to deny. They reached out, moving into each other's arms, seeking comfort and shelter from a fear they carried around in their hearts every day.

Unable to take the conversation further, they lay for a while, immersed in their own thoughts about their son who was down the hall asleep in his room. As if on cue with the first light of dawn, a bird outside Joe and Maria's bedroom window began with a plaintive chirp, a lonely chirp that went unanswered. The morning sun's rosy fingers reached through their window, throwing light across the bed. They shared a cautious, but heart-felt kiss, knowing that might be the last kiss for a few days because 'The Day' was almost here.

Back down the hallway, in the swallowing quiet of his room, Kougar had startled awake, his heart pounding, his body glistening with fear-drenched sweat. His throat convulsed in panicked contractions. The 'dream' had happened again. Once more he relived watching his little sister writhe, as she was being burned alive, right in her bed. The psychic trigger then fully pulled: *I could have saved her!*

A moan turned into a tight gasp as Kougar sat up in bed. His blue eyes darted around in the cruel, grey-blue light of a lurking dawn that couldn't extinguish the roiling shadows around him. He rolled out of bed and staggered to his dresser. He flung open a drawer and reached behind it where a pocketknife was taped to the back and snatched it free. Panting with fear, he opened the blade and pulled up his tee shirt revealing his left chest. Thin, white scars crisscrossed his skin. He needed to see blood. He needed to bring the pain. Then, in a barren corner of his mind, something stirred. The mocking laugh of his alter ego slipped out through his ears filling the air around him.

Put down the knife, you coward, Gaius' cutting voice said within him in an Irish accent. *The little cuts are only a temporary pleasure. Now, if you were going to thrust it all the way in... well, now you're talking. But you won't. Just sit here for a second and be with me; know that I have done horrible things, that I have contempt for fear, and that you could be like me; you could be... me. So, feel what I feel, know what I know.*

*

Kougar made it through the early morning hours by leaving his traumatized psyche like a spirit leaving a dying body, and submerging himself into the refuge of Gaius' world. He now stood in front of the bathroom mirror and stared with hooded eyes at what he was: haunted, a lamb ready to be slaughtered without a whimper. And there was that persistent, vague lack of recognition as if he was never convinced at what the mirror reflected. But this much he knew:

You're no boy and you'll never be a man. You'll always be... something else.

Kougar took one last look at the mirror, his deep blue eyes revealed nothing and looked right through him. His long, thick, blond-white hair was a mass of dreadlocks that spilled down on his shoulders like an unruly tangled wave. Knotted bangs hung down below his brooding eyebrows obscuring a face that was beginning to square with masculinization.

Kougar stepped out of the bathroom and passed by his bedroom window. If he had looked out he would have seen Mt. Bachelor. The late August morning sun revealed the mountain still had a few patches of snow just down from the pinnacle.

Kougar slouched sullenly into the kitchen. His mother looked up and quickly smiled, a cautious smile that annoyed him. Maria Phelps could see none of her olive skin and broad cheekbones in her son's face, or her almond-shaped hazel eyes that were arched with worry. But she knew her son and that *look.*

"Sleep well?" she asked, forcing her voice to be slightly hopeful. She tried to keep the slight tremor out of her hands but couldn't.

He gave her a veiled look and shrugged. "Ok."

Maria could read the anger below the surface and she felt the old, yet always newly felt pang of sadness that washed over her. "The nightmares?"

"Same old," Kougar replied vaguely as he walked by her.

Maria sighed, her eyes clouded over like the thousand times before. "Where are you going?"

"I'm going up to the high school and lift weights," Kougar grumbled.

"Okay, honey. Text me when you get there."

"I'll try to remember," Kougar said over his shoulder.

Maria knew that was as close to a yes as she was going to get. She sighed. Try as she could, she couldn't tamp down the helpless feeling she often felt when her son got locked up inside himself, and even with her mother's touch and love, she could not reach him. He seemed always beyond her, trapped behind a cruel sheet of ice.

Kougar walked across the front porch. He picked up his skateboard and made his way to the street thinking that being here in Bend was all right. Going from a city of almost ten million people to a town of barely eighty thousand—now that was some change! Bend had no freeways, with hardly a siren to be heard, just the train going right through town in the middle of the night, which sounded really cool to him. The outdoors were just moments away. Bend was situated in the high desert nestling up against the Cascade mountain range, surrounded by National Forests and BLM lands. His dad had bought him a used mountain bike and he was already tooling around Phil's Trail complex, the Mrazek Trail, all the way up to Mt. Bachelor across Dutchman's Flat passed Todd Lake and into Happy Valley. More than once he got happily lost. He did enjoy the time he was deep in the wilderness and ran out of water; nauseous and almost delirious with thirst and exhaustion, he finally made it down to Skyliner Road where he hitched a ride in the back of a truck, the driver telling him to helped himself to a half empty bottle of water that was rolling around in the bed of the truck.

Kougar skateboarded along the quiet neighborhood streets toward the high school, pumping hard to dispel his anger. Gaius, he thought, was never angry; he would shrug and laugh at the fact that 'The Day' was coming. But Kougar could only huddle in a crouch with no shield above him to stop the arrows of pain from raining down on him.

Grenfeld's Office

Mr. Grenfeld took off his horn-rimmed glasses, rubbed his eyes and looked up at Kougar who stood in front of him. It was the first day of classes at Mt. Bachelor High. Kougar fidgeted as usual, uncomfortable under any one's gaze. Mr. Grenfeld leaned back in his desk chair and studied Kougar for a moment, trying to figure out this young man's motivation. He couldn't help arching his bushy eyebrows at the sight of Kougar's dreadlocks.

He put his glasses back on and looked down at a sheet of paper containing the grade transcripts from Kougar's last school year. He looked it over carefully, murmured to himself, sighed, and looked back up at the disheveled boy who was pulling nervously at the sleeve of his grey turtleneck tee shirt.

"Well, Mr. Phelps, you certainly aren't setting the academic world on fire," he began, in a tone that suggested more of a question than a statement.

Kougar kept his eyes down and shifted his weight from one foot to the other and continued to fidget.

Mr. Grenfeld tilted his head and rubbed his white goatee. "Are you planning on going to college?"

Kougar kept looking down and scratched his nose nervously.

"Are you, Mr. Phelps?" Mr. Grenfeld demanded. "I can see from your grade transcripts, that you have just over a 2.0 GPA average. My class is an Advanced Placement class and you have to have a 3.8 GPA just to qualify to get in."

He leaned farther back in his chair while he let his words sink in. "So, you have barely a 'C' average," he continued, "and you didn't answer when I asked you if you were going to college."

"Maybe, maybe not," Kougar cut in with a mumble.

"What?" Mr. Grenfeld asked, his eyes squinting as he peered up at Kougar.

Kougar still kept his eyes down, shuffling his long legs. Kougar knew this might be a bad idea. He couldn't bring himself to look at Mr. Grenfeld but he could sure feel the teacher's hard stare.

"… I mean, it's not for everyone… but I think so," Kougar managed without a lot of conviction as he brushed back his long, corded blond bangs with a nervous hand.

Mr. Grenfeld let out an impatient sigh. "You think so? You have a lot of ground to make up GPA-wise. Everyone who takes my class is going to college."

He shook his head and took off his glasses and looked at Kougar, his eyes frank. "So, are you?"

For the first time, Kougar raised his head, and looked at Mr. Grenfeld for a brief moment, his deep blue eyes inscrutable. "Probably not," he said, barely audible.

The lines in Mr. Grenfeld's forehead knotted together as he tried to figure out the puzzle in front of him. Finally, holding back his exasperation, he slowly said: "Then… what are you doing here, Mr. Phelps? This is not an elective course. This isn't for just anybody. I can't—"

"I want to learn about death," Kougar cut in, eyes down, his voice a flat statement that had an edgy undertone and it caused Mr. Grenfeld to stared at the youth, trying to figure out this kid who wouldn't look at him. For the first time he glanced at Kougar's tee shirt that had a saying stenciled on it. He pointed at it and read the saying out loud:

"The end waits for every one... Indeed it does," he said wryly. "Why would a teenager like you wear a shirt with such a morose saying on it? Are you a budding philosopher, young man?" he asked, amusement in his eyes.

Kougar didn't respond. He looked up briefly at Mr. Grenfeld and then away, out the window. "I want to know why fear and death are so… strong." Kougar looked away from the window after his words disappeared through the incoming glare of light. For a brief moment, he showed Mr. Grenfeld his twisted sad smile... "And your class. …"

"The Transcendent Meaning of Love, Life, and Death in Literature," Mr. Grenfeld helped Kougar.

"It's one I would really like to take," Kougar finished with an understated conviction.

The old teacher arched one of his bushy grey eyebrows as if still analyzing the teen's cryptic smile... "So... death interests you?"

Kougar nodded and said just above a whisper: "Yeah."

Mr. Grenfeld grunted to himself and cleaned his glasses with his tie while he paused in thought.

"I would say that death is the farthest thing from every teenager's mind in this school—and rightly so."

"I ah, know a little bit about it, but not enough," Kougar said, his hooded blue eyes peering through his bangs.

"Okay then, you want to learn about death. Remember, this class spends most of its time with the other two topics: love and life. There are a lot of questions surrounding love and life that—"

"That's the thing: there's all kinds of questions," Kougar blurted out, his tone still low. "I mean, with love and life, there are lots of questions? Yeah, I get that, I think. I know I'm almost seventeen so I don't know much about those questions. They don't really interest me that much."

"Really?" Mr. Grenfeld asked skeptically.

Kougar rubbed at his chin nervously. He wanted to stop talking but couldn't help himself.

"I mean, with life, you know, you can think of the past, the present, what might happen in the future. I guess it would be the same with love—though I don't know anything about it. There would be love in the past, the present and maybe in the future. All of that is great. But death ..." Kougar trailed off.

"But death has no past, no present, no future, right?"

"Yeah, that's right."

Again Mr. Grenfeld leaned back in his chair and studied Kougar more intently. One of his thoughts asked if this young man might be thinking a little too darkly about death. Is there some deeper motivation going on here? He then noticed that Kougar had looked up and had met his eyes, if only briefly.

"I guess what I mean is that I want to know why there aren't really any questions to ask about death. Maybe one."

"There are many, Mr. Phelps."

"Why is death so much more… powerful than love and life?"

Mr. Grenfeld's face broadened with his smile and he chuckled. "Ah, now that's open to question and in my class we'll be reading some novelists and poets who tackle that debate. Some say that you can't separate life and death. As the great Greek philosopher Heraclitus said: life and death are one. In that vein, other thinkers have thought that if you have joy that you'll have to accept the grief that will inevitably come; that you can't have all the smiles without all the tears; that you can't have happiness without having, at some point, to suffer. It's part of the deal. You can't, in other words, have one thing without its opposite. The debate is as endless as what humans have and will, continue to experience."

A frown washed over Kougar's face. He moved his head slowly back and forth, his long, blond bangs rustling across his forehead. "I can see how you could have a debate about love, and about life. But death doesn't debate with anybody… not even God."

Mr. Grenfeld couldn't help having another smile. "I see you have thought about this 'death' thing deeply."

"Nah, but 'it' thinks about me," Kougar responded, an ironic curl started at the corners of his mouth.

"This is all kind of interesting, but all of that aside, you, as a student, don't qualify for the class," he said in a matter-of-fact tone.

"I know," Kougar said, looking down.

"This is really a class for those who are going to college. It's the cream of the crop."

"I know," Kougar replied, his voice resigned.

Mr. Grenfeld tilted his head and looked at Kougar skeptically. "I frankly don't think you could do the work. Can you write? Your grades certainly don't suggest that you can. How could you compete with the other kids? This is a seminar-style class, just ten students. There is a lot, I mean a lot of discussion, question and answering sessions. It's the Socratic Method. And there is the writing. Essays. We will even try our hand at some poetry writing. Expressing in written form and thinking about these three quintessential human experiences is what this class is all about. You can't just take notes, memorize a few things and have me give you a multiple-choice exam. There are eight spots for seniors, just two for juniors. You are a junior and you are clearly not in the top two hundred, let alone the top two in your class."

"I know," Kougar said firmly, a little frustration in his voice as he shook his shaggy head.

Mr. Grenfeld heard the frustration in Kougar's voice and his face softened and he stroked his sliver goatee. He studied the young teen's face for a moment looking for clues to help him figure this boy out.

"I must say," he sighed, "I have never had a request from a student as ill-prepared as you. Only the very, very academically ambitious ones apply for my class, those who want my class on their resumes." He smiled and continued. "I don't kid myself, no one would take my class if they felt it wasn't necessary in this hyper-competitive academic world we live in. Literature," he scoffed mockingly, "how does that prepare you for an academic career in science, technology, engineering and math? Right? I know those arguments from students, even from a few counselors. But you?" Mr. Grenfeld voice questioned.

"I want to be in your class, Mr. Grenfeld," Kougar said in almost a whisper. I could do the work. I know my grades aren't that good but I read. I read a lot. I read all kinds of things," and Kougar glanced quickly at Mr. Grenfeld, just enough to make eye contact.

"Like what? What kind of books?"

Kougar shrugged nervously. "Ah, just stuff. It doesn't matter. Dumb stuff."

"Okay, like what?" Mr. Grenfeld insisted, "What kind of stories?"

Kougar's feet shuffled under him as he squirmed. "Oh, ah, horror stuff I guess. About monsters... dumb vampire stories. Ah, you wouldn't know it."

"Hmmm. Sounds scary. You like being... scared, yes?"

"I am," Kougar said without thinking, grunted at his own words and looked out the window.

Well ..." Mr. Grenfeld finally said, "it's against my better judgment, but I will give you a shot. It just so happens that one of the two spots for a junior is unfilled. But I have to tell you that I'll give you the quick hook if you can't keep up. I am sorry, but that's the way it is. This is an elective course. You sign up voluntarily for the pain and disappointment so-to-speak, grade-wise." The old teacher smiled wryly.

"I understand, Mr. Grenfeld," Kougar said in a low voice.

"Very well, then, see you in class," Mr. Grenfeld said curtly and looked down and busied himself with the work on his desk. A moment passed and he realized that Kougar was still there.

"Anything else, Mr. Phelps?"

Kougar shuffled and began nervously. "I, ah. I ..."

"What is it?" Mr. Grenfeld asked still concentrating on the work before him.

"Well, I don't talk much, especially in a group of people. So, if I don't say much, it isn't because I'm not following or that I'm not up on what's being said, or that I don't have an opinion. I'm trying to work on that. It's just... hard for me."

Mr. Grenfeld looked up from his paperwork, his face softened, and there was warmth and understanding in his voice.

"Okay. I understand. See you in class."

"Thank you, Mr. Grenfeld," Kougar mumbled out his appreciation. He turned and quickly walked through the office door and out into the hallway that was teeming with kids. A tight, guarded smile was on his lips but then vanished as he thought about the real possibility of how tough the class was going to be. Well, if he flunked out, his mom would be disappointed but his dad, he wouldn't be upset, he knew. In fact, his dad, despite being a college math professor, really didn't sweat Kougar's mediocre grades. He seemed... almost relieved by his son's average academic performance.

He would probably flip out if I was an 'A' student, Kougar mused to himself. *That would rustle up some fears all right.*

Kougar's tall frame picked its way through the stream of students in the hallway, some rushing, some walking so slowly, especially the girls locked in some chatty conversations that seemed to Kougar to be competitions not real conversation. He arrived at his locker, and the word always occurred to him when he thought about his father: *helpless. He* worked open the combination lock and pulled out his skateboard. *Helpless... I hate thinking about that stuff.*

The Birthday

They both felt it… that distance. It spread between them like a deepening silence that choked off any soft words or thoughts of affection. The black-cloaked silence would not allow the respite of healing memory or allow them to turn to one another… only away, to stare off into the fathomless hole of loss between them. The inevitability of the dull numbness that possessed them on this day shamed them both. But they were too helpless to resist as the tragic glacier moved over their souls with its inert, hideous weight, every year on this day.

Joe sat in a deeply cushioned, leather recliner. His sandy, blond hair was combed back off his forehead that was furrowed with the pain of the past. He rocked the chair slowly as if trying to comfort himself; his clouded blue eyes looked off into the distance through the walls of the house. He tried to see back to a time before the cold, dark, spirit stepped between them, but the roiling black smoke of that tragic night stopped his vision. He knew tonight that that stygian spirit would lie down in bed between him and his beautiful wife. He would try, as he always did, to say something, but his words would go stone cold on his lips and only a sigh of grief would come out, like the empty wind through a scarred, hollow log.

"Joe," Maria's soft, low voice, finally managed, "Joe, it's Kougar's day, too. She tried to lock eyes with her husband but he couldn't look at her. Her words hung in the air and then disappeared into the silence. She stood in the kitchen, leaning on the tiled island, next to the sink. She brushed back the bangs of her thick, light brown hair that she let grow well below her shoulders because she knew her husband liked her hair long.

When was the last time he ran his fingers through my hair? She asked herself. *It certainly wouldn't be tonight. He would never be able to reach across the distance… nor will I. Oh, how I want this night to be over.*

"I know," came Joe Phelps's anguished reply. "I know... each year, I think it's going to be different ..." His words trailed off into nothing. Then, as if blown by a cold wind, his voice came back. "I guess we were cursed and blessed with Michaela and Kougar having the same birthday ..."

Maria knew what was coming next: the same scene, the same soul-aching dialogue in a tragic play. She tried to put up her hand in protest, but it was a feeble gesture.

"She was such a beautiful girl... so gentle... so loving—"

"Joe, please. Please don't—"

"So caring of others," Joe's grief-stricken voice continued. "She would have touched so many lives. She was the light in this world. She filled me with such joy and hope. I still can't believe she's gone... Oh, God."

Joe's eyes welled with tears and he covered his narrow face with his deeply veined hands, his pain as immediate as it had been seven years ago when his daughter, Michaela, his sweet Michaela, had burned to death.

"It's Kougar's birthday," Maria implored softly. "He's seventeen. We have to—"

"Yes, yes it is." Joe said the words quickly, trying to control his grief. He sighed deeply and wiped at his eyes.

Like always, Joe's words had washed over Maria like a heavy tide of grief, and each time she would try to swim against the dark waves that wanted to take her down, down under into that hole between them. Emotionally she would thrash around, kick hard with her legs, strike out with her arms—but the water was too heavy. Down she would go... and they would meet in the deep, open their mouths and the dark water would swallow their words.

In the hallway, just next to the living room where this sad scene was once again being played out, Kougar listened to his parents' anguish. They thought he had already left to go ride his skateboard around Drake Park. He had heard this annual conversation before and as heart-breaking as it was to listen to, he felt drawn to it, a part of him wanting to share their pain, to be a part of the family's shared lost. But he never could go into the room and 'be' with them. 'Something' wouldn't let him; 'something' didn't know how to… do that. If he didn't have his own tears to share with them, then he didn't deserve to be with them.

Where are my tears? Why do I just feel… rage?

Again he wondered why he couldn't be sad. But, oh, the rage he had in him bubbled under his soul, his blistered volcanic soul. He knew—and wasn't afraid—that when his rage finally surfaced to rise up like an enraged Phoenix, it would lead to his death. And he hoped that it wouldn't be for nothing, but there were no guarantees. And *it, all of it,* had happened for nothing… and *nothing* was all the explanation he could get. *Nothing;* and how that 'nothing' sliced at his heart with a jagged, sadistic blade.

He looked down at the saying he had stenciled on his black turtleneck tee shirt in gold letters: Be Happy If You Have Nothing In Life. He grinned, his lips twisting oddly. Not too many days would go by without Kougar thinking of how he would have traded places with Michaela. He knew Michaela had been his parents' favorite.

She was my favorite, too…

Kougar backed away from the wall where he was listening to his parents and silently moved down the hallway to the backdoor and let himself out into the late summer night. He didn't blame his parents for acting the way they did on his—*Michaela's!*—birthday. He never felt like celebrating it either. If Michaela could never be there, why bother?

Kougar had been very close to his sister. They were born exactly a year a part. They had been inseparable, no sibling rivalry; they played together like brothers. They were always interested in doing the same things. The fact that they had the same birthday made Kougar feel like Michaela was his twin. 'Irish Twins' his mother had told them. 'That's what you both are.'

Kougar walked around to the front porch and picked up his skateboard. He crossed his yard, dropped his board on the dimly lit street and started to get up to speed, pumping his leg hard, his wild, disheveled, blond-white dreadlocks blowing out behind him. He wanted to exhaust himself. Perhaps then, Michaela might leave his mind alone for a while. Usually, in the days leading up to their birthday, she would visit him often, popping up in his mind while he did the most routine things. At night his dreams would invariably be various horrible versions of the night the house burned down. Michaela's terrified screams would echo in the dreamscape, her burning arms flailing around like a pair of hellish tapers. And when he awoke to the alarm clock, he could still hear the screams, faintly, far, far off in the distance. After a moment, as he lie awake, staring at the ceiling, the screams finally drifted just outside of his hearing.

The last few nights, though, a different dream had come to him and he had been so happy to see Michaela free of the maniacal flames and smothering black smoke. He saw her in the meadow behind their old house in rural Virginia. The meadow was verdant with spring flowers that sprouted up among the tall, wild grass. A brisk, warm breeze flowed around like a gentle wave. Michaela entered at the far end of the meadow and waved to Kougar. He felt his face break out in a warm smile as he waved back and started to walk towards her. He couldn't wait to hold her in his arms.

Michaela stopped, gestured to her left, and a tall girl emerged from a dense line of trees that boarded the meadow. The girl walked up to Michaela, who looked up and they locked eyes for a moment. Michaela then offered her hand, and the tall girl took it softly. They then turned, and started walking towards Kougar through the swaying flowers and tall blades of grass.

He quickened his pace. How wonderful it would be to talk and laugh with Michaela once again. For a moment he looked at the girl who was holding Michaela's hand. For some reason, he couldn't get a good look at her. He didn't recognize her. Her face appeared fuzzy. Nothing about her seemed familiar. The soft, oval shape of Michaela's child's face was easy to make out. Her brown skin glowed, and he could see her looking at him with love. It always struck him how different she seemed. No one would suspect that she was his sister with her long, dark brown hair, the deeply, almond shaped, dark brown eyes, contrasted with his pale skin, blond-white hair and sharp blue eyes. Michaela took after her grandfather who had come from Mexico. He had been nicknamed 'El Indio,' for his copper skin, prominent cheekbones, and straight, jet-black hair. His genes had lain dormant for more than a generation and had then expressed themselves in Michaela.

Kougar was eager to reach Michaela and her 'friend.' He then realized that at a certain point, he couldn't close the distance between them. He walked faster but the distance remained the same. *I've got to get to her!* He broke into a run but the distance between them remained. He would then wake up and lie there, not with the fear and helplessness caused by the other dreams, but with the relief of having seen her the way he wanted to remember her. He was grateful for that…

"It was nice to see you, sis," Kougar said under his breath, as his speed leveled out. On his skateboard he flew through the darkened streets lit only by a few streetlights and the full moon. He hopped curbs and skidded sharply here and there, his wheels grating against the pavement. He wanted to leave today way behind him and he felt free as he rode swiftly, banking in and out from the sidewalk to the street, around garbage cans that had been set out for tomorrow's pick-up.

Kougar was breathing heavily as he pushed up the final hill and then coasted down into Drake Park. The Deschutes River rolled right through the park its dark waters reflected the full moon's light, flowing like a soundless, non-judgmental witness to what might occur along its banks. Only a little after ten in the evening, the park seemed oddly empty. The park butted up against downtown Bend and even on a Thursday night there should have been some walkers about. The tourists are all gone, Kougar reasoned, and it was the second week of the new school year.

The Park

Maya Virk and her cheerleading friends were finishing up a late dinner after cheer practice at the Burger Joint in downtown Bend. Maddie Johnson, Maya's best friend, dominated the conversation as always. She seemed to know the most gossip about what was going on with the 'in crowd' at school. Carley Campbell, Cheryl Schmidt, Amanda Wong, and Breah Kowalski were listening intently to Maddie as she described the woes of Katie Donner, the senior who seem to change boyfriends every few weeks.

Amanda just giggled under her breath like she always did, while not saying anything; Breah brayed out that big laugh of hers at anything Maddie said; Carley and Cheryl, made faces, sighed and snorted with exasperation and let out short, gasps of shock; Maya just sat there with a little smile as she took in Maddie's story.

Maya Virk was a natural beauty. Her slender figure was tall and moved with an easy femininity. Her oval face lit up with a gorgeous smile that came easy, genuine, and unaffected. Her liquid, dark brown eyes looked out through thick eyelashes with sensitivity and friendliness. Maya carried herself with a sense of maturity that made people think she was older. She was easily the most beautiful girl at Mt. Bachelor High, with her exotic, Indian looks. Her father, Raja Virk, was from India and had moved to American during his college years. He was studying to be a physician when he fell in love with the great forests of the Pacific Northwest and the Cascade mountain range. The vast open spaces of the great outdoors that teamed with animals, streams of salmon, the ecology of which fascinated and captivated him. It was all so unlike the urban sprawl and crush of humanity he had experienced growing up in New Delhi. He had changed his major and instead, got a Ph.D. in forest and land management and never returned to India.

Maya seemed oblivious of her beauty. Her easy, outgoing personality attracted all kinds of people. She made friends easily and not just with the 'in' crowd at school. She liked everybody and everybody liked her. She continued to smile as Maddie went on with her gossip.

"No way!" Breah cut Maddie off in mid-sentence.

"Yeah, way," Maddie replied. "It could have easily happened to her with that 'rep' she has. Remember last year, she missed, like, three weeks of school."

"Yeah, I remember," Carley chimed in. "They said she was out sick. Mono, or something like that."

"No, it was to have an abortion," Maddie said flatly, with dramatic conviction."

Silence. All the girls looked at one another with shocked expressions.

"Yep. That's right. I'll bet money on it. Remember she had been going out with that senior guy. You know, the guy who had to repeat his senior year because he flunked out. He was that jock who became academically ineligible for the basketball team. They said he could have been a star."

"That's right!" Cheryl burst out. "Eric Whitman! Boy, he was a cute guy. Right?"

"That one," Maddie said, nodding her head vigorously.

"Wow, that's heavy duty stuff all right," Carley concluded. "If it's true."

Maddie almost took offense. "I would be willing to bet my last—"

Maya's calm voice cut Maddie off. "Do you want me to ask Katie? I know her."

Maddie snorted, annoyed. "Jeez, Maya, you know everybody, don't you?"

"Her mom works with my mom at the Psychiatric hospital. I volunteer there and I have seen her when she has come to pick up her mom. We've talked quite a bit. I think she is a very nice girl."

"I'm sure she's a nice girl," Maddie replied, backtracking a bit. "But bad things can happen to nice girls. You never know. I mean, look at us here," she changed the subject, mischievously, "we're all nice girls with steady boyfriends!"

All the girls busted out laughing with Breah's huge laugh almost drowning out the others.

"Not me," Amanda piped up in her high voice, finally saying something. "Even though I might like it, no bad thing is going to happen to me," she concluded in a shy, but disappointed tone, her lips barely moved in an unemotional face. She was known to show her dry sense of humor every now and then.

There was a loaded silence as the girls exchanged astonished looks and then they all cracked up.

"All right, girls," Maya said as she got up from the table and brushed the crumbs off her cheerleading suit. "I've got to get back home."

"I'll drop you off," Maddie suggested.

"No, that's all right. I'll take a short cut through the park. I'm a little stiff from practice. I want to walk it off."

"Okay, see you tomorrow. Text me."

"Bye guys. Hey, good practice tonight. I thought we really rocked it. Good job. The first football game is in three weeks and we'll be ready. We'll be hot."

Maya raised her hand and all the girls started exchanging high fives, said their goodbyes, and piled out the front door of the restaurant.

Maya, with her purse slung over her shoulder, headed down Bond Street towards Drake Park, thinking of her agenda for tomorrow while also remembering Maddie's comment about bad things happening to nice girls. She was sure she would never let *that* bad thing happen to her. Of course bad things can happen and will happen to everyone eventually, her logical mind reminded her.

She shook off those uncomfortable hypotheticals just as she entered the park. The moonlight had been fairly bright and allowed her to make out the trees around her, and the various statues commemorating the

'Founders' of the city that lined the walkway. The park seemed deserted. She couldn't see any dog walkers or strollers. Large, old Ponderosa Pines towered above her, their limbs swaying in a breeze that blew down into Bend from the Cascades. She could smell the rain that was coming in about twenty minutes or so, she guessed, but she would be home by then. The moon then ducked behind a large bank of clouds and the park seemed to go dark. There were a few standing lamps around but they didn't give off much light.

Maya really didn't notice her surroundings as she had taken this route at night many, many times. She focused on the little bit of homework she still had to do when she got home. She then put on her earplugs, hooked up her iPhone and opened the music icon.

*

The large Man's heart jumped and began to thud against his chest while his breath quickened. *There she is!!!* He couldn't believe his luck. He had to take a moment and calm himself. He could feel slight tremors in his giant meat-hook-like hands as he gripped the steering wheel of his old Dodge van.

Back in town for three days and... bingo! There she is!

The Man had suddenly seen Maya in her cheerleading uniform as she walked down Bond Street. He had just been cruising around, mulling over plan after plan of how to do what he *had* to do, and *wouldn't-you-know? There she is.*

She hadn't changed, not one bit, The Man gladly noted, his cold, blank eyes taking in everything about her appearance. All of it downloaded into his one-track mind: her uniform... such a nice touch; it made his imagination spasm out in all the dark corners of his mind; her white, Nike cross-trainers; he grunted and thought, *they won't make her fast enough;* her long, flowing brown hair that looked so easy to grab on to; and her particular walk, her signature, the natural innocent swaying of her hips that made him stare...and stare so as to sear that motion into his

25

memory, his predator's memory; but that wasn't how he would described himself.

I'm no predator, he thought while he set his jaw righteously.

The Man again remembered, like it was yesterday, when he had first seen Maya on the track field. She ran the four hundred meter race. She was only a sophomore and had a great 'kick.' She was really pushing the seniors. He thought then that she would end up beating them out. He could easily see down into the track field from his van with his binoculars. The track field and the high school next to it, was very familiar to him. He had thrown the shot put here twenty years ago. He thought he still held all the school records for distance with the shot put and the state record for that matter. He didn't know why, but every track season, he would come down—some instinct compelled him—to check out the girls' track team. Nothing ever 'happened.' Then, last year, he came over to check out the team, looked through his binoculars—and something stuck him like a thunderclap. *There 'she' was.* And he was sure for the first time in his life.

He had scoured his mind for a way to approach her. *Let her know how I feel,* a voice in his head had asserted with the conviction of a sincere admirer and a dedicated fan. The voice argued for him to be open with her, to smile, to offer his hand, to speak honestly about the devotion he felt for her; to playfully ask her to just hang out so they could talk and laugh with one another, play some games, whatever. *She'll be the one and only date you never had,* the voice had concluded.

Yes, that's right, he had nodded. His overly large head bulging out from his shoulders, his neck tucked into huge trapezius muscles.

However, another voice had oozed out of the bowels in the back of his schismatic mind: *You'll have to make this girl talk. She's too young to really know what she wants. You will have to show her... Perhaps a little tough love will have to be the ticket. But, you'll have to be so, so careful!*

He had come close three times to having a 'moment' with the girl. But those failed missions had not been without profit. He had learned the girl's name was Maya, while he hid in some bushes on the street where she lived. She and some friends had passed by, laughing and talking amongst themselves when he had heard her speak in a sweet tone that sounded like a lullaby. It had excited him greatly. The next day, trembling with anticipation, he had almost shown himself to her while she was walking out to the back parking lot of the psychiatric hospital where she volunteered on Sunday afternoons. His shy side suggested that he put his mask on, because, well, his face could take a little time getting used to, and he didn't want to spoil their first meeting with the sight of his twisted, crooked grin that was set in a meaty, pock-marked mug of a face. It was enough that she would be able to see his blank eyes that were as dull as an old doll's.

When he was sure no one was around, he had opened the driver's side door of his van and unfolded his bulky six foot seven inch frame that strangely made no sound as his large feet touched the pavement. He had kept his van running, that was the first step in his plan. He had been so excited, even though his heart beat with its typical slow pound... pound... pound, and his breath had been deep and undisturbed.

Just when he had decided the timing was now, and he would finally have a nice talk with Maya, a primal instinct shouted a warning, and he pulled back with a quickness and speed that belied his ponderous bulk. All of a sudden, two hospital security guards rounded the corner of the building and headed straight for him. They would have seen him had it not been for Maya, who waved at the two guards who stopped, and walked over to her to chat. They wouldn't miss a chance to talk with the beautiful and friendly Maya.

It was then that he had really felt fear, for the first time. The prospect of being caught hadn't really occurred to him, but feeling the full force of the unknown implications struck him like a blow, almost knocking the wind out of his barrel chest. He carried around that same fear for a week, shaken to his core about what might have happened. He had to get away and get a hold of himself. So after a torturous week, he had left Bend promising to himself that he would return; because he knew, ultimately, that his love for Maya was stronger than his fear.

The large Man felt fate had dropped an opportunity into his lap as he watched Maya turn the street corner and head into Drake Park. He had gone through enough shame from that last time he tried to 'talk' with her. He was a different man now. He let his fear pass through him. He drove past Maya, not looking in her direction. He pulled over at the far end of the park and got out of his van. He made sure to grab his mask, something he always carried with him in the van, and in his pocket, his thick fingers touched the outline of a small bottle that was filled with chloroform.

That'll get the conversation started off on the right foot, he thought as he jogged down the walkway to get behind Maya. Suddenly, he heard a scraping sound on the pavement behind him. He whirled around to see some kid flash by him on a skateboard, heading off into another direction.

Practically taking up the whole walkway, Kougar had seen the big, dark shape jogging up in front of him. He knew that joggers and skaters could often be at odds. He calculated if he could squeeze by the huge man without offending him. *I wouldn't want to piss that guy off,* he cautioned to himself.

"Sorry, on your right!" Kougar called out, and he pumped hard to get by the man in a hurry. The man seemed startled and spun around, but Kougar was by him in a flash, and moved off to the right at the bend in the walkway that led uphill to another part of the park.

Just some kid, The Man grunted to himself. He stopped for a moment to watch Kougar disappear off into the distance. He looked around and saw nobody nearby. He went left at the bend in the walkway and quickened his jog. Up a head, about a hundred yards away he could see Maya making her way towards the walking bridge that led over the Deschutes River.

The Man knew he had to get to her before she reached the bridge or his chance would pass. He stepped off the walkway onto the grass so he could silence his footfalls.

Kougar liked to skate to the top of the slight hill, stop, turn around and then barrel down going as fast as he could. Nobody was around as far as he could see. He liked to do it a couple of times. He had time. No need to hurry back home and have cake. His birthday cake would go uneaten like it always did. If Michaela wasn't there to share it with him, why bother?

Kougar pumped hard and started back down the hill. He was in a mood to be reckless. This day always made him feel that way. *Let's go!*

The Man was closing the distance between he and Maya. Another fifty yards to go and he would be right on her. He was ready. The time was *now!*

Maya looked down at her iPhone and put on another song that she could listen to with her ear buds. The moon above her was then overwhelmed by a front of arriving voluminous black clouds. The restless, anxious breeze had strengthened and blew through her thick, rich hair.

Kougar was bombing down the walkway now. He thought if he wiped out he could always ditch into the grass. His blond-white dreadlocked hair whipped out behind him. In the near distance he could see that big jogger again and, also, someone, who looked like a girl with a short uniformed dress on. She was walking slowly on the path. Kougar didn't think much of it, just to observe that the big jogger was going to pass her before she got to the bridge.

Kougar then noted that the jogger picked up speed. For some reason, it made Kougar pick up even more speed. He was gaining on the jogger rapidly. The huge ponderosa pine trunks flashed by him like ski gates on a downhill slalom race. Kougar was getting ready to break off at another bend in the walkway to keep from running up into the jogger and the girl who was walking so slowly. She would just be in the way. And with his speed, he didn't want to plow into anybody.

The Man couldn't believe his fortune. Maya hadn't heard him come up behind her. Then, a break in between songs allowed Maya to hear the heavy footsteps coming up behind her. Startled, Maya gasped as she realized the big shape was coming for her! Instinctively, she ducked down in one quick motion, and The Man's ape-like arms grasped at the empty air.

Maya screamed out.

The sound pierced Kougar's ears and bolted right into his sub-consciousness. *Michaela!* He didn't think. He just acted. He adjusted his turn and stayed straight on the path.

Maya... (*Michaela*) screamed again as The Man tried to get a firm hold on her. She could feel his fetid breath on her face and the hideous strength of his vice-like hands as they tried to grab onto her.

Kougar could see that The Man was trying to do something to the girl and it wasn't friendly. He was trying to hurt her. 'The' memory of him sitting up frozen with fear in his bed, while his room was catching fire rose up in front of his mind's eye. His ears echoed with his sister's screams that poured out from the middle of the inferno in her room. He then acted on a desperate instinct. *Michaela!* As he was about to slam into the back of the hulking jogger who had one hand on the girl while the other hand fished around in his front pocket.

The Man and Maya only had a millisecond to turn to see Kougar's dark shape ram into them with a dull thud of colliding bodies. Kougar made sure that all of his impact would be right into the huge, bear-like Man. The Man's hand on Maya convulsed, jerked open, and she went sprawling off to the right. She rolled over onto her back and for a brief second, she could see a skateboard upside down its shiny wheels turning furiously. She quickly got up to her feet. She saw The Man and the skateboarder turning around and around in a grappling embrace. She saw the whirling figures head right to the edge of the sharp embankment and in an instant, The Man lost his footing and fell down into the river. Kougar yelled out: "Run Michaela! Run!" His words echoed out across the river's black water that flowed silent and deaf under the hidden moon. She walked quickly onto the bridge and started to run just like 'she' had been told. She looked back briefly to see her rescuer dart over and pick up his skateboard. He took one quick look at The Man who thrashed around

30

in the river like a grizzly looking for salmon, and then sprinted off in the other direction.

Maya ran and ran, her track-trained strides eating up the distance. Finally, she slowed to a walk. She was only one block away from her house. The rain started coming down from a black, starless sky. She lifted her head up and let the rain splash down on her closed eyes as she tried to blot out the vivid few seconds at the bridge. She stood still for a moment letting the rain bathe her face, feeling the adrenaline in her body subsiding. Standing with her gold and green Mt. Bachelor High cheerleading uniform on, her bare legs she felt cold. She hoped the rain could wash away the awful moment that had just... *happened*, like some wicked twist of fate.

Whew! That was more than creepy, she sighed to herself. No, she wouldn't tell her parents. She couldn't. They were overprotective of her as it was, and she was just starting to get some independence. Realizing that she was shaking, she breathed deep and felt herself calm down. It had just been one of those freaky, wrong-place-at-the-wrong-time, things, she convinced herself, trying to minimize the whole incident that still had its claws in her; that's all it was. That's it.

Yep, just one of those weird things. She then remembered Maddie's comment about bad things that happen to good girls... *Yeah, almost,* she thought as she let out a deep breath. And really, nobody, not her parents let alone Maddie, needed to know about it since ultimately, nothing, nothing *happened* all because of some stranger... some skateboarding kid. She wouldn't be walking through Drake Park anytime soon, though, that's for sure. Who had been that person on the skateboard? She knew that he had definitely saved her from probably a horrible experience. And, she wondered, who, who is Michaela?

*

Kougar's all out dash took him through the quiet streets that had settled down for the night. Winded, he finally reached his limit. He stopped and put his skateboard down. He had left the park far behind and found himself on one of the small streets that made of the old part of town. It was a block of small weatherworn Craftsman Bungalows, their overhanging eaves dropping heavily with the passage of time, and their low-pitched roofs hunkering down against the rain that Kougar just noticed. Drops of moisture dripped down his forehead. A lone amber streetlight revealed only Kougar's outline as if he was a disembodied ghost. A dog started barking at him from a couple of houses over, then stopped after its owner yelled a few gruff commands. He tried to remember exactly what had happened in the park, but it seemed like a blur in his memory; it flashed through his mind like a fast-forward tape: it showed the girl running across the bridge and the quick, sick, grappling with the huge Man. The Man had felt as thick as a Ponderosa Pine tree trunk. Kougar shuddered for a second to think of what would have happened if The Man had gotten a good hold of him.

That was very lucky.

In the back of his mind where the suffocating black smoke and murderous flames burned and scorched without end, he wondered: what if the whole thing at the bridge had gone badly and The Man had been able to crush the life out of him with those massive hands... would his sacrifice then be enough for Michaela?

He let that question work its way through his consciousness like a grinning death mask; it dared him to think that his death would be enough, but he knew different.

No, I guess it wouldn't... But it would be a start.

The Costume Dance

Kougar shook his head, his apprehension growing. He sighed nervously as he sat on the floor of his bedroom with his back against the wall, tapping his size twelve feet against the front of his bed. His stomach then began to turn and burn with acid. The familiar anxiety attack had begun.

But the wheels! He shouldn't have agreed to go to the dumb high school costume dance. But he badly wanted those high performance skateboard wheels that his mom had bribed him with. The thought of being in the midst of all those kids, the loud music, the dancing, plus all the *looks* he was going to get—it was going to be just too much.

Oh, man, oh, man.

"Look," his mom had persuaded him, her hazel eyes full of encouragement; "you have to start going to social gatherings with your peers. You are a junior now. And the event is for a good cause. I like the idea of the dance being a fundraiser. I don't care if you go for fifteen minutes, just hang out and listen to the music. You *have* to go. I promise you it won't be bad. You have to give yourself a chance. You might make some friends. Look, it's a normal thing to do."

"Yes, I am a junior and that just means I have all of next year to go to one of these *stupid* events," Kougar had countered.

Maria had wearily tilted her head to one side, gave her son a long look, and had let out a frustrated breath.

"It's always the same answer, isn't it? Next year."

"Yeah," Kougar had said quietly but hopefully, trying to get his mom to see his reason. "Yes, there is next year. I'll go next year when I know I won't have to spend another year with those kids…Yeah, I could do that. Okay?" He had almost pleaded, his blue eyes cast downward.

Maria then had clasped her hands together and tapped her two beautifully manicured index fingers while an obvious idea gathered behind her eyes. *At least he was talking about it and not just dissolving into a fit.*

"Christmas is a long way off, you know?" she had begun.

"What?"

"A long way from now."

"Yeah, so?" Kougar had asked, wearily.

And then Maria had dropped the game-changer: "A long time to wait for those new Skateboard wheels; the newest technology for boarders. That's what I hear anyway. And you said you are *dying* to get them. Right?" She had teased.

Kougar had taken the bait, hook, line and sinker. "Heck, yeah!" he had almost shouted, looking directly into his mother's eyes. Something they both knew he rarely did. His mother had noted it and a small smile had gathered on her soft lips.

"Well, if you go to the high school costume dance, your father and I ..." she had paused with great drama, "have agreed to get you the wheels ..."

Kougar felt the irrational panic starting, as an insidious queasiness gathered in his stomach. Even in the huge Commons area at the high school where the dance was being held, he knew, it would start to close in on him like the collapsing walls of a dark, smoldering closet... (The trigger slowly pulled) and fear always led him back and back. There would be no air, just smoke from a ravenous fire.

His hands clenched at the carpet underneath him. His chest tightened. He rocked back and forth and desperately looked inward for help... for relief... for a way to lose himself... to again be *not* what he was... He knew where to go, where he had gone many times in the privacy of his own room. 'He' wouldn't go to the dance... but *Gaius* could. He could submerge himself behind the mask and behind a *costume*. Safe...

Gaius managed to find his way behind the raised stage and stationed himself under the temporary metal stage supports in the shadows. This was the first time he had been out... out of the anonymity of Kougar's bedroom and in public. Going to the dance, as Gaius, was the only way Kougar was able to go. Other costumes wouldn't have given him the cover he needed. Gaius wasn't a costume... He was real... very real. He came over Kougar when the panic and loathing became too much. Kougar would then begin to fear his sense of self would collapse like the last thought of life and push his soul out behind him where it would look at him through the consuming blackness. At that moment, nothing would feel right and he couldn't sense anything that was... himself. 'Becoming' Gaius gave him an identity. With green eye contacts, seeing through shades of green, allowed Gaius, to see and be who he was.

Kougar had read all the vampire stories out there, he knew what vampires were all about, how they think, how they talk. He liked how they were apart, separate; that they were in control of those around them without having to *be* with them. They were always in control, except, when they were thirsty. Gaius was... necessary. He could see through the darkness because he didn't dream, he never slept; a transcendent force, Gaius stood astride life and death, aloof, inside the shadows he shrugged and had nothing but contempt for fear. He was everything Kougar wasn't.

Gaius was happy that the music wasn't as loud back where he was slouching in the shadows underneath the back of the stage. Skrillex's 'Kill EVERYBODY,' blasted out from the speakers in front of the stage.

Maya, her boyfriend Hayden, Maddie and Alex, sat with some friends at a table just off the dance floor. The table was littered with cans of soft drinks. Everyone was laughing and trying to talk above the loud music.

Maya, in keeping with her classy style, had come dressed up as a traditional bride from India. She wore a full-length gold gown with silver lace patterns. She had on a jeweled veil that covered the back of her head and lay across her shoulders. A chain of red rubies cascaded down her forehead. Rings bejeweled most of her fingers, and bracelets of gold and silver decorated her wrists. She just oozed beauty, poise, elegance, and a maturity that belied her age. All the girls had buzzed around her when she had arrived at the costume party with Hayden, who was dressed like

Arnold Schwarzenegger in 'Predator': sleeveless fatigues, combat boots, a sharp crew-cut, face-paint, and had a fake M-16 assault rifle slung over his shoulder. With all the attention Maya and Hayden had received, it was clear that they were the most popular couple at the dance.

"Maya, that is such an awesome dress," Maddie gushed loud enough to be heard over the pounding music. She reached out from the black folds of her witch's gown with a pocked-marked hand and touched the fine silk fabric. Maddie was sitting next to Maya at the table. Hayden, who sat on the other side of Maya, had a possessive hand on Maya's knee while he talked to Alex who had dressed as a zombie.

"Thanks, Madds," Maya replied, her gorgeous smile warm and genuine. "I have adored this dress for years."

"Years?" Maddie asked, surprised. "Whose dress is it?"

"It was supposed to be my Grandmother's wedding dress. But she never got to wear it."

"Wow. What happened?" Maddie asked.

"It's an old story and not a happy one. Maybe I'll get to wear it for her one day."

The DJ on the stage made an announcement in between songs:

"The Boys and Girls Club of Bend would like to thank again, The Mt. Bachelor High School Student Council for hosting this First Annual Halloween Costume Dance to help raise funds for The Boys and Girls Club of Bend. Let's hear it for Maya Virk, President of the Student Council, and all her council members that made this event possible. Great job, guys! Come on out and take a bow. Come on, Maya, bring your team out!"

Maya got up from her table and walked out onto the dance floor and was joined by the student council members in various costumes. Maya stood out like a jewel, glowing in her exotic dress.

The packed Commons erupted in applause, sharp whistles, hoots and hollering broke out among the throng of costumed kids.

"Hey, Madds," Maya began as she returned to her table, "I'm going to the restroom."

"Okay. I'll get us some more drinks and more popcorn."

"Cool."

Maya leaned down and whispered something to Hayden, who just nodded and continued talking to his friend. As she turned to go, Hayden reached out and pinched her on the behind. Surprised, she almost stumbled catching herself. It was certainly not a graceful move for the beautiful gown she had on.

"Hayden?" she almost gasped with shock and some embarrassment as she turned back around. She heard Alex and his friend laugh.

Hayden ignored her concern and thrust his chiseled jaw up, his fierce face paint giving him a hyper-masculine look. He reached out and took her hand and pulled her down to him.

"I just wanted to say," he whispered in her ear, "you look hot... very hot."

She gave him a quick smile. "I'll be right back."

As she walked to the restroom, she replayed Hayden's words back again. Yes his tone was soft, and she knew he had meant it. But there was another hint in his tone and she had noticed it lately, especially in his eyes: *Desire. Sexual desire.* One part of her was kind of excited by it; another part was afraid of what will happen when that time came— and her young girl's intuition told her that time was *soon.*

The restroom was predictably crowded. Girls were reapplying their costume make-up, giggling and joking. Maya said hi to a few friends and heard more compliments about her dress. She moved down to the sink at the end of the counter and began to re-adjust her veil, feeling the fine old fabric and wondering again about who had made it. She then noticed that all of a sudden the bathroom emptied out and she was by herself.

She looked into the mirror, her light bronze complexion seem polished, accentuating the sparkle of the red rubies on her forehead that spilled down from the middle of her parted, thick brown hair. She saw that she didn't have as many sun-streak highlights in her hair like she had had during the summer.

Her mind drifted again to Hayden's whisper. She liked him, liked him a lot. *But.* He would clearly be one of the most—if not the most—sought after boys in school, if they weren't together. He was the biggest star on the football team. Just a junior, he was already a highly recruited running back, and— she smiled to herself—would easily have an academic scholarship coming his way. He was athletic and very, very bright, good looking… and rich. His father was the most prominent lawyer in town. They lived in that big house in Broken Top. She admired these qualities in him and so did her parents who were very pleased that they were a couple. Maya knew that Hayden was going to have every success in life. With boys like Hayden, you could just tell.

But I'm not ready, she thought. *I don't know if I am in love with him. Sometimes I think so. I could be… should be. I just have a feeling. He won't wait for me. It has to be special, more special than anything I'll ever know. It only happens once, that first time. Only once… I'm not afraid. I just want it to be 'right'.*

She sighed as those things went through her mind, ran her fingers through her hair and headed out just as a pack of girls, squealing and giggling, jammed their way through the door.

Sophomores! Maya thought to herself. This dance should have been a junior/senior event only. She then saw a bunch of freshman girls headed her way and decided to duck down a small hallway and take a short cut that she knew well.

The maintenance hallway led to a side door that opened to the back of the stage. She could hear that the music had changed to some slow, ominous sounding rap music with a vibrating, pounding base. She opened the door and walked through and out into the backstage area.

From his place in the shadows of the stage, Gaius looked over as the sound of the opening door caught his attention. Under the backstage lights Maya's dress glowed and her jewelry sparkled against her cinnamon skin. Her flowing dark hair spilled down her shoulders and rustled as if she was walking into a soft breeze... Gaius watched her with an intensity that he had never felt before. It was like seeing beauty for the first time.

This girl. She is unbelievably... beautiful—and he realized he couldn't ever remember using that word. Involuntarily, he moved his lips to soundlessly say the word: beautiful, as she walked—no, flowed— towards him with that feminine poise that made her seem years older than she was.

Gaius watched Maya pass by, drinking in every moment with his green eyes. Never being able to be completely still, he subconsciously rolled his skateboard back and forth with a small movement of his left foot.

Maya was trying to figure out the rap artist's name that was motor-mouthing the lyrics of the song that was playing. Then, a glint of light on the floor to her right caught her eye. She saw the rolling wheels of a skateboard and they flashed into her memory of that night at the bridge in Drake Park, of those skateboard wheels that she saw for an instant that were spinning around as she lay on the ground. And she thought:

That person, whom ever it had been, had definitely saved me from something awful. Could it—

Maya caught herself in mid-thought and an instinct made her stop, turn, and walk towards the moving skateboard. Suddenly, it stopped.

Gaius' eyes widened with surprise, thinking: *She can see me!*

Maya finally made out the dark, shoed foot resting on the skateboard, and the long dark pant leg attached to it. The rest of Gaius' body was in the shadow of the overhanding stage. Maya stopped in front of Gaius but she still couldn't see all of him.

Gaius knew Maya was going to say something to him and he girded himself, knowing and feeling that he *was* Gaius, not Kougar. *Gaius, not Kougar...*

"Hey, are you here for the costume party?" Maya asked, her smile open and friendly.

Gaius didn't respond right away. Maya tilted her head to one side as if to say: well? He thought that was the most beautiful thing he had ever seen. He took a long, deep breath as Gaius welled up within him.

"Actually, I am," Gaius finally said, his tone smooth and formal, his Irish accent obvious. "And you?"

Maya thought the figure in the shadows was shorter, but when she heard Gaius' voice she had to look up.

He's tall, she thought, *and what an interesting voice. Not a kid's voice, but mature. It had depth. And that Irish accent! Cool.* Interested, Maya thought she would continue this encounter for a little bit.

"Of course I am here for the party. Can't you tell?" she asked in a modest tone and opened her arms to better show off her costume.

"Of course I can tell, but it seems to me, that you look like this all the time. You are quite beautiful; stunning, really," Gaius' accent purred.

Maya flashed a surprised smile and she almost blushed with an innocence that she was happy to feel.

She tried to keep a little composure, but she quickly smiled broadly and her deep, brown eyes glowed. "I don't think anybody has ever... ever given me a compliment like that before... and the way you said it. Thanks. Thanks a lot."

"It's the least I can say."

Now Maya really *was* blushing and fully intrigued. She tried to hide those facts and change the subject, though her heart wasn't in it. "Why are you back here instead of out there, in the crowd, enjoying yourself?"

"To be honest, my ears are easily bombarded by loud noises and the bright lights are...oppressive to me. I startle easily, beautiful lady," Gaius confessed, his voice even.

"Why do you speak that way?" she asked coyly.

"Of course I speak that way. Is it not the proper way to speak to a woman like you?"

Maya let out a warm chuckle. She was being charmed and she liked it "Do you really go to this school?"

"Someone does, but I don't."

Maya smiled at the evasive answer. "The boys here certainly don't speak like you."

"Well, to tell you the truth, I learned my English and grammar a long time ago, from teachers much different than you'll find around here." Gaius' voice rippled out of the shadows like a quiescent stream.

"How long ago?"

"I would say... more than a couple of grades ago."

"I see... Okay," Maya began excitedly, "I know who you came as. You are some famous Irish writer, aren't you?

Gaius slowly moved his face and upper torso out of the shadow of the stage. Maya pulled her head back in surprise and a slow appreciation spread across her face. Gaius long, disheveled, brown hair was brushed back off his forehead and tied into a thick ponytail. His complexion was pale; his eyes were an emerald green that looked intensely out from under moody, dark brown eyebrows. His lips were reddish and at one corner of his mouth, a little dried spot of blood was visible. He wore a tight fitting, white turtleneck tee shirt that revealed the coiling muscles of his deepening chest and long arms. Emblazoned on the front of the tee shirt was a Superman decal with the letter 'V' inside the decal not the letter 'S.' On the back of the tee shirt there was a saying in black letters: 'Immortality Is One Bite Away.' A few drops of blood marked his tee shirt near the neckline. He looked down at Maya, devouring her with his unblinking eyes.

Maya started to say something, but a feeling—and she didn't know where the feeling had come from—made her pause. Without intending to, she locked eyes with Gaius. She felt as if his deep green eyes were *reading* her...almost being *intimate* with her. A strange emotion stirred vaguely inside her and she couldn't help but feel that this 'eye-lock' she was having felt like a 'lip-lock'. Unconsciously, she put a finger to her full, red lips, and felt herself blush for a second time. With some effort and uncharacteristic shyness, Maya broke her gaze with Gaius and looked down.

"Uh," Maya began, trying to recover her poise, "that was a little weird... but cool," She smiled, as her ringed fingers gesture self-consciously.

"You felt... awkward," Gaius said as a warm, knowing smile started at the corners of his mouth and lit up his pale face. "I'm sorry. I want you to feel... comfortable with me." He moved back slightly, not fully back under the darkness of the stage. Off and on, shadows played across his face.

Maya recovered her poise but again, *something* wanted her to look and keep looking at this boy/man's face that was so attractive to her. He wasn't necessarily cute—but yet there was something charismatic about him.

"I am called Gaius," the Irish voice said.

Maya smiled. "Cool name. I'm Maya."

Maya reached out her hand. Gaius took his pale hand out of his front pocket and shook Maya's hand. Her surprised look came quick.

"Your hand... it's cold."

"What did you expect?"

Maya laughed and nodded her head. "You're good. That's really good. You have a very cool costume. And I can tell that you have bought into it. You play the part well. I'm impressed."

"Costume? Playing a part? Not me... I am what I am." And Gaius gave Maya a mysterious look that was partly a self-reflective one. "But, perhaps, sometimes we are better off being someone else than who we really are," his accented voice low, almost a whisper that carried a tone of revelation.

"You've got a point there."

She wanted to continue this very interesting conversation with the vampire. "So, you are a vampire, right?"

"I don't like to talk about it. It makes me self-conscious. That's not an enjoyable feeling for someone like me. I like to feel... detached. I prefer to observe."

"From a distance, right?"

"Precisely."

"What do you like to observe?" Maya prodded, enjoying the Q&A.

"A beautiful woman... like you."

Maya couldn't help moving her body into its most feminine pose "A lady, a woman," she began coyly, "can't you see I'm just a girl?" And she tried to look shy but hoped he could tell she wasn't.

"Nice try," Gaius' voice purred. "I see what any man would see."

"Really?" She noticed that Gaius fully appreciated her pose. She felt a new sense of empowerment flow through her sense of being. *I am enjoying this so much!* She didn't know when it happened, but she was totally absorbed in this bit of 'theatre'. She felt her real self had been lost and some *new* self was being created by Gaius' words.

"I have seen countless women in my long years... but you, you are unique."

"Unique," and she savored the word, especially because *he* said it. "What lady doesn't like to hear that word? Do all vampires speak like you?"

"I don't talk that often with others of my kind, let alone, know how they talk to their... prey."

The word 'prey' didn't register to Maya. She looked into Gaius' eyes and cocked her beautiful head to one side. "Your eyes... they are green. I thought vampire eyes were red."

The shadows moved across Gaius' face. "Despite what you have read, vampires are—" he smiled sheepishly—"are kind of like humans. We are all different, have different looks."

Maya probed some more. "How else are 'you' like a human?"

Gaius moved his face out of the gloom where the shades had played across his pale complexion. The intensity of his eyes softened and Maya could sense that his gaze carried words for her, words that she wanted to hear.

"I have… feelings… longings," Gaius said lowly, his Irish accent poignant with inflection.

Maya grinned. "I see. That's very interesting. Of course I know what you eat—I mean drink. Can you have feelings for what you are going to… kill?"

A pained look came over Gaius. "That has never happened to me… but I have… hopes."

"Why aren't you out on the dance floor or hovering around the crowd looking for a victim? You—"

"Prey. There are no victims. Only prey."

"Okay, prey. So why aren't you out looking for prey?" Maya smiled, enjoying the game.

Gaius moved his body out from under the shadows of the stage and looked intently at Maya. Again, 'that' something made Maya lock eyes once more with Gaius' deep, glowing green eyes.

"My *prey*," Gaius, said slowly, his voice, fatalistic, "my prey always comes to me."

Maya didn't realize how much *she* had bought into the make-believe/*real* scene she was in with Gaius. With an embarrassed smile, she looked down, but wanted to look right back up. She *felt* like she was just waiting for… something. No words, no more looking. Just waiting for—

Gaius reached out, cupped Maya's chin and lifted it up so he could look down into her eyes. All of a sudden, Kougar's anxious consciousness started buzzing from within. This encounter was going to shatter and reveal what he really was: painfully shy, uncertain, strange, emotionally stunted, verbally inappropriate—all the symptoms he had been diagnosed with as a child. This kind of closeness to a girl, this unbelievably beautiful girl, who, he now fully knew, was rocking his emotional world, was about to break down Gaius' sense of self and send him slinking off, a scared vampire running from its prey.

Maya felt the 'moment' take a hold of her and she played her 'part,' even though a strong and growing feeling inside her made her *want* this 'moment' to be *real. This is crazy,* she thought, *but I 'so' want it to be real.*

Gaius closed his eyes, gathering the force of his persona. *I'm not done. I like being who I am.*

Maya realized that Gaius' hand was not as cold as it was when he had first touched her with the handshake. It was warm and soft, but she could also sense that it possessed masculine strength. She looked at him with a feeling in her eyes that she could not now name, but she thought her eyes said: I am open to whatever you want to do. Do what *you* do.

Gaius dropped his hand and with both arms reached around Maya and drew her into an embrace. The feeling of their bodies coming together electrified them both. Maya took a short breath. Kougar within could feel his vampire's mask starting to break down. Powerful emotions that he had never felt in his life were filling his eyes, and subtle tremors crossed over his face as he tried to control his feelings.

"Are you going to bite me, Gaius?" she managed, softly.

"No, that would be a waste," he said in a vulnerable, low voice, his Irish accent husky with emotion. He lowered his face, his reddish lips just inches from hers. "I…I want to kiss you."

Maya felt ready for that and welcomed the "moment' to happen to both of them. She wanted to feel his lips press against hers; she wanted to release a torrent of newfound feelings that she was only now becoming aware of… and they frightened her with their intensity.

"But if I kiss you," Gaius' low voice turned tortured, "it would be… dangerous; our lives would never, never, be the same. I couldn't do that to you."

He could see that Maya almost begged him with her eyes to *do it* before the moment was gone forever. He pulled himself away from her with some effort. They shared a moment where they acknowledged with their eyes that they both felt let down. He then reached down and picked up the skateboard and tucked it under his arm. He had one last 'Gaius moment' in him before he walked away.

"I am glad that you were the one *prey* that I let go."

Kougar walked by Maya, trying to hold on to his Gaius persona as he locked eyes with her one last time. Once past her, he could feel the Gaius 'mask' was coming off. He quickened his step and walked through the door where Maya had entered.

Maya watched him go, still trying to come to grips with the intensity of what had just happened. *How strange and...wonderful that had been.* She tried to process the cascade of new emotions she had felt during that brief, but profound, encounter with 'Gaius.' The sheer power of it all left her a bit dizzy and almost in disbelief of what had occurred. She knew then that she had experienced something unique and very unusual. Something—a small voice said to her—that would never, ever, happen again. She knew—but not without some resistance—that she had just been an actress playing a part in a scene. There was no denying though that it had *felt* real, so real to her. She wanted to stay 'in character,' to stay in the world of Gaius' words… but that feeling was slowly slipping through and out of her like an unrequited ghost. Sadly, she knew that the whole scene with Gaius was just going to be a part of her daydreams.

I won't be able to tell anyone about this, she thought, *not even Maddie. She wouldn't get it. She wouldn't even begin to understand what it had felt like.*

Suddenly, she felt sad and sighed. She readied herself to plunge back into the crowd and join her friends at the table. She was sure they were wondering where she had been. Hayden would probably be annoyed with her.

That's all right. It was worth it...Gaius, she pledged to herself, *I won't forget. I will never forget… you.*

She then noticed an object on the ground where 'Gaius' had stood. *Ah,* she thought. It looked like a wallet to her. *Now, I'll know his real identity.*

She reached down and picked up the object and immediately felt the cold surface. *Ha!* It was just an ice pack, and it was slowly defrosting, drops of water dripped through her fingers. *Yes, that was a nice touch, the cold hand.* And then the quick thought came out of nowhere: *But I bet his lips would have been warm...* and she felt a sweet ache in her chest that she savored despite the pain.

She shook her head, almost blushing again. She dropped the ice pack and walked around the back of the stage and made her way onto the dance floor that was writhing with kids in costumes. She wove her way through the crowd and over to her table.

"Hey, Maya!" Hayden's voice admonished, his face looking more annoyed because of the warrior's face paint he wore. "Where have you been? We were looking for you. I sent Maddie to the bathroom to see if you were still there."

Maya sat down next to Hayden and put a hand on his leg and that seemed to calm him down.

"Oh, sorry," Maya said too quickly, but Hayden didn't seem to notice. "I lost my darn contact in the sink and it took a long time to find it. I must have just missed Maddie. I used a short cut around the back of the stage."

The music had stopped with the end of a song. The dance floor cleared and the background chatter of the kids rose up and then suddenly, it died down.

Gaius had persuaded Kougar for one last chance. Gaius knew this was it. He would never see Maya again. Kougar might. But that was different... so different. *That* didn't matter. *Look,* Gaius implored, *let's do the dance, then a quick look, and we're out.*

No, the inner Kougar had stated, with fear in his voice. *Hell, no!*

Come on, we can do it. I, Gaius, can do it. We read about it in that Vampire novel, over and over again: The Vampire Mating Dance. Remember? We did it hundreds of times in front of the mirror, just you and me in our own world. We have every move down. I'll talk to the DJ. That ten bucks you had stuffed in your pocket will come in handy. None of the kids will recognize the song, so we'll have the whole dance floor to ourselves. We are doing it for Maya and me. 'I' won't ever see her again.

No! came the inner Kougar's panicked reply, *we've never done the dance in front of people.*

Don't worry, soothed Gaius, *leave it to me. It's just the mirror, and me. Just like old times. Calm yourself. I've got this.*

"Hey look!" Alex pointed with a zombie finger at a figure that stood at the far edge of the dance floor. A spotlight caught the upper half of Gaius' body.

Then the iconic, rhythmic, lead guitar of John Fogerty ranged out in the song 'Run Through The Jungle.' Everybody seated in the tables around the dance floor turned to look at the tall, self-possessed vampire who moved at his own deliberate pace. They could see the lean, well-muscled chest under the tight tee shirt, and the long, powerful arms that swung in an easy, almost animal way.

Maya could hear the shouts: "Cool costume!" "Nice Look!" "That's it, dude!" Even Alex shouted out: "Sick look!" Maya felt her heart leap up and bang against her chest. *GAIUS!*

As the music blared out, Gaius, his face set in the haughtiest, yet unemotional face a vampire could manage, started his solo dance, his body moving to the rhythm of the music, his moves sensual and lithe, his muscles rippling under his tee shirt.

The costumed kids clapped their hands in in sync with the music. Everyone was transfixed. Maya, hungry to look again at Gaius, stared, enraptured at Gaius' composed, arrogant face. Gaius seemed oblivious to everyone around him; it was like he was in his own dance studio, using the mirrors on the wall to guide him.

Gaius stopped half way through the song. The kids kept clapping hoping that the vampire would get back to his dancing. Gaius found Maya's eyes in the crowd like a magnet. He gave her a full, unblinking, intense green-eyed look as he walked slowly toward her. He moved past her table as if he was in slow motion. John Fogerty's song continued to rock out.

"What's he looking at?" Hayden sneered.

"Well, he's not looking at your ugly face," Alex grinned, enjoying Hayden's obvious discomfort as the vampire stared at Maya. A long pause went by as if everyone was in slow motion, too. Then real time came back at last.

"What the... what kind of freaky crap is that!" Hayden started, anger in his voice.

Maya clamped down on his leg to keep him from getting up from the table. Even Alex reached over to help her.

"Whoa, dude," Alex laughed, "don't get flamed. It's cool."

"Yeah," Maya soothed, "what do you think you are going to do? It's just some kid in a costume. We're at a costume dance, remember?"

Gaius slipped through the crowd and vanished.

"Yeah, yeah," Hayden said reluctantly, his body slowly relaxing. "Yeah, I remember... but I won't forget that crap. Why was he looking at you?" Hayden looked in the direction where Gaius had disappeared through the crowd of costumed kids. He then glanced back at Maya looking for an answer.

"How the heck do I know?" Maya threw up her hands with emphasis. "I've never seen him before," looking innocently, but knowing she couldn't get Gaius' green eyes and pale face out of her mind.

The DJ put on a slow song and Maya saw her opportunity to distract Hayden. She stood up, "Come on, let's slow dance, everybody."

Hayden turned to Maya. "I would like to know who that freaky, wanna-be bloodsucker is," his voice still heated.

"Ah, who cares? I sure don't. Come on, let's dance."

Hayden eyes softened but the intense line of his jaw remained, his face paint looked ominous, and his voice still had that sexual tension in it. "Yeah, let's. It's about time." And he eagerly put his arm around Maya.

Maya didn't mind having Hayden's arms around her, and certainly didn't mind if Hayden kissed her, even right in front of everybody on the dance floor. They had been going steady for a year now, the most visible and popular couple at school. They seemed so 'right' together. Everybody said so.

But something inside her couldn't help but wonder what it would be like to have a long, slow dance with Gaius; to be able to look into his eyes the whole time; and maybe to... to loosen that ponytail of his and run her fingers through his hair.

Grenfeld's Class

It only took fifteen minutes for Kougar to skateboard to school, through the nicely manicured neighborhoods of Newport Hills and Northwest Crossing. Again he couldn't get over how deferring the passing cars were to him, slowing down, and giving him a wide berth. People walking dogs waved to him like he was a known neighbor.

He turned onto the road that led down into the school parking lot. The brown-bricked buildings of Mt. Bachelor High School spread out before him under the backdrop of the Cascade mountain range. Mt. Bachelor, Broken Top and just to the north, the Three Sisters mountains stood out, their very tops still showing slivers of snow from last winter. The school stood on the far end of the west side of town. Just behind the school the empty high desert forestland began. The Deschutes National Forest spread out for miles, through the Tumalo Falls area, and ran right up into the mountain range. Kougar had taken his mountain bike on all the trails, deep into the forest, getting to know the area fairly well. He didn't notice the view. He was thinking about the math tutorial hour his mom made him sign up for. While doing 'C' work in math was O.K. with his dad, the college math professor, it wasn't acceptable to his mom.

I guess I just have to suck-it-up, he sighed to himself as he coasted on his skateboard. Actually, that's exactly how his mom had put it. He wondered where she had learned that phrase. Not from him.

The rumbling roar of an accelerating motor sounded right behind him, breaking Kougar's chain of thought. A shiny, silver 335i BMW coupe flashed right by him, missing him by just a foot as Kougar quickly veered to his left and hopped off his skateboard. *Whoa! That was close!*

Kougar watched the silver BMW roar into the parking lot and dive into a parking spot. Four kids piled out of the new coupe. One big kid, a couple of inches taller than Kougar, laughed and pushed the shorter kid who had gotten out of the driver's side. They both laughed about something. The big kid, Kougar recognized, was Alex, the football player.

They had lifted a few weights together early in the mornings before the school year had started. He was an O.K. kid Kougar had thought then. They shared a passion for lifting weights. He had even asked Kougar to come out for the football team. Kougar had ironically laughed his 'thanks-but-no-thanks.' He then recognized the shorter kid, if six-foot is short. It was that kid who had sat next to Maya at the Costume Dance. He had that pigeon-toed walk that told you he was fast and athletic.

Kougar watched the pigeon-toed kid for a moment as he pulled up his board and walked toward the school entrance. If he was Maya's boyfriend, he sure as heck is lucky, Kougar thought.

For the first time, an odd feeling started to creep around the outside of his heart and then, in the pit of his stomach. He tried to ignore it as if it were some, brief, strange, sensation. He thought it would pass as soon as he hit the bustling hallway.

But it didn't. It… bothered him. Then the word flashed into his consciousness.

Envy! No... Jealousy!

Kougar shook his shaggy, dreadlocked head. He almost barked a laugh to himself thinking that it was useless to have such a feeling when there was nothing he could do about it.

Man, this sucks.

A kid's voice next to him brought him out of his little, newly found misery. Kougar had to look down to see who had spoken to him.

"Yo, dude. Nice shirt," a short, brown-haired kid with wire-rimmed glasses remarked. The kid gestured at the saying stenciled on Kougar's brown, long sleeve, turtleneck sweatshirt. It read: 'Look Under The Rock For The Next Revolution.'

"Thanks, man," Kougar replied as he shrugged.

Kougar moved through the throng of kids and headed toward his locker. He needed to grab some books and to put away his skateboard. He couldn't stifle this new sense of irritation that was growing inside him, and couldn't stop from banging his hand against his locker. He filled his muscled chest with a deep breath and let it out with emphasis, hoping he could expel this new, edgy angst. He then felt a newly formed current of strong, watery, emotion was surging through him. He felt himself being tossed and tumbled around by the wild current, while Maya looked on, from the safety of the river bank, holding hands with *that* kid, her sweet face watching his head struggling to stay above the roiling waters.

His hormonal chemistry no longer lay dormant within him. He stood against his locker as it rocked him like a body blow. He was confused... and angry at this new force that involuntarily ebbed and flowed.

I wished I had never seen her; never noticed her.

Finally, Kougar tried to reason harshly with himself, that he shouldn't be so stupid about it. After all, he was sure that he wasn't the only one who felt attracted to Maya, even as deeply as he did. He pushed away from his locker and got back into the stream of kids heading off to class.

Get in line, dude, he thought bitterly. He hated being in any line. He could see himself and a bunch of other goofy, awkward, boys in a long line, waiting, hopelessly, hopeless.

He snorted derisively to himself. *That is really weak. Dude, you are weak.*

He decided he hated this newfound weakness in him and he was going to battle it head-on. The big-picture voice in him was saying again: 'you can't want what you want.' Yes, he *wanted* with every fiber of being, that his sister Michaela could still be alive; he wanted his father not to be ashamed of him... And now, he wanted what he should have *never* wanted: to get next to Maya and to have the strength to be able to look into her eyes.

Yeah, fat chance, Romeo... you, are no Gaius, that's for sure.

He figured that if he concentrated on being angry; to keep repeating how obviously hopeless the whole prospect was, that he could make the ache in his heart subside.

Damn. Damn. I don't like it.

He wandered around the hallways until the last minute before the new class hour started, working on his solution. He looked up and saw that he was in front of the tutorial room. He never looked forward to doing math, but he did look forward to the distraction of trying to figure out how all the darn algebra symbols work. He would even enjoy some torturous word problems. *Bring it on!*

He opened the frosted glass door walked through and closed the door behind him. The tutorial room had four separate desks in U-shape cubicles with chalkboards. The room was lined with bookshelves with all kinds of math textbooks. He slowly walked down the row of cubicles. The first three were empty, and as he came to the last one, he could see a girl who had her back turned to him as she wrote out some algebra symbols and equations on the chalk board. She wore a pink sweater with her blue jeans. Her curly brown hair cascaded down her back.

Oh, great. A girl, Kougar thought quickly to himself as his lips drew into a grim line, but he did notice—something he was doing instinctively now—how shapely her figure fit into her clothes. *Nice. Okay. Try not to be so damn shy!*

Kougar had figured his student-volunteer tutor was going to be some nerdy, math-geek kid with thick, black, horn-rimmed glasses.

A girl.

He hated the prospect of looking dumb in front of a girl.

Oh, well.

Kougar thought he should say something, but he didn't want to interrupt the girl while she wrote on the blackboard. Finally, he tried to say something but the mumble never made it passed his lips. He gave up and decided to wait for her to finish.

"Didn't think you would be seeing a girl math tutor, did you?"

The girl's soft voice flowed into his startled consciousness with an unbearable familiarity. She continued to write on the board with her back to him.

"Don't worry. I won't bite or call you stupid. Math is not easy. Most people don't just get 'it.' You have to work at it until it makes sense. I am here to help you do that."

Maya Virk turned around and flashed her warm, beautiful smile. She looked up at Kougar with her kind, liquid brown eyes.

"I'm Maya; Maya Virk, your tutor. She reached out her hand.

Kougar froze. He hoped his frozen face didn't look too stupid. He looked at her hand for a moment as if it were imbued with some supernatural ability that might grab a hold of his soul as well as his hand. An awkward moment passed between them that seemed like five minutes.

Maya didn't break off her smile but she dropped her hand. She looked down at a piece of paper on the desk.

"You are," and she looked again at the paper, Kougar Phelps. Right? Kougar, now that's an unusual name. I like it. It's cool."

Maya smiled in that quick, easy, way of hers.

Kougar shuffled his feet, trying to get the numbness out of his body. He was trying to come to grips with how close Maya was to him. *It's face to face!* He then remembered how mad he was as the new feelings in him started to spike. He avoided looking directly at her for only the briefest of seconds, which still felt like he was staring at her.

"Ah," he finally managed harshly, trying to control his anger. "Ah, I think there is a mistake. Yes, there is a mistake."

And with that, Kougar turned abruptly around, his long, dreadlocked blond hair bouncing around his shoulders. He quickly beat a retreat to the door.

Maya called after him, her tone confused. "You're Kougar, right?"

Kougar was already through the door and gone.

"Now *that* was awkward," Maya said out loud because she knew no one else was in the room. She then sighed a question mark, trying to process what had just happened. She had no answers except that that 'differently' looking kid didn't want a girl for a tutor.

The next few class hours went by in a haze for Kougar. He kept playing that scene in the tutorial room over and over again in his head. One part of him argued that he had done the right thing; the only thing he could have done: leave in that angry huff. The other part argued—and as the minutes passed, more and more convincingly—that just being near to her was worth it despite his almost overwhelming sense of shyness and the fact that she was someone else's; that she would always be someone else's.

He thought he heard his geography teacher assign some homework, something about reading the chapter regarding how physical environments shape human cultures. In history class, he stared out the window, picking up bits in pieces of the teacher's lecture on how slavery shaped the southern states of the Union.

Finally, he found himself in the last class of the day, the one he always looked forward to: Mr. Grenfeld's AP lit class. The class was in a small seminar room with dozen or so desks and chairs. Mr. Grenfeld stood behind a tabletop lectern that sat on a large desk at the front of the room. He was looking down through his glasses at his lecture notes. The 'cream-of-the-crop' seniors were coming through the door. They all seemed to know one another.

Of course, all the smart kids do, Kougar sniffed. Naturally, he sat in the last row of desks. There were two desks and he was in the corner one. No one else sat in the back row. The other kids had kind of sized him up and no one volunteered to sit next to him. They all wondered what he was doing in this class. His shaggy looks were in contrast to the basically clean-cut boys and fairly dressed senior girls, none of who Kougar had thought to really look at. He just listened and observed from the back. Four weeks into class and Mr. Grenfeld hadn't made a point to call on Kougar.

Well, so far, so good. Kougar knew though, sooner or later, that Mr. Grenfeld would arch his bushy, salt and pepper eyebrows and search him out with those intense, academic eyes.

I hope something stupid doesn't come out of my mouth.

Mr. Grenfeld cleared his throat while shuffling his papers.

"I usually don't allow this because we are some weeks into the class, but I will make an exception because of who it is. Maya Virk is going to join us. Perhaps some of you know her. She easily qualifies for this class and I think she'll be a great addition, and add to the already smart and stimulating discussions we've been having. She, along with Kougar back there, would give us our two juniors... Ah, there she is."

Maya blew through the door.

"Hello, Maya," Mr. Grenfeld greeted.

"Hi, Mr. Grenfeld, sorry I'm late. I had to make sure with Admissions that I was okay to join this class. I'm so excited." She looked around and flashed her lovely smile.

Obviously, all the kids knew Maya and greeted her as she made her way to the back row of desks. She was in the middle of saying 'hi' to Matt Barnes, when she noticed Kougar sitting in the back row and couldn't help the brief, puzzled frown that came over her face.

"Oh, hi, again," Maya said, ironically, out of the side of her mouth, as she sat down in the desk next to Kougar.

Kougar, with his chin cupped in his hand didn't look at her but gave her a small wave with his other hand as he tried to fight down those new feelings that welled up again as Maya sat next to him.

Damn, she's sitting so close! She can't know, or ever know what I'm feeling. The shame would be unbearable.

Mr. Grenfeld cleared his throat again. "Ah, Kougar, since you and Maya are the only juniors, I'm going to pair you guys up for our in-class writing exercises. Perhaps," and Mr. Grenfeld smiled mischievously, "perhaps she can get you to say something."

All the kids laughed at Kougar's expense, but it was all, from their point of view, in good fun. The grim line of his mouth said he wasn't about to laugh.

As the kids had their chuckle, under the laughs, Maya turned, looked at Kougar, and said in an annoyed voice:

"Kougar Phelps, right?"

"Ah, yeah, that's me," Kougar mumbled back.

"Why did you leave the tutorial is such a huff?"

"Ah, like I said, there was a mistake," Kougar said, half-heartedly, not knowing what else to say, as he brushed nervously at the long bangs on his forehead.

"What kind of mis—"

Saved by the beginning of Mr. Grenfeld's lecture Kougar cut Maya off.

"Shish," and he pointed at the old teacher who was beginning to pace back and forth behind his lectern.

Kougar didn't see—because he wouldn't look—the quick look of frustration that came over Maya's beautiful face. He just wanted to stare at her. It took all of his willpower not to. The war inside him had definitely started. His throat-tightening shyness battled with his increasing boy/man chemistry. All the new hair on his body, his deepening voice, his expanding muscles, and those new, impressionistic, racy dreams—all of it, was starting to create, hormone by hormone, desire by desire, instinct by instinct, a different Kougar. Just recently, without warning, he felt he had to smack his lips shut or a mad growl would shout out of his chest and he would morph into a single, raw nerve.

He could hardly hear Mr. Grenfeld's words as the conflict within him raged. Outwardly, his face was impassive as a teenage statue. Then, as the frontline of one part of the battle buckled, he looked at Maya with all the stealth he could manage.

Unable to resist, he employed his plan to take the most furtive glances at Maya that he had the courage to try…

The lean-forward-in-the-desk-quick-look.

The lean-backward-in-the-desk-quick-look.

The quick-look-around-at-everything-look.

The drop-the-pencil-quick-sideways-look.

It's working, he thought to himself with relief. *She hasn't noticed. Nice work.*

"Ah, Mr. Phelps?" Mr. Grenfeld began as he pointed to Kougar.

Kougar was deep into his surveillance strategy and didn't hear the old teacher calling on him.

"Mr. Phelps," Mr. Grenfeld prompted again.

Maya turned to Kougar; her voice had a mocking edge. "Hey, 'Kougar,' that is your name, right?"

She pointed toward Mr. Grenfeld who was waiting for Kougar. All the kids turned back to look at Kougar and they laughed at his awkward moment.

Kougar felt started for a moment under all the scrutiny.

"Oh, ah, yes?"

"Well, good. I am glad that Maya did get you to say 'something'," Mr. Grenfeld said, his words poking fun while he smiled through his thick glasses.

"I know you are concentrating on writing your notes, but I would like your take on Hamlet's conflicted intentions. Everyone else has had their say."

There was a definite quiet pause as Kougar tried to gather his thoughts. He could feel Maya's mocking, amused, gaze. Mr. Grenfeld tried to prompt Kougar.

"You might say, as many of us here have hinted at, is that humans have…a flaw; a very deep flaw; but what do you think that flaw is?"

Kougar squirmed in his desk and shook his shaggy head as he always did when he was nervous. He could sense Maya's amusement growing, and without looking (there was no way he was going to do that), he knew her mocking smile would be spreading across her face.

"Ah," and he waved a diffident hand in the air. "Ah, I pass."

The kids snickered again. Maya just kept that smile on her face.

"Come now, Kougar," Mr. Grenfeld encouraged. "Do you have an idea of what that deep flaw could be? It could be anything. It could—"

"We all need too much," Kougar began so lowly that the class couldn't hear him. Mr. Grenfeld leaned forward and cupped a hand to his ear. Maya heard Kougar and her mocking smile slowly vanished. A soft look of curiosity and attentiveness came over her face.

"Say again?"

"We, us, humans, we need too much," Kougar managed to say louder, his eyes looking down at his desk.

The whole class became quiet. Kids shifted in their chairs so they could look back at Kougar. Mr. Grenfeld stroked his silvery goatee as he studied Kougar, surprised, but not surprised.

"So, that's a flaw? Doesn't seem too bad of a flaw. We all have it. Hamlet is human."

Kougar kept his eyes down as he drew an invisible design on his desktop. He let out a sigh from deep inside him.

"He's too damaged. He's too… ashamed to let himself have that flaw. He says …" Kougar paused, and stopped drawing his psychological design for a moment. His torso twisted slightly as if some inner spirit wanted to speak for him. He slowly grabbed at his chest trying keep the voice within him down. But he relented with a shrug of his shoulders and spoke in a low voice that seemed like a confession.

"Hamlet says no to Ophelia, no to love. He wants to do battle with all his passions and… eliminate all of them. He hopes that might save him, 'if' he is worth saving."

The class was still quietly absorbing Kougar's words, searching their own experiences. Mr. Grenfeld cleared his throat with his own thoughtfulness.

"Why? Why does he reject Ophelia?"

Again, Kougar felt compelled to glance at Maya, but he forced his eyes to look away and started to draw his design once more. She still observed him in curiosity. 'Something' in her wanted Kougar to turn his head to her so they could have a long look at each other, and perhaps, she might be able to figure out what was behind Kougar's deep blue eyes that were partly hidden by his long bangs. Then, for some reason, a waylaid thought passed through her mind:

He's odd looking in a cute way, but certainly no Gaius.

Perturbed, she gave her head a slight shake. Again, the face of Gaius came to her mind like an old love song imprinted on her emotions, her fantasy emotions. She couldn't get over how the scene between her and the vampire, Gaius, at the costume dance had been... so wonderful... so exciting. She had nothing, nothing to compare it too or the way it had made her feel. She couldn't speak of it. She was afraid that just the attempt to explain it to Maddie would diminish its original power. It was a special secret that she was happy to carry around. A part of her was dying inside to find out who was behind the disguise of Gaius. Often, she found herself taking the long way to class to scan the hallways for a boy that might have, could have, been Gaius. She felt a little silly looking. After all, she was plenty happy with Hayden, even if she did find the kid who played Gaius, what then? Not being in that magical scene at the dance would surely make it an awkward moment. Despite that part of her that was curious about who 'played' Gaius, she knew in her heart that she really didn't want to find out. Gaius really didn't exist except in her memory, her panting memory. Her heart quickened as she remembered how sensually he danced. She almost blushed remembering his searing, green-eyed look; a look that saw all the way into everything that was making her a... woman... and no longer a girl.

"Well?" Mr. Grenfeld prodded Kougar. "Why do you think Hamlet rejects Ophelia?"

"When you are in love, ah, you are powerless, right? So, Hamlet is ashamed of that. Powerlessness. To be or not to be. That is a stupid question when you are suffering from love. He doesn't want any piece of that. Love is an illusion. Both people 'have' to agree to be flawed. Hamlet won't go there."

Mr. Grenfeld rubbed his chin in thought. One by one, the other kids turned their looks away from Kougar and back to the old teacher. They were all surprised at the depth of Kougar's analysis. They were all reassessing their opinion of the quiet, dreadlocked junior, especially Maya.

Mr. Grenfeld harrumphed deep in his throat. "Ah, interesting take, Kougar. But those ideas were not in your essay."

"I know."

"Why is that?"

"They just came to me right now. I guess I had a Hamlet-like epiphany."

Chuckles murmured through the class. Kougar's face expressed surprise and then embarrassment. He wasn't trying to be funny. Mr. Grenfeld nodded with a big smile on his face.

"No, not the kind of epiphany that Hamlet had about his madness and its consequences... Maybe, it's about my own little madness."

Kougar's matter-of-fact voice trailed off with a strain of embarrassment as he heard his own words and what they said about him.

Saved by the class-ending bell, Kougar got up quickly and was the first one out the door as he heard Mr. Grenfeld's instructions.

"Next week, we'll start on the poetry section. Come prepared."

Kougar moved quickly through the throng of kids in the hallway. He felt the side of his face was still burning under Maya's gaze. He tried to shake it off.

Talk about the spotlight!

"Hey, Kougar," came Maya's voice, insistent, like a command from behind him.

Kougar stopped in his tracks, almost frozen, Maya's voice having a strange control over him, compelling him to turn around and look at her. He managed not to turn around to face her. She walked by him and leaned close to his ear. He could almost feel her full, promising lips on his ear. His heart thudded in his chest; he stood stock still like a deer in the headlights. He wanted to sprint away but his legs were set in stone.

"Yo, dude," came Maya's accusing whisper in his ear, "if you want to look at me, don't be so sneaky about it. That's rude."

Maya's whisper lashed coldly, but intimately, at his ear. Yes, the words stung, and he felt stupid. He also thought her disdain had been worth it. Rejection felt... oddly good.

Maya's hair brushed lightly against Kougar as she passed him. She didn't look back, but hoped—for some silly reason— that Kougar would be looking at her as she walked away.

Of course Kougar looked at Maya's retreating figure, noticing how beautifully she walked. It was like a language that spoke to all that he was physically becoming. All of a sudden, that language turned bittersweet—another new emotion that rocked his inner world. The admiration in his eyes slowly faded. Anger spread from his black pupils as reality imposed its facts on him. Maya will always be with somebody else and it doesn't take a Hamlet-epiphany to know that's how it is.

Confrontation with Hayden

It took Kougar a good fifteen seconds to finally get his legs to move. His anger finally subsided. During that time, the traffic of kids poured around him like he was an odd rock that protruded up in the middle of a fast moving river. No one noticed the glassy look in his eyes that seemed like an empty computer screen that was trying to boot-up.

He made his way to his locker with Maya's whisper still cutting at his ear. He strapped on his backpack, grabbed his skateboard, and slammed his locker shut. He wanted to just get out and ride hard. Maybe, if he could go fast enough, to tear all out on his board, he could leave behind the unwelcomed emotions that were creating havoc in his mind. He felt he was morphing into…something; some new identity within him was birthing amidst the tornadic gusts of his newfound roaring needs, desires, anger… and fears.

Kougar burst though the exit doors. He hopped on his skateboard, and headed down the sidewalk picking up speed like a runaway train. He weaved in and out, buzzing by shocked kids who were startled by his hurtling form, his dreadlocks whipping out behind him.

Hayden Murphy parked his silver BMW next to the curb waiting to pick up Maya. He was anxious to see her. He didn't have any classes with her and while they usually sat together in the cafeteria at lunch with their friends, he had to miss lunch to get his car tires rotated. He was eager to hug and kiss her beautiful face and feel her respond to his embrace. He was looking forward to tonight. They had agreed to do some homework together over at his house. His parents were going out for dinner and a movie. Hayden knew that Wednesday night was date night for his parents. He and Maya would be alone. And, as far as Hayden was concerned, they didn't get enough alone time. She had her cheerleading practice and he had football practice. He was a star but he worked at it. His family was full of overachievers and he wasn't going to be an exception. Maya and Hayden were so busy with academics and they both were open about how they competed with each other to get the higher GPA.

Yeah, we push each other. I'm beating her this year, Hayden thought to himself with a slight, fierce grin on his lips, and a look of determination in his brown eyes. He pulled his rearview mirror down to see if his hair was in place. He rearranged a few wayward locks of his reddish, brown hair, took another look and cocked his head to the right as he always did when acknowledged to himself that things were cool.

Their friends always said how they seemed so great together. He had to admit that they were *perfect* together, and every day, he realized that more and more. He leaned back in his car seat and sighed, flushed with the absolute conviction that not only was Maya the most beautiful, talented girl in school—she was all his. He was in love and who, *who* could blame him! Who wouldn't want to be with Maya? Ha! Who wouldn't want to hold her beautiful body, to have her look at you with those gorgeous eyes and to be seduced by 'that' smile? And, most importantly, to have *that* particular smile that was only for him?

He definitely loved Maya. He *wanted* her. He thought 'it' will happen, and an over-the-top anticipation poured through his body and made his imagination run wild and steamy.

His mind drifted in and out of their possibilities together, what the future might hold for them. He didn't see any obstacles, let alone another rival—Hayden's revelry stopped abruptly as he looked in his side mirror. He could see a kid, a tall kid on a skateboard, barreling down the sidewalk towards him.

A back door in Hayden's memory snapped open, and the image of a tall kid dressed as a vampire and giving Maya that obnoxious stare that everyone had seen, flashed across his mind. He had looked for the probable suspect a couple of times, even asking—without Maya with him of course— a few heated questions of a few kids. Nothing. The memory of how provocative *that* stare had been made him press his lips together tightly.

The kid on the skateboard, Hayden could still see in the mirror, was rapidly approaching the car. That kid was really flying. He was going to pass right by Hayden's driver side door. Some male instinct sparked up in him like lightening and his arm blurred into action. He pulled on the door handle and the door flew open right in the kid's way.

Kougar had only a split second as he saw the car door flash open in front of him. He pitched off his board and went sprawling in the grass, his backpack came loose, and his skateboard went under the open door. It kept hurtling down the sidewalk until it veered off and banged into landscaping rock.

Hayden got out of his car and walked slowly over to Kougar who was writhing on his back. Kougar's face scrunched up as he tried to catch the breath that had been knocked out of him as he hit the ground and his elbow had struck him in the stomach.

Some kids walking by stopped to check out the scene. Hayden waved them on. "He's all right." He turned to Kougar. "My bad, dude," he said, with a forced sincerity. "I didn't see you coming. You were hauling ass, that's for sure."

Kougar tried to take in a few deep breaths. He lifted his hand and managed to croak out with a gasp: "No… worries. I… was… going too fast."

Hayden got down on one knee studying the tall kid who was trying to catch his breath, hoping to find any clue that would tell him if this kid could have been that vampire at the dance.

"Just try to stretch out, raise your arms and take a deep breath. I know what to do. I have taken a few helmets in the gut to know. There, that's it."

Kougar finally got his breath and focused on the kid looking down at him. He blue eyes suddenly narrowed and then widened with recognition.

It's Maya's boyfriend!

Hayden offered his hand to help Kougar up. Kougar quickly gathered himself and stood up, refusing Hayden's outstretched hand.

"I got it."

"Suit yourself," came Hayden's curt response. "Wow," he began, flatly, "you were really going fast. Sorry about that. I never saw you."

"Like I said, no worries."

"I don't know you."

"I don't know you, either," Kougar said back in the same tone, looking away, while he brushed the dirt off his shirt.

"That's a surprise. Ah, you must be new. I'm Hayden. What's your name?" he almost commanded.

Kougar paused for a second knowing what was going to happen next. It always did with certain people and he knew that Hayden was one of those.

"Kougar."

Hayden looked puzzled for a second. "Cougar? Like the cat?" his voice mocked and he put on a crooked smile.

Kougar didn't look at Hayden. He kept his eyes focused over Hayden's shoulder. "No. It's spelled with a 'K' not a 'C'."

Hayden started to size Kougar up, observing first that Kougar had him by a couple of inches and looked like he did some weight work with his muscled chest and arms.

I bet the kid is pretty strong. I wonder what he could bench.

Hayden noticed the messy dreadlocks, baggy pants and read the saying on Kougar's tee shirt.

This kid's a freak all right. There's no way he was at the dance.

Kougar still kept his eyes off of Hayden's. In a confrontation like this—and he knew it was, even though Hayden had apologized. *What a half-assed apology.* That's how things had always started. He could feel the tension underneath Hayden's words. In the past, he would have just looked at the ground and let what was going to happen… happen. But something new in him made him look up and then down into Hayden's eyes.

They stood there for more than a moment, studying each other, making calculations. Next to them, on the sidewalk, kids passed by, chatting and laughing, not noticing the subtle drama next to them. The 'stare' then turned into something that surprised Hayden, not Kougar: a little test of wills. Who would be first to look away?

For the first time in his life, the rage that Kougar had always carried around for himself started, ever so slowly, to look outward, right into Hayden's eyes; right into Maya's boyfriend's eyes... A new, deep voice thudded up from his gut and into his mind:

A couple of black eyes and that kid won't look at you that way anymore.

Before he thought about it, before he realized he had changed his mind, Hayden asked, still not looking away from Kougar's eyes:

"Were you at the costume dance, dressed up like some wanna-be bloodsucker?" And Hayden finished off the last two words with tight emphasis.

Kougar tilted his head back in a moment of surprise. He then paused while two conflicting sides were battling inside him. One side said to say: *'no;' and then just pick up your board and leave. It's not worth it. 'It' will just happen again. What will you say to mom about what went down?*

The other side, the new one, said: *hey this time it's different. This kid isn't just a bully. He's Maya's boyfriend! Something you'll never be. Never. So, stand your damn ground and tell him like it is; like it was at the dance.*

As much as he wanted to go with the new resolve he couldn't, he knew. *I have to keep paying the price. It's only right. It's easy. Just tell this kid the truth and he'll go off, all right. It's just another way to let the torch fall... Let it fall.*

Hayden signed impatiently. "Were you at the dance?"

Kougar readied himself for what his truth might ignite. He wouldn't fight back. He *had* to take it.

Kougar's flat reply was almost out of his mouth when his peripheral vision caught sight of 'that' walk. Maya was approaching down the sidewalk behind Hayden.

Holy crap!

Kougar quickly changed his mind as Maya walked toward them. He couldn't let Maya see him take a beating.

"Ah, no. I didn't go to the costume dance. Too many little kiddies there."

"I was at the dance. Do you think I am a little kiddie?" Hayden's voice was thick with anger.

"No, dude. It's, ah… it's not my thing. I don't do dances."

"Are you sure?" Hayden took a close look at Kougar's face."

"As a bloodsucker? A vampire?" Kougar pretended to be puzzled. "I would never be a vampire. They're pale sissies."

"Yeah, you've got that right," Hayden said gruffly.

"Why do you ask?"

"Hey, guys!" came Maya's sunny voice that startled the two boys out of their standoff. "Oh, hey, Kougar, what are you—"

Hayden's annoyed voice cut in. "You know him?"

Maya gave Hayden a puzzled look because of his tone. "Yeah, he's in my AP Lit class. I didn't know you knew each other. Kougar doesn't speak much so I was surprised to see you two talking." Maya smiled at both of them but she could sense the awkwardness between them. "What's up?"

"I don't know him," Hayden almost hissed.

"We, ah, just met. We had a little accident," Kougar said, his voice even. "I was going a little too fast. Hayden opened his car door just as I was passing by. I had to ditch my board and took a little tumble. It's all good… I guess I'll be on my way."

Kougar had kept his eyes off Maya because he was afraid he would just stare at her. He gave Hayden a quick studied look, and then turned away, picked up his backpack, and headed down the sidewalk to get his skateboard.

I wonder what the hell she sees in him?

For a long moment, Hayden and Maya both looked at Kougar as he walked away, his long, dreadlocks slightly swaying back and forth. Hayden's blunt, but incredulous tone broke the silence.

"That freak-boy is in your AP Lit class?"

Maya was thinking about what Kougar had said in class. *His take on Hamlet was pretty cool. That was a surprise.* And then she wondered how he could be in Grenfeld's class if he was looking for a math tutor? He couldn't have that high of a GPA.

Hayden asked again, his voice annoyed. "I said, how can that freak be in your Honor's Lit class?"

Maya responded with her own annoyed voice. "I don't know, and hey, he's not a freak."

"He's not? Are you kidding? Look at him."

"He's just… different."

"I'll say," and Hayden blew out his lips for emphasis. "I mean, look at that tangled mass of hair, and he's the only junior here, that I've seen, who rides a skateboard."

"He probably doesn't have a car."

"That's obvious. He definitely isn't from around here. Some out of state freak all right."

"Jeez, Hayden," Maya's voice now scolded, "will you stop with the 'freak stuff' already. Who cares what people look like?"

"Well, anyways, he's a weird dude, that's for sure."

"Can we go now? I've got to get home, change clothes and get back here to run through some cheerleading routines. Don't you have football practice?"

"Yeah, yeah," Hayden said out of the corner of his mouth while he still looked after Kougar who had picked up his board and was skating off.

"Let's go."

Maya tugged at Hayden's shirt and then walked around the side of the car and opened the passenger door. Hayden couldn't help the parting shot that came to his lips. He tried to keep his voice down, but Maya heard him and sighed loudly from inside the car.

"Freak."

Hayden and Maya

Hayden burst through the locker room door and jogged over to his locker, his cleats clicking on the ground. Usually, the locker room banter would be in full swing, a lot of smack talking and horsing around, but all the players were quiet and dog-tired. Coach Jones had worked all the players really hard today in preparation for the game against cross-town rival Bend High.

Hayden's best friend, Alex was already dressing his large frame. He watched Hayden tearing off his jersey and pads.

"Whoa, dude, you should be too tired to be in such a hurry. I saw that Coach put the offense through some extra work. You guys need it," Alex smirked. "Don't worry, defense wins games." And Alex raised his voice, his leader's voice, so his fellow defenseman would hear. "Defense wins football games, right boys!

"Ooh rah!" Alex's defense belted out in tired voices.

"What's that?"

More energy this time: "Ooh rah!"

"I am going to be late," Hayden remarked, throwing his cleats into his locker. "Damn offensive line. They took forever trying to learn the new trap plays. Jeez, it's not rocket science."

"Well, that's why they play offensive line. They're too dumb to play defense." Alex laughed and a few others within hearing distance laughed, too.

"Real funny, dude," Hayden shot back, not amused.

Hayden ripped off his socks and underwear.

"Buddy," came Alex's mocking voice, "There are only two things you are ever in a hurry about."

Hayden started to head off to the showers. "I don't care but I'm sure you are going to tell me anyways."

"Yeah, two things: when I am buying lunch, and when your hot girlfriend calls your name. You go running, right, Lover Boy? That's where you're headed, I'll bet any money on it."

Alex was always a smart-ass Hayden thought as he heard the scattered laughter of his teammates. Before he got to the showers, he turned around.

"Yeah, that's right, you big meat. Who here wouldn't? If one of you said no, you would be a liar, that's for damn sure. And, she won't be calling any freakin' one of you losers. Suck on that, boys.

Hayden ducked into the showers amid the catcalls and hoots. He heard Alex's laugher that rose up above the din. No mistaking that deep belly laugh.

Hayden was late in picking Maya up. He knew there was no chance that she would be late. Maya stood in front of her house, hands on hips, a backpack full of books on the ground next to her. She wore a slight pout on her lipstick lips.

Damn, she knows that little pout of hers drives me crazy, Hayden thought as he pulled up to the curb.

He cocked his head sideways in that way he did when he was really taking in her appearance. Maya was one of the few girls in school who made it a point of always wearing lipstick. It was another item on the list of things that Hayden found irresistible about her.

I'm definitely going to kiss those lips tonight. Hopefully, we'll get through the homework quickly.

"Hey, dude," Maya said, irritated, "you're fifteen minutes late. Got stuck horsing around with Alex, no doubt."

"No way. Sorry, babe. Coach kept us late preparing for Bend High."

Maya opened the car door, threw in her backpack, and buckled herself in.

"Not ready, eh? That's not a good sign."

Hayden blew off her misgivings with a wave of his hand. "Ah, it's nothing. We have one sophomore tackle that we have just put in. The senior who plays that position, you know, Pete Farris?

"Yeah, I know him."

Hayden shook his head. It shouldn't surprise him but it always did. "I should have known that you knew him." And then they both said it together like it was rehearsed:

"I know everybody."

Maya flashed that wickedly beautiful grin of hers as Hayden winked and laughed through his handsome smile.

"Anyway, Pete's out, he twisted his knee—can't tell you how much that sucks. He allows me to bust the big ones. So this sophomore has to man-up, but he's slow. And Pete, hell, he is a road grader; I would just follow his big butt, then cut back and be gone. That's how I broke all of the state sophomore rushing records. If this kid doesn't get his assignments down, they might get to me at the line of scrimmage. I need a little more room."

"That's not good."

Maya looked out the window at the maple trees that lined Mt. Washington Drive as they headed to Hayden's home in Broken Top. The leaves had turned and some were already feeling the weight of fall. Reluctantly, they began to lose their grip on the whitening boughs, and dropped off like they were sad, and world-weary. They had had their time in the warm sun, and while they were full and green, in the prime of their photosynthetic nature, they felt an exquisite sense of order. Maya liked the underlying order of nature; she liked the order of numbers and musical notes, and she liked order in her life. The spontaneous and rash had no claim on her. Her life was goal-driven and structured to achieve. Even her imagination was ordered within limits, and she was very conscious of her choices and feelings.

But the experience she had with Gaius at the dance, showed that the door of order could bust open, and the crackling, hot wind of fate, could ignite all the excitement and passion—and yes, the unfamiliar longings that she now knew, lay dormant at the bottom of her heart.

Lately, when the night turned its most obscure, just before the first, thin blue rays of dawn tried to push through the expiring dark, she would find herself awakened by a nascent wave of emotions that were surging in her depths. She remembered Gaius' smoldering eyes when he pulled away from a kiss that she had wanted and the way it didn't happen had left her surprisingly empty. Just a week ago, strange tears had welled up in her eyes for no apparent reason as she practiced her piano. The absence of that kiss poured longings into her daydreams; like the one she was having now while looking out Hayden's car window. All of a sudden 'the' daydream would just insert itself into her conscious thoughts. She was helpless to stop it and had to follow its path. Then, suddenly, the path would dissolve into a ghostly, evanescent awareness. An awareness that went hungry.

It troubled her that her thoughts often turned to Gaius. *He's not real, just some kid in a costume, with a cool accent.* But it had felt so real to her, so strangely sweet.

The more she thought about it, she knew it wasn't fair to Hayden. She almost felt that she was not being true to him. The rawness of her daydreams made her feel like she was practically cheating on him. Her life didn't seem so ordered now. She was distracted. On top of the Gaius thing, that crazy, close call experience she had when the huge man had tried to grab her while she walked through Drake Park, haunted her, despite her rationalizations. She shuddered as she remembered his vice-like grip. All of what had happened to her in the past few months had, to her surprise, started to overwhelm her because all of it was—unspeakable. There was really no one she could confide in, certainly not her parents or friends. Her Indian Grandmother, Sania, had died three years ago. They had been very, very close.

Oh, I miss her so much! I need her now.

She knew Hayden had been talking and tried to pick up the thread of their discussion. And while she did this, something in her told her that she and Hayden were coming to an end point for now but didn't know how that 'end' would happen. Maybe later they could get back together. She wanted time to deal with what was going on inside her. It wasn't fair to be with Hayden when she felt she was unable to 'be' with him. And certainly she was unable to love him with the type of love she now knew her heart might be capable of. She liked Hayden very much and truly enjoyed being a couple with him. She couldn't help taking into account the popularity benefits, the accolades that came from just being together. Also, her parents were very happy with Hayden and very supportive of their relationship, especially her dad.

Maya finally turned an ear to what Hayden had been saying, her daydream and thoughts had flashed by in seconds.

"... We may have to pass the ball more to open up the running game, and play a little 'hurry up.' Catch the defense napping."

"Yeah, that's a good idea," Maya added in just to let Hayden know she had been listening.

Hayden turned onto the drive that led into Broken Top. Maya was used to Hayden's gated community. But she always felt it was kind of stupid to drive through a gate and by the guard station, just to get to your house. In Bend of all places! Maya lived in the old part of the River West neighborhood in a modest house. Her father, Raja, liked the quaint, old street they lived on with all the mature, ponderosa pines that towered over all the homes on the block.

"Whatever you guys decide," Maya finished her thought, "we can't lose to Bend High. Those guys will rub it in our noses. Who could bear the shame?" And she flashed a grin at Hayden. "S'dude, you better run your butt off. You have to give me something to cheer about. I don't want to see all the long faces at school on Monday."

"No worries, babe, we got it."

Maya never got over the size of Hayden's house. It was three times as big as hers, with all the rooms designed for individual activities. There was one room for sewing, one for working out and yoga, two for offices, a media room, not to mention the four bedrooms. Making small talk, they made their way through the front door, a tall wooden double door that led into the house. The vaulted ceiling towered above them as they walked into the great room. Maya couldn't help but look up at the broad, wood-beamed ceiling. The entrance to the house felt like she was entering a fancy hotel. Beautiful paintings adorned the walls and small, elegant sculptures were set into arched niches. A stacked rock fireplace rose up in the middle of the room, all the way to ceiling. Three huge windows looked out onto a patio and beyond that, a rolling golf course. The sense of being surrounded by beauty, comfort and security, always seduced her.

Maya and Hayden, textbooks scattered around them, sprawled out on the huge, thick and luxurious throw rug in front of the fireplace. Maya sat crossed-legged with a biology book in her lap. Hayden lay on his stomach, propped-up on his elbows as he plowed through his Calculus homework.

The last few minutes, Maya could feel Hayden's glances as he looked up from his book. She knew he wanted her attention, wanted to pull her away from her work. It was a little game they played: he would keep looking at her until she relented, closing her book with a loud, impatient clap. She would then give him an irritated look and say: 'what?' He would give her a mischievous, knowing smile and say with a husky voice: 'what do you think, beautiful?' They would then fall eagerly into each other's arms and start down the amorous path.

This time she felt like she was going through the motions, not in the spirit of the moment. She kind of hoped that Hayden would see this and return to his homework, but he didn't pick up on her muted spontaneity. Maya's biology book still lay open on her lap as she turned her head to look at Hayden, her eyes neutral, saying neither 'yes' nor 'no'.

"Come here, beautiful," he said lowly as he went to her, pushing the book off her lap, and putting his arms under hers as he laid her on her back. Her initial reaction to resist fell away like a fallen branch in a river that had become unmoored from between two rocks in a fast flowing current. She let the powerful current take her. She wanted to distract

77

herself; she 'needed' the distraction. What better way than to let Hayden's lips find hers and feel his athletic body against hers.

Yes, maybe this will chase away those daydreams. Let it... flow.

Hayden's weight pushed on her, sinking her deeper into the plush rug beneath her. The current took and took her as she bounced from rock to rock in the roiling white water. She could see herself walking along the riverbank watching, watching the intense current carry her along. How nice, to just lay there and let things happen as long as she felt... distracted—problem solved. As Hayden lips pulled deeply on hers, her body naturally responded to his, an anatomical response that she just observed.

She vaguely noticed his warm hand had entered through the two buttons in her shirt and began to caress her bare skin as she continued to watch from the riverbank with that new, passive look in her eyes. The current suddenly quickened, and she felt his hand move up and quickly cup her bra-covered breast.

She heard herself murmur in protest as she grabbed at his hand. "Hey, buddy... Not... so... fast.

Hayden's hand still cupped her breast as Maya tugged at it, trying to slide it off, even though the initial feeling had been pleasant and promised a lot more distraction.

"Come on, babe," he whispered warmly into her ear, "this time is so right."

Maya had known for some time that 'this' moment had been coming. Now it had arrived. She murmured again, a weak protest.

"What about your parents?"

"They won't be back until late," he managed as his lips moved down her neck.

"But," came a weak whisper.

"This is so perfect, babe. We both want it... We both need it. I love you. I love you so much... I know you love me."

"You think?" A weak question.

"I know it's scary, but I'm not afraid. I'm not afraid of what this moment means for us."

She realized her breath had quickened without her control and its sound surprised her. The current was really going fast now.

"But, I—"

He cut off her breathy protest as his lips moved ardently on hers and then down to the other side of her neck. Both their hands were still locked on her breast in an unmovable, but exciting impasse.

"I know it might be hard for you to admit that you love me so I'll admit it for you."

"Do I?" Another weak question from under her quickening breath.

"Yes."

For some reason the river scene suddenly disappeared from her closed eyes and she opened them. She could feel Hayden's body moving on hers. She rolled her head sideways and looked out the huge window onto the patio. Her eyes suddenly widened with shock. *There he was!* Gaius was sitting calmly in a cushioned, wrought iron deck chair. His green eyes watched her thoughtfully, no judgment in them, just a slight curiosity.

"Damn!" Maya closed her eyes, found her voice and shattered the fragile, intense moment. She rolled out from under Hayden's embrace as he reluctantly let go. She opened her eyes and quickly looked out at the window. Gaius was gone. The chair was gone.

"What... what's the matter, Maya?" Hayden's voice struggled while coming out of his passion.

She paused and slowly sat up cross-legged. She couldn't look at Hayden's still ardent eyes. That would be too much to handle right now, she knew.

"Well?" he almost barked impatiently.

Her voice was low, almost steady, but a nervous hand brushed her tousled hair off the side of her face. "I'm sorry, I can't go there... I'm not ready. I know you are but... I can't. Sorry."

Hayden studied her for a second while a different emotion started to well up within him. His voice turned harsh and full of disappointment.

"You know what? You'll never be ready …" His tone then turned into impassioned reason. "We *should* be ready. This is our moment, our time."

Still not looking up at him, Maya thumbed the edge of her biology book and couldn't help the twinge of sadness that crept into her words.

"Maybe you are right. But… it's not my time. I'm sorry."

Harshness returned to Hayden's voice. "Sorry? That's a hell-of-a thing to say right now." He barked out a laugh. "You know, you have never said you're sorry to me. Never, as long as we have been together... Man, that's weak."

"Sorry."

"Stop saying that. I get it."

"I… I think we need… a break."

The sound of the word 'break' was an emotional blow to Hayden. His body recoiled back from the blow. It took him a moment to wrap his mind around the finality of that word.

"A break …" Hayden scoffed, blowing through his lips in frustration. "Right, that's what we need, a damn *break.*"

"Hayden… I am serious. I know you are ready. I understand that. I'm not. I'm sor—"

"Will you stop with all the sorry stuff?"

"I need some time alone."

"Look. I'm sorry I touched you. You know I respect you. I'm sorry I wanted you. I'm sor—"

"Will you stop saying sorry?" Maya cut in with her own exasperation. "You don't have to be sorry for that."

"But I am."

An awkward pause settled in between them. Hayden started to say something, and then changed his mind as he tried another way to reach Maya. He had to get her to reconsider. *This is all so stupid!*

"Why do you need time alone? Can you tell me what's wrong? Look, I can wait. If you think we're rushing into it, I can—"

Maya finally looked up at Hayden, her eyes pleading. "No... No. It's not fair to you. You're ready. I need to be alone for a while."

"How long do you need to be alone, Maya? Do you need a week? Two? A month? How long do you want me to wait?"

"I'm not asking you to wait."

Hayden tilted his head back and sighed heavily, getting desperate. "I don't mean wait for 'that.' How long do you want me to wait until we can be together again?"

Hayden's eyes suddenly softened and pleaded with a vulnerability that she hadn't seen before. It made her stomach turn into knots.

She looked away before his eyes made her burst into tears. "I don't know when we can be together again. I just need to be alone."

Hayden's eyes hardened again. "So... you're just rejecting me. That's really what it is."

"No, Hayden. No. That's not it. It's me... It's me. You are so far ahead of me."

"Ahead? What does that mean?"

"I'm not... I'm not in love with you."

Hayden quickly pushed the hurt aside, not accepting her words. "But you *do* love me. I know it. Like I said, for some reason you can't admit it."

"Maybe I do... But right now, that's not good enough. Look, it has nothing to do with you. It's just me."

"Can we talk about it?"

"No. I'm sor—I know, you don't want me to say that, but I am."

"Jeez, Maya, what's the big secret? Why can't you tell me?"

"I can't. All right?"

Hayden's face showed a sudden insight, almost hoping yet fearing. "Is there... someone else? Another guy?"

Maya rocked back with immediate irritation. "Hayden, for God's sake, no, of course not. You know I'm not that way. Jeez, what a thing to ask."

Hayden got up and paced back and forth, his mind spinning until it came to an end. Reality...

"We're done then," came Hayden's flat voice. "Right?"

Maya just nodded her head slowly. Hayden realized he didn't like the vulnerable feelings that had just passed through him and that he had shown to Maya.

"All right, we're done... So, you want to be alone. You know I won't be alone. That's not who I am," he almost threatened, anger in his voice.

"I know. You can date whoever you want. It's only fair. You can move... on. I want you to. If something changes in the future, it changes. But we can't go on like it will."

Hayden's voice came bitter, sarcastic. "S'kay, I can go out tomorrow and start dating and heck, so can you... You know I'll start dating... soon. There are a lot of girls I could call right now and hook up with. I could—"

"I know you could. It's... it'll be all right. It has to. Don't look for me to be dating anybody anytime soon, *that's* who I am.

"Fine. We're done... I get it. Let's go. I have to study my playbook for Saturday night's game."

"No. Don't worry. I can walk."

"You can't. It's a long—"

"Don't worry. It's not that far. I need to think," Maya said as she gathered up her books and put them into her backpack.

"Yeah," came Hayden's voice with its disappointed edge, "you do that."

The easy familiarity and affection between them was suddenly gone like it had been a lie. Awkwardness crept into their thoughts and movements. The air around them tensed and they suddenly couldn't look at one another. An uncomfortable long pause went by as they both tried to come to grips this new feeling between them.

"This is odd," Maya finally said.

"You can say that again," Hayden agreed as he shoved his hands into his pockets.

"Ah, I'll, I'll see you around, then," Maya tried to sound like small talk but felt stupid.

"Yeah… 'see-you-around', or whatever that means, "Hayden replied, his voice sounding ridiculous to him.

"All right. Okay," was all Maya could think of to say.

She turned around and headed out the door. She knew Hayden's eyes were following her and she wondered what he was thinking. She had no idea.

Waiting with a Purpose

Maya and her cheerleading teammates finally got the intricate routine down they had been practicing over and over. At last, the timing was perfect. It was a pretty detailed routine with all the jumps, tumbling and other stunts.

"Whooo!" Maya shouted out at the end of the routine. "Yeah, girls, way to keep those toes pointed! Great! Let's call it."

All the girls clapped and started to gather up their gear and head off the field to the locker room. Maya was captain of the Cheer Team and she had worked them hard. Homecoming was coming soon and she was determined to have them prepared. She liked the hard work. It was a helpful distraction and kept her mind off certain things.

The first couple of weeks since she had broken up with Hayden had been difficult and, yes, strange. She hadn't realized how much Hayden had been a part of her daily routine. He often picked her up to go to school and, if they were both around after football and cheerleading practice had ended, he would take her home. In the cafeteria, at lunchtime they always sat at the same table with all their mutual friends, and they had texted each other constantly. Now...nothing.

Well, done is done, she reminded herself.

Her best friend, Maddie, happily became her transportation. They had the first class of the day together, biology, so it was convenient. They could compare notes before class and Maddie would always make her laugh with her quirky sense of humor. She and Maddie had 'started' another table at lunchtime. Maya thought it was interesting watching who split off from what was now 'Hayden's' table. She made it a point to say to herself that it didn't matter whom. Maddie certainly was keeping tabs and her sarcastic comments were stupid-funny, but funny.

"Boy, how *awkward* was that?" Maddie began in her typical dramatic style."

Maya was packing her gear into a backpack. She and Maddie were the last two on the field. The football team's practice had ended thirty minutes ago.

"What's that?" Maya asked, innocently.

Maddie snorted in surprise. "What's that?" She said obviously. "Hayden walked right by us and didn't even say a word. He didn't even look our way."

"Oh."

"You mean you didn't notice. Everybody else did."

"It's all right… I guess it's hard for him."

"I'll say. Jeez, Maya, I still think you are crazy. I thought you guys were so perfect together."

"I know you think I'm a prude. But I—"

"No honey, just a stupid prude. I mean, just because he touched your tit. In my book, tits are like arms, touching them is no big deal. It doesn't have to lead to anything. Heck, it's just like holding hands." She gave Maya a devilish grin.

Maya gave Maddie a shocked look with a touch of mockery in it. "Madds, you are as bad as they come," and she punched Maddie in the arm. "No, it's not just that, as I told you, he was ready for more and I know he was going to keep wanting more. Maybe that's just normal. I guess."

Maddie's tone was indignant. "Duh, girl. It would raise the hair on your arms just to tell you half of what goes on in this school. Jeez, Maya for someone who is so 'with it,' I sometimes think you are in a bubble.

"Well, whatever. Obviously, I'm not ready to be normal yet. Besides that, as I said, I just need a break. Now that's normal, I think."

They started to walk off the field when the overhead lights went off. Maya had failed to zip her pack all the way up and her light sweater fell out and dropped to the ground behind her.

"Okay, whatever you say."

"Yes, it *is* okay. I'm over it. I know he has to be mad at me. But he'll get over it too."

"You've got that right. The girls are already starting to circle. Leah Thompson was licking her chops looking at him the other day in the lunch line like he was a piece of fresh meat!"

"Ugh, that's gross."

"Ha! Pardon the pun! But, not only her, there was Cory McPhear—"

"So... so let 'em!" Maya tried to end the conversation thread. "I know that's the way it's going to be. We're not together. He should move on."

Maddie shook her head in feigned exasperation and started to give Maya a good lecture. "I still think you're nuts. I mean he's like the primo-catch of all catches. Girl, you should run to him and get on your blessed knees and beg him to take you back."

Maya tried to take a swing at Maddie and missed as Maddie ran off with Maya in pursuit.

Madds! You are so annoying!"

"Beg! You should beg him to take you back!

The girls laughed hysterically all the way to the locker room. Maya was sure glad to have a best friend like Maddie.

*

The Man looked down into the athletic field through his small binoculars from inside his dirty, white late model Dodge van. He shifted his weight feeling his right rear buttock had fallen asleep. There were many girls to look at as they tumbled and jumped around in their beautiful cheerleading uniforms. But he only had eyes for one girl. She was the most beautiful, the one who attracted his innermost being like a magnet. He felt a small tremor as he watched Maya's skirt flop up as she was frozen briefly upside down in a move during the routine. He couldn't help noticing how shapely her legs were all the way down where her thighs vanished under her tight, soffee shorts. He felt his imagination squirm in and out of the images in his roiling mind.

He didn't know how long he would have to wait for another opportunity to present himself to her. He didn't care. The passage of time meant nothing to him, only that he was getting closer. That inevitable fact powered his faith and fueled his love. He would be ready whenever the moment came again. He was always ready, like an expectant lover, his heart open to chance, to the fateful chance of their embrace.

He carefully noticed the other girls leave the field. Only Maya and one other girl were left. They stood talking. Who knows what girls talk about? He had no clue. It doesn't matter what they say. Even mutes have something to say. But he liked the way their voices sounded, way up high, like little birds. He had never heard Maya's voice. He imagined it to be like a fluttering flute. But he had heard her scream. He heard it at night when he went to bed with the light on. He knew she was trying to tell him something, something special.

He quickly noticed that something had fallen from Maya's backpack. He waited… The field lights went out. The girls walked, then, ran off the field. He waited. Time went by. He waited. All the cars were gone from the school parking lot. He got out of his van cautiously, like a bear emerging from its winter den after hibernation. He slowly scanned all around him and lifted his head like he was a grizzly standing on its hind legs sniffing the wind. He walked down the hillside. With surprising agility for a man with his heavy bulk, he hopped the fence and darted with an unusual quickness over to Maya's sweater that lay on the ground. He snatched it up like a prize and left as quickly as he had come.

Sneaky Peek

Kougar could smell the deepening fall as he boarded his way to school. He took in the clean, crisp air, of the high desert, so different than the bulky air in L.A. that seemed crowded with dense urban smells.

The close call with Hayden some three weeks back still bothered him with small episodes of nervous adrenaline, which he tried to subdue with more intense weight lifting and shadow boxing with the speed bag.

Jeez, what if Maya had seen me get my butt kicked?

The prospect of it all gave him a sick feeling in his gut. He had just felt helpless as always in that situation. He couldn't—wouldn't—bring himself to raise his hands and ball them into fists. He knew this was the way it was and the way it had to be.

The price is never fully paid. I'll always bring the lions to me. One day, I'll apologize to my parents... One day.

He had never looked forward to school, just too many things he wanted to avoid: the crush of students in the hallways, the 'looks' that he could always see from anywhere, like he had eyes in the back of his head, boring classes. He knew his appearance was hardly typical, especially at Mt. Bachelor High, which really tended to the 'preppy' side. Back in L.A. there were more than a few similar to him, though certainly not enough for him to blend in. The lions would always find the one who went his own route away from the anonymity and safety of the herd.

Now, however, he looked forward to school—well at least to Mr. Grenfeld's class. The prospect of Maya sitting next to him filled him with an anticipation that was at once both exciting and fearful, a combination he had never felt in his life. He continued to try and take the most furtive and secretive glances at her. The temptation of her close proximity was all but overwhelming. He wanted so much just to stare at her beauty, to take it all in, moment by slow moment until his visual thirst had been quenched—for the moment! The subtle perfume she always wore with its sensual scents of sandalwood, rose, and dried lilac imprinted on his senses. He liked that he could lie in bed at night and summon those fragrances to the air around him.

Once, while Mr. Grenfeld was giving a vigorous lecture about how reading great literature can encourage readers to act more morally, that it is one of the few things that can touch our spiritual souls, our human souls, Maya just said lowly, without turning to Kougar: "Hey, Sneaky-Peek, stop being so obvious."

One thing he could do, when the timing was right, was to stare at her from afar, down the hall, across the cafeteria, or through the window as she stood, gathered with some friends on the large lawn outside the science wing. Most of the time she was unaware, but a few times, she happened to glance around and catch him, and allowed their eyes to lock on for a brief moment. Her gaze never showed that she rejected him, or that she was disinterested, just that she seemed slightly curious. He certainly wasn't looking for an invitation—no, no! That was never his purpose. He looked because he had no other choice. Thoughts about Maya would suddenly arise in him, hardly ever the product of his conscious mind. She had opened a door from behind a door that he never knew existed.

He wondered how long 'these' thoughts would go on, how long they could refuse his control. He hoped he would finally be able to deal with it like he did with all the other would-be emotional thoughts that had tried to cross his path: with silence and a cool heart. He was unsure if those two trusty weapons could shield him. It was enough now just to observe Maya, to notice things about her and to keep his distance. He certainly noted that she and Hayden no longer walked together in between classes, or sat at the same lunch table. But most important to what lay behind the door that was behind the door in him, was that they no longer seemed to be a couple. No kisses, no handholding, no quick embraces before class started, none of that. Nothing, not even a 'hi, how are you doing?' Nothing... Now, that was interesting. It peeled away the sharp edges that cut at him when he had seen Maya and Hayden embrace. He was grateful for the relief.

Can't say I'm unhappy about that. Good for her.

Kougar braked to a halt and popped up his board that he then snatched with one hand. He walked up the steps and mingled in with the mass of students who were filing though the front door of the main entrance to Mt. Bachelor High. Very few kids were as tall as Kougar. As he made his way down the main hall, his dreadlocked head could be seen above the rest. The walls were lined with painted posters of various 'cheers' aimed at the upcoming Homecoming game against Redmond High. It was another high school event that he wasn't going to attend. But he was having second thoughts about that only because he could take a seat in the stands and watch Maya and her cheerleading squad.

A handful of freshman girls were giggling and chatting right in front of his locker. They all stopped at once, as if on cue, and looked at Kougar as he approached. Kougar could see one girl's lips start in a whisper. He thought he made out the word 'weird' the way her mouth moved. They then scattered off in different directions. It made Kougar think of a small flock of blackbirds that all of a sudden had stopped chirping on a low hanging branch when a black cat came strolling towards them. They all then tensed and burst into flight.

A tight smile started at the corners of his mouth. He was still getting used to how big he was and how that might affect people who saw him. In the past, being small, kids might stare at him because of his appearance: disheveled blond dreads, ripped, ill-fitting jeans and wrinkled shirt, but they never moved away from him like they were scared. They just stood and stared.

Good. I'm a big freak now.

For his mom's sake, he hoped that his days of being bullied might be over for a while, but he had no control over that. He was going to be who he was and if that attracted bullies, so be it. At least his size might be a deterrent, and keep him from being hurt or bloodied so easily.

He put his board away, took off his jacket, grabbed some books.

"Yeah, dude," came the squeaky sophomore's voice from the same kid who had noticed the saying on Kougar's tee shirt before. "Nice, shirt."

'Waiting to morph, waiting to live', was stenciled in white letters on the back of Kougar's black tee shirt.

Kougar just turned around and nodded at the short kid who nodded back, his thick glasses making his eyes a little bigger than they were. Kougar noticed the kid's khaki pants and neat sweater.

"It's cool," the kid said with admiration. "Cool. I would like to morph."

Kougar just nodded again and then asked, looking down on the preppy little geek, "Into what?"

The kid couldn't help a deep sigh and his over large eyes looked inward for a moment and then up at Kougar.

"Something... something a lot different," the voice squeaked wistfully. The kid then walked away, his backpack covering all of his back and sagged down on to his backside.

Could I be different than I am? Kougar ran that question through his mind as he walked to class. The question had never occurred to him before. He didn't really know. But something within him was morphing whether he liked it or not. He was just waiting, waiting like a spectator, watching his life unfold without him. Who is more real? Him? Or the avatar he felt like he was observing? He couldn't decide. When you have no sense of control, 'decisions' are illusions. Hamlet knew that.

His mother had sensed a change in him but she kept questions and comments to herself as if she didn't want to bring attention to what was going on with him. She didn't want to make Kougar self-conscious about a change that she hoped would be for the better. If he wanted to talk to her about it, she wanted to keep that door open, even though her son had never confided in her, let alone told her anything personal. And her heart ached because of it. She had her own ideas (hopes) about her son's personality quirks. She hoped Kougar's character would keep growing, that maturity and time would reshape it away from the crushing shyness, avoidance of people, the irrational stubbornness, and OCD traits and the deep pain that hooded his eyes at times. She didn't want to believe (and didn't), much to her husband's frustration, that Kougar's diagnosis of late onset Asperger's was a fixed thing. Her husband's experience with his father had made him accept, fatalistically, the doctor's diagnosis. If her hope eventually turned into a dead end, she wished with all her heart that he would find his way in life, find some measure of peace, fulfillment and happiness.

The class hours went by quickly and then it was lunchtime. Kougar sat alone as usual in the cafeteria. He could see Maya sitting at a table with some friends. Hayden was at his table with 'his' crowd.

Maya noticed Maddie and Alex looking across the aisle at one another. Maddie gestured at Alex to come over and sit with her. He gestured the same way back at her. Maddie shrugged her shoulders and so did Alex. Both shrugs weren't really heart-felt.

"Hey, Madds, go ahead and go sit with Alex. It's all right. It doesn't matter to me. I could sit at the same table with Hayden, but I know he would be very uncomfortable. He needs time. I get that. So go ahead if you want to."

Maddie turned and gave Maya a mischievous grin. "Ah, no worries, honey, it's a game Alex and I have been playing for a couple of weeks. We're really just hangout buddies. He wants more but I'm not into it. It's all so messy."

"No way," Maya started in surprise. "I thought—"

"Breaking up is hard to do, but not for us," Maddie smirked. "You and Hayden 'had' something to break up. Alex and I, well, we just let go of our bodies."

Maddie slapped the top of one her textbooks with her open palm and let go a devilish laugh. Maya just shook her head with a chuckle.

"Boy, Madds, you are too much."

Carley and Cheryl both heard the end of the conversation and surprise spread across their faces as they both said to Maddie at the same time:

"You're not with Alex anymore?"

"Truth be told, girls, I was never really *with* Alex. How can you be with Alex? He's got a *big*—" and she narrowed her eyes and looked around at her audience to see if they got her pun. Gasps were heard from all the girls except Amanda who just giggled under her breath. "Yeah, a big ego. He's just a big 'player,' that's all."

"And you?" Breah chimed in while she chewed on an apple.

"Well," Maddie said as a matter of fact as she brushed her hair back, "I'm a *player,* too."

"Two players can't *be* together," Maya said with a grin spreading across her face, "But they—"

"But they can hang out together!" Maddie finished Maya's sentence.

All the girls broke out in loud laughter, nudging one another. Maddie's mirth rose above the rest. Kids sitting at the surrounding table turned to see what all the hilarity was about.

Alex looked over at Maya's table sensing the 'joke' was on him somehow and he couldn't help a smirk, knowing Maddie's sarcastic sense of humor. Alex didn't really care. Maddie had been, and is… fun.

Despite himself, Hayden glanced over as well, not looking at all the girls, but at Maya's gorgeous smile. He looked away quickly, and as he did, his eyes came to rest on Kougar, who was sitting alone at his own table across the cafeteria. His eyes focused hard and they told him that Kougar was looking at Maya. Yes, that freaky kid was staring at her. Hayden mumbled something under his breath and finally looked back down at his lunch and took a bit of his sandwich. It tasted like paper.

God, that kid bugs me!

After lunch, Kougar's math class dragged on for hours it seemed like. He was so relieved when the period bell rang that he almost leaped from his chair. He moved quickly down the hall, weaving in and out of slow walking kids until he got to Mr. Grenfeld's class. Maya was already seated. He slowed down to act nonchalant and made his way to the seat next to Maya. She gave him a small greeting smile that he likened to

Christmas tree lights coming on. All he could do was nod back like the shy mute he was. He sat down and watched the other students filter into the class one by one. He then felt her gaze on him. It seemed like a spotlight.

"Hi Kougar, or is it Sneaky-Peek? Which one?" Maya low voice asked politely.

Something in Kougar made him relent and a sheepish smile spread across his face. He turned briefly and looked at Maya whose eyes teased, but were friendly.

"Ah, you got me. I guess I'm both. Sorry about that. I really don't mean to be rude."

"I know you don't. That's why I don't mind. I've seen you check me out from far away." Maya continued her low voice that sounded like a purr to Kougar. "Now we're sitting next to each other. A friendly look is a friendly look. No big deal."

Kougar sifted his weight nervously in his chair. "Maybe not for you, but for me... yes."

Maya had not expected the straight honesty in Kougar's tone. Her eyes reevaluated Kougar's profile. "Well, no need to sneak. I won't bite."

"So you say," came his skeptical reply. "If I were you, I wouldn't want anyone who looked like me to be—"

"Look, you are not me. I don't care what you look like. But you obviously do. You should chill about that."

Kougar was about to say something to further his point but he stopped before the words got out of his mouth.

"All right," he began as a matter-of-fact, "So I don't scare you out with my ah, scraggly dreads and the stalker-look I give you?"

Maya turned and flashed Kougar her beautiful smile and she couldn't help but chuckle.

"Stalker-look. Dude, you are funny."

Kougar's voice turned serious. "Well, what if you knew that I wasn't funny ha, ha, but... *funny*?"

94

She scoffed softly so the other kids who were settling in their chairs couldn't hear. Mr. Grenfeld started to shuffle his notes to begin.

"I don't buy that. You are making yourself out to be creepy. Nice try. I can see you're not. I think what you look like, the hair and all that is probably just a mask. Maybe you just want to be someone you're not."

Kougar's low, almost whispered retort didn't come out with all the conviction he had wanted. "You should judge a book by its cover, besides, you don't know anything about me."

"Nice try," Maya smiled through her words, not turning to look at him. She just looked ahead to Mr. Grenfeld who was giving some closing comments on theme of death and how it had been dealt with in the literature they had covered so far.

The classroom conversation sounded to him like it was coming from another room as Kougar's thoughts turned inward, trying to come to grips with Maya's words. He was surprised how they rolled into his consciousness like rumbling thunder that was getting close to his exposed refuge of familiar truths.

I don't know what she thinks she 'knows' about me. I'm stuck with 'me'. My parents are stuck with 'me'... We are all stuck with the fact that Michaela is gone.

Kougar continued to brood, the discussion around him was muffled by his distraction. Every so often he made out bits and pieces. Suddenly, he realized that all the kids had turned around and were looking at him. Maya had that same curious expression in her eyes, the kind she had when she caught Kougar looking at her from a distance. All the kids had one hand up in the air.

"So, with a show of hands, it looks like everybody here in class would like to die peacefully in their sleep, given the choice," Mr. Grenfeld noted. "Everybody but you, Kougar. How would you prefer to go? Tragically perhaps, like Hamlet?"

"Tragically?" Kougar started, clearing his throat as he tried to speak up. "No, I don't have enough guts for that."

"Then how? It's your choice, any choice."

Kougar looked down at the floor while his brief life flashed before his eyes and then raised his head and said flatly:

"I want to die for a reason."

Gaius?

Kougar's response to Mr. Grenfeld's question was so simple and plaintive; it struck a chord in Maya. A thoughtful pause filled the classroom as everyone reassessed their wish to die peacefully in their sleep.

"Well, it's certainly hard to disagree with that," Mr. Grenfeld smiled and nodded. "I think Kougar really summed up what we all should have taken away from the subject we have been covering in the first part of this class. Dying peacefully in our sleep maybe too easy a way out—if, we're lucky enough to choose. So—"

"Or unlucky," Kougar cut in with a bitter emphasis.

The ending period bell rang.

"It's a double edge sword, isn't it?" Mr. Grenfeld admitted, appreciating Kougar's perspective, thinking to himself that the dreadlocked student probably had a story to tell, if he was able to.

"Now it's on to what is most alive in us, the poetry of love!" he said loudly above the sound of the bell, the shuffling of books, and creaks of chairs as the students headed out of class.

Maya found herself walking next to Kougar as they approached the door. For the first time, she studied him, thinking to herself at the same time: *why?* She noticed how tall he was, his broad and muscular chest and long, strong arms, the profile of his squaring jaw. A tiny smile made it to her lips, as she couldn't ignore the mass tangle of Kougar's blond hair that seemed to sprout out in every direction, covering his forehead and falling down to one side of his face to the other depending on how he moved his head. His baggy, wrinkled jeans and well-worn, extra-large, faded, turtleneck sweatshirt with the enigmatic saying stenciled on the back, gave him a messy, grunge look. But there was something vulnerable and honest about him that made her feel for him in a caring way. She could see in his diffident way of speaking, his shyness, the way she felt he hid behind his appearance that there was really nothing 'freaky' about him.

He just seems a little lost.

Something in her wanted to make friends with Kougar. He always seemed to be by himself.

Maybe he might want to be friends.

"Hey, how's the math going?" she asked in a friendly tone.

Kougar gave a guarded shrug and muttered under his breath. "Ah, math …"

"I'm sure you're getting it," she said, making it sound like small talk.

"Ah, not really. I guess it's not my thing. It's all Chinese to me, besides, I always run out of fingers and toes," he finished sheepishly. Maya laughed warmly.

"I know I can help you with that."

Kougar just grunted uncomfortably under his breath.

"Is it because I'm a girl?"

They made their way into the hallway. Maya could tell Kougar was uneasy and she waited patiently for him to reply. A couple of Maya's many friends said 'hi' almost as a question as they passed by, noticing that she was walking and talking to a big kid whose weird appearance was unusual for Mt. Bachelor High. Kougar saw their expressions and then looked down at his feet, embarrassed for Maya, not for himself. Maya took his silence for an answer.

"So, it is because I'm a girl, huh?" she asked with a soft understanding in her voice.

Kougar turned his head and cocked an eyebrow at her. It was a look that he hoped she couldn't read as he said to himself: *it's a heckuva lot more than that!*

"Ah, yes… and no," his voice trailed off.

98

Maya pursed her lips, puzzled. They walked another ten steps or so in awkward silence. She tried another way, determined to make a friendly connection with Kougar. She *always* made friends.

'Hey, I'm going to drop off a book by the library. Want to walk over with me?" Maya smiled her friendly, devastating smile.

A moment of shock spread across Kougar's face that he quickly tried to hide.

"Come on," she encouraged.

Kougar allowed himself to take the first, real look into Maya's liquid brown eyes. He let the briefest light of longing appear in his gaze as he took in her beauty. A small, lost smile found its way to one corner of his mouth. Remembering the looks on the faces of her friends who had passed by them, he didn't really want people to see her with him.

"Look, I don't want to… *waste* your time." His tone turned downward with a sigh of reality. He veered out of the flow of kids off to side and stopped next a line of lockers. Maya followed.

"Don't be silly, you wouldn't be—"

"Hey," and he shook his shaggy head, "I know you are just trying to be friendly. But, I don't think we should be friends."

Maya was taken back. It was certainly not what she expected him to say. She couldn't help the unfamiliar feeling of self-consciousness that spread across her face. She ran a nervous hand through her hair.

"Oh …" she managed, and then asked something she had never had to ask, and she felt silly and coy all at the same time. "Is there something you don't like about me?

Again, the lost smile tugged at one side of Kougar's mouth. "That's funny… something wrong with you. That's really funny."

She narrowed her eyes. "Well, I'm not trying to be funny," she said, her voice serious.

Kougar's smile vanished with a sigh. "I believe you."

"So, what is it" Maybe I'm too—"

"Hey," he said through an incredulous chuckle, "don't worry, it doesn't matter. It *really* doesn't matter."

They both looked at each other: Maya wanted a better explanation but didn't know what to say to get it. A few wrinkles of frustration spread across her forehead. Kougar finally put an anxious hand to the back of his head and scratched at an imaginary itch. Determined, Maya almost started again with the same question but Kougar raised a hand to stop her.

"Look, don't worry about it. Ah, I gotta go."

Kougar split off from Maya's side and headed down the hallway. A stray thought made her curious. She let Kougar get ahead of her and then she followed him, studying the movements of his walk. In a flash, she saw it in her memory. When he had said the word 'waste,' something about the way his lips moved jarred an image to life in her mind.

No... No way, she thought.

Kougar arrived at his locker. Maya studied his every move as bits and pieces of images accelerated through her awareness. The way his head tilted as he put some textbooks away in his locker, the angle of his body... He pulled out his skateboard and one of the metal wheels spun and picked up the reflection of the hallway lights.

Kougar closed his locker and started to walk away. Maya followed, the question bubbling on her lips. She started and stopped her insistent query; finally she couldn't help it. In the middle of the hallway, filled with students, she stopped and sent out a half-hearted probe.

"Gaius?"

The flow of students moved around her as she stood looking at Kougar's back. He kept walking. Fighting the urge to just turn around and stop her foolishness, she tried once more. This time she summoned up some courage she didn't really feel and barked the words out as if she was certain.

"Hey, Gaius!"

Kougar froze for a moment as Maya's voice filled him with panic. He didn't turn around. He couldn't turn around. No way he was going to face her. He managed to push against the paralysis. He got his legs moving slowly at first, and then his stride quickened, carrying him down the hall until he disappeared into the stream of kids.

Maya watched him, her mind spinning.

Oh, my God! It's him! That's impossible. He can't be Gaius!

Her thoughts reeled into her like blows and she moved over to the wall and leaned against it.

I can't believe it. There is no way he could be! No way!

Images of Gaius' charismatic but not handsome face scrolled through her mind. How could she forget the haunting, smoldering green eyes that had looked right through her, making her feel like she was barely dressed? Her memory could clearly play back his smooth, confident voice, and his words of such conviction and honest truth; words that had opened a door to a deep longing; a longing that had crept up upon her with a puzzling stealth that continued to mystify her. The seduction of it all had surprised and stunned her. She tried to reconcile these thoughts with Kougar, the terribly shy, disheveled, dreadlocked kid with the uncertain manner of speaking. Kougar's overall awkwardness contrasted so much with Gaius' easy, experienced, self-assured manner. To her, everything about Gaius was more man than boy. And Kougar?

Not even close! Besides, he doesn't even want to be my friend!

"Hey, Maya, there you are!" came Maddie's exasperated voice. "Where have you been?"

Deep in her thoughts, Maya didn't acknowledge Maddie, as if she didn't hear her. She was coming to grips with the new feeling of being hurt and irritated at the same time by Kougar's rejection.

"What's the matter? You've got a strange look on your face. Are you all right? Jeez, you look like I do once a month," and Maddie laughed at her own joke. "Hey, now," she insisted.

Maya slowly came out of her lost, jumble of thoughts and her eyes finally focused on Maddie. "Oh, hi, Madds... I, ah, I was just going to drop off a book at the library."

Maddie looked at Maya skeptically. "Are you sick or something?"

"Sick of school, I guess," she said, surprised by her own words.

"I'm with you, sister! Let's go. You can drop the book off tomorrow. The girls are waiting outside. We want to get on the same page for cheer practice."

Again, Maya didn't seem to hear Maddie. Maddie let out an impatient sigh and grabbed Maya by the arm and ushered her along.

"Come on! Jeez, girl, you're like a zombie!"

Maya let Maddie tug her through the hall. They made their way out the school's front door, down the steps and over to where Carley, Cheryl, Amanda and Breah stood talking and laughing.

Kougar was across the parking lot when he saw Maya and Maddie emerge through the front door. He was ready to board off when he stopped to look at Maya, again, marveling at her beauty, which he could see, even at a distance.

God, she's beautiful. And she wanted to be my friend!

Another voice in him said again, like always: you can't want what you want, especially *that*. Not *you*... not the way *you* are... You are no Gaius.

Kougar snorted derisively to himself. He didn't need a mirror in front of him to see the look of mockery on his face. Now Maya knew he *was* Gaius.

Ha... She has no idea about 'where' Gaius came from. How could he explain to her that he was not *really* Gaius, not pretending, but that he had *needed* to be Gaius? When the trigger pulled Gaius would... come. Maya would want to know.

It'll sure be freaky when I tell her she doesn't need to know, that she 'couldn't know'. Ha! She really has no idea! Damn. Damn!

He took a deep breath and steadied himself. He tried to envisage all the ways he would answer her coming questions. Every scenario that flowed through his mind made him out to be a weird fool. For the first time, he wished that Gaius had taken that kiss at the dance when he had the chance. Even behind his mask, Kougar knew it would have struck him like a thunderbolt and afterwards, he could lie awake at night and feel her lips on his, an undying memory of outrageous daring and luck—thanks to

Gaius. At least that would have been some consolation for the outright, throat-constricting embarrassment that was coming his way. A desperate measure flashed through his mind: maybe he could drop out of Grenfeld's class. That would be an hour out of the day where she couldn't interrogate him. But maybe, just maybe, he could make her not believe it. If he just said 'no' enough times, she would come to see that it was just a strange coincidence that really wasn't true. She would have to look elsewhere. Certainly the contrast between him and Gaius was just too strange. She wouldn't be able to connect the dots.

Heck, I can't connect them. I told her that I was not funny, ha, ha... but 'funny'. She needs to chew on that until there's nothing.

He gave a fatalistic shake of his head and blew out his lips with a dejected sigh. Still, his eyes were drawn to Maya and he watched her talking with her friends. Even at this distance her skin glowed and her long, brown hair glistened in the sunlight. He felt he could be content with only looking at her from afar, maybe even having a few harmless words between them while in Grenfeld's class. But now the harmless words would be impossible.

Damn. Damn.

A little ways down the sidewalk, Maya briefly noticed Hayden and Alex standing in a crowd of their football buddies. She and Hayden locked eyes awkwardly. His look seemed lost, sad. She kept her eyes neutral. She quickly turned back to her friends.

Hayden sighed and gazed out across the sports field, turning his back to his buddies so they couldn't see the heart ache on his face. The sound of a high-powered car revving up distracted him to look over to the parking lot. His unfocused eyes suddenly narrowed and locked on to Kougar.

What is that 'freak' looking at?

The words almost erupted out of his throat like a growl. He could clearly see Kougar was staring at Maya. He watched for a moment as a rage built up in him. He finally muttered thickly under his breath.

"That's it. I have had *enough* of that crap."

Alex, who stood next to Hayden, heard his buddy's unusual tone. "What's that?"

Without a word, Hayden took off jogging towards Kougar, a sneer growing across his face. Alex called after him.

"Dude. Hey, Murph! Where are you going?"

Alex started after Hayden. He looked back to the other guys and barked over his shoulder with a smile. "Time to go, see you boys at practice."

A chorus of derisive snorts rose up from the boys as they turned to watch Alex jogging after Hayden across the parking lot. They shrugged and started to head off to the locker room.

Kougar saw Hayden coming his way. He wasn't really surprised. Based on his last encounter with Hayden, he knew something like this was going to happen. Sooner or later a lion would come for him. But not here, not so close to where Maya was. He didn't want her to see Hayden put him down; didn't want her to pity him. How could he explain to her that he had taken Hayden's blows willingly and not out of fear? In a few minutes, it was going to get ugly. He took a deep breath and let it go as he looked out past the school to mountains in the distance, their pinnacles lit with the deep golden light of the waning sun. The sun will fall… He will fall. So be it.

Kougar dropped his board and started to skate. Hayden and Alex were about fifty yards away. He could have put the pedal down and raced off and there would have been no way Hayden would have been able to catch up to him. Why put off the inevitable he reasoned to himself. He just wanted to go far enough off campus and find a side street.

Alex could see that Hayden was making a beeline for Kougar. Alex recognized him from the weight room.

"Are you going after that kid on the skateboard?" Alex said through deep breaths.

"Yeah, that freak. That busted freak! He bugs the crap out of me. He's gone far enough," Hayden puffed back.

"Hey," Alex's voice was wary, "be careful. I know that kid. We've lifted before. He is one strong dude. Don't let him get his hands on you. He'll squeeze you like a zit. And I've seen him on the speed bag, too. He can box," Alex panted out... "Hell, what's he to you?"

"He's a freak," came Hayden angered response.

"Let him go. Don't be flamed, bro. You don't know what you might be getting into. The kid's strong. And weird. You never know."

"I don't care," Hayden panted back as he quickened his stride into a run. We're going to get something straight," Hayden finished, in between gasps for air.

"You'd better let me help. This kid—"

"Stay out of it," Hayden cut Alex off. "I got this."

Maya didn't care what time the girls wanted to practice. She barely heard the discussion as she kept trying to link the dots between Kougar and Gaius. She let her gaze wander off. Out of the corner of her eye she noticed some movement. Some boys were running across the parking lot.

Hey, it's Hayden and Alex! What the?...

Out ahead of the boys she could see Kougar riding his skateboard. She watched for a moment and then made the connection.

They're running after him!

She could tell by the intensity of the chase that Hayden wasn't trying to catch up with Kougar to have a friendly chat.

Darn it, this is getting out of hand!

She knew how aggressive Hayden could be and what he might do. It was going to end badly—*for Kougar, that's for sure!* Without a word, she dropped her backpack and bolted off, startling her friends, who called after her with cries of surprise.

"Hey! What's going on!? Where are you going?" Maddie yelled after Maya who was hitting her track stride.

All the girls looked at each other with puzzle expressions.

"What's up with her?" Breah said.

"I don't know," Maddie said. "That's weird."

"Where is she going? Why is she running? Carley asked, her eyes big with surprise.

"Don't know, but I'm going to find out. Let's go, girls. Come on!" Maddie shouted as she started off. Carley, Cheryl, and Breah reluctantly followed.

"What about the practice time?" Amanda muttered under her breath. She was the last one to take off and tried to catch up to her friends.

Kougar headed down the first side street of mixed businesses that all had nice manicured lawns and a common, small park area with more grass, some trees and a few benches. He could hear the heavy, running footsteps of Hayden and Alex gaining on him but he didn't look back. And he thought what he always thought.

The price has to be paid.

Hayden saw Kougar cut down the side street using the sidewalk. He was furious, his rage driven by the depths of his despair and helplessness over the break-up with Maya. All the emotion that he had kept bottled up within him burst to the surface. The rage told him that the only way he was going to feel better was to stop that freak, Kougar, from looking at Maya. It disgusted him to see that. Kougar had no right to stare at Maya. It was *wrong*.

Hayden kicked his stride into a higher gear, just like he did when he burst through the tackles, past the linebackers, and into the open field. He turned sharply across the corner lawn, hopped a few hedges, and cut Kougar off, right in small park area in between the businesses. He ran right up Kougar's back, knocking him off his skateboard. Kougar went sprawling. His backpack went flying and when it hit the ground, it split open, scattering its contents.

Hayden stood over Kougar, breathing deeply from his long sprint. With his hands on his knees, he looked down at Kougar and growled thickly through his teeth.

"Now, look, freak, you're going to stop the staring. Got that?"

Kougar always went into a calm mode when 'it' was about to happen. For a quick moment he wondered if 'it' was going to hurt.

Hayden seemed like a mad dog looking down at him. As Kougar got slowly to his feet he said calmly:

"What are you talking about?"

Hayden sneered and moved right up to Kougar's face. Their noses were only six inches apart. Kougar could feel Hayden's hot breath on his face.

"Don't freakin' play games with me," Hayden continue to growl, his jaw working with rage. "Right this damn second, you are going to stop staring at Maya, you freak. It's disgusting! You hear me?!"

Alex had arrived on the scene. Hayden had left him far behind in his mad dash. He thought the scene was about to blow up between Hayden and Kougar.

"Hey, man, Hayden," Alex voice warned, "come on, cool it."

"Shut up, Alex," Hayden shot out of the side of his mouth. He moved another inch closer to Kougar's face. "No more stares. Got it!"

Kougar expression was of the utmost calm which Hayden began to notice. It made his eyes flame and his fists clench.

"I think this is a free country. I believe I can stare at whatever I want," Kougar said in a low, calm voice, his unworried eyes showing no interest in Hayden's convulsing features.

Kougar's calm demeanor enraged Hayden and pushed him over the edge. He took one step back. Kougar knew what was coming and he didn't put up his hands.

"Stare at this then," Hayden spit out and his clenched fists snaked out, striking Kougar across the face in a quick sequence, a right then a left. Kougar's face turned back with each blow. Taking a moment to absorb the blows, a slight grunt coming out with each hit, Kougar finally turned his head back. Blood started at the corners of his mouth. He made no move to stem the trickle of blood down his chin. Being a couple of inches taller than Hayden, he just calmly looked down into Hayden's furious eyes. A moment passed. Kougar spit some blood out and again, said calmly:

"Free country."

"Don't look down on me, freak!" Hayden snarled and his fists snaked out again punching Kougar in the stomach. The air rushed out of Kougar's lungs in a whoosh. One more stomach punch and Kougar went down on his knees.

"Hayden! Stop it!" Maya shouted frantically, as she sprinted into the fight and plowed right into Hayden. She took him to the ground and he gave no resistance, the fight going out of him.

"What the hell is going on here?!" Maya shouted at Hayden in between deep breaths.

Kougar, on his knees, tried to regain the wind that had been knocked out of him. Hayden got to his feet, his expression subdued. He couldn't look at Maya. He glanced down, his face filling with emotion. Maya angrily took two hard steps and pushed Hayden in the chest, knocking him back.

"What are you doing!?"

"Hit me," mumbled Hayden.

"What?" she blurted out in shock.

"Hit me."

"Hit him," Kougar said between shallow breaths, still clutching his stomach.

Maya looked at Kougar and back to Hayden debating whether she should give Hayden a nice slap across the face. He certainly deserved it!

"What are you doing here?" Hayden said in a low voice. "This is none of your business. What do you care about that freak?" And Hayden gestured at Kougar who was still gathering his breath.

"He's my friend."

"No I'm not," Kougar said, finally able to look up, his mouth bloody. Maya's eyes widened at the sight of Kougar's bloody face.

"See?" Hayden muttered. "None of your business."

Maya's friends began to arrive, Maddie in the lead. Maddie was about to shout out something but stopped, as she took in the seriousness of the situation, nothing funny to be said right now. The other girls followed Maddie's lead and didn't say anything, feeling shocked by the scene in front of them. A real fight!

"He," and Hayden jabbed his finger at Kougar, "has been staring at you, like you're a piece of meat. It's not right," Hayden stated harshly. "He can't look at you that way." And as much as he tried, he couldn't keep the sound of pain from creeping into his voice. "He can't."

The emotion in Hayden's words gave Maya the answer she was looking for. Her eyes softened but her voice was firm.

"Hayden, you know it's over between us... You've got to move on. This should have never happened. I can't tell you how angry I am at you. Jesus, Hayden, you hurt Kougar. Are you kidding? He didn't deserve it. He's a friend."

"No I'm not," Kougar reminded her.

Maya rolled her eyes in exasperation. "Will you stop with that," she said sharply. "Yes you are, dammit."

"I love you, Maya," came Hayden's tortured voice and his emotion now poured out of his eyes.

Hayden's unexpected words lingered in the pause they had created. Maya's shoulders slumped a little as she sighed. It broke her heart to see him so defeated, so much in pain. She still cared a great deal for him. She hadn't realized he had been so hurt.

Could I have done it another way? She agonized to herself.

She walked over to him. She could see his eyes welling up with moisture. Tears. Maya shook her head wondering how it had come to this, how Hayden, who always seemed so strong, so confident, could be reduced to this display of emotion in front... *of everyone!* It cut her deep. Her eyes felt hot.

"Hayden... you're were just too far ahead of me."

"I can wait," his raw voice whispered out.

"I'm sorry. I'm sorry it's o—"

"Maya ..." Hayden managed to say. "Does it look like it's over for me?"

"I'm sorry." It was all Maya could manage.

Everyone stood quiet for a moment. Carley and Cheryl had a hand to their mouths as they absorbed the drama. Amanda just looked on, her mouth pulling tight, her eyes blinking back an unexpected emotion. Maddie wanted to go to Maya and hug her but held back. Alex shoved his hands in his pockets and tried not to look at Hayden's pain-filled face. Kougar's raspy voice broke the silence. He still clutched his stomach with one hand.

"Well... I'm sorry, too."

Maya shot him an irritated glare. "What are you sorry about?"

"Yeah, freak," Hayden said quickly, anger, replacing the pain that had been in his voice.

"You're the one hurt!" Maya almost shouted, still irritated.

"I'm the one who's really hurt," Hayden interjected.

Maya rolled her eyes at Hayden and let out an exasperated sigh.

"I didn't mean to stare. Sorry, it won't happen again," Kougar said, as he rocked back off his knees and sat on the ground. He could feel the corner of his lips puffing up from the impact of Hayden's blows.

"Good," said Hayden with some measure of satisfaction. "I'm done here." And he looked at Maya with dry eyes, but pain still lingered in the corners of his expression. "I guess we're really done, too."

"It just wasn't our time now, Hayden. It's not," Maya said sadly.

"Yeah," Hayden shrugged, "just not *your* time. I get it."

If a hug could have wiped all the hurt off of Hayden's face, Maya would have been more than happy to embrace him for all the time they had been together, the feelings they had shared. But she knew her caring affection would not be returned or well received. She just bit at the bottom of her lip under Hayden's heavy, last, pain filled gaze. The girls opened a space for Hayden as he walked between them, Alex followed. Maddie opened her mouth to make a comment and Maya knew it would be something breezy because Maddie didn't like awkward situations. Maya stopped Maddie with a wave of her hand.

"It's all right, Madds. I'll see you guys in a little bit. Okay?"

Maddie gave Maya a look to see if she was going to be all right. Maya nodded.

"Ok. Let's go, girls."

The girls said their concerned, muffled goodbyes to Maya while looking warily at Kougar. They walked away talking softly amongst themselves. Maya went over and sat down next to Kougar, wincing at the sight of his bloodied mouth.

"Is it bad? Here, let me help you." Maya started to tear off a piece of her nice white, long-sleeved shirt. Kougar stopped her.

"No, it's all right. It really wasn't that bad. I've had worse," he smiled grimly through puffed lips. He pulled up his shirt to wipe the blood off his face. "I've got a rag right here."

"It's stupid for *you* to feel sorry, okay? It was so wrong for Hayden to do what he did to you."

Kougar leaned back on his hands and decided that he had to confront the inevitable right now.

"I feel bad you had to see it."

"I saw it all and it was horrible... Why... why didn't you protect yourself?" Maya voice was anguished. "I kept hoping you would put your hands up but... I guess you were scared and couldn't react. I was too late getting here. I could have stopped it."

"I wasn't afraid."

"I don't understand. Then why didn't you pro—"

Kougar started to squirm a bit, moving his head and pursing his lips, trying to keep the words he wanted to say from escaping. He cut her off with a dodge.

"It doesn't matter. It's over."

Maya moved closer to Kougar and looked him square in the eyes, something Kougar could only take for a couple of seconds before looking away.

"Okay, so you weren't afraid. Why let him do that to you? You are bigger and I think, stronger than him."

Again Kougar moved his head around uncomfortably and sighed slightly as he mulled over his thoughts. Maya wouldn't let it go.

"Why?"

Kougar finally decided what to say but it was hard for him. He tried again to put her off.

"You wouldn't understand."

"I think I can manage."

Kougar took a deep breath and let it out through a small smile and looked down, his unruly blond bangs almost covering his eyes.

"I… I had it coming," he began, his voice flat, emotionless.

"What?" Maya's disbelieving voice whispered out loudly. "Are you kidding?"

"I've had it coming for a long time. I don't know when that time will end... For some people, there isn't enough punishment; for some people, the price is never paid."

Maya sat back and studied Kougar's dreadlocked profile looking for a clue… something to help her.

"I don't understand. What's with all the punishment stuff and the price to-be-paid thing?"

Kougar lifted up his head and gave Maya a crooked smile, wry amusement in his deep blue eyes.

"You still want to be my friend? I've got layers and layers of freak stuff. Hayden is right to call me a freak. I don't think your buddies would like it if we were friends. Didn't you see the stares when we walking down the hall?"

"Not really," Maya said quickly, trying to downplay what she had noticed.

"Nice try."

"Look, friends are friends. I don't care what small minds think. It's not like—" and she tried to stop the awkward words before they came out of her mouth—"we're going to be together." And she added quickly: "I mean friends are friends. No harm in that. I have a hundred friends."

Kougar thought for a moment, a puzzled expression made its way across his forehead. He had missed entirely the 'together' reference and Maya's momentary embarrassment.

"A hundred friends... mmmm. How can you be a friend to a hundred friends? Wow. I couldn't imagine that. Heck, two friends would overwhelm me."

Maya smiled and chuckled. "I just know a lot of people, that's all."

They paused for a moment. Then Maya said in a serious voice that was tinged with regret.

"I'm sorry I was late getting here. I could have stopped it."

Kougar shrugged. "Maybe this time but not next. He obviously still loves you."

"He'll get over it," she said, trying to convince herself. "He'll have to."

"I'm glad a few punches in my face helped out."

"Jeez, Kougar, you are so weird."

"I am," he said seriously while nodding... He paused, gave Maya a quick glance, and then looked inward, trying to find some courage. He could see that Maya was dying to talk about 'it.' It had been hovering around their discussion. Maya finally started it and Kougar cut in.

"You're Gaius, you—"

"No. It's not like that."

"That was you at the dance?"

"Ah," he sighed sheepishly and looked down, "that was Gaius, not me."

Maya gave Kougar a puzzled smiled. "I don't understand... It *was* you. Just a costume, yes—" she said, her tone full of certainty. *It was real for me!* Her mind flashed back to the scene between her and Gaius behind the stage, and the way she had felt came flooding back.

Kougar squirmed and said in a defeated voice. "It's not a costume."

113

Maya was still caught up in images and feelings of that night. She knew he had felt what she had. His eyes had said so. *It was real for you, too!* Hope tugged at her heart as she thought this to herself.

"Sometimes it's better to be someone you're not," Maya quoted, remembering Gaius' words.

Kougar again looked down and declared in wistful, but honest voice, "I am no Gaius, that's for damn sure. You *have* to believe me. He is everything I'm not."

"You mean everything... all the things you said during that—"

"Gaius."

"The kiss you wanted—"

Again Kougar cut her off, adamant. "That he wanted."

Maya breathed out a slight, skeptical chuckle as she remembered the intensity of that moment. "That's kind of hard to believe. I could swear that you—I mean, Gaius was ..."

"Yes *he* was. Anyways, it doesn't matter," Kougar began quickly. "I mean, look at you and... look at me." Kougar snorted sarcastically.

Maya let the sadness gather in her eyes, but there, in a small corner of her heart, she would keep alive that night and what it had meant to her. Is it enough that those memories stay an ethereal cache of smoldering feelings—and yes, hungers—that would never be made flesh? *It had better be!*

"Ha!" Kougar laughed nervously, "TMI, that's for sure." You should have never found out. Now I feel weirder than I am."

Maya just looked at Kougar, trying to see Gaius in his face, hear him in Kougar's voice.

"Hey, ah, I gotta go... Thanks for calling off your mad dog. I had a feeling that he wasn't done."

"It was the least that I could do. ..." And Maya held out her hand and smiled. "Friends? And don't worry, you can stare all you want. Hayden won't bother you again. So, friends?"

Kougar paused for a moment then took her hand warily.

"Well, not really."

Maya's smile broadened. "Okay, we can be not-really-friends, then."

"All right," he relented, and then looked around at his scattered backpack items.

"Here, let me help you."

"It's all right, I got it."

"No worries."

Kougar started gathering books. Maya saw some items about twenty feet away and went for them. She noticed a cell phone that was flipped open. She acted without thinking. She punched in her number and hit 'talk.' She heard one ring then quickly closed the phone and picked up some notebooks, pens and a calculator. She walked back to Kougar. He opened his backpack and she put the items in.

"Thanks... I hope this doesn't happen again... I know it was hard for you," Kougar said, with regret in his voice.

"Hard for me? Dude, you're the one who got punched. I don't get you. How can you worry about me? You've got it backwards."

"It's complicated, I guess," Kougar laughed sheepishly. "Now, I have to figure out what to tell my mom," and he touched at his puffy lips. "In the past, when I got bullied, my dad would just say we're moving and off we would go to a new area, a new school."

"Do you think you'll move again?" she said with a concern in her voice that surprised her.

"They know the signs. I'll have to—"

"You have to finish Grenfeld's class," she said, trying to be persuasive. "You have to. You've put too much work into it just to drop out."

"That's a good argument," he said, encouraged by her tone. "But my dad... he worries about me. It almost seems like he's getting bullied, not me."

"You can't move, I mean, it's ridiculous. You just got here. Don't you like it here?"

"Yeah, it's cool. I like all the stuff you can do," and he laughed, "except stare, without being hassled. I dig mountain biking."

"You do?" Maya's face brightened.

"Yeah... you?"

"I love it. I've been riding since I was ten."

"Cool."

"We'll have to ride. I know all the trails and where to go."

"You, me?" Kougar sounded confused. "I don't think we—"

"Hey, just because we're not friends doesn't mean we can't meet up on the trail and decide to ride for a while... harmless stuff."

Kougar cocked an unsure eye at Maya as she beamed a smile back at him.

"Maybe... Maybe someday," he said without conviction, and then quickly changed the subject. "I gotta go."

Kougar leaned down and picked up his skateboard and one of the wheels cycled around a few times and it caught Maya's eye. The memory flashed across her mind of her sprawling on her back on the grass that night at Drake Park, and seeing for a brief instant, the upside down skateboard, wheels still spinning. She thought of all the ways she might ask Kougar in a roundabout way about what had taken place. They all seemed stupid, contrived, so she just started to tell her story.

"Hey," she began, "one night, about three months ago, I was walking home through Drake Park and some guy, some huge man tried to... to grab me." She couldn't help clutching at her arms for comfort as she relived that awful experience. "And someone, on a skateboard like yours, ran right into the man, knocking him off me and I ran away. That somebody... might have saved me from something horrible; might have saved my life."

Kougar's face turned reflective as he studied her intently while she told her story. *So it was Maya!* He never knew whom the girl was that had been struggling with the big thug. But, her screams had sounded so familiar that they had just galvanized him into a course of action; an action that he hadn't consciously chosen. He decided not to reveal his part. It would be just too complicated.

"Wow, I guess you were lucky. I have skated Drake Park at night and I know it is dark in some places and if you get up enough momentum, it's hard to stop."

"Was it you?" she asked directly.

"Who me? Me? No, no, obviously, I would have remembered that, for sure. I mean, take a gander. Do I look like a hero to you?"

"I don't know what a hero looks like."

Kougar put his backpack on and brushed his long blond bangs back off his forehead with his hands.

"Well, it ain't me."

"Yeah, well, anyways, this guy on the skateboard didn't know who I was."

"Like I said," Kougar added quickly, "the guy on the board probably had too much speed going and couldn't stop, and it happened to help you out. A nice coincidence if you ask me. That's it," he said as if to convince himself that his explanation was accurate. "Yeah, that's it."

Maya just looked at Kougar and he could tell she wasn't too persuaded by his 'take.' She just tilted her head to one side, pursed her lips, and studied him. Kougar felt like she was reading his mind. Time to go.

"I ah, I guess I'll see you around."

Kougar turned to walk off. Maya watched him for a few steps and then she called out to him.

"The guy didn't know me. He shouted at me: "Run Michaela, run."

When Maya said his sister's name, Kougar froze. The scene that night flooded back through his mind. He tried to remember what he had yelled out that night. He couldn't recall. He wasn't sure because everything had happened in hyper speed. But he must have said it. He didn't turn around but started to walk away. It was just another thing he didn't want to explain. Talking about Gaius had been enough. But Kougar's pause told Maya what she suspected was true.

It was you!

"Kougar, I know it was you. It *was* you. You saved me!" she shouted after him as he continued to walk away. Kougar shook his shaggy head and came to a slow, difficult stop, and turned around.

"It just happened, that's all," he shrugged and said, lowly, trying to downplay the whole thing.

Without thinking, Maya walked quickly up to Kougar and embraced him. His face locked up with stunned surprise. She couldn't imagine what would have happened if Kougar hadn't knocked that man off of her. A quick tremor of fear went through her body, and, as she pulled Kougar closer to her, her trembling subsided. She couldn't help but to image that she was also clinging to Gaius's tall frame and pressing her head against his muscled chest. A cascade of emotions overawed Kougar's mind by the contact with her body. The beauty of all that she was amazed him but also filled him with fear. To be flushed with euphoria and anxiety at the same time staggered his sense of self. He felt these two feelings could easily be turned into an addictive drug.

Slowly, awkwardly, fearfully, he finally returned her embrace with timid arms. A couple of heated moments passed that hinted at something between them, something deep and tidal. She felt Kougar's overwhelmed shudder. She realized how uncomfortable he was, and with difficulty, she withdrew. They stood for a second, each measuring how the touching of their bodies had been much, much more than a harmless hug and how it surprised both of them. Maya broke the loaded silence with an embarrassed grin.

"Sorry, I didn't mean to invade your space. I, I just wanted to thank you for helping me; for saving me," and her eyes moistened with gratitude. "Thank you."

Kougar cleared his voice nervously. "Well, it was just one of those things," he said, as he tried to laugh it off.

"Yeah, right," Maya forced herself to laugh back, "just one of those things."

Kougar sighed. This had been one stressful conversation. "Hey, thanks for the help with Hayden. I guess that makes us even, then."

Maya smiled, her deep brown eyes glowing. "Even? No, I don't think so. You are a real hero."

"Ha!" Kougar couldn't help grunting a sarcastic laugh through his puffed lips. "Not even close." And with that, he turned and, with some urgency, walked off.

Maya watched him go. Her mind was really reeling now. So, Kougar *was* Gaius and now he was the one who had saved her that night, and, the one who let Hayden punch him out.

It's all so confusing. Who is he, really?

One part of her wanted to find out and the other part... just wanted to be with Gaius, to have him devour her with his eyes. She couldn't help the wild imagining that blew down from the forested mountains at the back of her mind, that if her lips melted under his, that it would be just like going... all the way. She shook her head in surprise at her untamed fantasy while all the shades of red played across her face.

Kougar turned the corner and slowly pushed along on his board. He could still feel Maya's weight against him and her arms around him. He felt like he had been held for the first time in his life. His heart had thudded alive as if from a deep dormancy when she had pulled herself close to him. So much of his emotions had always been about fear, pain, rage... and loss. When she had pressed her head into his chest, the smell of her hair filled the air around him with a fresh, furry, herbal scent that had almost made him light headed.

Forget about it, his subconscious reminded him. That was as close as he will ever get to Maya, besides, she was just being nice; just giving him a 'thank you' hug. *Yep, that's it.* But still, he couldn't get over going from being smacked around by Hayden and then right into Maya's arms! The irony of it all struck him suddenly and he barked out a sarcastic laugh that he cut off quickly as he felt a sharp pain in his ribs were

Hayden's heavy fists had pounded him. He bent over, grunted, and clutched at his stomach with one hand, his mind chasing away farther and farther from what should never, never be considered.

Just minutes old, the embrace with Maya seemed more and more like a dream and not something that had actually happened. *Good!* The actual substance of her body against his would diminish dream by dream, and finally—he knew—it would dissolve into an insubstantial bodily mist that would smoke through his grasp.

And that's the way it should be! Freaks like me shouldn't stare, shouldn't hope… shouldn't feel things they shouldn't. Period. Freakin' period!

Kougar felt a warm, mineral taste in his mouth and he realized that he had bit the corner of his puffed lip. He spat out some blood-filled saliva. He wiped an angry hand across his mouth feeling a grim satisfaction at his pain. He pounded the pavement hard picking up speed until he was speeding recklessly, swerving around parked cars, hopping curbs. He hoped for some kind of violent collision, a sudden impact that would rock his body with pain, the kind that would bring him closer to Michaela. Hayden's blows hadn't moved him that much closer to her.

One day soon, he announced to himself, *I'm going to be with you. I promise.*

The Decision

Kougar arrived home without face-planting on any car windshield. *Not that I didn't try.* He popped his board up and snagged it in one practiced motion and tucked it under his arm. He took two long strides up the front porch stairs. He dropped his board next to the patio bench and then walked through the door and into the living room. He was hoping he could make it to his bedroom without being seen. It would be easier to explain the cuts at the sides of his mouth if he could tidy up his face and put on a clean shirt.

He knew his mom was at home. He saw her car parked in the driveway. He scanned the kitchen. *Good.* He didn't see her. As he walked by the kitchen island, his mom, Maria, stood up from behind the kitchen counter. She had been looking for a new sponge in the cabinet under the sink.

"Oh!" came Maria's startled cry as she saw Kougar's face and bloody shirt. All her fears poured into her voice and she couldn't keep the panic out of her trembling tone. She put a shocked hand to her mouth.

"Oh, Kougar! Son, what happened to you? You're hurt!"

She rushed over to Kougar and softly put her hands up to his face, trying to examine his injuries.

"It's nothin', mom," came his calm voice as he turned his head away from her inquiring hands.

"Nothing?" she gasped in horror. "Did 'it' happen again? Who was it? Who did this to you?"

"Mom, mom. 'It' didn't happen. Okay? I was goofing around with some kid in the gym and we decided to spar with the gloves on a little bit, nothing heavy. I accidently dropped my hands and put my face in the front of a few combos." Kougar grinned sheepishly. "That's why I don't box for real."

"No bullying?" she asked warily.

"Nah, nothing like that. Just trying to have fun...a little fun. That's all," he grinned again, hoping to convince her.

"You call a bloody face fun?"

"Like I said, it was an accident. The kid didn't expect me to drop my hands. I thought I could just dodge my head. I guess I wasn't fast enough. It was kind of funny."

"Well," Maria said, her voice relieved, "no more of that kind of fun, all right? Imagine if your father had seen you and not me?"

"Yeah, we would be on our way out of Bend right now." Kougar laughed through his words and then his tone changed, his smile vanished. "He would have figured that somebody got to me again... It always seemed like he was getting bullied, not me."

Maria let Kougar's words sink in. She thought for a moment, her pretty face softening. She then spoke in a low voice, an ironic grin formed on her lips.

"In a way he was. Believe me, he felt the fear and pain that you did... He did."

"Well, it didn't happen to him. He never got punched or kicked like a dog. I didn't ask him to feel... anything for me."

"He's your father."

"Yeah, tough luck for him," Kougar said, looking down.

"And me?" Maria looked at him, her eyes plaintive, hurt sounding at the edges of her tone.

Guilt spread through him as he squirmed. He let out a sigh, and pulled at his bloodied shirt.

"Ah, mom..." and Kougar brushed a painful hand over his forehead and through his dreadlocked hair and he spoke with hesitant difficulty. "I ah, I am sorry how those things might have... hurt you."

Maria looked deeply into Kougar's eyes, trying to reach him, realizing how rare this discussion was. "Of course they did, son. I am your mother and I love you. I always will. You can't be hurt without it hurting me."

Kougar finally looked down, unable to match the intensity of feeling in her gaze. He shoved his hands into his pockets. He had to pause to gather his thoughts, to try and say the right thing. *But what if it came out bad?*

"I… I want you to believe that all of those times, the bullying, it didn't really add up into anything for me. I'm all right. I can take it."

"Kougar!" came Maria's disbelieving gasp. "Honey, how can you say that? You don't have to take it. It's not your fault. You were a victim."

The jungle of knots and emotional twists within him suddenly coiled tightly. They tied off any more attempts to 'explain' himself. *There's really no use in that,* came a flat voice from deep in his zero sum heart.

"Look, like I said, all those times don't add up to anything for me."

Maria walked slowly over to Kougar as if to ask his permission. He didn't stop her this time and she embraced him tenderly, maternally. She wanted to hold on and never let go of this rare, mother/son moment. She could feel him getting uncomfortable so she drew back, her hands on his shoulders. She looked up at her tall son and nodded, her eyes moist. She could see that the childhood structure of his face that had so resembled hers was now broadening into a masculine version. But the riotous blond-white hair, and the deep blue eyes of his father, looked back at her; they pleaded, saying what he couldn't.

"Jeez, look at you. My boy, my sweet boy, is almost a man."

Kougar shrugged, a little embarrassed. "I don't think 'sweet' is the right word, but I would like to get the awkward boy-thing over with."

"Oh, son. It's just a small phase that all boys go through at some point. You are no different."

"Yeah, just freaky different."

"No. Kougar, it's not like that. Believe me."

"I could have had a friend today."

Maria's face brightened. "Really? But I don't understand. What do you mean 'could have'?"

Kougar shook his head deciding it was just too complicated, his emotions tangling into a knot that he felt he just couldn't untie.

"It doesn't matter."

Maria tried to read into Kougar's obvious disappointment. "Hey, just because this person didn't want to be friends with you, doesn't mean that you wouldn't be a good friend. People make or don't make friends for all kinds of reasons. It's not a big deal but I'm sorry it didn't work out."

"No need to be sorry. I... I didn't want to be friends."

"Okay. Fair enough. You have your reasons."

"You've got that right," came Kougar's clipped response. "It would just turn out... bad."

"Bad for you?"

Kougar sighed and cleared his throat to get out his last thought. He looked down at his bloody shirt and then looked up at his mom.

"No, her. It would be bad for her."

"Her?" Maria asked in surprise.

"Yeah."

"Well, son, you don't know that. Sometimes you have to—"

"Well, never mind." Kougar waved a hand at her to stop the discussion.

"But son, I think—"

"Mom, I said never mind," Kougar's flat, stubborn voice came out tight. "It doesn't matter."

Maria gave her son a long look, trying to read behind his words, knowing that if she tried to really question him, she wouldn't get any answers. She was all too familiar with that tone, his way of always ending a discussion that tried to go deep. There was that door, that impenetrable door that she could never open. She had only been able to knock on it. But today, that *door* had cracked open ever so slightly, ever so painfully. She studied him for a moment. She tilted her head, finally deciding that the 'boxing' story was just that: a story. He had his reasons. She would never know them. But the 'friend' story, that was painful for him. That hit home. Sadness welled up within her. If only he would let her share his pain.

"You all right?" she finally managed.

Kougar breathed in, his throat finally relaxing; his jaw stopped its tight contractions. "I'm good. Don't worry. I'm good. I'm going to clean up." And then he laughed. "It's been a bloody day."

Maria watched her son disappear down the hallway towards his room, his broad shoulders swaying back and forth underneath the fall of his long, twisted locks. She thought how special this moment had been for her. She folded her arms around her, savoring it For Kougar to let her embrace him like that, as fleeting as it seemed to her, was something to be grateful for, like the first raindrops of spring. She had always thought, that with her mother's love and affection, she could soften his hard, unfeeling edges; edges that weren't cruel or hateful, just hard, like pitons sticking out of a granite rock face. She had made sure that he didn't see her tears when she had tried to get close to him only to be turned away. Over the strained and unrequited years, she had finally made an uneasy peace with Kougar's ways, his boundaries. Her hope, her every day prayer, was that Kougar could somehow, make his way back to her, to finally let her in.

Open the door, my sweet Kougar. Please, open the door.

Kougar peeled off his clothes and walked into the bathroom that was attached to his bedroom. He took a quick look at his face in the bathroom sink mirror; dried blood at the edges of his mouth and a slight black eye that he was surprised to see. One of Hayden's blows must have traveled up his cheek and glanced off his eye. He touched a hand to his ribs and winced slightly as he pushed on a spot that he knew would bruise up tomorrow. He grunted and thought: *That Hayden sure packed a punch.*

He was glad Maya had showed up when she did. It could have been a real beating. He actually felt sympathy for Hayden. That poor dude was so in love with Maya. He was so flamed. He didn't know for sure, but he had an idea what Hayden was going through after losing someone like Maya.

Kougar ducked into the shower and felt the sting of the water as it entered the small cuts on the sides of his mouth. He pressed his lips into a tight, grim line as he reaffirmed his decision, his 'only' possible decision, to not be friends with Maya.

Of all people, why did it have to be 'her'? I'll have to unfriend a friend that never was. Now, I can't even look at her from far away. All of it ruined because of Hayden's fists and her wanting to be my friend. Damn.

His mocking chuckle sounded under the fall of the water that streamed down his face. He would have to avoid Maya for a few days, to keep strengthening his resolve. He would tell his mom that he would like a couple of days off from school. He didn't feel well. She would be able to look behind that excuse and give him his two days. His dad wouldn't say anything as long as his wife felt it best. That would give him tomorrow and Friday and with the weekend, he would, by Monday, be the freaky Iceman that he was. All of it, he hoped, will have passed over like a sudden, violent sandstorm that removed all tracks in the sand in its aftermath, leaving a bony dryness that said nothing had ever thought or walked through here.

The Game

Maya's cell phone pinged again. She let out an exasperated sigh and texted Maddie back:

> ...No, not going to Home Coming w anybody.
> Ugh..!

Maddie replied:

> ... Dang! Don't get so flamed, GF..!

That was the third time Maddie had asked her. Maddie finished her text:

> ...How many poor boys u turn down, Miss
> Hottie...?

Maya, right back:

> ...A few...A few. ☺ Didn't feel like it...

Maddie:

> ...U r such a heartbreaker! ZOMG! Maya Virk not
> going to HC! That's a crime! LOL! Maybe u r
> waiting for that dreadlocked kid to ask u. Ha! I'm a
> no go, too. ☹ Let's crash Cooper's HC party. Just
> single bitches lookin' 4 fun! ☺ Hope we rock it
> tonight at the game! I'm out! Pick u up at 6...

Maya:

> ...Cool...

Maya texted back and tossed her phone on the bed and lay down next to it. She picked it up and studied a number on it. An annoyed sigh blew through her lips and her fingers drummed on the bedspread. Finally she sat up and muttered under her breath. She turned on her phone, highlighted a cell phone number and punched in a text:

> …Hey, u missed Grenfeld's class last two days. R u ditching..?

Maya shook her head feeling foolish but hoping Kougar would text her back. She was surprised how she had looked for him in the halls and was more than a little disappointed not to see him in class. She kept thinking that, for some reason, Kougar didn't like her. That really bugged her. It was a thought she had never had to contemplate in regards to anybody. If someone hadn't liked her in the past, she didn't know about it. She stared at the phone… It didn't ping… and it didn't ping. She pursed her mouth in frustration. Her mind filed through all the things that Kougar might not like about her. She decided it could be any one of them.

Jeez, what's his problem?

A sudden, unfamiliar insecurity began to spread through her like fingers of troubling questions. At first, she tried to just observe this new feeling like she was a detached scientist, but her forced sense of neutrality was quickly overrun by one thought: *He really doesn't like me. What else could it be? I tried to be nice to him,* she thought, as she felt sorry for herself.

She stared at the phone and before she knew it, she pouted out a text:

> …U mad at me..? ☹

She stared at her phone for another couple of minutes, her face flushed with a growing sense of being more and more ridiculous.

Nothing… No ping. She shook her head and tried to get a hold of herself and with some effort she managed to think to herself:

Why should I care?

Yes, he was Gaius *and* he saved her that night but he was just that kid, Kougar. Just Kougar, she had to remind herself: messy dreadlocks, hair all down in his face, baggy jeans shot through with holes, riding a skateboard like he's a freshman… and just geeky shy, with nothing going for him. Nothing that she could see, except that he saved her, probably saved her life… and he had 'come' to her as Gaius, his green eyes burned into her memory.

Why didn't he kiss me? That would have told me so much! Now, I'll never know!

The mystery enflamed her and she hated not knowing. She felt a strange ache under her arms, deep in her chest. She sighed impatiently, and thrust her hair back off her shoulders and stood up.

Just leave it alone, sheesh! It's all just stupid. Stop it! She commanded harshly, shouting inside her mind. She sprawled back on her bed seeking to compose herself, but the comfort and softness of her bed felt like she was lying on a rack of nails, her thoughts reeling with disturbing 'what ifs.' She just wanted to give it a rest, hopefully to forget all of it, all the roiling turmoil within her… Gratefully, a creeping fatigue crept through her mind and she drifted off into a fitful sleep and dreamed of her Indian grandmother who scolded her for not playing the piano and dancing. Her grandmother's Indian accent with British overtones sounded through her dream in a broken stream of old stories that were full of wisdom and warnings; warnings about beauty and consequences, and something about fears.

Suddenly her eyes popped open. She turned her head to one side and caught sight of the clock on her dresser drawers and gasped out in a panic.

Yikes! I'm late!

Her cell phone pinged. Maddie was outside. Maya sprang off the bed and became a whirlwind of activity. She put a change of clothes in her backpack, put on her cheerleading uniform, quickly brushed her hair out and then dashed downstairs and passed by her mom, Lisa, who was in the kitchen preparing dinner. She closed the oven door and straitened up. She still had her nurse's outfit on, an apron tied around her waist. Her sandy, brown hair hung just below her shoulders. Her nurse's uniform didn't hide her lithe figure. Lisa's hazel eyes flashed in surprise.

"Hey wait! Where are you going in such a hurry? I'm making dinner."

Maya came to a hasty stop. "It's Homecoming Game tonight!

"Oh, that's right. You going to the dance with Hayden?"

"Mom," came Maya's irritated tone, "we haven't been together for over a month."

"Oh, yeah, that's right," Lisa tried to sound genuine. "Sorry. So, who are you going to the dance with?"

"I'm not."

"Not going to the Homecoming dance? Oh, honey," Lisa said, feeling sorry for Maya.

Maya turned and headed to the front door in a hurry and yelled over her shoulder: "No worries, mom, it's all right. I'll be back around eleven! Bye!"

The stands were full to bursting with fans from both schools. All the people in the east stands could take in the harvest moon just above the tops of the Cascades that stood in the background. It was a beautiful, cool, late October night. Maya could hardly hear the cheers of her team above the yelling spectators, which had kept up all game long. Both school bands tried to play louder than the other.

The game was going down to the wire, every penalty flag brought cheers and heavy boos.

Jeez, thought Maya, *we're cheering our butts off and nobody can hear us. It's crazy loud!*

Hayden had been running hard all game. He was slow to get up on more than a few times when the other team gang tackled him, piling on… and on.

There was under a minute to go. Mt. Bachelor High was driving down the field. Every yard Hayden gained seemed to be after contact. He kept driving his legs mindlessly, grunting out in determination until the whistle blew him down. Mt. Bachelor High was behind by six points. They had to score a touchdown.

Maya and her team had stopped the formal cheering, not wanting to turn their backs on the action. They didn't want to miss any of the game with a victory hanging in the balance. Maya and Maddie clutched and grabbed at each other during every play, screaming with excitement. All the eyes in the stadium were transfixed with the scene on the field—except for one pair.

The Man frowned as Maya and her cheer team stopped their routines. He stood in the last row at the top of the stadium in the farthest corner from the field. He had been watching Maya the whole game through his small opera binoculars. This was the first time he had attended a Mt. Bachelor High football game. He didn't care about his alma mater's football team. He came for Maya. He felt close to her, yet so far away… from embracing her.

Everybody knew that Hayden was going to carry the ball and the defenders on Redmond High knew that, too. There were going to be no surprises, no trick plays. It was going to be smash-mouth, running in between the tackles football. Hayden 'was' the offense, with over two hundred and twenty yards gained and three touchdowns so far.

The Mt. Bachelor fans were in frenzy when the team came out of a time out. They were on Redmond High's twelfth yard line, third down and five. The last play, Hayden ran it up the gut with no gain. He was met at the line of scrimmage by a wall of defenders. They didn't take him down. He kept pumping his legs, his forward progress stopped as he was pushed back by swarming defenders, the ref's whistles blowing madly.

A huge groan went up from the Mt. Bachelor stands. This was it: fourth down, ten seconds to go. Maya could hear the cries of encouragement for Hayden. She and Maddie added their voices to the calls. They clutched at each other in nervous anticipation.

Mt. Bachelor took its last time out. Everyone knew that for all the discussion that was going on between Mt. Bachelor's coach and quarterback, it was essentially: give Hayden the ball; he was the star and he had been the horse that had carried his team this far.

As both teams got set at the line of scrimmage, shouting from both stands reached a crescendo. Maya couldn't hear herself think. Maddie squeezed her arm like a vice. The Mt. Bachelor quarterback tried a few harsh counts to get the other team to jump off sides. The Redmond defense just waited patiently, bunched up with nine players stacked in the box, linebackers, and safeties right on top of the defensive linemen.

Suddenly, Mt. Bachelor's offensive line lurched forward into a tangled mass of players. Two defensive linebackers burst through a hole in the line. Hayden's fullback took on one of them and Hayden lowered his helmet and launched himself digging his cleats into the ground. The helmet-to- helmet crack sounded above the roaring crowd. The linebacker staggered back and down under Hayden's impact. Hayden made it to the line of scrimmage and saw a sliver of an opening between two linemen. He juked and stutter-stepped himself sideways and squeezed through the gap. Daylight! Hayden burst through the mass of bodies and headed for the goal line. The strong safety and the other linebacker converged on him from either side. He girded himself for the wrenching collision that was coming. He pumped his legs for all he was worthwhile a primal growl rose up from his lungs. He was going to carry those defenders into the end zone with him!

Hayden was closing on the goal line. The two Redmond defenders hit him on both sides at the same time, the sound of pads crunching together under the heavy impact, echoed in Hayden's ears as his breath whooshed out of him in a sickening gasp. Both of the opponent's' helmets pushed through Hayden's arms and pinched the football out of his grasp. The football squirted out onto the ground and a couple of Redmond defenders dove on it.

Groans of disbelief rose up from the Mt. Bachelor stands while Redmond High's fans cheered deliriously. The game clock clicked to zero. Hayden lay still on the ground while the Redmond defenders danced around him, elated in victory. Alex pushed his way through the celebrating players and knelt down next to Hayden.

"Murph! Murph! Hey, man, you all right?"

Hayden mumbled as he tried to gather himself up to his hands and knees.

"My fault... My fault." Hayden managed to breathe out. I had it. I had it... I let everyone down."

"Ah, man. It's not like that. You played great. We had other opportunities.

Hayden lifted up his face guard and spat out in disgust and dropped his head and shoulders under the weight of the crushing loss.

"It came down to me. I dropped the football."

"Dropped the ball! Are you kidding?"

"I dropped the ball," Hayden insisted is a gasping breath.

"Serious, dude," Alex almost shouted as he helped Hayden to his unsteady feet. "It was a perfect hit."

"A hit's a hit," Hayden shot back through dry lips as he swayed slightly.

Alex tightened his grip on Hayden. "Nobody was going to hold on to that ball. They crushed you. It's not your fault. Forget about it."

The Mt. Bachelor fans were still stunned. Some stood, others sat back down as if they were waiting for the game to continue. Finally, the exit started. Maya and Maddie hugged each other, a hug of consolation. Maya looked over Maddie's shoulder to where Hayden was, still on his hands and knees, Alex bent over him. She felt so sorry for him. A month ago she would have run out onto the field to be with him, help him, hold him, to try and lessen the pain of defeat. A part of her felt bad that she couldn't, and she was a little taken back at the small, but strong desire that wanted to. It would just be...awkward. She sighed, her memories tugging at her. But she knew, ultimately, that Hayden had a strong sense of self-confidence. *He'll be all right.* She wondered, though, why some girl wasn't out there with Hayden. She figured he would have a girlfriend by now.

Maya and Maddie let go of each other. Maya caught sight of Maddie's tears. She was more than a little surprised because Maddie always seemed above it all with her ever-ready sarcastic remarks and funny observations.

"Oh, my God, Madds." Maya said almost as a question.

Maddie grinned sheepishly back through her tears. "I guess I really wanted us to win. Bad loss."

"Yeah, definitely a tough one. There's next week though. We're still in first place. Redmond has two losses. We just need to win the last three and we'll be at state. See?"

"Yeah, you're right. It'll be all right. I'm just practicing the tears for when I have a real breakup with a boyfriend, I'll know how to do it."

That was more like the Maddie that Maya knew. They both laughed. The field was emptying, some of the kids in the school band walked by the girls carrying their instruments, still talking in shocked tones. Carley, Cheryl, Amanda and Breah made their way over, milling through the exiting spectators.

"Ugh, bummer!" Carley muttered under her breath.

"How sucky was that?" Breah snorted out.

"Redmond sucks anyways," Cheryl stated.

"No worries, girls, it's party time. We're still in first! Hey, let's go change," Maddie began, an excited glint returned to her eyes, her sadness and tears long gone. "Let's head to the locker room, get ready and head over to Cooper's Home Coming party. There's got to be somebody's boyfriend I can steal. It'll be fun!"

The mood of the girls picked right up, now that it was okay. They elbowed one another and made snide comments.

"You guys go for it; I'm out," Maya said as she stuffed her gear into her backpack.

"Out?" came Maddie's shocked reply. "No way, come on, girl we'll—oh, I see. Hayden's going to be there."

"Well, he's had a tough night already. But actually, it's all right. I'm not worried about that. It's long over. I've got some stuff to do."

"Stuff?" Maddie eyed Maya skeptically. It's Saturday night. What 'stuff' is there to do except party with us righteous girls? Right, girls?!"

All the girls voice their agreement.

"True. True," Maya smiled. If I get bored I'll buzz on over and look in on you hotties, make sure none of you get 'stuck' in the bathroom with some senior. I'll see you guys in the locker room. I'll get the gear," Maya said.

The girls headed onto the field and began hugging and consoling the players that they knew. Maya started to gather up their cheer props putting them in a large duffle bag. She said hi to a few friends who passed by her.

"Nice job, Maya," one said. "The cheers were really cool. Bummer about the game."

"Awesome stuff, Maya!" another said. "You girls were really on it."

"Thanks, Bobbi. Thanks, Sue. We did our best. I think the team did, too; just bad luck at the end. We'll win next week!"

"Yeah," both the girls said at once. "See ya."

For a moment, Maya looked out across the field. The Redmond team had already exited in their excitement, anxious to get on their bus, go home and celebrate. They might not make it to state but they did beat the favorite, Mt. Bachelor High in their Homecoming game.

Maya saw Hayden walking alone, head down, the last Mt. Bachelor player to leave the field. Maddie saw him and walked over. She put an arm around Hayden. They then stopped and Hayden embraced her. Maddie patted his back, consoling him as any friend would. Maya could see that Maddie turned her head to say something in Hayden's ear, through his helmet. If anybody could cheer Hayden up, it would be Maddie. *Good job, Madds.*

Maya scooped up another cheer prop, closed the bag and slung it over her shoulder. She looked down to end of the field. Hayden and

Maddie were still in each other's arms. Still. Maddie had stopped patting Hayden on the back. She watched the way they held on to each other. It seem to last too long. A little notion vaguely suggested that it might not be just a 'hug' anymore, but as an observer, she just observed.

Pursued

Maya took an extra-long shower, relaxing under the cascade of warm water, as her fatigued muscles started to unwind. She couldn't help feeling pensive, as her thoughts kept turning inward. So many puzzling things to think about these days! She was not used to this new sensation of being a bit overwhelmed. She hoped the falling water would help clear away the clouded film on the window she was trying to look through to see things for what they really were. She had cheered hard during the game and felt a little worn-out from trying to yell above the noise of the fans. She was relieved not to be going out tonight with the girls. They were way too wound up. Maddie and the girls had already changed and had headed out, definitely ready to party. Maddie had whipped them up into a bunch of crazy girls. As they left, Maddie had given Maya an extra strong hug, saying it was too bad Maya wasn't going along because she always kept them in line, kept them out of trouble. She was the big 'Sis'.

Maya was the last one on the locker room. She dressed, stored away her cheerleading gear in her locker and then realized that she must have left her jacket on the field.

As she made her way back onto the football field, she looked up into the night sky. The full, harvest moon was now partly obscured by some fleeting clouds that had swept over the Cascades. A swath of stars glittered above her like a million tiny jewels. But some portent in her mood made her think of a million tiny spider eyes…watching. The dark outlines of the various school buildings seemed abandoned rather than empty of students. She saw the parking lot was almost deserted, except for a few scattered cars of the night cleaning staff. A crisp, cool wind rustled up from out of nowhere. It swirled rather than blew, as if it started up from right underneath her. She folded her arms across her chest for warmth thinking that she would need her jacket for the walk home. She welcomed the walk, a chance to have some quiet time alone with her thoughts, to figure things out. She could have snagged a ride home with

Maddie but she didn't want to rush and be in the middle of all that hyped up energy the girls were feeling about going out and hitting up Cooper's Homecoming party.

The stadium lights were still on. Empty field, empty stands. She looked around, across the field and saw in her memory the last play of the game: the screaming and jumping fans, Hayden running hard, looking like he was going to score the game winning touchdown as he met those two defenders at the goal line—and then, the sickening sight of the football squirting out of Hayden's hands... Game over.

It'll be a while to get over that, she thought, as she felt sorry for him.

She saw her white jacket on the ground, next to the player's bench. She walked over and picked it up and put it on. She felt better as the cold wind didn't reach her body. She decided to sit on the bench for a while to take in the empty quiet of the stadium that, over an hour ago, had been packed full of frenzied fans, horn-blowing school bands... And now, nothing, nothing, no visible record of the heart-breaking or elated emotions, or of physical trauma experienced by the players—the drama of it all...nothing, but an empty, clean field. She wondered if her thoughts could become like that football field, clean, with defined chalk lines, no visible drama, a new grassy slate, unburdened by what had happened before.

She took out her cell phone and looked for new texts. Had Kougar texted her back? No. Nothing. She sighed in frustration, thought for a moment and then tapped out a text:

> ...Sitting in an empty stadium. We lost. Heartbreaker. Just wondering what u r doing... Friends..?

She sat for a while, figuring that her text, like the others, would not be replied to. Determined, angry...and yes, hurt, she forcefully pounded out another text:

…Friends..?

Ugh, she said to herself. She felt ridiculous but couldn't help it. Something in her made her want to try and make a connection with—her cell phone pinged. She looked at the message, hopeful. She read Kougar's text like it was an exclamation point:

…No…and don't text back…

"What is his problem?" she whispered to herself, exasperated. She read his text over and over, then put her cell phone down on the bench next to her and looked out feeling as empty as the football field.

Kougar cursed under his breath while he texted Maya back. Anxiety flooded through his body. He wondered how she had got his number. The knots started to turn in his stomach.

God, she is stubborn. I don't want to be friends. I can't be. I don't. I—

I do, Gaius within said, in his clear and confident voice.

Kougar had been lying on his bed. Something in his mind shifted with the clear sound of a heavy iron key turning inside of large rusty lock. He sat straight up when he heard Gaius' voice. Kougar had always let Gaius talk to him when Gaius was…in charge, when Kougar had needed to 'become' Gaius, to escape from the black, loathing closet of what he was, to be free of himself. But mostly to forget his pain, especially if the images were getting too intense: the roaring flames, the burning figure, arms and legs flailing against the consuming fire. *And the screams…* If only for a while, in the secret of his bedroom, in front of the mirror, feeling the power and confidence of Gaius the vampire, time would be… lost.

Let me out, Gaius within said again.

It doesn't matter …You, don't matter, Kougar reaffirmed to himself.

139

I matter to her, came Gaius' insistent voice. *She wants to see me and I want to see her... Let me out.*

No... No way, Kougar shook his head. The whole thing with Maya was just becoming too much. *She has 'no' idea what I am.* Kougar drew in a shuddered, panic-ridden breath.

Kougar got up and paced back and forth, finally coming to a stop in front of the mirror above his chest of drawers, his breathing had deepened, his muscular chest starting to rise and fall in agitation. His face displayed the struggle going on within him. There was no way *he* could go to Maya. His fearful blue eyes looked back at him, suggesting a caged animal.

Let me go to her, Gaius whispered in his ear. *Stay in here. Safe...*

Kougar let out a harsh, anxious grunt and stalked off to the bathroom. He opened a drawer and pulled out a contact case and opened it. Green contacts. He reached back into the drawer and brought out a pale colored makeup jar and a brush. Continuing, he picked out a can of brown spray-on hair color and brown eyebrow mousse. He brushed the makeup on. He sprayed on the hair color, turning his blond hair brown and lightly brushed in the brown eyebrow color. He looked in the mirror, smoothed his hair out and pulled his long tangled locks back into a tight ponytail. Kougar put on a black turtleneck tee shirt with the superman logo that had a V instead of an S in the middle of it. He leaned over and put the green contacts in. He breathed deep, letting his mind and body unlock and relax, letting 'it' happen. He opened his eyes and looked into the mirror. Confident green eyes stared back at him, a slight hint of amusement in them.

Gaius.

He turned his back and the mirror revealed the saying stenciled on the back of his shirt:

'Immortality is only one bite away.'

*

Maya sat for another fifteen minutes or so, her mind a battleground for what to do next. She thought of all kinds of texts she could send back, angry ones, funny ones, disinterested ones. Or,

The next time I see him in Grenfeld's class, I'm going to get in his face and ask him what his problem is. I need an answer!

The Man sat in his white Dodge van, still parked on the street above the stadium. He stared at video on his smart phone, a video of Maya as she went through her cheer routines during the game. He was transfixed by the way she moved, the expressions on her beautiful face, expressions that only he could fully appreciate; that only he could see were actually a subtle communication only for his eyes.

We have our own language, the dull, bottomless voice sounded in his empty mind. He had seen Maya exit the football field. His hungry, deep, patience made him curious to wait and see when she left the girls locker room, which he could see from his van through his binoculars. He knew that the one who hunted for love had to be lucky. Luck and love, his mind twisted with the thought, go hand in hand.

He finished staring at the video. He pulled out his keys and started to put a key in the ignition when a movement outside his van caught his attention. A tall figure in a black tee shirt walked quickly by, a long, brown ponytail dangling down below the shoulders.

The Man watched, with no real interest, the figure—some kid—walking down the sidewalk. The figure disappeared around the corner of the street that led around the back of the school and out into a surrounding neighborhood. The Man took one last look down onto the lighted football field and his predator's eyes saw something that made him do a double take as he drew in a sharp breath. He quickly brought up his binoculars to confirm what his tight-fisted heart had hoped.

It's her! And he almost shouted out the words but clamped his jaw shut and then, swiftly, like a transformation, went into his calm, hunter's mode. He quietly slipped out of his van and made sure not to close the driver's side door with any noise. He looked down at Maya sitting on the bench, under the lights, with no one around. It was an offering, he thought, as if she sat on an altar and offered herself to him. He moved his huge body with no more sound than a grizzly bear's ghost as he made his way down to the fence that surrounded the field. He made sure to stay in the dark shadows that spaced about ten feet apart along the fence. He darted into each shaded area, paused and then darted again, making his way around behind Maya.

All of a sudden the football field's lights went out. It startled Maya for a second then she thought, *Closing time. Time to go anyway.*

Maya sighed and stood up, shaking her head that was still full of unresolved thoughts. She took a second to get adjusted to the darkness and started to make out the school's outdoor lighting that framed the outlines of some of the buildings. She headed off the field, forgetting her cell phone that lay on the bench where she had set it down. She was getting close to the exit when she heard a jingling fence sound back behind the stands. Out of the corner of her eye she thought she saw a hurtling shape cutting across the corner of the field. She froze in mid-stride and a gasp of fear shot up within her and got stuck in her throat. An instinct made her bolt under the cover of the stadium stands into the mosaic of the support structure that spread out like a thick forest of steel beams and poles.

She found herself pressed against some beams, not realizing how she had got there. She tried to calm her breath as her mind flashed back to that night in Drake Park. But that was different. Yes. It was some drunk; *but here, at the high school? What if...* She thought she had pretty much buried that night under a thick layer of just one-of-those-freaky-things-that-can-happen. More and more she felt like it had happened to another person. But now, that thick layer had just dissolved in a sickening hyper-second.

She held her breath straining her ears for any sound; any hint that there was someone out there. The wind whispered coldly and loudly in her ears and the thudding of her heart echoed in her head like a quickening base drum. Twenty seconds passed by and she heard every second click off. Her panic started to rise. Nothing. She decided to stand still and wait, to try and get a look at whom or what was behind her. It was probably just her imagination, galvanized by the thought that surfaced from the murky depths of her fears of how The Man had clutched at her with his massive hands.

She realized she was probably seen ducking under the stands. She tried to look through the twisted field of support structure for any movement. But it was too dark under the stands, darker than a small closet. With the wind starting to pick up, she couldn't hear any sounds but her own quick breathing. She had to move!

She darted this way and that way, not knowing where she was going in the tangled mass of support structures. She kept going deeper and deeper, far back under the stadium. She was getting confused and couldn't figure out her bearings, which added to mounting sense of fear. She felt every time she moved that whoever it was, was countering her move, getting closer and closer to her. She had to swallow down a desire to shout out for help. She reached inside her jacket pocket for her cell phone. *It's gone!* She drew in a panicked breath remembering she had left the phone on the bench.

The Man had cocked his head and nodded as he noticed Maya's cell phone on the bench, the little sliver of vague moonlight glinted off the metal casing. Another reason that tonight was the night, he thought without emotion. Now, he stood where he was, just under the stands. A few thin slivers of frosted moonlight peaked through the back of the stadium stanchions and allowed The Man to vaguely see Maya dashing this way and that, in a crude circle. He knew his body would be enshrouded in darkness with the occluded moon behind Maya. A humorless grin twitched at his lips as he noticed that despite her frantic movements, she was getting no further away from him. Finally, she stopped and stood still, listening as the wind swallowed the sounds around her. The Man imagined the support structure under the stands was like a metal trap that Maya had walked into and now her leg was caught and she couldn't move away from him. He watched her for a while, without blinking, curious, his mind blank. His heart beat slowly, so slowly, his breath came in smooth and relaxed, as if he were asleep.

The Man stepped out from under a corner of the stands. It was time for a face-to-face with Maya. She would be nervous at first, no doubt. He would have to get her to relax. He put on his knitted facemask and then reached in his pocket for the vial of chloroform and a piece of cloth. He put a few drops in the cloth and put the vial back in his pocket. He could see Maya in the middle of the support structure, waiting for him. He nodded and started to head back under the stands. *I know she'll like me...*

"Hey now, big man," came Gaius' calm, Irish voice from a bench in the first row of the stadium, "what's with the winter face mask? It's not that cold. You know, you missed the game... It's all over."

The Man halted in his tracks for a moment, then turned to look up where the voice had come from. He saw Gaius's long frame stretched out, reclining on a spectator's bench, propped up on one elbow. He judged the distance between them, calculating that in two strides he would be up the stairs and then he would choke that funny kid's voice off.

"I know what you're after... I'm after the same thing," Gaius continued in the same tone, his green eyes watching the Man with an animal alertness.

The Man grunted under his breath and made a move toward Gaius, to see if he could spook the kid. Gaius didn't twitch a muscle and continued to intently gaze at the Man.

"Leave her to me," the Man's voice rumbled out from a deep hole, his large lips wrinkling the fabric of the mask around his mouth, "and I won't hurt you."

Gaius slowly rose to his feet and looked down on the Man and said with slight amusement in his voice: "Being hurt, even being killed, I haven't had to worry about that for a long, long time. I could care less... but maybe you might."

Gaius reached down behind the bench and picked up a baseball bat and patted his palm with it. He could feel a rage starting to simmer within him. Gaius' calm voice started to thicken with a steely resolve.

"I just reached into a trash can and look what I found, a cracked baseball bat. The handy things people throw out... Like I said, the game's over."

This kid was a brash little sucker; he sounds like a foreigner, the Man thought as he shifted his ponderous weight from one foot to the other. He figured he could take the bat from the kid and break it over his head or he could crush his throat and that stupid accent. That might be fun, but Maya... would have the time to get out of his reach. He stared at the kid in frustrated rage, his dark eyes, like two black marbles reflecting a distant fire.

The standoff lasted for ten unblinking seconds. A grunting cough barked out of the Man's mouth as he shook his head, reluctant to back down. He turned swiftly away and stalked off and in six giant strides he was across the field and easily vaulted the fence in one powerful thrust of his legs.

Maya decided to make one more mad dash for what she thought she could see was an opening that led out onto the field. Her shallow breaths of fear almost had her gasping. She had rather face what ever there was out in open space where she could use her speed. Track was her sport and she was fast. She felt trapped under the stands in the midst of all the mass of twisted steel supports. She took in a deep breath and then dodged her way around the beams and then the opening loomed and she burst through it. She looked behind herself fearful of what she might see pursuing her. Her heightened awareness only had one second to warn her of DANGER as she slammed into a looming shape in front of her. Strong arms reached around her. A panicked scream erupted from her lips as she pushed back from the shape that was holding on to her. She vaguely heard the voice from her memory as she thrashed around, arms flailing.

"Maya. Maya. It's all right," Gaius' voice soothed.

Maya opened her eyes and looked up into a pair of warm, green eyes.

"Oh, Gaius! It's you!" and Maya threw herself into Gaius' arms in desperate relief, clinging to him, seeking comfort in his muscular embrace.

"Hey… It's all right. I'm sorry I scared you."

"Oh, my God, I'm so happy to see you."

Maya finally got a hold of her wits and looked around fearfully, scanning the dark football field.

"Hey, we should go. Fast."

"Why? What's the matter?"

"I think there is somebody out there. Someone was following me," Maya said, fear in her voice.

"It was me."

"You?!"

"Yes. Me. I was following you, trying to decide if you wanted to see me or not."

"You?"

"Me."

Maya took a moment. Her whole body drew in a deep breath and a sigh of relief poured out of her, releasing all the tension of those few frantic moments, letting the fear recede.

"Like I said, I'm sorry if I scared you," Gaius said sincerely as he gently squeezed her shoulders.

Maya allowed herself a smile and a small laugh. "Wow, you really had me going, that's for sure."

Amusement showed in Gaius' eyes. "After all these years, I guess I have a way of sneaking up on people, but almost always," his look narrowed, "I never have to resort to that."

The serious look in Gaius' green eyes made Maya realize that, *ah yes, Gaius is a vampire!* And her memory quickly, and anxiously, returned to their first meeting. She had wanted so much to get back into the magic of that seductive encounter.

"Ah, here's your phone. You left it on the bench."

"Thanks. I can't believe I forgot it. Oh Gaius, I've missed you so much. You have no idea. I was so afraid that I would never see you again."

"I had to come …"

The moon came out from under the clouds and cast its pale light onto Gaius' pale face. His lime-toned eyes smoldered. The thought burst into Maya's consciousness as she looked into his completely composed face: *He's not pretending!*

Gaius began with smooth conviction. "I am… what I am …"

A small smile of revelation started at his lips that seemed to Maya to be warm and seductive. "And I am here to see you… to admire you. Having lived so many years as I have is to know that time is limited, so limited… it could all stop like a frozen clock." A little shrug of despair ran through his shoulders. "I don't get out of the shadows very often. I can't tell you how… how fragile things can be. You don't know how important you are to me."

Gaius' gaze was mysterious and intense and Maya felt it looked right into her soul.

"I… I feel the same way. I can't stop thinking about you."

"You are so innocent, so special, such a beautiful woman—"

"Hey," Maya cut in, her smile full, a tinge of red embarrassment flushed her cheeks. "I'm just a girl."

Gaius kept the intense glint in his green eyes and his voice continued, serious.

"Not in my eyes. In my time, *girls* had pigtails, were still able to sit in their daddy's lap and were able to jump up into their mother's arms. You would have had a dozen marriage proposals by now, or easily could have a bouncing baby on your knee. You would certainly *be* something to be… desired."

"Gaius," Maya laughed and couldn't help herself. "You're funny. You're so… so—" and she stop herself from saying 'so into it'.

Gaius cocked his head slightly to one side, not getting her meaning. "Now listen to me."

Maya's smile slowly receded and for the first time, she thought she could see a cloud of fear come over Gaius' face.

"Look. You have to promise me something. Okay?"

"Sure. Anything."

"If you are going out at night, take your parent's car or get a ride. No walking around at night alone." A tinge of fearful anger crept into his voice and he tightened his hand on Maya's shoulder. "I mean, here you are, in this dark field, all alone."

"I was only getting my jacket that I left here during the game. I tried to text Kou—I mean, I was just sitting here for a while lost in thought. I was thinking about you, actually. The field lights went out, and now here you are. But you did put a scare into me."

"I don't want you to be afraid. Someone like you should live without fears. Fear leaves a mark," Gaius let his last words trail off as if he didn't want to say them.

"I know you might not be from around here, but this is Bend. Getting bit by a dog might be the worst thing that could happen to you here."

"This might be Bend, but I'm from the shadows. I've lived most of my life there. Every place has its shadows."

Maya tilted her head to one side and smiled trying to make light of Gaius' words.

"Things in the shadows. Things like you?"

Gaius narrowed his eyes and shook his head, his voice coming out, just a little more than a whisper.

"Much, much worse than me, things with twisted minds and horrible, violent desires. I... I couldn't bear it if you were hurt by anything. So, promise?"

"Okay, chill," Maya smiled through her words. "I promise."

"Good," Gaius flashed a smile at Maya that was so confident, it suddenly turned his pale, plain face into a handsome one, something Maya didn't miss noticing. "Let me walk you home?"

"Absolutely." And Maya felt the thought flash through her mind and disappear with a slight pain: *Kiss me now, Gaius. Now!*

She looked up at Gaius, her soft brown eyes full of permission. He gave no hint that he knew what was in her gaze and just smiled back patiently, a patience that his face said was difficult. She moved close to him, their lips inches apart. She whispered:

"You told me that your prey always comes to you."

A small smile of modesty spread across Gaius' face that Maya thought was so revealing, so easily masculine, so charming. His shoulders shrugged slightly.

"Yes... I can't help to want what I want," his accent lilted. "But, you're not my prey... you are a prayer that has been answered. I might be what I am, but I have a non-beating heart that still longs, that still hungers for... an impossible love." A look of vulnerability then came into Gaius' green eyes. "Buried under the burning pain and soul shattering agony of my 'change,' lies a memory, the memory of a time when I thought the sound of my heart was a call... a call to another who would be the only one to hear it... No one ever did."

"No one?"

"I have lived a very long life with that memory."

"I'm here."

"Yes." Gaius' smile was happy... and sad. "Like a prayer."

They held onto the intense moment with Maya wanting it to evolve the way it should, their lips so close. Gaius said, finally, with difficulty:

"If we let it happen... everything will be different. Right now... the way we are... it must be enough... for now. Trust me."

Maya let the passion slowly ebb out of her body. She sighed wistfully. "There's so much to talk about. I just can't get over that you are here." She noticed Gaius' tight-fitting tee shirt. "Here, take my jacket, you must be freezing."

Gaius just shook his head and grinned. "Every temperature is just right for me."

Maya ran her hands along Gaius' arms. "You're cold. You need—"

Gaius cut her off with a tilt of his head and a look that said 'duh'. "Of course I'm cold."

Maya nodded thinking that it didn't matter to her if he was pretending or …not, or 'what' it was. Gaius was more real than anything she had ever known.

"You might 'be' cold, but I know you're not… Hey, I'm starved. La Rosa, the Mexican place, is just a couple of blocks from here—oh, you can't—"

"It's okay. That's very considerate of you, very perceptive. I'll sit with you and have a glass of water. I can tolerate a little of it. It tastes horrible, though," Gaius grinned sheepishly.

Maya was relieved that the restaurant was fairly empty, the dinnertime rush over. Pendulum lights hung down from the ceiling keeping the light soft, and the dark orange hand trawled walls gave off a quiet warmth. Initially, she didn't see anyone she recognized and that was good. She didn't want any interruptions while she was with Gaius. She asked the hostess, a slender girl with short, strait, blonde hair that allowed anyone to see the two colored tattoos on her neck, for a booth. Her nose was pierced with a diamond stud. Maya realized that she recognized the girl. She had graduated last year. The tats and the nose piercing were new. Maya pointed at a high-backed booth way over in the darkest corner where she thought Gaius might be more comfortable. She did notice how the hostess took an unsubtle moment to look at Gaius, his pale, 'gothic?' looks, how his muscular chest strained against his tee shirt. Gaius showed no indication that he was being 'looked' at. The hostess seated them, giving Gaius a last glance. Maya crinkled her face, annoyed. The hostess was so obvious.

"Nice," Gaius said through that charismatic smile of his. "Very private."

"I feel bad eating in front of you," Maya said sheepishly.

"Never mind... It's okay, really. It will be kind of interesting to watch you. It will stir up vague... memories."

"I am sure you must miss out on a lot. There is so much yummy stuff out there."

Gaius sighed, his lips parted in a crooked grin. "Well, I never have to worry about gaining weight or having to go on a diet. And, I get to ...ah, drink as much as I want. I don't worry about carbs and sugars."

Maya took a moment to process what Gaius said and couldn't help laughing loudly, genuinely. "Now that is really funny. I hadn't thought about that ..." She looked at him for a moment, the question just popped into her mind, without pretense. "Are you all right... being with me?"

With his intense gaze, Gaius showed Maya his answer. She thought she could read his deep attraction to her but also picked up that it wasn't without difficulty. A tiny self-conscious smile touched his mouth.

"I am right where I am supposed to be," Gaius said lowly, his voice husky with emotion. He reached his hands across the table. "May I?"

Maya clasped her hands to his. Their hands move softly against one another with a feeling as deep as any kiss. She vaguely noticed his hands were warm but she imagined them to be... cold ...She looked into his eyes and started to say something but stopped. She wondered if certain questions would... ruin the spell that they both seemed to be under.

"What is it? Gaius's accent lilted. "You can ask me anything and I'll try my best to answer. I am... almost an open book for you." And he smiled warmly.

"I know you are Irish, that accent and all. But the name Gaius, I really wouldn't know, but it doesn't seem like an Irish name."

"Ah, you are right. It's not. My full name is Gaius Aloysius McCaughey. My dear mother had a 'thing' for Roman names. I am named after some supposed ancestor, who, ah… thought that courtship was having his way with one of the native Irish girls from a prominent family. You see how the continuation of life and violence are… so intertwined."

Maya tried to read Gaius' eyes but couldn't. They seemed to be shades of green ambiguities. "I bet you are full of stories."

"Countless …" Gaius' mouth turned a little grim, and with a slow shake of his head, he seemed to try and banish those memories from his mind. "Most are not happy ones. They would not seem real to you. That part of the book is closed. I would not burden you with them."

"Nothing about you would ever be a burden to me."

Gaius grinned and chuckled, his small laugh a mixture of pain and wistfulness and his emerald eyes said: you don't know what you are saying.

"So you say."

"I do," Maya added as she squeezed Gaius' hands with hers. "You might not believe me …" And she searched for the right words as an experience or two bubbled up into her consciousness. "I, I think I can understand how, for some people, things happen to them that make them into two people and they are more… comfortable that way."

Gaius leaned back and studied Maya, while he silently struggled to keep his sense of self and to keep Kougar's consciousness submerged. Her words had surprised him with their insight.

"Interesting theory for a 'girl' of your age. Can't say I know what you're talking about. I mean, how… would you know that?" Gaius asked, his voice wary.

Maya realized how uneasy Gaius seemed. She could sense a fragility creeping into the space between them.

"Hey, it really doesn't matter… It doesn't matter to me. I just want you to know that I… understand, and that I am so happy you are here."

Gaius relaxed back into the kind of moment he wanted to be in: to be fully 'with' Maya.

"I am very glad of that, so, enough with musings which don't come from the heart, that don't do justice to what's important. I used to always think that the future had no need of me... that my life was something that lived in the past. But now, I look at you and I want to have the right kind of dreams again. I am so lucky to be with you."

They left the restaurant and walked down the street lined with small commercial businesses and then into the Northwest Crossing neighborhood, a newish housing community full of stylish conformity. Maya and Gaius strolled arm in arm, quiet, lost in their thoughts of one another. The night air had cooled to a chill with the passing of time. Fallen leaves littered the sidewalks and crunched under their feet. Halloween decorations were displayed on many front porches. Suddenly, breaking their mutual silence that they were enjoying, Maya's cell phone pinged. She stopped and pulled out her phone.

"It's either my mother or Maddie with some sort of sarcastic comment. She and the girls are at Cooper's party. Oh, it's Amanda. "Maya read the text:

...I'm glad u r not here...

"Humph," Maya mused as she texted Amanda back:

...So, bad scene.?

Maya's phone pinged immediately:

...Yeah. No fun...

Maya put her phone back in her pocket.

"Trouble?" Gaius asked.

"Oh, no. I'm really glad I didn't go to the Homecoming party; soooo glad. I never would have seen you. Everyone there will be talking about the dance tomorrow night and who's going and who's not."

Maya pulled herself closer to Gaius as they walked on. They entered a small park full of trees, landscaped shrubbery and sitting area with wooden benches.

"So," Gaius began, "you are going to the dance tomorrow night? I mean, I am sure you are."

"No… not this one."

"I find that hard to believe. Obviously you—"

"I didn't want to go."

Gaius came to a stop and took a moment to figure out how to ask what he 'had' to ask.

"Ah, there is no one in your life? No one special?"

"Yes …Yes there is."

"Then why—"

"You… I've decided that you are very much in my life." And Maya squeezed Gaius' hands.

"After one dinner date?" Gaius gave her a crooked grin.

"No. It started at the costume dance and the way you danced for me."

"You thought that was for you?" Gaius asked innocently.

"I haven't been around as long as you have, but the *way* you looked at me… I just figured, yeah. Yeah." Maya smiled with the memory of it.

"Ha! Now that changes everything. I normally don't dance *with* a 'girl' on the first date but I couldn't forgive myself if you didn't have a Homecoming dance… Shall we? I bet you have a nice slow song on your phone that you can play for us." And Gaius' quiet, confident smile spread across his face. Maya giggled and smiled back, her brown eyes shining.

She pulled out her phone and scrolled through her music and picked one out and set her phone on the bench while the song came on, Adele's 'Love Song'. As the romantic acoustic guitar opened the song, Maya and Gaius came into a dancer's embrace, their eyes locked on to each other's in a silent communication of mutual fascination and gathering love.

Maya felt Gaius' eyes melting her and she said under her breath: "You must trust me... I 'know' who you are."

Gaius sea-green eyes glowed with intensity as he took in her words. Emotion filled his throat.

"You don't know what it's like to finally be discovered, after all these years in the shadows."

"If I could stop time, I would do it right now," Maya whispered.

"Well, being an old... 'soul,'" his Irish accent purred, "I can tell you that this moment is the real eternity, not the one I am living in. For us, this moment will always be a part of eternity. Do you believe me?"

Maya felt Gaius' words filled her with such heavy meanings that her heart fluttered with a lightness that made her feel like she was hovering in his arms.

"I do... I do."

Without a word they moved and swayed until the guitar strains slowly finished the song.

They turned down Maya's street. Gaius had his arm around Maya's shoulder and she had her arm around his waist. Some clouds parted and the moon came out fully, casting its light on the ground around them. They came to a stop outside of Maya's house which seemed nestled under a couple of towering ponderosa pine trees. They looked at each other, knowing the 'scene' had to come to an end, *hopefully just for now,* Maya thought to herself. She panicked for a moment as she came to grips with all of the unknowns spanning between them like a bouncing, creaky suspension bridge that swung precariously to and fro, high above the jagged depths of an alpine crevasse. She could see the anxiety spreading on Gaius' pale face.

He knows what I'm thinking...

Gaius tried to say something but it never escaped his sad lips.

"When ..." Maya began, not knowing what else to say, "When can I see you again?"

For a quick second Gaius' eyes turned desperate as they searched inward and found... nothing. He struggled, his mind spinning, trying to grasp on to an answer that never came. His words came out quickly, more despairing than hopeful.

"I want you to know that I want to. I do."

"But you won't," Maya said, her voice matching Gaius' sad tone.

"There… are a lot of problems. You have no idea."

"I just want to be Kougar's friend."

Gaius barked out an ironic laugh, shaking his head slowly as he looked down.

Gaius' face showed the pain of his words. "Don't waste your time. I'll come to you when I can… *if* I can."

Maya started to speak and Gaius put a couple of tender fingers to her lips to stop her. He gave her a frail smile.

"Don't... There's *no* other way."

Gaius gently moved his fingers from Maya's mouth and let them caress her cheek and finally, down her neck. He gave her a last, smoldering green-eyed look, turned away and walked off quickly. Maya watched his retreating figure, her eyes glistening from the newly found pain that started in her heart, like a song that no one would ever hear.

Troubling Thoughts

Maya tossed and turned under her bedcovers, the feelings of the night still passing hotly through her body. She felt Gaius' fingers softly touching her face... *Gaius is Kougar... Kougar is Gaius.* The thought kept playing over and over again. And—*I don't think he's pretending... does he?* It didn't seem to her that Kougar was play-acting. He 'became' Gaius, or needed to 'be' him. Maybe Kougar had just taken pretending to an extreme level. She wasn't sure. She had tried to tell Gaius that she understood—in her way— the dual personality thing.

As she lay there, looking up at her bedroom ceiling she remembered, on a couple of occasions, while volunteering at the psychiatric hospital where her mother was a Head Nurse, her mom had taken her to a room where they talked with a patient who 'had' multiple personalities and fully believed 'who' they were. Her mother told her that this patient was, at times, aware and unaware of her personalities and talked about 'them' in the third person. Her 'alters' had made her life chaotic and she had to seek help. There are more than a few people, her mom said, who have dissociative personality disorder that can manage to function at a basic level in life. Only when the personalities endanger the patient or others is there a clear reason for some kind of intervention...

Maya couldn't help the thought that slowly made its way into her mind:

Does Kougar... have some kind of mental problem?

She tried to put the implications of that question through all her interactions with Kougar. 'Mental problem' seem too strong of a description to her. Sure he was an odd—well, different... *yeah... odd.* He was very, very shy. Certainly he came off as nervous. His hair, the disheveled look; the way he kept himself apart... how he just let Hayden pummel him, saying he deserved it! And what about Gaius!? How could Kougar 'become' Gaius so completely with the flawless Irish accent, his way of speaking, and his I'm-comfortable-in-my-own-vampire-skin manner? And… of all things, the way Gaius looked at her, touched her, the depth of his feeling and passion for her! It was all so… real!

She also couldn't forget that Gaius had said that Kougar has… problems… All of these thoughts flicked through her mind like new lightening. It took all her emotional strength to try and step back from what Gaius meant to her, how he made her feel and how she just wanted to be with 'him' all the time …The reality of not knowing when she would see him again, if ever, made her lay over on her side and curl into a ball with pain. Her eyes filled with fresh and deep emotions, as she played back Gaius' words… something about 'an impossible love.'

Why did he have to come tonight? She agonized to herself. Now, there were no more turn-offs on the road she was on. Again, Gaius' voice sounded in her mind: 'I had to come.'

I need to know! I need answers!

She thought about talking with her mom, but inwardly, she shook her head. No, she couldn't go there yet. She needed to—*I have to get Kougar to talk to me!*

She had to believe—wanted desperately to believe—that Kougar could… feel, and *does* feel, what Gaius shows when he looks at her. She knew, from the furtive looks of Kougar's blue eyes, that he felt something. And that something was frustratingly hard to figure out. Kougar seemed attracted to her and repelled at the same time. She decided the only way to get to Gaius was through Kougar. What could she do? What could be done to make them… one and the same?

She sat up in bed with a resolve. She picked up her cell phone off the nightstand. The phone's light illuminated her face in the darkness of her room. It was just after three in the morning. She thought for a moment then tapped out a text to Kougar:

> …Hey…TMRW is Sat. If u r riding somewhere, I can meet up with u. B4 u get all flamed, we don't have to go as BFFs. It would be cool to be able to ride with someone who really knows how

to ride and could keep up with me. U know how
to ride... right? ☺

She thought that throwing a challenge at Kougar might push one
of his buttons. At least the ball was out of her court for now. She hoped
her spinning mind would slow down and allow her to get some sleep. The
last few seconds of her phone mode shined on the ceiling above her as she
lay back down. She thought she could make out Gaius's profile in the
shadows outlined by the fading light of her cell phone's screen. She
missed Gaius already. She had definitely decided that she wanted him in
her life. But how, how could that be realistic? He... *wasn't* real. It kept
coming back to that: he *wasn't* real. Her aching heart told her different.

A troubled sleep finally arrived and her dreams erupted with
rapid, focused and unfocused montages of her with Gaius: walking
together, holding hands, laughing, dancing in the park, looking deeply
into each other's eyes at the restaurant, chasing each other under the soft
lights of the football field. In each scene, Maya notices that Kougar is
watching her and Gaius, his head tilted down, his brooding blue eyes
looking out from underneath his brows. Gaius is confidently oblivious of
Kougar's somber observation. She knows she's having the time of her life
with Gaius. Her radiant smile for the charming vampire and his seductive
smile for her overwhelms their senses. Despite Maya's joy, she can't help
but feel the intensity of Kougar's moody, foreboding stare, and when she
glances toward him the happiness on her face turns thoughtful. Gaius
finally catches up to Maya on the field and they fall to the ground with
Gaius rolling on top of her, pinning her arms down.

Maya laughs deeply, thrilled with the touch of Gaius' body on
hers. Their laughter finally subsides... She turns her head and sees
Kougar sitting on the player's bench watching them. His melancholic
look is turning angry. She looks back up at Gaius. Their eyes share a
mutual fascination full of passion... and awakening emotions.

The moment is now, Maya thought. *Now!*

She closes her eyes and lifts up her lips. She doesn't see that the look of love on Gaius' face suddenly hardens with the triumph of his natural appetite. His green eyes flash brightly. She hears him whisper as he leans down to kiss her:

"The courtship was really, really fun."

She felt him bush across her receptive lips and moved down to her neck. She could feel his passionate embrace tightened quickly with a desperate strength. She had a brief second to realize something was wrong when she heard Kougar's angry voice ring out.

"Gaius! Get off her, you blood sucker! Not her! Not this time."

Gaius's electric eyes glared with hunger at Maya's soft exposed neck. He then pulled reluctantly away with a frustrated snarl.

"What business is it of yours, freak?" Gaius spat out at Kougar. "Go home and hide in your bedroom like you always do."

"She's not for you," Kougar replied thickly.

Gaius barked out a sarcastic laugh. "Well, she sure isn't for you, freak."

Kougar looked at Maya, his expression full of regret and unrequited hope that slowly turned to acceptance. His voice came out slowly, like a verdict.

"That's right… She's not for me …"

Gaius turned back to Maya and clasped her firmly. Maya's breath quickened with terror. She squirmed in his grasp.

"Gaius, Gaius. No." Maya pleaded.

Gaius growled at Kougar his voice full of his lust and hunger. "Now, go home. You don't want to see this. It'll just turn into a nightmare for you and," Gaius enjoyed a twisted grin, "you don't need another one. Too bad you don't have the courage to take yourself out. Sissies like to suffer …. Okay, have it your way."

As Gaius bends down to bite Maya's neck, Kougar roars out and hurtles himself forward and knocks Gaius off Maya. They both tumble and writhe together on the ground. Gaius wins the struggle to get on top and starts to strangle Kougar. Kougar bangs his fists uselessly against Gaius' body.

"Stop! Stop it!" Maya screams…

Maya woke up in a sweat, breathing hard, her screams ringing in her ears. She looked around for a second trying to orient herself as reality slowly crept back into her mind. She sighed and shuttered a bit realizing how real the dream had felt to her. She got out of bed and opened her window blinds to let the morning light in to extinguish all the shapes and shadows of her dark dream that might be lurking in the corners of her room. She gazed out into a bright morning of fall colors, all reflecting the enigmatic shades of transition. Everything suddenly seemed mysterious to her. She wondered if that was the point: there really weren't answers, only more questions, some more dangerous than others… some full of tears; some that led to the lonely dead-end that lies at the back of every heart flushed with love.

She turned away from the window and walked over to her nightstand. She checked her phone, not really expecting a return text from Kougar. No new message. There wasn't even a text from Maddie, which surprised her. She definitely should have heard from Maddie by now. She could have used some funny gossip about Cooper's party last night to boost her mood. Maddie could always do that for her.

Maya took her long face out of her room and headed to the kitchen. Her mom was pouring herself a cup of coffee. Maya could smell bacon cooking on the grill. Even though her expression didn't show it, she was happy to see her mom.

"Hi mom," Maya said, a little subdued.

"Oh, hi, sleepy head. I looked in on you a few times but I didn't want to wake you. You were dead asleep. I bet you and the girls really cheered hard last night; too bad about the game. It was so close!"

"Yeah, it was. Hey, where's dad?"

"He had to go into the office for a bit this morning. Do you need to talk to him? I'm sure he wouldn't mind if you gave him a—"

"I just wanted to give him a hug," Maya cut in, realizing what she wanted, "just a hug. I haven't seen him lately."

"Oh, sweetie," Lisa Virk sighed, put down her coffee cup and took Maya into her arms. "Honey, is everything all right?"

Lisa smoothed Maya's hair with her hand, tucking it tenderly behind one of her ears.

"I'm all right. That was a tough loss last night."

Lisa searched her daughter's face looking for clues to her downcast mood. It was not like her daughter to be down. Something else had to be bothering her, she knew.

"Do you want to talk about it?"

Maya's smiled was puzzled. "The football game? Ah, nah, that's all right. It was sad. That's all. Poor Hayden."

"I heard all about it from Hayden's mom."

"You called her?"

"No, she called me. We're friends, you know. She says Hayden is inconsolable."

"He'll get over it. He's Hayden."

"I am sure he will... Anything else bothering you?"

Maya sighed deeply. "No, I'm good."

"Sure?"

"Mom, I'm good. I'm going to clean my room. It's a mess, and the downstairs and grandmother's room. I'm sure it's been awhile."

Lisa looked thoughtfully at her daughter, giving her a moment if she wanted to 'say' anything. "Okay. I was going to get to the downstairs tomorrow. You don't have to."

"It's okay. I got it."

"I'm going to meet up with your dad a little later and we are going to Sisters to the Farmer's market and the art fair. Want to go with us? That would be fun."

"Ah, thanks, mom, but I'm going to take my mountain bike out for a ride ..." And then she said with quiet hope: "I'm going to meet up with a friend. It'll be nice to get out before the weather turns bad."

"That sounds great. Be careful with the rocks. Don't take any chances. Be safe."

"Mom... I always am."

"I remember when you broke your collar bone when your wheel got stuck between two rocks and you fell on your shoulder. It could have been worse."

"Mom," Maya replied back, with an annoyed sigh. "Don't worry. I'm just going out for a little ride."

"Okay. Good. I'm cooking up some breakfast."

"Thanks but I'm not hungry yet. I'm going to start cleaning and do some homework."

"I'll leave it on the stove. Just heat it up when you are ready."

Maya nodded and her long face returned, a look that her mother picked up on. Lisa moved to embrace her daughter and then held onto Maya's shoulders.

"Hey," she soothed. "Remember, your father and I love you very much. You are such a beautiful girl, so smart. We want you to be happy. We have so much respect for how well you do at school, how you conduct yourself, and how mature you are. We are confident that you will make the right choices for yourself. And, remember, we are always here to help you make them if you need us. It's okay to need help. We all do."

"Thanks, mom. I know."

Maya turned and walked down the hall to her bedroom while Lisa looked after her retreating figure, her face full of love and... worry.

Maya entered her room and surveyed what needed to be done. She let out a determined breath of air and went about cleaning and organizing her room with a purpose, hoping to get her mind off of Gaius/Kougar and the likely fact that many of her questions will go unanswered. She put in her earplugs and clicked on Katy Perry.

She got into her cleaning with a flurry of activity wanting to forget... to forget. She finished her room in an hour. Still on her mission, she headed downstairs with a dust rag and the vacuum. Downstairs consisted of a great room with a ten foot by ten foot parquet wooden dance floor to one side with a wall mirror. She sighed for a moment as she looked back on all the hours she and her grandmother had spent on that floor. It was their secret time together. On the other side of the room sat a shiny black, grand piano. In the middle of the room a couch and two chairs faced the piano. A small hallway led to a bedroom and bath. As Maya reached the bottom of the stairs she inhaled and her memory caught the faint smell of Indian incense. Maya pulled out her earplugs. For a moment, she thought she could see her grandmother sitting at the piano playing a soft, hauntingly sweet melody and smiling.

Maya walked over to the piano while her mind filled with her grandmother's music. With one hand she started to dust the top of the piano and then, with the other hand, she reached down to the keys and slowly played out the refrain of her grandmother's evocative and tender song. When she wanted to be close to her grandmother's spirit she would play this melody, her hands touching the keys like falling rain. She remembered her grandmother telling her that only the fingers of one hand could reach the deepest emotions of the piano.

I have to play more and dance. She would want me to.

With her grandmother's playing still in her ears, she walked over to the wall that had pictures of Sania Virk as a young woman in her various dance dresses and in her beautiful saris. Maya smiled and dusted off a few picture frames as her grandmother's radiant smile looked at her and again, Maya admired her elegance and the graceful poise of how she stood and moved that the pictures could only hint at. The family resemblance was strong in the facial features and bodily shape with only her grandmother's darker hair and skin being the obvious difference. Her father, Raja, would always remark how much Maya took after his mother: the talent for music, mathematics, dance… and beauty; so much like your grandmother, he would say, and then would add quickly with a painful smile: but hopefully, not too much like her!

Maya finished cleaning the downstairs. She put the vacuum back in the cleaning closet. She walked by the kitchen the still lingering smell of cooked bacon stirred up hunger pangs. She picked up a strip of bacon and was getting ready to take a bite when she heard her cell phone ping.

'Bout time, Madds! Maya thought, irritated.

Chewing on the bacon, made her way down the hallway to her room. Fully expecting a snide remark to start off Maddie's text, she saw it was from Kougar:

> …KGB trail, junction 48. 12 pm. I'll wait for 5 minutes…

Maya looked at the clock on her screen. Yikes! It was already eleven fifteen. It would take her a half an hour to pedal hard out to Phil's Trailhead and from there to the Junction 40. Maya made an annoyed face as she replied to Kougar's text:

> …I'll wait for 5 minutes, too!…

Maya stripped off her clothes and hopped into the shower. Under the streaming water she tried to gather herself, letting out a deep breath. For a brief moment she summoned her wiles as she watched the soapy water slide past her shapely hips and down her beautiful, light cinnamon-skinned legs. Almost unperceptively, a few fluttering thoughts drifted through the back of her mind that made her… 'look' at herself; a new nascent look, it stirred up harbingers of sensual tidings as insubstantial as a heated mist… With an inward focus, her feminine subconscious secretly put itself on full alert. Her mouth turned into a determined line as she swore to herself that she was going to somehow make Kougar her friend.

The Ride

Maya pedaled hard, her breath deepening with exertion. She pumped, throwing herself against her pedals, keeping her knees in for more efficiency. She knew that Kougar would stick to his five-minute wait time. The air felt cool in her lungs. Fall was hanging on in the high desert. The sun radiated its yellow/white rays that made the landscape appear hyper-clear, as if it was under a magnifying glass. The snow line on Mr. Bachelor and the Three Sisters kept getting lower and lower. The Crater Bowl at Broken Top was already covered in snow. She hurried up Skyliner, past the last neighborhoods of Broken Top and Northwest Crossing, and finally past her high school. A few maple and vine maple trees stubbornly held onto their yellow and red wrinkled leaves. As she turned onto the trail that led off of Skyliner to Phil's Trailhead in the Deschutes National Forest, the bright, mustard yellow tops of rabbitbrush that spread out on both sides of her, had lost their summer bloom and had turned an opaque white as stark as exposed film. Rusty colored pine needles crunched under her speeding, knobby wheels.

Her black tights kept the cool wind off her legs. She wore a snug black and white, long sleeve dry fit with a three-quarter zipper, which unconsciously, she left zipped all the way down, revealing the smooth skin of her throat and upper chest. The outfit seemed like a body suit that showed off her athletic body. Her long, brown hair blew out from under her helmet as she picked up speed to get to the junction where she hoped Kougar was waiting. Maybe she would beat him there and then she could wait for him and appear a little annoyed when he 'finally' showed up. No such luck, she knew, as she checked her wristwatch. It showed that she was already five minutes late! She bunched her thigh muscles, got up off her seat and sprinted.

On top of a flat boulder, Kougar sat on his used, Gary Fisher hard tail, his arms crossed. With a mixture of dread and curiosity, he watched Maya approach through the trees. He had to admit that she was fast.

She can get after it, he thought as he rubbed his chin. He also thought that he should have left. She was more than five minutes late. *Why did I wait? This whole thing is going to be awkward.* These thoughts turned his attitude from apprehension to surly, fearful and surly.

Maya almost spun out of a sharp turn between two tight trees in the trail that led her where Kougar sat on his bike. She came to a skidding stop as the disc brakes on her dual suspension, yellow Trek bike protested.

Breathing deeply, she looked up at Kougar and tried to shade her eyes. The sun was directly above him and he appeared like a dark shape. She took a moment and then moved to one side so he was out of the sun's rays. She saw that Kougar had on some mirrored blade sunglasses. A bright yellow bandanna corralled his blond dreadlocks into a thick bunch over his shoulders. His white, turtleneck sweatshirt pressed against his muscled chest and he had the sleeves rolled up, showing his strong forearms. His calf-length jeans were faded with a frayed hole here and there. With his arms still folded across his chest, he looked down at Maya. It helped that he had the sunglasses on. It felt good... and necessary, to hide his eyes. Maya just looked back up at him...

Finally, Maya said: "Boy, you sure are talkative."

"It's easier when there aren't so many people around," Kougar said as he tilted his head to one side.

"Don't be nervous. It's just me."

Another pause passed between them. Maya pulled off her helmet and shook her long brown hair free, hoping Kougar would appreciate her beautiful flowing hair. Maya could see Gaius' forehead as Kougar looked at her... but nothing else of him, certainly not the voice, and the seductive accent. Nothing...

"You're late... I should have left," came the toneless voice.

"I would have," Maya shot back quickly.

Kougar gave off an agitated sniff and looked off into the distance, than back to Maya. She wished she could see his eyes to try and 'read' him. But the mirror reflection of his sunglasses gave off a steely look as impersonal as the metal eyes of a robot.

"Sick bike, sister." Kougar said, awkwardly, as his metal eyes looked at her.

"Sister?" Maya's slight grin gave away her surprise.

"Yeah, I watch T.V. like everybody else."

"Thanks. Das coo," Maya's grin turned crooked. "Gary Fisher... that's a nice hard tail. You don't see too many hard tails anymore."

"Yeah it's not like your cute, dual suspension. I know it's getting out of style but I like to feel the bounce of the trail under me... A hard tail takes more skill to ride. Period," Kougar said flatly, looking away from her.

"Really?" Maya's skeptical voice asked with an edge.

She checked out Kougar's whole set up with an analytical eye. "No clips? You don't ride clipped in?"

"I'm a skateboarder," he said, obviously, as if she should have known. "I don't like having my feet stuck."

"It just takes a second to clip-out."

"Too long for me."

"What about all the pedal bounce when you hit some rocks?"

"Just because my foot comes off the pedal doesn't mean my foot is not still connected to it," Kougar replied, his tone impatient.

"Connected? Like, with some kind of spider web or something?" Maya grinned sarcastically.

"That's one way to put it."

"And, no brain bucket for your head?"

"Nah, too much extra weight. Besides, my head is empty so it's hard as a rock."

Maya nodded, a line of mockery tugging at her smile. "Funny. Brave or stupid?"

"None of the above."

"Well, we'll see how empty your head is when you bang it on a tree or a rock… Look, I'd feel a lot better if you had a helmet."

"That's not how I roll. And it doesn't matter why," came Kougar's surly reply. "Look, I didn't dis on you, that you look like you're going to a photo shoot and not a ride."

"Oh, you noticed?" Maya flashed her beautiful smile.

"Whatever."

"I didn't say you look like you should be on a skateboard and not a mountain bike."

"Same thing, just with two wheels…" Then, surly: "You know, we don't have to do this."

"I want to see what you've got."

Kougar tilted his head back and Maya could tell he was rolling his blue eyes behind those sunglasses. Kougar snorted, his mouth turned into a grim line.

"What I've got? You're funny."

"Why aren't you laughing?"

"All right," he began, angry, "I'm not out for a stroll. I'm going to head down KGB to the Express Way, pass the Chicken, up Phil's, to Voodoo, take the fire road to hook up to Grand Slam, then out to Storm King down to COD through the rock garden and back." He then looked at Maya, sizing her up. "Probably over two hours… but I like to bomb it when I can. I won't wait for you. I won't be stopping unless I have chain snag or something like that. I'm just out for a ride. I'm not here to chat. Ah, sorry."

A little bemused grin pulled at Maya's lips as Kougar went through his directions. The grin broadened into a smile as her eyes accepted his challenge.

"No worries, dude, I think I'll be able to hang… and, ah, sorry, I won't wait for you either."

Kougar took off his blades and gave them a cleaning with his sweatshirt. Something in Maya made her look for Gaius' warm green eyes, but Kougar's annoyed blue eyes locked onto hers for a brief second, then, they looked away.

He still doesn't really look at me when I'm looking at him. He's hiding behind those sunglasses.

Kougar put his blades back on. "If there is something bad on the trail watch for my signal—if you are close enough to see it."

"You're going to lead?" Maya asked, with a little mocking edge to her tone.

Kougar didn't answer but scoffed under his breath. He came to a balance point on his bike and hopped sideways down to a lower boulder, 'walked' his bike with a couple of hops down to the third lower bolder and then to the ground.

Maya had to nod. That was some good balance.

"Nice."

"Remember, I'm just riding… you're just riding. We aren't riding 'together'," Kougar said, making sure to say the last word with enough emphasis that Maya understood.

Maya just teased back. "Jeez, you're soooo mean."

Kougar tightened the fit of his riding gloves and said flatly, as if he didn't hear her playful tone: "Just keeping it real."

Kougar pulled his water tube up to his mouth and took a swig, gave Maya a brief look with his mirrored eyes, and pedaled off down the trail.

Boy, that wasn't a great start, Maya thought to herself as she started after Kougar. She didn't get why he seemed angry with her. Nobody had ever responded to her that way when she was obviously trying to be friendly. Well, Gaius did tell her that Kougar had problems. She had to find out what they were. She had to find a way… a way to break down his barriers. She needed to get his attention… his respect. She thought of one way and she hoped she was up to it. Failure was not an option. Resolve found its way into her pedals as she matched his speed. He was already *moving* at a brisk clip, which she thought was a little too fast for this trail. If she didn't pay attention to loose spots and take the proper angle around the corners, she was going to spinout, and fall behind, something she was determined not to let happen. No time for daydreaming. This ride was going to be physical.

I'm going to stay on his six.

She could tell that he was testing her, if she was willing to push it. Kougar's blond dreadlocks bounced around his shoulders as he pushed the pace through the winding, up and down trail. It had some rock patches, nothing that she couldn't ride over easily if she took the correct line. Kougar got out of his seat on the mild up-hills to keep his speed up and Maya did the same. She *had* to stay with him. She was already breathing deeply.

Kougar rifled through his gears, getting the maximum efficiency possible. He was just going to methodically ride away from Maya. He kept his turns tight, made the most of the slight down hills, mashed over the small rock patches. He heard her voice in his head: *I want to see what you've got.*

He was going to show her right away as he pushed way beyond his normal pace, having to brake often in the turns, his back wheel fishtailing. Another fifteen minutes of this and she'll get discouraged, he felt confident.

Kougar streaked along as the trail passed through thick conifer stands of Lodgepole pine and Western juniper. Wide outcroppings of bare slate rock towered over him. Here and there, a few Manzanita bushes stretched out their hard, red stems into the trail. They whipped at Kougar's bare shins as he flashed by with too much speed to avoid the bushwhacking. The cuts trickled with blood that ran down in a line and stopped at the tops of his socks. The stinging lash had felt good, a just punishment for having agreed to this stupid ride. He should have never texted her back. He should have just barked a few laughs at her taunts and left it at that. He was annoyed and frustrated. *Yeah... but why frustrated?*

He growled to himself as he almost skidded out of a turn: *Why can't she just leave things the way they are?* Despite himself, he just wanted to have a 'few' faraway looks at her, maybe a couple of sneaky glances at her in Grenfeld's class. They didn't need to talk. *And what's with the friend stuff? I've never had a 'girl' for a friend. Never needed one.* He scoffed. *What's the point!?*

"Whoa!" Kougar exclaimed, startled, as he barely refocused himself to turn his handle bar sharply away from a tree trunk that pinched into a part of the trail. He took a quick look back behind him and a tight, satisfied grin touched his lips. Maya was nowhere in sight. *I dusted her. Yeah, that's what I got!*

He started to run up the base of Hell's hill, getting as much momentum he could before gearing down for the climb. *Now I can ride in peace.*

Kougar settled in to the long grind up the hill. Behind him, he heard the shifting of gears and glanced back. *Maya! What the—!*

I've got him! Maya gloated to herself.

"On your right, *dude*," Maya said out of the side of her mouth at she started to pass Kougar. The flash of her smile infuriated him. He bit on his lip and tried to get up out of his seat and pump hard to keep up with her. Maya just sat in her seat, toying with Kougar, her legs spinning fast. Having had enough fun, she turned to him.

"You didn't know I was a track star did you? See you down the trail."

With that she shifted, stood up, sprinted up the hill and was gone…

Maddened, Kougar took himself to his pumping limit and beyond trying to keep up with her. *Holy crap!* Both his sides ached as his breath came in deep gasps. He was not even half way up the hell hill and could no longer see Maya. *Man, she's gone!* Despite his anger he couldn't help but admire her 'kick.'

Kougar put his head down and pumped and pumped, finally cresting the hill. His chest heaving, he looked down the trail. No sign of Maya. He cursed under his breath and pedaled off in a furious pace, gears clicking, his chain creaking under the pressure.

Fifteen minutes later with his breakneck pace and still no sight of Maya …*She's gone. I'll never catch her. Damn!* He tried to burn out all the energy in his legs wanting to at least get a glimpse of her before his strength gave out. Nothing. Realization set in and he knew he couldn't keep up his current pace. Mercifully, he ratcheted down his speed. His heart pounded in his ears, sweat poured off his face, his bandanna was soaked.

He rounded a corner on the edge of a ridge. There she was. On top of a small boulder she sat on her bike her arms folded across her chest. Behind her, the Deschutes National forest spread out like a green blanket of evergreens flowing all the way up to the last tree line. From there bald rock face alpine terrain rose up into the snow-covered tops of the Three Sisters, which sparkled in the bright sunlight. Farther north along the Cascade range he saw Mt. Jefferson's jagged peak, and Mt. Washington, standing alone, a huge pyramid of a mountain, and farther still, he could vaguely make out the outlines of Mt. Hood. It was an exceptionally bright day.

Maya's helmet was hanging from her handlebars and her long brown hair moved in the slight breeze. She took a slow swig from her water tube. Still trying to catch his breath, he looked up at her. Kougar saw that she seemed fresh. No sweat… anywhere! She watched him with a slight smile on her face.

Kougar pulled off his soaked yellow bandanna and his dreadlocks spilled out down over his forehead and shoulders, a tangled mass of hair. They waited… who would be the first to speak? Finally, Kougar: "Why did you wait for me?"

"I'm not a meanie like you."

"Man, you climb like a monkey," he had to admit with admiration in his voice. "Never seen anything like it. I didn't think a girl could dust me like that."

"Well, I'm half Indian," Maya grinned, crookedly. "I have a little monkey's blood in me. My people believe the monkey is courageous, smart… and very, very fast."

"You sure are."

"But above all, the monkey is curious and always friendly," she said as her brown eyes twinkled. She looked at Kougar for a second and his mirrored eyes returned her look. She turned around and took in the view.

"Wow, it's so beautiful. Isn't it?"

"Yeah," Kougar nodded as he followed her gaze. "It's a lot better view than you get in L.A."

"How was that scene?"

"L.A.?"

"Did you like living there?" Maya asked, hoping to get Kougar to talk… about anything. She was encouraged by the opening and tried to stay in the natural flow and not to seem like she was 'trying' to get him to talk.

"Well, it's not Bend that's for sure. Here, everywhere you look, it's just white people."

"What about me?" Maya asked quickly. "I've got the ethnic look, don't I?"

Her words were almost like a command to Kougar as he couldn't help but look at her… fully. Finally, nerves broke off his gaze,

"Ah, yeah… you would fit in perfectly in L.A. You could pass for—I mean, not that you obviously don't here. I mean—"

"What do you mean?" Maya tried to play with Kougar's inference. She was hoping that he would take it as just a little teasing. Playful. But she knew she was treading a fine line and that he could abruptly clam up. "Pass? Like I could be Hispanic, or Middle Eastern, or Native American, or even a light-skinned black person. I guess I 'could' pass."

Kougar mumbled a small embarrassed laugh and looked down. "Ah, if you say it like that. Yeah. But me, well, I am what I am. There, I didn't pass for anything but white. White and always alone… not a good combination." Again the small, troubled laugh.

Maya couldn't help but catch Kougar's phrase: 'I am what I am.' She remembered clearly and Gaius' words sounded in her ears like he was standing next to her: 'I am what I am.' Kougar's voice shared nothing of the accent or intonation of Gaius' but something about the 'declaration' of the tone seemed... connected.

Feeling a little boxed-in, still looking down, Kougar tried to diminish the 'ethnic' analogy. "I mean... you know, you, ah... certainly pass here."

Keeping up with the gentle teasing Maya replied: "You mean as a white person?"

Kougar looked up quickly, the answer bubbled up and came off his lips like the obvious answer: "You could 'pass' anywhere. Anywhere. Yeah, anywhere because you, well you—"

"I what?" Maya cut in, her teasing sharpening.

Kougar squirmed and picked at the sleeves of his sweatshirt, trying to figure out just how to say 'it'. The words blurted out: "The way... you look."

"The way I look?" Maya asked while pretending to be puzzled.

Kougar struggle to keep from saying what shouted in his mind: *You're beautiful!* He didn't want to say that and have her laugh in his face... or worse!

"I mean... hey, look at me... and look at you."

He fought back the words. Maya dropped the puzzled look and reconsidered her playful tact. She softened her eyes realizing that he was struggling with something honest and true to him. A wave of compassion spread across her face as she recognized how hard it was for him to express himself.

"It's okay. Don't worry about it. I was just play—"

Then it jumbled out, almost painfully: "You're beautiful and I'm, I'm—"

"Wait," Maya stopped him. Something inside Maya knew where Kougar was headed and her heart suddenly ached. She wouldn't let him say it. "Don't say it. Don't—"

"And I'm kind of a freak." Kougar's words spilled out. "You'll always do way more than just fit in. You're the most popular girl in school."

"No I'm not," Maya quickly said, trying to dismiss Kougar's description.

Kougar just scoffed at her attempt. "Hey, I don't know anybody at school and even *I* know that you are."

Maya pursed her lips in thought and came down off the boulder and moved next to Kougar, brushed her hair back with one hand and looked at him. His mirrored eyes looked back at her for a second, then back to the sprawling view of nature over her shoulder.

"Take your sunglasses off. I can't see your eyes. It's hard to really tell what you're thinking."

"Good…"

A pause spread between them. Maya tilted her head and decided to say what she knew in her heart.

"Kougar, you're no freak."

He let her words pass through him, almost like a benediction. He noticed her tone sounded a lot like his mother's… He… almost wanted to believe her.

A slow, sarcastic smile moved painfully across Kougar's lips. He took off his blades and turned his head and gave Maya a brief, hooded look, his blue eyes clouded with the trauma that lie in the depths of his heart, his soul… and his memories that were as fresh and immediate as a scorching blister. The intensity of Kougar's fleeting look staggered Maya inwardly like a mind-meld. Then, as quick as it had come, the story in his eyes blanked out. The 'moment' had been too ephemeral for Maya to get a hold of 'what' had flashed between them. But rolling waves of emotion welled up in her and spilled over the levies of her conscious mind. She 'had' to make sure to keep the moisture out of her eyes.

"That makes only you, my mother and my dad—well, I believe he thinks it but won't say it ..." And then he said cryptically: "It's a small price to pay ..."

Kougar fought down a sharp desire to just turn and flee. Panic filled him as he realized what Maya must think of him after his 'weird' cryptic confession. He didn't know what made him stay, what made him say what he had; was it a nascent, enigmatic sense of hope?

"Anyway!" he almost shouted, desperate to change the subject. "Let's finish the ride. I think I've recovered from the dusting you gave me."

Maya smiled, relieved, glad that Kougar hadn't all of a sudden decided to just turn and pedal off by himself, putting an end to her— *their*— chance to become friends. Kougar retied his bandanna around his head, corralling his dreadlocks. He remembering her words, they still moved through him like a fragile key that began its stealthy attempt to open a door within him.

"Cool," Maya beamed. "Let's go."

Maya watched Kougar pull his mass of tangled, blond-white dreadlocks into place, prompting something in her that made her say as she cocked her head to one side: "If you ever want to trade hair, let me know."

Kougar quickly gave Maya a puzzled look of disbelief. "What? Are you kidding?"

"Nope," Maya said, shaking her head with conviction.

Kougar studied the ground for a second, and then looked up and over Maya's shoulder. "That would definitely be a problem for you."

"How so?"

"I don't think you would like to be on the outside."

Maya grinned. "I think I would find a way to deal with it."

Kougar shook his head. "You don't know what you're saying."

She knew this was risky, but she desperately wanted to figure Kougar out. Why did Gaius say she should stay away from Kougar? And 'what' were the serious problems he had? What made Kougar... 'become' Gaius?

"But why do you want to be on the outside?"

Kougar sniffed, looked away off into the forest. "Want? It's not like that." He felt an odd need to defend himself. "It's just the way it is."

"I don't believe that. You don't have—"

Kougar cut Maya off with a tight sigh. "You don't know what you are saying. You don't... know me."

"Sorry... I know I don't... But I want to," Maya replied quickly in such a genuine voice that Kougar, involuntarily, was drawn to her eyes. She tried to hold his gaze to hers, but his skittish eyes jumped away from hers like a blue bird taking abrupt flight off a suddenly twitching branch. "And I would definitely trade for the hair," she smiled trying to ease the tension. Luckily, Kougar wanted to do the same.

"All right... Let's go."

"Great. Let's do it."

"But hey, do a guy a favor, take it easy on those up-hills. Don't hurt my feelings." And Kougar paused for a second as if he was weighing something, and then gave her a quick smile.

Maya matched his smile. "It's just a matter of weight. I weigh a lot less than you do. There's less gravity pulling on me. I am sure you would smoke me on the down hills."

Maya could tell, that for the first time, Kougar had really smiled at her, however brief. It was genuine, not like the guarded half smiles or the sarcastic ones. She did see some of Gaius in that smile but not the ease, the confidence... the seductiveness. It gave her hope. She felt that she had at least a foot in the door.

"Okay. We're almost to Grand Slam, and then we'll hook up to Storm King. You go first. You're faster than I am. I don't want to hold you back."

"No worries. This isn't a race."

"It was," Kougar shot back quickly.

"It's not now. I like riding with you. This is fun." And Maya flashed her beautiful, reassuring smile. "You lead."

Kougar put on his blades. "If you insist."

"I do."

Kougar swung his bike around and pedaled down the trail with Maya following behind. The bright sun flashed through the trees and as the cool wind blew across Kougar's face, it came with a timid realization. *I like to ride with you, too,* he managed to say with a cautious voice to himself.

They took a quick switch back and turned onto Grand Slam and headed into the old growth forest, thick-trunked Ponderosa pine and Douglas fir towered above them blotting out the sun. Patches of sweet smelling Buckbrush, Manzanita, and Grouse whortleberry, their small red berries, now dried and shriveled, shaking in the wind, spread out on either side of the single track. They raced along the trail when they could, their disc brakes letting off tight friction sounds when pressed too hard, and they grinded out the up hills, gears clicking, legs spinning fast.

Not really wanting to, but unable to stop, Kougar's thoughts kept returning to Maya, just Maya… just to the thought of her. Wow… He shook his head as he streaked into a corner and pumped the brakes to avoid a couple of sharp rocks that jutted into the trail. He could have never imagined a day like this. He struggled to come to grips with it. But then there were the words that were always in the back of his mind. They pulsated lowly and their letters glowed in a smothered red: *Stay on the outside… Stay on the outside.*

Maya was thinking, too, how improbable this outing was. Her thoughts were squarely on Kougar and her indomitable desire to know him and solve the 'mystery.' She could see the muscles in his back bunched up under his tight sweatshirt when he pulled on his handlebars to pump up a hill. She refocused on the trail, as she knew they were headed to a six-foot drop off. She figured Kougar would back off his speed and

179

ride down the steep, rocky drop that had an old tree log lying across the trail at the bottom. But she saw that he was picking up speed.

What's he doing? He's going to jump it! He won't clear the log!

Before she could shout out a warning, Kougar was launching off the drop. He pulled on his right handlebar and turned a three-sixty.

"Wow," Maya said under her breath as she watched the trick. She slowed her speed to ride down the drop and hopped over the log by pulling her front wheel up. She rode over to where Kougar sat on his bike.

"I thought you were crazy, but you did it so easily."

Kougar just shrugged and his blades looked at her. "It's just like doing a three-sixty Ollie on a skateboard. Easy."

"That was cool."

Kougar took a long draw on his water tube. Maya did the same. A silence gathered between them. Not one that had any tension or awkwardness; just an enjoyable silence between them. No need to say anything... Just thoughts.

Presently, Kougar said:

"See that road there about thirty yards off to the right?" Kougar pointed toward a small dirt road that just seemed to start right in the middle of the forest. Maya followed his pointing finger and finally saw the curve of a road.

"Oh, yeah. What about it?"

"It's an old logging road. About an hour and a half down that road on your bike you will see a rusty bucket that I nailed down on top of a sawed-off tree trunk. Park your bike and walk into the forest right by that bucket. About thirty yards in you'll see a deer and elk trail. Walk on for about thirty minutes and you'll come to the base of a steep, rock-face. I have a rope hanging down. Walk up that rock-face with the rope about hundred and fifty feet and you'll come to a ledge."

"What's there?"

"It's just a place where I go when I... well," he decided to say it another way: "when I need a place to go," he finally said lowly. "It's like an island. I've pitched a tent there. Over the summer I stocked it with some stuff, a sleeping bag. The view is awesome. If you listen carefully, you can hear the Big Cascade River Falls in the distance. I've hiked it many times. Have you seen it?"

"Once. It's hard to get to. But it's cool."

"About seventy-five feet straight down. I wonder what it would be like to jump that."

"Obviously you wouldn't want to," Maya said warily. "The fall would probably knock you out and the cold water would freeze your muscles and you would drown. Simple as that."

"Yeah… but what a ride," Kougar said mysteriously, a tone of finality in his voice that Maya didn't pick up.

"I prefer to ride a mountain bike," Maya countered. "So, you've spent the night out here? Alone?"

"Yeah," he sighed and then said, almost to himself: "It's a chance… to hear only the sounds that are 'supposed' to be here."

Maya couldn't keep the surprised tone out of her voice. "Your parents, they let you—"

Kougar shrugged as he talked over her. "I told them where I was going."

"Wow, they give you a lot of freedom."

Kougar smiled with tight irony. "Well, sort of."

The sound of wheels on the trail made them look back up the trail. A couple of bikers with professional riding gear on were headed fast toward the drop. They had high-end bikes, a Santa Cruz and a Kona. Both had Oakley blades on that reflected the trail. They jumped off the drop and easily landed past the log, dust rising up where they landed and they bombed down the trail.

"Hummph," Maya grunted. "Serious dudes."

"Yeah, maybe," Kougar replied. "Let's see."

With that, Kougar whipped his wheel around and accelerated down the trail.

"Hey, wait—" Maya blurted out and then hurtled down the trail after Kougar. She knew the Rock Garden was coming up. She hoped Kougar wasn't thinking about doing anything stupid. Her mother had told her to walk the places where the rocks were bad. She always walked the Rock Garden. It was brutal, way too technical for her. Up ahead, she could see the determined angle of Kougar's body as he turned into the corners, gaining on the two riders as a long down hiller led right into the Rock Garden. The two riders adjusted their speed to take time to pick their line, and head methodically into the rocks.

Kougar drew up quickly on their backs. At first Maya thought he would crash right into the back wheel of second rider. She felt a sliver of fear tingle up her spine. *What's he doing!*

"Kougar!" Maya shouted. "Oh, sh-!" she almost swore. As she pedaled down the hill she saw Kougar veer off and start to pass the riders as they entered the rocks. *He's crazy!*

Kougar came up hard on the back of the second rider.

"On your right, Mr. Spandex," he called out calmly as he surged pass the riders. They looked at him in shocked surprise as they saw his speed and the fact that he had no helmet on. Kougar entered the rocks.

Images flashed through Maya's mind of Kougar pitching over his bars and sprawling onto the rocks in a hideously twisted heap. She could only watch, her breath suddenly stopped by fear.

Kougar hit the first patch of rocks with a little more speed than he should have, he thought, as the front wheel twisted and then bounced violently upward. Kougar fought his bars and leaned his body toward the line he wanted, hoping to get the angle of his front wheel right. In mid-air, his stuck his right leg out to use its weight to steady him for the briefest of seconds, to keep from tipping over. The jagged rocks roiled underneath him bouncing him hard left, then right. So many quick, spit second decisions that seeing wasn't enough. He had to 'feel' where the rocks were and what angle he wanted his wheel to touch this or that side of a rock.

It was like riding a bull out of the chute. Hold on and use your balance. Try to keep your wheels straight and time your pedaling just right. Bam! His front wheel slammed right into a flat steep rock. His front wheel staggered and popped straight up, almost going backward, stopping his momentum. Just in time, he twisted his front wheel and lurched forward with his body. His wheel came down to land on the side of the rock and that gave him just enough forward motion to get back on his line. A few more stomach lurching bounces threw him off his pedals as he headed down the steepest part of the Rock Garden. He fought the panic that told him to brake. But he knew he needed the speed of the bike to catch up to his feet if he wanted to continue.

Maya could see he was in trouble. But she had thought that the instance Kougar entered the rocks. Nobody that she knew ever made it through the Garden without getting off or clipping out to put a foot down. She found her breath.

"Give it up, Kougar! Stop! Stop now!"

Kougar committed to his speed and leaned forward to keep his front wheel down. In a flash he saw the barest line, almost a crack, between two jagged rocks. Miss it and he was going down hard and his body would be broken. He had a brief second to aim his wheel and tried to squeeze his legs close to his bike frame and then... he shot between the rocks his wheels fitting through the rocky keyhole. *I'm through!* He shouted in his mind and then knew what he had to do at the bottom—and that quickly!

His momentum rocketed him down a steep incline into a hard hairpin turn. Turn, or he would crash into the trunk of an ancient Ponderosa pine that had been split in two by lightning. Its ominous, jagged outline stood at the bottom of the steep drop. He pulled hard on his hand brakes and bent his left handlebar almost to the ground as his back tire fish-tailed around and slammed into the trunk bouncing him back like a pin-ball off a bumper.

Whoa! That was extreme! The elation rose up in him, replacing the fear that had shot through him during the rock-ride. A few minutes later the two riders made their way carefully through the rocks, using their feet like oars to steer away from rocks to maintain their balance. At the bottom they rode by Kougar who sat on his bike, his arms crossed. As one rider passed, he turned to Kougar and spat out as he looked Kougar up and down:

"Freak."

Kougar grunted and said under his breath: "So I've been told."

Maya finally made her way to Kougar, walking her bike through the rocks. She couldn't believe that she wasn't running to where Kougar had fallen in his crazy, lunatic attempt, to ride through the Garden. But there he was, upright and waiting for her, sitting calmly on his bike. She coasted down the incline and drew up beside him, pulling off her helmet in an angry motion.

"Jesus, Kougar! That," she gasped out in angry amazement, "that was the most *insane* thing I have ever seen! I mean, are you kidding!? You could have broken your neck or smashed your head like an egg. No helmet. For God's sake! I don't get you! You scared the hell out of me!"

"Sorry," Kougar said calmly, like 'it' was no big deal.

"I mean, at school, you seem so shy, so—"

"Scared?" Kougar cut in.

"Yeah... scared of me, Hayden, scared of kids in the hallway, scared of speaking up in Grenfeld's class, and now what you just did. I don't get you."

"Being scared is one thing."

Maya shook her head. "One thing? Don't you understand fear?"

Kougar sighed and looked off into the forest and finally turned his blades to Maya and said lowly:

"I know everything about fear."

Maya continued to shake her head, not understanding Kougar's words. "Well, it sure doesn't seem like it."

184

Kougar looked out over the Rock Garden. This was the first time he had made it all the way through without stopping. He had fallen once, luckily sprawling perfectly between the rocks with only a hip bruise to show for it.

"Sometimes… it's not about fear or being scared," he said as he continued to look out over the jagged sea of rocks behind them. "Sometimes you just want to do something to see what it 'feels' like."

"I think that's stupid," Maya said, anger still in her voice.

"You're probably right …"

"So why?"

Kougar looked at her, his mirrored blades inscrutable. "Why not?" He said, like it was obvious.

Maya let the anger drain out of her voice as she realized something. "Well, look," she began, softly, "you can't ever do that to me again, okay? Be crazy on your own if you want to, but not in front of me… I couldn't take watching you get hurt. That's not my idea of a good time. I mean, watching what Hayden did to you was enough. Believe me."

Kougar tilted his head to one side as he took in the meaning of her words and the tone of her voice that resonated within him like a soft caress.

"You think?" Kougar replied, a trace of stubborn skepticism in his question.

"Yeah… I do," she said, her deep brown eyes displaying the depth of her feelings.

"I'll consider it, then."

"Good. Now, can we finish this… exciting ride in a very boring way? She smiled and Kougar returned a small, thoughtful smile. She hadn't seen that one before. He turned and rode off down the trail.

"No extreme tricks!" she shouted after him.

"No tricks!" he replied over his shoulder.

The Dance

After an hour of steady pedaling, Kougar and Maya arrived at Phil's Trailhead. During the ride back down COD, Maya kept going over what Kougar had said to her. She felt he had cautiously let her in a bit. She had called for a few 'water' stops and tried to make some small conversation, keeping things light, no more talk about fears or questions about him that he would be uncomfortable with. He had to come forward. But he seemed preoccupied, quiet, and didn't take up or respond to her friendly comments. Questions about Gaius were hanging on her tongue but she dared not go there. Yet…

They pulled up next to the large posted map of Phil's trail complex. Kougar leaned his foot against a boulder and Maya did the same on the other side of the rock. A sudden stiff breeze blew a bunch of dried leaves across the almost empty, unpaved parking lot. Something made both Kougar and Maya watch the leaves swirl around until they stopped. Kougar was silent. He drew a couple of swallows from his water tube and wiped a hand across his mouth. Maya took off her helmet and combed her hair out with her fingers. They just stood there, like time for them had stopped and they didn't know how to go forward, to let life's clock tick off the seconds of their lives… The ride was over.

The one feeling that Maya had, and it had been growing within her on the ride back, was that she didn't want this day to end. There was something final about this day. Her instincts signaled that somehow, she had to make something happen and she knew, deep in her heart, she *wanted* to make something happen.

"That was a great ride. I had so much fun. I never thought we—"

Kougar had just been waiting for her to say something. He eagerly, and a little awkwardly, jumped in. "Yeah, it was a, a cool ride. I, too, didn't think that …well, you know." He looked away nervously.

Maya helped him out with a small laugh. "Yeah... I know. Me neither."

Another pause swelled between them and Maya decided to go all in. "Hey, what do you got going now?"

Kougar struggled to keep from saying that his mom had stuff for him to do around the yard, leaves and pinecones to rake up. Stuff like that.

"Ah, I, ah I've—"

"Do you like the piano?" Maya cut in, not wanting Kougar to finish his sentence.

"Piano?"

"Yeah, I play the piano and I give lessons."

Kougar's blades just looked at her for a second. "Is there anything you can't do?"

"Well, I can't ride a skateboard or do what you did today in the Rock Garden. That was really sick." Maya flashed him a big smile.

Kougar looked away. "My mom has always bugged me to learn an instrument, something I could be, ah, creative with or whatever. But I knew I would suck, so I didn't."

"No, it's not that hard," she began, excited.

"Like math?" Kougar shot back at her.

"Well, yeah, it's kind of like math, notes and numbers have a similar relationship, but there's no emotion, no feeling in math... Come on, let's go to my house."

Kougar shrugged his shoulders and fidgeted with his handlebars, moving them back and forth. Being out in the woods with Maya on mountain bikes was one thing, but to go to her house, that was a totally different deal, fraught with all kinds of risks.

"Nah... I can't. I've—"

The imperative of what the day had meant to her and what it might hold for them pushed her to insist with all her charm.

"Oh, come on, Koug, it'll be fun. I won't bite."

Of course Kougar noted her use of the nickname his parents used with him and her warm and beautiful smile, framed by her long, flowing hair.

Kougar shook his head. "I don't think so... Out here it was kind of okay, but, your house? I mean ..." and a growing apprehension stirred in him. He pawed nervously at the ground with his worn sneakers. "I mean, what happens, ah, what happens when your parents—"

"See you?" Maya cut in and then said quickly, almost too quickly, "So? Besides they're in Sisters and won't be back until dinner." Of course she knew if her father got a look at Kougar... he would definitely jump to conclusions. She could see his face now, the stern, disapproving cloud passing over his dark features. Her forehead involuntarily winced as she promptly pushed that image out of her mind. She looked at her watch. "It's only three right now. Come on," she encouraged him.

Kougar looked down at his pedals and said lowly, fighting his conviction. "But we're not... friends."

Maya laughed loudly and fully. Kougar liked to hear her laugh that way.

"I know that. Hey, most of the people I give lessons to aren't necessarily," and she held up her hands and gave the 'in quotes' sign, "my friends. They are my students. Come on, unless you have some big date to get ready for."

"Yeah, right," Kougar scoffed and then grinned. The irony was rich.

"Follow me," Maya said, settling it all, and sped off down the trail toward Skyliner. She didn't know what was going to 'happen,' but the day was still going on and she felt she would know what to do... She looked back and smiled. Kougar was following her.

They turned down Maya's street in the River West neighborhood and they rode up Maya's driveway.

"Here we are," Maya said.

She got off and punched in the code to open the garage door. She walked her bike into the garage and leaned it against the wall. She looked back at Kougar who stood in the driveway almost like he was stuck in a trap.

"Hey," Maya soothed, "come on, park your bike in here. We don't want to leave a nice Gary Fisher out on the lawn. You never know. Lots of college kids walk through here to get to the bars on Galveston, especially Ten Barrel."

Kougar reluctantly parked his bike next to Maya's. He took off his blades and removed his bandanna and his blond-white dreadlocks spilled out over his shoulders and down the sides of his face and just over his eyebrows. Maya could see his blues eyes were uneasy. Maya opened the door that led into the kitchen from the garage.

"Come on," Maya motioned to Kougar.

Kougar followed her into the kitchen. Maya stopped by the refrigerator and opened it pulling out half of a sliced apple.

"Want a snack? I bet you're starved after that long ride. Apple?"

"No. I'm good."

"Sure?" Maya asked as she bit into the apple.

"I'm good." Kougar said again with the same muted tone.

"Let's go downstairs." Maya headed down the hallway off the kitchen. She had to wait while Kougar's walk-the-plank steps caught up with her. "My room's down the hall." She almost giggled self-consciously to herself. "Ah, you don't need to see it. It's just a girl's room. Not that interesting. Give me a quick sec' to pull on some jeans and a shirt. Wait here."

Before Kougar could give into his nerves and just bolt this scene, Maya returned, coming back down the hall with some tight, faded jeans on, black socks on her shoeless feet, and a form fitting short sleeve, black tee shirt, with a V-neck. She came to the stairway that led down. "Down this way."

Kougar slowly followed her down the carpeted stairs having to duck his head as the stairwell dropped at an angle to open up to the low basement ceiling. The light from the ground level basement windows threw two broadening shafts of light, one, onto to the worn, wooden parquet dance floor, and the other glistened on the black, grand piano. Between the two windows a large, sliding glass patio door was covered in drapes. Kougar looked around, taking the room in as a couple of thoughts drifted through his mind: he couldn't imagine playing the piano and the dance floor looked like a place he could make a fool of himself. *I'm no Gaius,* he reminded himself.

Maya wandered over to the piano and moved her hand over its glossy finish like a caress.

"I used to spend a lot of time here when my grandmother was still alive." And Maya lost herself in her memories as they passed by her mind's eye like a collection of film-darkened scenes. "She taught me many things …" Maya smiled. "She was so beautiful and wise. She had a wonderful talent for music, dance and… math."

"Just like you, eh?" Kougar added.

"Funny you say that. My father is always saying," and she took on her father's tone with his Indian accent: "That Maya, she is so much like her grandmother—but hopefully, not too much like her!" And she laughed, almost sadly. "It's a family joke."

Kougar just nodded back, not really understanding what she meant. Maya continued.

"I think if she had grown up here, in the states, instead of India, her life would have been so different. Here, her talents could have set her… free. The way she played and danced. You couldn't take your eyes off her. Such grace."

"How did she die?" Kougar asked.

"Oh," Maya sighed, finally realizing at long last: "the doctors said that even though she was healthy, there was some weakness with her heart …" She looked over at her grandmother's pictures on the wall and felt the tug of an all-encompassing tide of unlikely emotions that she had experienced over the last month. "When memories are all you have, you can only live so long with a broken heart… an abandoned heart. It finally

190

took her. That's what I think." And Maya closed her moist eyes for a moment as she let the stream of newfound insights continue their truthful journey through her little girl memories and into her young woman's soul.

Kougar's eyes focused thoughtfully as he forgot his unease and let himself get caught up in Maya's story.

"A broken heart?" Kougar half said and half asked.

Maya wandered over to the wall where her grandmother's photos hung. Kougar followed her and looked at the pictures of Sania Virk. She looked like a character out of an old, foreign film. The beautifully draped saris and a radiant smile that matched Maya's.

"As she always told me: she was only meant for one man. And the man she chose was not to be the one allowed for her."

"Allowed? You mean... her parents didn't like the guy?"

"I guess you could say that," Maya said through a small painful laugh. "Back then, life in India could be very strict for girls and certainly for wealthy ones like my grandmother. The culture is very different from here. Her father had picked out husbands for her and she just shook her head. She was a free spirit, way ahead of her time. She just wanted to play her instruments and dance... and to love truthfully."

"So? What's wrong with that?" Kougar asked, puzzled.

"You don't understand. She 'had' to get married. That's what... that's what her duty was to her family. So it went for some years until she met my grandfather. I never knew him. Neither did my father."

Kougar was still puzzled. "They didn't get married?"

"No. They couldn't. He was a very skilled carpenter, an artist with wood, my grandmother said, and very handsome. But her father thought he was just a construction worker."

"Ah, not allowed," Kougar said, getting it.

"Right. He was doing some woodwork at my great grandfather's house. Every day he would walk by my grandmother's music and dance studio at a certain time and my grandmother would be there, dancing, or playing the piano. The big doors to the studio were always open because of the hot weather. He liked what he saw and my grandmother liked what she saw."

"Did they talk?"

"With the eyes, yes. My grandfather didn't want to disrespect my grandmother's father by talking to his daughter."

"So how—"

"She danced… and he watched."

"When did they talk?"

"One day, he came to watch her dance and she was waiting for him with a suitcase and they left together. Then, they talked."

"Whoa. How do you just look at someone and then leave with them and then—"

Maya cocked her head at Kougar, annoyed. "You don't get it, do you?"

"I guess not," Kougar looked down.

"They knew… they just knew …. What do you know, Kougar?" Maya asked unexpectedly with a slight tease in her voice.

Kougar was totally taken by surprise. He sputtered for a couple of seconds. "Ah, who, me? What do I know?" He sighed and looked around for an answer that finally came to him as he shook his shaggy head once. "I know that you make me nervous. That's what I know."

Maya laughed. "No need to be nervous. I'm just a girl."

Kougar didn't look at her but had to confess in muted tones: "Yeah, so I've noticed."

"Oh, you have?" And Maya flashed her beautiful smile.

"Yeah," Kougar almost muttered.

"Let's play some piano. Let me show—"

Kougar lifted up his hand. "You go ahead. No need to try and teach my ten thumbs and me. I'll just listen to you."

"I'm a really good teacher."

"I'm sure. Look, it's hard enough for me to just 'be' here. You know what they say: Don't try to teach a pig to play, it's a waste of time and it just annoys the pig."

Maya laughed, undeterred. "It won't be like that."

"Trust me. It will be for me. Just… play something."

"All right. Come sit over here," and she motioned to the couch facing the piano."

"I'm all right," Kougar's wary voice said.

"Come on," Maya coaxed.

"I'm good. Really." And he shuffled his feet in place.

"Okay."

Maya sat down at the piano and adjusted the small standing mirror on top of the piano to focus on the view of the keys below.

"What's the mirror for?" Kougar asked, wondering.

"Oh, it's to keep me from looking down at my hands. It allows me to keep my head up as my grandmother said— to 'show' what I am playing. I can glance at the keys without dropping my head."

She rubbed her hands together for a couple of moments as she looked down at the keys suddenly lost in thought about her grandmother. She heard her grandmother playing her favorite composition. She started right in with the refrain, working the notes softly with her right hand, building and building the hauntingly beautiful melody and momentum.

Little by little, minute-by-minute, the sound and pitch of the keys entered Kougar and he felt a softening begin deep within him, a slight unwinding of a traumatic knot. It was a siren's call to peace that had never resonated in him before. This was… new. He was drawn to the sound. Slowly, under the spell of the music, he made his way over to the piano.

Maya watched him approach. She tried to look him in the eyes but he kept his eyes down. But she could see the subtle play of emotions across his face. She kept playing and the music kept luring Kougar closer. Finally, he sat down on the piano bench next to her, fascinated with her finger work across the keys that made such soothing, and evocative sounds. The spell deepened. The scarred and burnt door of his past began to open ever so slightly, and the music's light poured in through the trembling crack.

It came to her, and she knew what to do. Maya adjusted the mirror as she played, so the angle could take in both their eyes—*if he would only look,* she thought. He could then look at her without having to gaze 'directly' at her. The piano mirror would provide a… safer way.

She knew that in order to have a chance, a chance for them to get started, she had to get him to look at her long enough, so she could tell him with her eyes what she was beginning to feel and that he could be safe with her.

Come on, Kougar, she summoned with all her heart. *Look at me! Please.*

Finally, the music allowed him to do what he would never do… this close. He looked into the mirror. For the first time, they really saw each other, not just each other's eyes, but what they held within, all the words their mouths couldn't say now. Unspoken words were always ahead of what's possible to be spoken. *Boom.* The base drum was pounded once, no sound, just a deep reverberation of feeling spread out between them. They held onto their mutual gaze while Maya finished the song with the last refrain slowing, and slowing, until she rested her hands upon her lap.

After a moment, as the last sound of the piano faded out, Maya reached up and tilted the mirror down. For Kougar, Maya's eyes blinked out as the mirror reflected the black and white piano keys.

Maya turned to look at Kougar, and slowly, he turned to face her. They locked eyes… It was safe. Maya let a smile gather across her face. Kougar's full smile moved through his features, clouded as they were by his mass of blond-white dreadlocks. They paused, savoring the moment.

Presently, Maya said under a soft giggle, "Did you like the song?"

Kougar sighed as he took in all that had happened… all that 'had' happened because of the music. "It, ah, it was beautiful. I've never heard anything like it."

"It was mostly my grandmother's piece and I have added things over the years. I guess you could say, it's our song. I feel close to her when I play it. I played some notes that were new. The song just went there. It surprised me."

Maya could fully feel her grandmother's presence. The music had elated her and with Kougar here, and 'really' looking at her, she felt inspired and suddenly she realized:

"I've never told anybody about my grandmother."

"She taught you to play?"

"Yes... and to dance." Maya got up quickly from the bench, her eyes shining. "I know that there are sides to you that nobody knows about."

Kougar thought deeply for a second but being with Maya now felt safe to him. "That's... probably a good thing."

Something about Kougar's gentle, tortured shyness made her feel that she was totally safe with him, able to say anything or show anything. Again, she felt the inspiration.

"I'm going to show you something that I've never shown anybody. It's one side of me that none of my friends know about. I'm—"

"Not even Hayden?" 'Something' had made Kougar blurt out the question.

For a second, Maya met Kougar's question with a puzzled smile. "No, not even him. I... ah, never felt comfortable enough for that. You're not Hayden."

Kougar grunted under his breath. "That's for sure."

"I mean that in a good way... in a different way."

The inspired look returned to Maya's eyes. "I'm going to dance for you. It's an old Indian dance, a special dance my grandmother taught me. I use different music than she did but the dance is still the dance. The dance has two purposes. It's for the entertainment of an audience ..." She paused, becoming self-conscious as a wave of innocent shyness passed over her face as she changed her train of thought nervously. "Obviously, I don't have the right costume on." Maya smiled, her cheeks glowing an unaccustomed red under her smooth, light, cinnamon skin.

"What's the other purpose?" Kougar asked, intrigued.

Maya laughed softly, shyly, "I sort of know and... don't know what it is. You'll just have to use your imagination," she said seductively, smiled, and turned away.

Maya walked across the wooden floor, the mood of the dance beginning to work its way through her body. Just off the dance floor she slid behind a three-paneled floor screen that had Indian designs on it, decorated elephants and riders. There was a table with a Bose iPod sound system and a wooden drawer with jewelry that had belonged to her grandmother. She put on sets of thin gold wrist bracelets that tinkled together and long golden earrings. She scrolled through the music and picked out Loreena McKennitt's 'Marco Polo'. She gathered herself for a second, rolled up her shirt, up just past her belly button and tied a knot to hold it in place. She was fully with her grandmother now, the quiddity of her ways moved through Maya like the silent flow of a vast river under a full moon.

Kougar watched Maya go behind the screen. He had no imagination or experience to know what kind of dance Maya would perform. If it were anything hypnotic like the song Maya had played on the piano that started the whispers of surrender from parts of him that festered with fear, loathing and guilt—what would happen?

Maya came out from behind the screen. She walked smoothly, with a dancer's coordination and a confident, maturing femininity. She stopped at center of the dance floor and the music started: the slow bongo drums, guitar and sensual violin filling the room. With her hands, Maya slowly pulled her flowing hair down over her face. She then placed one hand over her heart, then the other. She heard her grandmother's words: *Find your focal point. Put your energy there...* She summoned and she summoned... She was going to offer her heart... the single, ageless original motive of the dance; the other purpose she couldn't articulate to Kougar.

She began. Slowly she raised her hands and parted her hair and looked right at Kougar, her liquid brown eyes telling him that this time, this moment, was where they were supposed to be. She dropped her hands to her knees, her hips swaying to the music. She allowed—and the music allowed her— to isolate each part of her body: every roll of the shoulder, the hypnotic flow of the arms, while the tinkling, gold bracelets gleamed at her wrists, the gradual, slow sensual swaying walk towards Kougar, all of it merging into the whole as her body felt the caress of the music.

Kougar's gaze was unblinking. He was transfixed; transported he felt, beyond any boundary of his limited imagination. He… couldn't take his captivated eyes off Maya. The overwhelming novelty of it all froze him as he sat, watching from the couch, his sensibilities bombarded by all that Maya was, and all that she was becoming.

In front of him now, Maya grounded her bare feet and continued the swaying walk that had every appearance that she was moving forward. She gradually raised her hands to again brush her hair down over her face. Her undulations got slower and finally, smaller. She placed one hand on her heart then the other. She paused there and just like in the beginning… she summoned and she summoned. And then she raised a hand to part her hair away from one side of her face then the other and locked eyes with Kougar. For a moment, she thought she could see Gaius's green eyes flashed through Kougar's blue eyes and their warmth and feeling merged. Hope surged in her heart as she smiled and savored the image. The music ended. She broke the spell as she 'just walked' over and sat down next to Kougar on the couch, her bracelets tinkling. Kougar looked down for a moment, trying to grasp everything that he had seen… and had felt. He shook his head, puzzled and turned to look at Maya. He sighed in amazement.

"You never showed this to anyone?"

"No," she said, again with that small, shy laugh.

"What's it for? I mean, why don't you perform—"

"It's not 'just' for performing."

"I don't understand. Why do—"

"It's for a time like this… It was for you."

Kougar sighed deeply. "Wow. It was… incredible. I have never seen anything like it."

"And… you won't," Maya said softly, with a knowing, half smile tugging at her full lips, no vanity in her tone. She realized she might never dance that way again. It was like a singular, evocative phrase in a poem that can't be written again the same way, or voiced the same way again. With her internal revelation, her half smile broadened and she said:

"It was a one-time thing."

Questions reverberated in Kougar's mind. *Why?* Tumultuous feelings, new and old, swirled and sparked within him as he struggled to come to grips with the whole mysterious and exhilarating day with Maya.

"Why?"

"Why what?" Maya asked, hoping for her chance… their chance.

"I mean… today. Why today?" Kougar managed, as words failed him.

Maya paused, lifted her hand.

"Friends?"

Kougar could only bust out a small startled, ironic laugh. Maya continued to hold out her hand.

"Friends?"

Kougar's mouth moved with his internal, fear-ridden doubts that clawed up from the depths of 'what-ifs' at the back of his mind. Maya cocked her head to one side with that beautiful look of hers and her eyes said: 'well?'

Kougar shifted around in his seat. Paused and then finally said, his voice almost a whisper: "For now," and he grasped her hand, while a faint voice at the edge of his lost hopefulness added: 'and forever…' The touch of her skin widened his eyes with a subtle jolt of electricity.

"Good friends?" Maya pushed with all of her charm.

Kougar nodded… but still had to say: "For now."

Maya relented and laughed. "Okay. For now… Boy, you're a hard one."

Kougar looked at her and confessed in a low voice full of all that had gutted and torched his life: "No, not hard... Just alone."

"Not anymore," Maya said, full of the conviction that lighted her eyes.

Kougar replied with a wary smile. It was all he could say. Then: "Ah, I gotta go."

Maya just nodded. The day had to... end.

Kougar turned and moved toward the stairs and they walked up without saying a word, but their thoughts were on each other. They reached the top of the stairs and started down the hallway. Kougar was waiting for Maya to say something, something he wanted her to say. And then she did.

"Ah, hey," and Maya tugged at Kougar's elbow. He turned around. "I had a great day with you... a wonderful day."

Kougar nodded. "It was... very cool."

Maya nodded back and they both nodded for a second, thinking the conversation should go further, that certain words would be said. But for right now, the nodding was enough. They both shared a small knowing laugh. Kougar turned again and walked through the kitchen and out the door to the garage. Maya pushed the garage door opener and the door lifted, the sunlight pouring in. Kougar walked his bike out to the driveway. Again, they both felt that more words should pass between them—perhaps even something more... Finally Kougar moved his mouth to speak and Maya waited with sudden expectations.

"So... what happened to your grandmother when she left with that guy?"

Maya had to let out a small laugh at her silent hopes.

"Oh... well they travelled around the country for months, perfectly happy, full of joys. Then one day my great grandfather's men found them and took my grandmother back home. She was pregnant with my father. She was kept under constant watch and was escorted everywhere. She caught a few glimpses of my grandfather but was never allowed to see him. After the baby came, she received a note from my grandfather's sister who said that one day, as they were walking down the street, an abandoned house was on fire." She had to pause as she realized that she had never told this story before, hadn't thought about the grandfather she never knew in… years. The old pain of his absence in her life came back to her like a flood. She sighed as she gathered herself. "They could hear the sirens of the fire trucks coming. Without a word, he turned and walked toward the burning house. His sister tried to hold him back but he kept going. He entered the house and was… consumed by the fire."

A small tremor of scorching memories crept through Kougar's body and he almost fell back a step.

"Hey," came Maya's surprised voice as she reached out to grab Kougar's arm, "are you all right?"

Kougar took a moment to push back down the surge of burning memories, and to get a hold of himself. "Yeah, I'm good… It's just… It's kind of shocking. I mean, why would he do that?"

Maya paused and again, she reaffirmed to herself what her newfound insights had said to her.

"He died of a badly… badly broken heart. He was first. And my grandmother finally did, after all those years."

"You think?"

Maya nodded.

"Wow …" Kougar said lowly. "That's heavy."

Maya couldn't help the small smile that spread across her smooth lips.

"Funny you say that. My grandmother used to say that life's heavy. You carry it the best you can until you can't and that's good enough."

A pause developed between them. They looked inward, each with their own thoughts. Finally Kougar spoke. "Your grandfather, what was his name?"

"Mahesh."

Kougar mulled over what he was going to say, then it poured out. "Your grandfather, Mahesh, he was a brave man."

"Brave?" Maya pursed her lips as she considered this new thought about an old tragedy, but it didn't stand up to how she had always felt... "Possibly... But, I think he was just weak," she said with an old conviction. That's why my grandmother loved him so much. She said it was his last act of devotion. It comforted her, but it has always made me angry. He could have outlived his despair. Time could have given him an opportunity to know me, to know his son, my father. His sacrifice was for... nothing. That fire burned out a big part of my life."

Kougar nodded, his face twisted with memories. He sighed through a muted laugh. "Yeah, I guess a fire could do that." And his voice seemed to turn inward. "But I don't think he was weak. Weak people don't walk into a fire. He was brave. Brave people don't wait; they don't hesitate. That's why they're brave. Cowards play it safe."

Kougar mounted his bike and put on his blades; they turned towards her.

"Believe me, I know. See you in class."

Something about the distant overtones of pain and regret in Kougar's voice made Maya want to anxiously confirm what she had hoped had happened today. As Kougar began to ride off he heard Maya call over his shoulder:

"Friends, right?"

Kougar didn't turn around. He stuck out his arm and gave her the thumbs up sign.

It was coming clear to her that something... something bad had happened in Kougar's life. All the hints were there: the covering mass of blond dreadlocks; the neglected way he dressed; his timid, shy, halting manner; the pain that drifted through his mysterious words; riding recklessly without a helmet; letting Hayden pummel him—and Gaius! She had to fight down the urge to run after him, to stop him, to pull off his blades and to hold him and ask—no, tell him, that she could, and would, share his pain. In the distance, her mind's eye could see the writhing and flickering of a scorching fire… and she wondered if, in some terrible way, those very same roaring flames had burned a blackened, lifeless path through Kougar's past as they had hers. Of course her life was only an evolutionary possibility when her grandfather, Mahesh, had willingly walked into the consuming embrace of the fire. She never *saw* those flames do their work. Kougar, she felt, had—*had!* seen them… *do* something.

The Test

Kougar reached over to his nightstand and flipped open his phone. He pushed aside his unruly hair so he could see the phone display as it lit up part of his face. He saw that the time was 2:05am. He then opened his text messages and reread what Maya had texted him as he went to bed:

Maya: Hey, Koug, epic day! ☺ I was… afraid u wouldn't like me. The way u took off at the beginning of the ride. I thought u were trying to get rid of me!

Kougar: I was… ☺ Sure glad u were so fast. And the way u smoked me. LOL! That was sick.

Maya:… U know, u are so easy to talk to.

Kougar: Hmmm… No one has ever accused me of that! It's always been better to just not say anything.

Maya: I feel like we've been BFs for a long time. LOL!

Kougar: Whoa, there! But… u r my first real friend.

Maya: No way!

Kougar: Yes, way. No one has ever played the piano and danced for me… that was awesome… U r awesome. I can't get over what went down today.

Maya: Yeah, me neither. ☺ I didn't think it would happen… but… but…

Kougar:… But what?

Maya: I'm kind of chicken to say it… Oh, well, here goes …. I think I like you… I like you a lot. ☺

Kougar: Me? ………… no way ….

Maya: Way. ☺ ☺ ☺ I'll let you sleep on that.

Kougar: I'll need to!... See you tomorrow.

Maya: Definitely! Can't wait!

Kougar: Cool.

Maya: So… I'm awesome?

Kougar: Yeah …Yeah, you are…

Maya: Cool. Sleep good! ☺

Kougar: Don't think I'll be able to.

Maya: Me neither!

Thank God for texting, Kougar thought as he closed his phone and set it back down on the nightstand. There was no way he's could have said some of the things he texted. *I would have been too freaked!... Man! She likes me a lot? Man...* Kougar kept rerunning Maya's words through his head as he heard the evocative echo of the piano keys as she played that unforgettable refrain, and, while images of her sensually subtle Indian dance moved before his mind's eye, imprinting his memory with innocent seduction. The force of all that she was overwhelmed his senses; it smothered the ever present red warning lights that blinked on and off behind his heart with a dogged fate. He blew out a low sigh as he gazed up into the opaque darkness of his bedroom ceiling. He could hear a faint pounding drum of a question starting somewhere within him. The slow drumming grew until it rose up and pounded the question into his ears. *I'm all in now, aren't I?* He searched for the answer hoping it would be etched in the growing shadows above him... Nothing.

*

Maya, too, gazed up at her bedroom ceiling, sleep evading her as her mind kept replaying the most unlikely day of her life. An epiphany grew within her, that all along, she didn't want to stop at just being friends with Kougar. She was driven by the emotional mission to help Kougar move toward Gaius. She wanted Kougar and Gaius to become... one. She felt—and had to hope that as Kougar came out of his shell, that he was *really* more like Gaius. If she could get him there, then, anything would be possible and the possibilities thrilled her. Then, as if her window cracked open and a bitter cold breeze blew across her bed, a sudden, nagging reality almost checked her excitement: *What about my parents, especially my dad? And what about my friends?*

She figured that a few of her friends might, *might* not *get* Kougar, and wouldn't understand her *choice*... What would Hayden and 'his' group say? She calmed herself believing that she was who she was: being 'Maya' with all her popularity and her myriad of friends and acquaintances, would make being with Kougar no big deal. Being Captain of the Cheer Team, Student Council President, in the race for Valedictorian of her class, and certainly a potential Prom Queen—all of this had to give her the clout she needed to make her choice... okay.

She breathed out an angry sigh as she pulled up the bedcovers to her chin. *It's not like I'm some loser!* And with that she dispelled her misgivings. She tossed and turned for a while, thinking as she did, that she was sloughing off her ignored doubts. Fitfully though, sleep came, and excitement trickled, then ran through her dreams as they resembled a disjointed narrative of a 'Beauty and the Freak' story...

Maya woke up to a text from Maddie:

> ...Hey girl, I'm coming by to pick you up for school. Don't say no... ☺

Maya replied:

> ...K...

I have to make it easy on her, Maya said to herself as she headed to the shower and the thought now just registered with some mixed feelings: *Maddie's with Hayden.* She knew the thought should sting more than a little but she was too distracted by what was going on with Kougar to really dwell on it. *Maybe later... Who knows?* Knowing Maddie, she believed that Maddie wasn't trying to make a point. *A point? No, that's not her. But, Hayden?... Yeah.* She felt surprised as the thought annoyed her in an anxious way. But a quick notion assuaged her unwelcome agitation: In a sense, Maddie was taking Hayden off her hands with particularly good timing. *Yes, that's the deal ...Yes.*

Maya and her parents were having some small talk as they sat at the kitchen island, drinking coffee and eating cereal. Her father, Raja, was fully dressed in his Chief Forester's uniform, and her mother, Lisa, was still in her robe.

"Can't believe this weather," Raja said as he raised his coffee cup to his lips and drank. "Hardly any snow yet. Up on the mountain, they've had to make and groom their own snow."

"Yeah," Maya chimed in. "The skiers at school are really bummed."

"I sure don't mind the snow being off the roads, that's for sure," Lisa said as she glanced down at the morning paper.

Maddie's car horn sounded from the street.

"Oh, that's Maddie. Gotta go." Maya gathered up a few books off the counter and started to head out.

"Hey, where's that hug your mother said you've wanted to give me? Too busy, eh?" Raja asked with mock hurt in his voice. "You've got to pay attention to me. Now that Hayden's gone, I'm the only man in your life," Raja teased and Lisa laughed. "And the most important one, I might add," Raja added with a twinkle and a big smile.

"Of course you are, dad," Maya said as she hugged her father.

Maya kissed her mom on the cheek as she passed by with her books in hand. "See you later. I've got cheer practice so I'll be a little late for dinner."

"We'll wait," Lisa called after her.

Maya closed the door behind her and headed down the walkway toward Maddie's car. Her dad was right, winter had yet to come to Bend, except for the real high country and the very tops of the mountains. The mornings were cold but the sun kept at it, its unseasonably warm rays heating up the afternoons into the mid-fifties.

Maya opened the passenger side door of Maddie's car and climbed in.

"Hi, Madds!" Maya said cheerily.

Maddie paused. "Hey" she said through a half smile.

Maya read the guilt all over Maddie's face. Another pause gathered between them. They both said each other's name at the same time and stopped. Then, they both said "I" at the same time and stopped. Maya got through this time.

"Madds. I know. I'm all right with it."

Maddie squirmed in her seat, clearly tormented. Her words gushed out: "Oh, Maya, I wanted to be the first to—"

Maya held up her hand and let go a small laugh. "Madds, you're the last one to tell me. It's okay. Really."

Maddie continued to gush: "I didn't do—I mean ..."

Maya just nodded and looked out down the road in front of them. "I know."

"I couldn't. You know, I wouldn't ..."

"I know."

"You're my best, my very best friend. I ..."

Maya continued to nod and said softly, trying to reassure Maddie. "I know. No worries, Hayden and I have been over for some time now."

Maddie finally just slumped in her seat as she sighed.

"It just happened... It felt... right. Oh, do you hate me? You should."

Maya turned and reached out to hold Maddie's hand and smiled warmly. Maddie let a tentative grin spread across her face. Maya squeezed Maddie's hand.

"I know how things can just *happen*."

"Hayden was so down after that game. He totally blamed himself. He seemed so lonely... I just wanted to cheer him up and... and ..."

"He needed you and you were there for him."

"I totally wasn't expecting that we... that we would get together."

"That's how it happens. You'll like Hayden. He's... He's has that... thing. That 'something' about him."

"You know, you're right. Oh, Maya, I'm so happy that you're okay with it. I mean if you were pissed, I would definitely call it off."

"Yeah, right," Maya cracked back quickly.

"I would!" Maddie almost shouted, hurt, drama etched across her face.

Maya thought that she knew Maddie better than Maddie did, so, she took her admonition with more than a little skepticism, but smiled at her anyway. Something in her though, certainly not part of her better nature, gnawed at her when she thought of Maddie and Hayden together. After all, Hayden had been her first real boyfriend. And that submerged part of her hadn't gotten over Hayden.

"Don't get flamed, girlfriend," Maya said through a laugh. "Let's go, we'll be late for class."

Maddie pulled away from the curb, both her hands on the wheel. She turned right on Galveston and started to laugh under her breath.

"What?" Maya asked.

"You know I was like your secretary at the party that night. Everyone wanted to know where you were and more than a couple of guys asked me about you."

"No way," Maya scoffed.

"Oh, yes way, girl. John Wright, you know, the track dude. He asked if you were dating anybody. He's a cutie."

"Yeah, a sprinter. He's one fast dude. He blew away the competition at state last year. He's always asking me to race."

"I think he stuffs his running tights, that's what I think."

Maddie had a devilish grin on her face and Maya made a big shocked face, tinged with embarrassment.

"Oh, my God! Madds! You think?! Hey, now that you mention it. Yikes! That's too funny!"

"And 'Louis'," Maddie exaggerated the French pronunciation, "That hottie exchange student from France, asked if you had a 'lover'. I told him you had more than a few!" Maddie pounded the steering wheel and let out her famous braying laugh.

"Madds! You didn't!" Maya shouted, horrified.

"I couldn't resist! And he seemed so impressed!"

Maya and Maddie had a good laugh, just like old times, the subject of Hayden relegated to the background…for now. Maddie pulled into the school parking lot.

*

Kougar could see his breath as he boarded through the cold morning. He never hurried to school but this time he did. He was eager to get a look at Maya before class started; even to—if she was alone—walk up and talk to her, to see her bright, beautiful smile that was like the sun to him.

Things are different now, Kougar kept thinking to himself. *She said she liked me a lot.* Kougar's unbuttoned frayed jean jacket billowed out behind him as he skated into the main school entrance. He popped up his board and walked through the school doors, his too-long tan old cargo pants spilled down over his old Nike cross trainers, the bottoms tattered by the constant friction with the ground; his blond-white dreadlocks spilled down over his shoulders and partially hid his face. On the front of his long-sleeved, dark blue turtleneck, there were words he had stenciled in white script letters that said: *New Days Are Really Just Older... Days.* He almost didn't put the shirt on as he dressed this morning. The words didn't speak as loudly to him as before but they did utter a persistent whisper. A hand of fate pulled the turtleneck over his head.

As was typical, a group of freshman boys turned to look at Kougar, who was at least five inches taller than any of them. Their circle parted to let Kougar pass through while they muttered comments about his appearance to each other under their breaths. Being used to it, Kougar ignored them.

He knew where Maya's locker was. He might catch her there, hopefully by herself. He would pass by and wait for her to call him over. Hopefully. He came to a turn in the hallway and something made him slow his purposeful strides. He took a tentative step around the corner and looked down the hallway to Maya's locker, while a stream of kids flowed by him. Kougar's heart leaped. *There she is!*

Maya approached her locker from the other side of the hall. She had on form-fitting blue jeans with a white V-neck sweater. Kougar got

THE PIANO MIRROR'S POWER

caught up just staring at her like she was walking toward him in slow motion. He started to move forward and then real time kicked in. Three boys, a couple of seniors, Kougar thought, and a kid he had seen sprinting around the track during the summer when he was at the weight room lifting weights, came up beside Maya, calling her name. The whole group stopped beside Maya's locker. They started talking.

Kougar could see Maya flashing smiles and laughing with the boys. The sprinter even tugged playfully at Maya's elbow after making a comment that Maya laughed at. Kougar could see that the boys' eyes were full of Maya. He could tell that they all... 'wanted' her, and each boy's face lit up when under Maya's gaze. IT was as plain as any painful day... He had seen—from a far— this scene played out many times, but today, it seemed like an agonizing new revelation.

When it seemed like Maya looked away from the boys for a second, to look up the hallway to where Kougar was standing, he backed up behind the corner. A jolt went through his mind, like the flash of a scorched meteor. He suddenly got the taste of burnt, metallic ashes in his mouth.

This is WHO she is. This is her world. There is no way I could or should be a part of that world. It's not right. What an idiot!... No... what a freak.

The impact of his thoughts flattened his back against the wall, his mind reeling with reality. Something within him heaved and rolled belly up. He finally got a hold of himself, nodded, while his lips formed a hard line of finality. Destiny's door opened in his mind and he knew exactly what he had to do to show Maya just what being friends with him was going to mean. Prescient images imposed their narrative on his actions now and to be. He felt like he was about to do stuff he had already done. He pushed off the wall and walked down the hall, an imperative lurch in his stride.

In math class Kougar just stared out the window, letting the stages of disappointment, pain and self-mockery pass, blow by blow, through him while he pushed his teen-aged, fear-ridden rage down the ever-gaping lonely hole that he carried around with him. Finally, he again accepted what the truth of him had always known and what Maya would soon find out. It would be a kindness, he reasoned. *She really doesn't get it. She doesn't get it.*

The period bell rang and Kougar filed out of class he started down the hall, clutching three books to his side with one arm. Something made him change directions. He turned left down a hall that passed by the basketball gym. He came upon a group of boys that he knew would be there before he saw them. Among the group were the three boys who had been talking with Maya at her locker. They were in an animated conversation. A couple of the boys had on their Mt. Bachelor High School Letterman's jackets. They stopped talking and turned to look as if Kougar, like a mangy, lone cowboy, had just walked through a pair of swinging half-doors and into a hostile saloon. Even the piano music stopped. Their mocking eyes told him what their mouths were saying to each other under their breaths.

As Kougar passed by, the sprinter, the kid who had tugged playfully at Maya's elbow, felt the power of being part of a group, sneered a few words just loud enough for Kougar to hear.

"... Yeah, dudes, he's got to be the freakiest kid in school. I bet he's got some meth rocks in his pocket. And look at that rat's nest for hair; every day is Halloween for him."

All his friends chuckled derisively and nodded. In every past situation such as this, Kougar would just... take it—*he had to!*— and keep walking, his shoulders hunched over, hoping his tormentors wouldn't follow and verbally pile on, or worse, give him a few shoves in the back... But not this time. This time had already *happened* before; it merely let his actions unfold again. *Freaky is as Freaky should do!*

Checking himself in mid-stride, Kougar turned and with the quickness of a cat he moved into the midst of the group of boys and with his free hand, grabbed a handful of the sprinter's shirt just under his chin, and in one violent motion, he snatched the sprinter up off his feet and slammed him into the wall and held him there, while the sprinter's feet dangled under him. The other boys were frozen by the unpredictability of the moment and shocked by Kougar's raw power.

Kougar looked into the sprinter's eyes and said in a tight voice: "You want to reach into my pocket to see if I have any meth rocks?... No? Or maybe, you like it just where you are. I should—"

The sound of a clear, whistled version of "uh-oh," interrupted Kougar. He turned to see Alex walking up with his usual swagger.

"Yo, boys," Alex began in a calm but scolding voice," you shouldn't tease the animal when's he not in a cage." And then his voice changed to a complimentary one. "You should know that Kougar is freaky strong. No offense, Kougar."

Kougar released is grip on the sprinter who landed awkwardly on his heels.

"None taken, Alex," Kougar replied.

Alex joined the group and smiled at Kougar and said for the other boys benefit:

"Kougar here can bench three bills." He looked at the sprinter. "He took it easy on you, John." Alex then turned again to Kougar. "I didn't think you had it in you. I've seen otherwise."

"Some days are different," Kougar said.

"That's good to know. I'll be sure to tell Hayden that you gave him a pass. Hey, my offer still stands: come play football with us next year. You could play right behind me, outside linebacker. I'll stuff the holes and you can burst in and throw running backs around like rag dolls. Come on, dude, it'll be epic."

Kougar grunted, and, as he began to walk away, the boys parted to let him pass. He stopped, and turned to Alex and said sheepishly:

"Thanks, anyways, but I, ah… I don't like physical confrontations." With that, Kougar moved off, the three books undisturbed in the cradle in his left arm. He heard Alex say over his shoulder:

"Yeah, except for some days," Alex said through a grin.

Kougar could feel the boys looking after as he passed back through the pair of swinging doors and headed out of the saloon... He turned a corner in the hallway and leaned against the wall and drew in a big shaky breath that he blew out in a long sigh. He could feel his despair driving him along with the predictability of an imploding Greek teen tragedy.

I didn't want to do that. But I had to... I had to. It's for her. Her and me: friends?

Maya waited eagerly for Kougar in Grenfeld's class. Kougar was the last one to shuffle in through the door. He looked around to see if there were any open seats not next to Maya but there weren't. With a look of fatalism, he walked- the-plank and sat down in the desk next to Maya as the period-starting bell rang. Maya flashed Kougar a warm, knowing gaze. Kougar never looked at her.

What's with the long face? Maya asked herself. She reached over and touched Kougar's arm.

"Hey," she whispered a greeting through a small smile.

Kougar finally turned his head to her but didn't—and couldn't—meet her eyes. He replied in a whisper that Maya could hardly hear.

"Hey," he managed as the words spilled off his lips into nothingness, while his mind kept processing a thought in a robotic like fashion: *disengage... disengage...* He didn't see Maya's concerned expression studying him.

"So, scholars," Mr. Grenfeld began as he took off his glasses and collected his thoughts, "we've been exploring, in this class, how great literature has dealt with the seminal themes of humanity: death and love. Some authors have talked about the meaninglessness of death, the tragedy of it—say, in Hamlet's case—while others suggested that humanity reveals its true character only in the face of death. For those who accept it, impending death comes with a certain clarity of spirit and crystalizes those enduring human values that are important and have stood the test of time and the rise and fall of human civilizations; it lifts the veils of petty trivialities, the mundane routines and stale emotions of everyday life that clouds, and obscures what our known mortality is supposed to teach us. For the wise of us, then, death is the ultimate teacher. Now, we have been looking at another great teacher of life: love. Ah, love, the antithesis of death—yet, it comes with its own kind of pain. However, could we, as a species, have achieved anything anthropologically significant without love? I think not and a couple of the poets we have read would agree with me. Death is final, but love... love can transcend, love can be resurrected again and again. We have read and read, so today, let us write, write a poem of love."

Protesting groans echoed around the class and the students squirmed in their chairs. Mr. Grenfeld held up his arm.

"Be not afraid my young, intelligent friends," Mr. Grenfeld encouraged, "this is an exercise only; a safe way to express that which perhaps you haven't had the chance to, because common words, common language, fail to say it all. Using your own unique, poetic muse, will allow you say it differently, more... completely. It will be a collaborative project. You can do this exercise with two, three, four or five people. Nobody has to write a poem all by themselves." Mr. Grenfeld grinned. "The anxiety will be shared. Pair up with the person next to you. You both will write six lines about love, anything that you love: a sport, a book, an animal, a person... anything that you have a love for. Then, we will alternate each line, put them together and *voila,* we have a sublime poem. Because love is the unifying theme, you will be amazed how the lines tie themselves together with a little imagination."

"We got this, Koug," Maya said in an excited, low voice. Anxious snickers, giggles, and laughter spread through the class while squeaks and groans of desks being scraped on the floor rose up as students squirmed in their seats.

"Sssssssh," Mr. Grenfeld hissed loudly. "Quiet. Good poetry is written in silence. Raise your hand when you and your partner are done."

The students set about their task, with intermittent sighs of awkwardness breaking the silence. Maya gave Kougar a few soft looks and then started to write. Kougar just looked down at his blank paper. Everything right now seemed blank to him. *Blank. Blank. Blank.*

The minutes passed by. Many of the students seem stumped, at a loss for words. Mr. Grenfeld could tell many were struggling.

"Come on, scholars, this is not rocket science."

"Yeah," came a quick, stressed reply from one senior, "rocket science is easier."

Again, a wave of nervous laughter passed through the class. Maya paused and thought and then wrote, paused and thought and wrote again. She looked over at Kougar a couple of times, hoping he would look back at her. She wanted to show with her eyes what she was writing, but Kougar just kept his eyes on his paper... his blank paper.

Hands started to rise as various students finished.

"When you finish, put the poems together and write them out alternating the verses of both poems."

Maya finished her poem. She looked over at Kougar's paper and saw that it was empty.

"Come on, Koug," she whispered encouragement, "it doesn't matter. Write whatever. It's just an exercise. You could even make something up."

Kougar managed a quick glance at Maya through a drooping spill of blond bangs that hung over his eyes.

"Is everyone finished?" Mr. Grenfeld called out. "Raise your hands if you are done."

The whole class raised their hands except for Maya and Kougar.

"Maya?" Mr. Grenfeld asked.

Maya just shrugged her shoulders and pointed a finger at Kougar.

"I understand that the poetic muse is a fickle thing, so we'll give Mr. Phelps a couple more minutes."

Kougar gave Maya another look through his bangs. The smile on her face almost shattered him. He looked away quickly and then started writing. In a flurry of scribbling, Kougar dashed out his poem.

"Done?" Maya asked as Kougar set down his pen.

"Done," came Kougar's tight, fragile whisper.

Maya reached over and grabbed Kougar's poem and she set about to quickly put the two poem verses in order.

"We won't have time today to get some readings, but we do have time for one and since Maya and Kougar are juniors, they have the privilege of going first," Mr. Grenfeld grinned as he spoke.

There were sighs of relief that spread through the class. Kougar looked frozen in his seat, eyes down. He slowly drummed the fingers of his right hand on the desk, and it seemed that his fingers kept time with a ticking time bomb. Maya finished writing out the poem. Her face looked puzzled but she tried to smile through her growing disquiet.

"Go ahead, Maya. We are ready to hear our first collaborative poem," Mr. Grenfeld said with curiosity in his voice that said everything about Maya and Kougar screamed 'opposites.'

"Okay," Maya said through a nervous smile. She quickly glanced at Kougar who still had his head down, his drumming fingers still doing their countdown. Maya began to recite:

"Funny, I said: I like you,

After I knew that I loved you.

Two—"

Kougar's drumming fingers stopped and his hand smacked down on his desktop. He bolted up out of his seat and quickly exited the classroom. There was a quick moment of silence that Mr. Grenfeld cut through.

"Obviously, the stress of writing good poetry can get to anyone," Mr. Grenfeld chuckled along with the class. "The most famous of poets were terribly self-conscious. A great beginning, Maya, but, please, start again."

Maya looked at the open classroom door that Kougar had rushed through with that same puzzled look she had when she read Kougar's part of the poem. She took up the poem in her hands and started reciting again, feeling instinctively the confessional and emotional impact of the words.

"Funny, I said: I like you,

After I knew that I loved you.
Two oases in the desert, one ugly, one beautiful,
Will always be far apart.
Funny, how an old dance has new steps.
When Gaius speaks a girl listens, because
Even a young vampire knows what it is to love.
Two opposite molecules in a teardrop
Will never find each other,
Because the desert burns all things.
Funny, my heart knew it before I did,
That you and Gaius are really one,
The one who, in the end, let me be an Indian."

An astonished and thoughtful silence went through the classroom quickly followed by a cascade of impressed comments and "wows," as students turned to look back at Maya, whose innocent expression said, for her part, that it was all true.

Mr. Grenfeld called out in surprised admiration, with a tone of I-told-you-so: "Yes. Yes. See? *Voila!* We have a real poem. Well done, Maya and Kougar."

The period ending bell rang and the girls of the class huddle around Maya as they exited, giving her compliments:

"….So cool."

"…Oh, my God, Maya, you're so brave…"

"…I want to meet this Gaius…" Laughter.

"…Geez, that Kougar, he's always a moody one. I don't know how you sit next to him. He's creepy."

"…I'm glad that your part was about love."

"….Ha! Ha! Maya, you're a poet and don't know it."

"…. For sure!"

Maya tried to play everything down. "Jeez, girls, it was just an exercise, like Mr. Grenfeld said."

"Seemed real to me," one senior girl with bright red hair said, thoughtfulness in her tone.

"Well," Maya said and then gushed: "A girl can only hope, right?"

"You've got that right," the redhead seconded.

Maya scanned the hallway for Kougar, hoping he would have waited for her.

"See you around, girls," Maya said as she headed off in a hurry, hoping she would find Kougar at his locker before the next class started. She had questions for him.

Geez, does he think we'll always be 'far apart'?

Kougar watched Maya leave the classroom amidst the pack of senior girls and knew that she would head for his locker. Along the way she waved at friends, while some friends, girls and boys, walked along with her for a while. Kougar followed, some distance behind her, watching the evidence of her popularity, which just helped to confirm what he *had* to do.

She came to his locker, paused for a moment then pulled out her phone and shot out a text. For a moment he battled with the thought of going up to her and saying what needed to be said, but there was no way he could say those words to her face. Panic spread through him at the thought of it.

I'll just have to show her. That's the only way.

Maya turned away from his locker and started toward him. He quickly ducked into a Boys bathroom and leaned against a stall, sighing angrily at his own cowardice. He pulled out his phone as he heard a text come in. It was Maya:

> ...Hey... what's up? Where r u? R u mad at me????" ☹

Kougar flipped his phone shut. *Mad at you? No... But I 'have' to be.* Pain and angry destiny made him shake his head like a frustrated beast. *I'll see you at lunchtime.* He would definitely *know* then; the final test. A candle's flame, behind all that he was, flickered its hope weakly. The reality of his seventeen years moved to extinguish the shrinking taper.

Kougar stood behind the open doors to The Commons that served the students as a gathering place and cafeteria. He watched Maya as she sat at 'her' table with friends, everybody chatting, texting, and laughing. Maddie, Amanda, Cheryl, Breah and Carley were at the table along with John Wright, the sprinter who Kougar had confronted earlier in front of the basketball gym, along with two other senior boys that Kougar didn't know. The table next to Maya was Hayden's table. Sitting with Hayden was Alex, the four boys who were with John during the confrontation, and a couple of cute girls. All of them definitely 'looked' like the 'in' crowd at Mt. Bachelor High.

I'm sure word has gotten around by now, Kougar thought: That new kid, The Freak was going to beat up John until Alex intervened. The Freak was dangerous, probably 'high ...'

Kougar had taken a little time to walk behind the school kitchen to the dumpsters. He rubbed some discarded grease on his worn jeans. He tore at the end of his long sleeves, letting out the hems, exposing the threads. He ratted his dreadlocks up into a sprawling mass. The test had to be tough... fatal. *I am what I am... and I am... what I look like,* he thought to himself as he looked into the ever present, invisible mirror that always followed him around.

As Kougar looked out over the Commons, he almost talked himself out of his plan, out of what he had seemingly done before. It almost 'felt' rehearsed. His face roiled with his conflicting thoughts, his heartbeat started to race and his breath became shallow. A part of him hoped beyond what little hope that had begun stirring within him with such uniquely new excitement after that incredible day with Maya. That part hoped that despite her surrounding friends, she would rise up to greet him with her beautiful smile, even give him a close friend's hug and ask him to sit and hang out. She would then tell her friends about what Kougar did in the Rock Garden out at Phil's Trail—but Kougar knew reality more than reality knew him. Persistent scorching memories will always have their way with him; will always have their day, over and over again. He stuck his hands into his pockets, hunched his shoulders, and walked through the door down the main walkway, his dreads swaying against his shoulders and against his forehead, just below his eyebrows. Again, he had the feeling of walking in slow motion as kids sitting in tables along the walkway turned to gape at him. He fitted his gaze directly on Maya as he walked toward her table. Maya was talking animatedly with Maddie and in the middle of it, something made her stop and glance up and down the walkway. Her eyes widened a little at the sight of Kougar walking towards her, with a weird slouch. One by one the others at Maya's table turned to look at the advancing Kougar. The same happened at Hayden's table. Kougar took a second to take in the stares and knew that what had happened in front of the basketball gym had spread. A couple of kids nodded and he could see John touch Maya's arm and point his finger toward him. Hayden had the 'I-told-you-so' look on his tight face and Alex just wore an expression of faint bemusement.

What's he doing! Maya thought, her apprehension starting to rise as she heard the derisive comments about Kougar rising up from her friends.

Kougar kept his unblinking gaze on Maya as he continued to get closer and closer to Maya's table.

Panic started to gather within Maya. *What's he doing"? Does he want to confront John again? What's he going to say?... No, not now! Not this way! Not here! Maya's anxiety-ridden thoughts blurted out inside her mind.*

Kougar watched as the panic—not a welcoming— spread across Maya's beautiful face. Behind his heart, that fragile taper of hope blew out like a distant blinking star collapsing in on itself.

He saw her full, red lips contort themselves into a soundless *NO as she slightly shook her head.*

Kougar still eyed Maya intensely. Here, he channeled Gaius and all that 'he' had felt. But Maya's distressed face told Kougar everything he needed to know. The test had worked, but it definitely came with a silent, wrenching price. The corner of Kougar's mouth twitched with controlled emotion as he stopped in front of Maya and looked at her though his twisted, blond-white bangs.

"Hi Maya," Kougar began without a trace of the dramatic scene he was in, "thanks for the invite, but I can't do lunch today. I've got to see how my meth lab is doing." Kougar turned and pointed at John and grinned. "Sorry about this morning, dude, I'm just a little sensitive." He then looked back at Maya who seemed frozen in the middle of a horrible thought. "Hey, it would be cool to meet up another time." And Kougar couldn't dampen down the shattered, empty tone of his last two words.

He put his hands back in his pockets, gave Maya a tragic wink and walked off, his shoulders slouching. He heard Alex chuckle in the silent wake of his exit. Then the comments burst out.

"...Oh, my God, Maya—"

"...Did you really—"

"...What a freaky guy. Can you believe it?"

"...He's filthy. What kind of joke—"

"...I'm surprised they don't kick him out. He's—"

"...Did you invite him to lunch? I mean he's got to be kidding. I think—"

"Maya," came Maddie's voice, next to her, "what was that all about?"

Maya just sat, dazed by all that had just gone on with Kougar. She felt the sting of the pelting comments. She could feel the panic returning.

"Maya?" Maddie insisted.

"Oh, you know, he's just that odd kid in Grenfeld's class," Maya finally said quickly with a shrug of her shoulders, and she instantly hated the betrayal in her hasty words. "I don't know what his deal is. He had that issue with Hayden remember?"

"Oh, Yeah," Maddie replied. "That was intense."

"Outside of that, I don't really know him."

"Didn't you stay there talking to him after we all left with Hayden and Alex? I mean, what did that kid say about it all?"

"Oh," Maya began, with a dismissive wave of her hand, even though self-loathing filled her heart, "he didn't say anything, really. I... just... felt sorry for him."

Maya didn't realize that she was starting to stand up during those last deceiving words. She almost wrapped her arms around her stomach as she felt the painful blows of her deception. Her eyes moistened as they remembered the devastated last look Kougar gave her before he left. She then bolted from the table and walked quickly down the main path of the Commons. She found the Girl's bathroom, lurched inside and leaned against a wall, her breath coming fitfully in labored despair. She slowly let her back slide down the wall to sit on the cold floor.

"Jeez," Breah blew through her lips, "that guy really upset Maya."

"Wow," Amanda echoed, "can you blame her?"

"Come on, you guys, let's go find her. Let's go!" Maddie said urgently. "Spread out, when one of you finds her, send a group text."

Maya's Cheer Team got up from the table and hustled down the main pathway.

Hayden watched the girls run after Maya and turned to mutter to Alex who was sitting next to him.

"I knew that kid was a freak the minute I saw him. Maya shouldn't have been nice to him. That was a bad game plan."

"I don't know," Alex said as he chewed on his sandwich, "nothing wrong with freaky, especially on the football field. I say we find a way to get that kid to play with us."

"Serious?" Hayden retorted.

"Serious, dude," Alex kept chewing, "You should have seen him pick John up with one hand like a sack of potatoes and pin him up against the wall. That's serious strength. I have a feeling about that kid. You just

TIM MULLANE

have to use 'freaky' in the right way. You're lucky he didn't blow up on you, when you were smacking him around."

"No way," Hayden shook his head. "No way."

Maddie passed by the Girl's bathroom and then stopped, turned back around and entered the restroom. She saw Maya sitting on the floor, her back against the wall, her knees drawn up, almost in a fetal position had she been lying on her side.

"Maya! Hey, are you all right? Don't let that weird guy freak you out. He's just strange. Forget about it."

Maya finally lifted her head up from her crossed arms, and parted her long brown hair with her hands. Her face seemed under a dark cloud and her words barely got off her lips.

"I think I just ruined my life."

Maddie blurted out more breath than letters: "What?!... Maya, are you kidding? What are you talking about?"

Maya looked off through the walls of the restroom and into the distance, which held... nothing for her.

"I just hurt someone so innocent and so... vulnerable. I'm just like the rest." And the loathing could be heard in her self-accusation.

Maddie said, almost annoyed: "What are you saying? I mean I saw the way he looked at you. Jesus, it looked like he wanted to... to do 'something' to you. I couldn't tell if he wanted to kiss you or... bite you."

Maya let out a low ironic laugh at the real implications behind what Maddie had just said.

Appalled, Maddie drew her head back and grimaced. "You're laughing?"

Maya sighed. "You don't understand, Madds."

"I sure as hell don't."

Maya looked away again and then back down in shame.

"I was afraid."

"Yeah, who wasn't? He was creeping everybody out."

"No, I was afraid for a different reason, and I can't stand myself for it."

"Look, I'm your friend. All of us, we're behind you. We'll help you. We won't let him touch you. You have friends. We care about you."

"I know," Maya said weakly and then finished sadly: "I know I have… friends."

*

Kougar exited the Commons and walked out the high school's front doors. The image of Maya's rejection of him kept playing over and over again in his mind; her startled fear, and embarrassment. EMBARRASSMENT! Yes that's definitely what he had seen on her beautiful face. Now, he knew; knew all of it. He broke out into a run across the parking lot to try and ease the ache upon ache that gathered within him. He was going to run and run until he collapsed, then maybe, he could get some relief.

He ran through the Northwest Crossing neighborhood at a full sprint. He could feel his lungs starting to burst. When he finally couldn't get any more air out of his lungs he came to a lurching stop right in the same spot in that small park where Gaius and Maya had danced together. He bent over, hands on his knees, his chest heaving. He finally gathered enough breath to straighten up. He looked around. Gradually, a flickering of in-and-out memory came to him, of Gaius and Maya and the dance they had had here. But he 'knew' that it was Gaius, not him, who had held Maya close during 'that' dance. Kougar would never have that chance… ever. He shook his head to try and clear the disjointed images from someone else's memories.

None of this should have happened!

The exhilarating ride out to Phil's Trail, that damn piano mirror, the unbelievable dance that Maya had performed for him. Just him! But, all of it was just a bad joke …. *On me…*

The cell phone in his pocket pinged. He almost didn't want to look at the text. It was Maya:

…Kougar…Kougar! Please!!!…

Kougar wrenched his eyes away from the text and snapped his phone shut. A shudder of despair ran through his body almost bringing him to his knees as he stumbled.

We could never be friends… Never… Ever.

It was ending, Kougar felt… *Good…* There was one more thing that would end it, period, and it had to be done. Again, he felt like he had *done* it before. This one, this last act, would sting. *She needed to be stung.* Because, that's what you get when you tempt the wrong kind of fate.

The Bridge

Kougar skateboarded down Maya's street, slowed, and came to a stop. He saw two cars in the driveway of Maya's house. Just under the branches of a huge Ponderosa Pine tree in the front yard, he could see in through the big picture window of the living room. He saw Mrs. Virk walk by and then a few minutes later, Mr. Virk walked by the window.

Kougar had boarded by the high school to make sure Maya was practicing with her Cheer Team on the football field. Behind him, a snow blanketed Mt. Bachelor had loomed up, as he had looked down onto the field his vision filtered through an angry despair and a creeping dusk. He had seen Maya sitting on a bench, hunched over, her arms resting on her knees, while her team was jumping and tumbling about doing one of the Team's routines. He had seen Maddie go over and pat Maya on the shoulder in a consoling way…

Kougar turned his focus back to the house… He decided that standing there as the minutes ticked by, waiting for a moment of courage to possess him wasn't going to happen. It never did. But despair can be a form of courage. Enough of it makes consequences irrelevant. He smiled grimly.

This is it. Time to make an impression.

Kougar kicked up his board and put one hand in his pocket. His posture took on the same ambiguous slouch that had formed his body as he had made his way through the Commons to Maya's table during lunchtime. He had on the same grubby jeans, fraying long sleeved turtleneck and torn up tennis shoes. And, as always, the ever, over whelming sight of his mass of blond-white dreadlocks spilling all around, framed his whole, freaky teen appearance.

He stood for a long moment before the front door, like a tall zombie that had come to a stop and shut down, blue eyes unblinking, almost glazed over. He then slowly blinked and came alive. He pushed the doorbell.

He heard steps coming toward the door. The nicely finished oak door opened like the lid of an antique black box of unknown contents; contents, he knew, would not be welcomed.

Raja Virk's head pulled back involuntarily and his eyes widened a bit as he took in Kougar's whole 'look.' There was a heavy, unpredictable pause that grew between them. Kougar tried to grab a hold of what he had rehearsed to say. Raja couldn't help the frowning stare of suspicion that emanated from his face. He realized that all he could do in those few seconds was... stare at the... apparition in front of him.

Kougar finally broke the awkward silence with a sheepish grin.

"Ah... hello. I'm here to see Maya."

It took a moment for Raja to accept that 'this' kid wanted to see his daughter. But... *It can't be,* Raja thought.

"You know my daughter?" came Raja's wary question.

"Who is it, Raj?" Lisa Virk called out over her husband's shoulder and Kougar saw Mrs. Virk walking up to join her husband at the door. A concerned and curious look came over Lisa's face as she saw who was at the door.

Kougar met Lisa's eyes briefly and looked away.

"Ah, hi," he said to Lisa in a low, tentative voice.

Raja continued with his guarded questioning. "Maya knows you?"

Kougar tried to make his voice normal and to imply the obvious. Again, he grinned sheepishly.

"Ah, yeah she knows me," and then he shrugged innocently and lifted up his one free hand. "We're friends... good buddies. That's why I'm here. She told me to stop by. We're in the same class." And Kougar peered down at Raja through his twisted bangs.

"I see," said Raja, his words coming to grips with the facts. "You're friends?" he managed to get out the disbelieving question as Lisa put a comfort-needing arm around her husband's waist.

Kougar pressed on. "Is she here? She'll tell you."

Raja closed his mouth because he didn't want the same question to come out. Lisa spoke for him.

"Maya's not here …" and she gestured to Kougar that she was asking for his name.

"Oh, I'm Kougar. Kougar Phelps."

"Well, Kougar," and both Lisa and her Raja looked at each other quickly at the odd sounding name, "she's not here right now. She's at cheer practice."

"Okay. Just tell her I was here. I'll stop by another time. Thanks."

Again Kougar gave them the sheepish grin, turned and walked off. He could feel Mr. and Mrs. Virk looking at him as he slouched off: Mrs. Virk would be pursing her lips together, her pretty face concerned, and Mr. Virk, a dark cloud would be passing over his visage right about now.

"I'll tell you," Raja almost spat out, his Indian accent becoming heavier when he felt anger stirring within him, "that Maya is too damn friendly sometimes. They're good buddies?" he mocked to his wife. "Are you kidding me? What makes a kid want to look like that?"

"I guess he is a little… different looking," Lisa said trying to downplay her own impression.

"Holy cow, I'll say," Raja scoffed.

"You know how popular she is."

"Too popular if you ask me," Raja replied flatly. "Next thing you know, she'll want to date someone like him." And Raja shook his head in disgust.

"No," Lisa tried to soothe her husband, "not our Maya. She's open-minded, but I don't think 'that' open-minded."

Raja grunted and grumbled a warning as he looked into the future, fearing the worst.

"Well, we can only hope. At some point that's all parents can do," Lisa said, hoping for the best. She started to turn around and walk back to the kitchen. Raja stayed in the open doorway glancing down the street where Kougar had disappeared.

"Maybe," Raja said as he shook his head again, unable to get the possible picture of Maya with someone like Kougar out of his mind. "I'll let Maya know that her 'good' buddy stopped by."

"Don't be too sarcastic," Lisa said over her shoulder as Raja reached into his pocket and pulled out his cell phone and started texting Maya, his thumbs working with emphasis.

"That would be too nice," Raja said lowly to himself as he concentrated on his texting screen.

*

Kougar turned off Maya's street knowing he had just pounded the final nail in the coffin of his friendship with Maya. He should have never felt like he was... safe with her. That was a very stupid move. He smiled grimly as he recounted the look on Maya's father's face when he opened the door. The bitterness just kept mounting and mounting in him, one sacrificial step after step, dragging him along... a victim again, but this time it was not as a willing one—and, how it hurt to have let someone in. He had always been shielded in the amour of his trauma. But this... how *it hurt.*

His cell phone pinged with a text message. Now, he thought, she should know what he knew: *Game over. Game over...* He flipped open his phone to Maya's text:

> ...I guess u met my parents... Why? Kougar, this is killing me...

Kougar skidded to a stop with an angry sigh. He quickly replied his fingers working furiously:

> ...I think your dad approved. I thought he was going to invite me in...

Maya sat on a bench on the side of the football field in her cheer practice outfit. She let go a distraught sigh as she looked at Kougar's text. She pounded back a reply:

> ...Sarcastic. Real funny...
> ...Doesn't matter. But he had a right to know that   we r good friends. AND all your friends needed to know just how friendly we r...Welcome to 'reality.'
> ...No more texting. I need to c u. NOW! We have to talk face to face.

Kougar pushed on his board for a while weaving in and out from behind parked cars. He stopped abruptly and replied to Maya's text, his thumbs pressing down hard on QWERTY keyboard:

> ...Right, no more texts...No more nothing...I don't know why u 'did it'... to me. Why... me? Doesn't matter, really... Don't text me again...

> ...No wait, Kougar! Please! I've got to... Meet me at the bridge at Drake Park... the place where u probably saved my life! 7pm. I'll be there! I hope u will   be there too. Please! I'm so, SO sorry about what happened in the Commons! ☹ I'm so SAD... ☹

Kougar angrily flipped his phone shut and skated off pushing with all his strength picking up speed until he was topped out. Without looking, he burst across Century Drive, barely missing two cars going in the opposite direction. Their horns blared out and their braking tires screeched.

He reached his house flying into the driveway. He slammed down hard with his heel and in a long skid he came to a stop barely an inch from the garage door. He bounded up the stairs to the porch and flung open the front door, which he closed loudly behind him.

The sound reverberated through the house, startling his parents. His father quickly looked up from a stack of students' papers that he was grading as he sat in a chair in the living room. He caught the sight of Kougar walking with agitated steps—the type of steps he had seen before and they didn't bode well, he knew.

"Son... Kougar," Joe called out after his son. "What's—"

Joe voice stopped as he saw Kougar lift his arm up, dismissing him. An uneasy feeling started stirring in Joe's gut as the not-to-distant memories started working through him.

Maria Phelps heard the door slam and the sound—and what it might mean—slowly startled her and she looked up from the sink where she was washing greens for a salad. As Kougar blew by the kitchen, she tried to keep a calm tone in her voice; a tone she had learned over the years to use with her son when it seemed like he was going to blow up in anger.

"Hey there. Why the rush?"

Kougar said nothing as he continued down the hall to his bedroom where he quickly shut the door behind him. Maria followed and came to the door and tried to turn the doorknob. She knew it would be locked. Joe had silently walked up and stood behind his wife and put a comforting hand on her shoulder. She glanced back at him and they both shared a hopeful thought. Joe knew to let his wife handle this. She was the only one who had a chance, a very small chance to reach their son when he was starting to get 'worked' up. The signs were definitely there.

"Son ...Hey," Maria began, "what's the matter? Can we talk about it?"

Maria let the silent pause play out, as she knew it was the best way. Don't push it... just wait. It has to be on Kougar's terms... always... Finally Kougar's muffled, but tight voice came from inside his bedroom.

"I'm all right. I'm just going to chill out for a while. You and dad go ahead and eat. I'm not hungry right now."

"Son," Maria soothed, "just come sit with us. We'll—"

Kougar's muffled voice cut her off. "No, you and dad go ahead… It's all right… I'm good."

"Sure?"

"Yeah… I have a lot of homework to do."

"Okay, honey."

Joe and Maria exchanged a look. Joe nodded as if to say it wasn't as bad as he had thought, and Maria's smile acknowledged the same.

"Homework?" Joe whispered. "Good." And he reached down and took a hold of his wife's hand and led her back down the hall to the kitchen.

Kougar sat on his bed and felt the familiar inchoate panic start to spread within him like a creeping, soundless, pressure. The slow trigger started to pull. With the help of his despairing anger he pushed back down what would have predictably spiked through him and surrounded him with scorching, claustrophobic flames.

His cell phone pinged with a message. It was Maya:

…See you in a few minutes. Please!

Kougar started to rock slowly back and forth stewing in a cauldron of whirlwind emotions that he let buffet him about. He kept rocking, until… until he had only one emotion left after the gritty, boiling internal sirocco had laid him bare, bare and as sharp as any bone of despair. He knew 'he' couldn't go to Maya… but one 'part' of him… could, and that 'part' had to get him there. He would leave the light on in his room and climb out of his bedroom window.

Maya showered quickly and threw on some clothes, a pair of runners, and grabbed her coat. She hurried out the front door saying to her mom and dad that she was sorry about running off but the girls were meeting for dinner at Croutons to finalize their routine for the football playoff game against Bend High, and that she would be back soon.

Moving quickly down her walkway, she realized she had just directly lied to her parents for the first time and felt a pang of guilt.

No choice, she soundlessly mouthed the words. She looked at her watch, took in a deep breath and sprinted off, her long track-trained strides eating up the distance hoping, hoping to God that Kougar would be there. As she ran through the cold, early December night, she had so many things to say to him. She flashed by houses decorated with Christmas lights. A few blow-up Santa Clauses waved at her as she passed by but their brightly lit faces did not cheer her. Her heart ached with the pain of how she had hurt Kougar and the way she had betrayed him because of a stupid, *stupid* fear.

She sprinted into the park and stopped for a moment to catch her breath. In the distance she could see the lamplight reveal a figure leaning against the bridge railing. It looked like Kougar. Her heart leaped! *He's there!*

She took off, eager to say what was in her heart. She had to get him to understand. She *had* to. She was in love, a most unlikely and surprising love. Her poem had said so.

Her heart leaped again as she got closer and could see that Kougar, with his back to her, had on a black, short sleeve turtleneck on with a saying stenciled in white letters: You Are One Bite Away From Eternity.

"GAIUS!" Maya shouted with joy as she closed the distance between them. Gaius turned around just in time for Maya to leap into his arms.

"Gaius, I'm so happy you're here! I've missed you so much."

She held herself tightly against Gaius' muscled chest. But something was *wrong.* Gaius wasn't returning her embrace. She slowly drew back and looked up into the sea green eyes that looked down on her. Something else, something stern and resolved, looked back through those green eyes. Gaius's pale face had a different cast and the smooth forehead, outlined by brown eyebrows, had a single serious line etched in it.

"Gaius?" came Maya's soft question.

"He helped me get here," Kougar's voice finally replied. "It's just me."

"Kougar?"

"Yeah... Freaky, isn't it? It gives you an idea of what's wrong with me."

Maya shook her head slowly. "To me, there's nothing wrong with you. I... I understand."

"Look at me" Kougar insisted, annoyed. "How can you say that?"

"It doesn't matter," Maya said softly.

"For such a smart girl, how can you be so stupid?" Kougar scoffed. 'It' will always matter. Didn't today teach you a thing or two about you and me?"

Maya looked off into the distance back to the Common's where the scene flashed through her mind of how she had betrayed Kougar.

"It taught me that I'm selfish and mean. I'm so sorry about what happened. I never wanted to hurt you. I—"

Kougar cut in with a matter-of-fact voice that had an edge to it. "You were just being who you are, just being in your world."

"No... I was afraid," Maya smiled sadly... "But I'm not anymore."

Kougar's mocking low laugh barely made its way off his lips... "You would be if you could see what's 'in' me." And his mouth framed his emotional anguish. "Gaius is a twisted fantasy. Five-year-olds have an invisible friend, not someone who is seventeen. Don't you get it? He's the opposite of what I am."

Maya again shook her beautiful head. "I don't believe that. He's real. I know it."

"It's all make-be-LIEVE!" Kougar's voice shot up then went down through the hole in him in a sarcastic bark. "It's twisted. Would you like to hear about my diagnosis? I have a lot of symptoms."

"It doesn't matter," Maya shot right back.

Kougar's feet started to shake with agitation and he started to pace around letting his emotions work through him, otherwise, if he stood still he would just blow like a geyser of angst. Finally he stopped pacing and said in a confessional whisper while he looked down at his feet and saw Gaius' reflection.

"Gaius... He can take me away... from things I can't stop from happening... and feeling. Can't you see?... I'm broken? I'm just a walking... scar."

"No... I don't see that." And Maya reached for Kougar's arm.

"You're blind!" Kougar turned away from Maya and walked a few steps away, his breath quickening, the line of his jaw was set, revealing his attempt to control his emotion. With his back to Maya, he tore open his shirt to reveal the left side of his chest. He turned back to Maya, and even in the low lamplight above them, lines of crisscrossed scars ran across his chest where he had cut himself, over and over again. They glistened in the light and seemed to move as if they were alive and fresh. His voice started thickly. He cocked his head; the glooming blue light in his eyes could be seen behind the green contacts.

"At one point, I had a... particular habit. This is what I am."

Maya slowly moved to Kougar, her eyes full of compassion, her heart aching at the sight of the self-inflected scars and the fact of how she had hurt him in the Commons. She reached out her hand, wanting to softly touch and soothe the pain that lay beneath those wounds. Just before she put her hand on his chest, Kougar recoiled from her descending touch and stepped back.

"I won't be your pet freak," Kougar said thickly.

"Kougar, no, no, that's—"

"I won't let you prove that you are big enough to include 'me' as a friend... Why me?" and harsh anguish poured through his words. "Why didn't you leave me alone?"

"Because I care for you. You heard my poem."

"That's the worst joke of all."

"It's no joke. I lo—"

Kougar cut her off quickly his voice turning angry, his facing darkening. "Don't... don't even go there. It's all a little cruel, really, the piano, the dance... I have a feeling you're something of a fake; yeah, just a fake. I guess that's the price you pay for being the most popular girl in school."

"That's not fair. You're so wrong. Why are you doing this to me?"

"I need to find someone of my own kind. I can't imagine who that would be, maybe in another lifetime, but it sure wouldn't be someone like you."

"Stop, Kougar... you're... hurting me."

"I don't believe you. How could the beautiful Maya Virk be hurt?"

"Just like you," her fragile whispery voice and her eyes telling the truth of her words.

"Yeah, right," Kougar said right away before the full weight of her honesty could wash over him.

Maya tried to move closer to Kougar but he backed off. He regarded her warily, like she had just entered his cage.

"Look, I know something bad happened in your life; something very bad, and I'm sorry. But you don't have to be stuck back there, always stuck being a victim."

"*Be* the victim? What the hell do you know? I'm alive! Only victims die!"

"Kougar, will you please hold me. Please."

"I... can't. My life... your life... we were never meant to hold each other... ever," Kougar said with a mixture of loss and implacable reality as he looked into Maya's deep brown eyes. He shivered for a second as the cold air finally asserted itself on his skin.
"It's so cold."

With that, Kougar turned around and headed down the bridge. Maya watched him for a second and then hoped that she could call him back but her voice knew the answer.

"Kougar."

Kougar kept walking without a pause on the bridge that led over the Deschutes River. It flowed, he noted, with the same disregard it had for anything that rocked and rolled with wanted and unwanted feelings. He knew now he could never see Maya again. He had to convince his parents that the same 'stuff' was happening once again. The bullies were back. Something bad was going to happen to him. He couldn't return to school. They had to move again.

Flight

Maria Phelps was glancing at the morning paper while she drank her coffee. She would read a few paragraphs and then look up as if someone was calling her name. She had felt the disquiet growing within her. Kougar didn't emerge from his room all last night. In the past, the type of agitation he was clearly experiencing last night would've precipitated a blow-up. She hoped that the way he tried to control his anger really meant that he was maturing, learning to cope. But another part of her feared that his attempt last night to push down his growing agitation hinted at something 'big'.

She then glanced at the clock on the stove and realized Kougar would be late for school. As she walked down the hall, she cradled her coffee cup in both hands as if seeking comfort from the warmth of the hot brew. She stopped at her son's bedroom door and knocked on the door and said with the tone of routine in her voice:

"Hey Koug, honey, you've got to get going or you'll be late for school."

She waited patiently for a reply. Silence.

"Honey?"

"I can't go today," came Kougar's low, muffled voice.

Maria looked down at the doorknob thinking it was probably locked.

"The door's open."

Maria entered and saw her son sitting cross-legged on his bed fully dressed but there was a charged stillness about the way he just sat there, Maria noted, as she studied him. *He's definitely holding something down.*

"You can't go to school today?" Maria asked

"No," came Kougar's flat reply, as he stared out through the window.

She looked at Kougar's profile and how he sat like a stone statue, which she knew, could morph into a writhing agitation in a volcanic second. She had to be cautious.

"Did you finish your homework last night? Your father and I were happy you were working hard on it."

Kougar continued to look out the window seeing nothing.

"No, I didn't do any homework. I lied."

The pause between them sounded like the increasingly loud pounding of a drum. Maria searched for the right thing to say. *Be careful, now…*

Kougar turned his head quickly and looked at his mother with eyes opened, pupils full like a cat that was suddenly aware of being cornered.

"I can't go to that school again," he began tightly, his jaw set. "We have to move."

"Honey, why? I thought you were doing well here. You said you liked it way better than L.A."

"I can't do it anymore."

Maria studied her son again, seeing how much he had grown over the last year and a half. He was practically a man. She realized she had to nudge him toward more self-sufficiency. His adult life was right around the corner. She took another tack.

"What can't you do?" she asked, letting a slight impatience color her tone.

Kougar's eyes narrowed as he was almost taken back by her accusation. His voice started to rise.

"I can't. Simple as that."

"Son, you're seventeen. One more year and you'll be in college."

"Yeah, right."

"Seventeen, and you're telling me you can't go to school. Come on."

"I'm going to call dad, talk with him. He'll understand how I feel. He always did."

"No, he didn't understand. He was afraid for you. We can't move this time. Your father has a good job and so do I. We both want to set down some roots. Son, it's time."

"*It's* happening again."

"What?"

"You remember that day I came home messed up and I told you that I had been goofing around, boxing with some kid. That didn't happen."

Maria put a nervous hand to her face as she suspected the worst. "What happened?"

"Some kid punched me out."

"Why?"

"Why have they always done it?"

Maria pursed her lips together and sighed with a decision.

"All right. You and I are going to school right now. We're going to the Principal's Office. You are going to say what happened to you and who the kid was who attacked you."

While Maria spoke Kougar started shaking his head more and more vigorously.

"No!!!" Kougar erupted. "I can't do that!!!" Kougar leaped up and started pacing around.

Maria watched her son for a moment giving him a moment after his outburst.

"If you want to blow up like you've done since you were ten years old go ahead. I'm still going to be here. I am your mother. I will always be here. I will always want what's best for you. I will always help you... Now... let's go. We'll do this together."

Kougar barked a sarcastic laugh between his lips, knowing now what he had to do.

"No," he began angrily, "I'll go. I'm seventeen, right?"

Maria just nodded slowly. "That's right," she said calmly, her tone firm. Kougar brushed by his mom and hurried out the door down the hall.

Maria watched her son retreat down the hallway and she hoped her new tact would work. She felt there was no other way with the passage of time bearing down on them. She felt the urgency of it all. *He's got to deal with it. He's got to rely on himself. He has to try. Just try!*

Kougar flew out the front door and gave it a good slam. He snatched up his skateboard and boarded off. He wasn't going to school. *Hell no. I'm out. I don't want to see or talk to anybody. Nobody!*

*

Maya scanned the hallways, passed by Kougar's locker, and she continued to text Kougar. No answer. Her morning classes went by like a slow montage of irrelevancy. She repeatedly glanced out the window hoping to get a glimpse of him. She took a few restroom passes just to walk the halls looking for him. Nothing. The only imperative she had was to get Kougar to trust her again, to get him to believe the truth of her feelings.

I've got to find him! I'm going to make him believe me. Oh, Kougar. Kougar! It's my fault... all my fault.

Maya waited outside Grenfeld's class desperately hoping that Kougar would come walking up with that unkempt appearance and give her that guarded, shy smile which said that he would give her another chance. She waited. She could see Mr. Grenfeld arranging his notes and beginning to start his intro to today's class. The period bell rang. She walked back and forth for a second weighing her thoughts. She broke off her chain of thought and her instincts took over. She strode off quickly.

Kougar waited behind a big Ponderosa Pine to watch for his mom as she left for work. He saw her exit the house, get into her car and drive off. He slowly boarded back. He was set with a determination as he opened the front door with his key and headed to his bedroom to get some things that he stuffed in a backpack, water bottles, some clothing items and bathroom stuff. He grabbed his riding gloves and his blade sunglasses. He walked into the kitchen and picked a few canned goods out of the pantry. He zipped up his backpack and fastened it on. He opened the door to the garage and walked in. He put on his hiking boots and wrapped a rubber band around his right pant leg to keep the bottom of his jeans from being caught in the chain. He pulled his mountain bike off the wall and walked his bike outside the opening garage door. No breeze blew. The unseasonably warm weather was still holding on stubbornly if only for about four hours of the day. Then it would get cold, and where he was going, the night would be very cold. Leaving now around ten in the morning, he should get there sometime around one in the afternoon.

With his gloves and sunglasses on, he rode off headed for Phil's Trail and then he would go deep into the forest, deep into the anonymity of the natural surroundings that would give him the separation he needed. There he would figure out where he would go next. Any long desolate road would do. After all, when you are in the emotionally barren, scarred wasteland of the desert, to go in one direction is just as good as any other…

Maya had found out from a friend who worked in the school administration where Kougar lived. He only lived five blocks from where she did. *So close all this time,* she ironically thought.

She hoped she would find him there and she would have her chance. She was prepared to deal with his anger. She just needed a chance.

She walked up the steps to Kougar's house and knocked on the door. She waited. No answer. She rang the doorbell and called out Kougar's name. She listened. Nothing. She tried the doorknob and was surprised to find it opened to her touch. Maybe he was somewhere in the house, not answering the door. She walked inside calling Kougar's name. She looked around and wandered passed the kitchen and down the hallway. She peeked into a bedroom on the right and saw a jacket that Kougar had worn before laying across a bed. It must be Kougar's room.

"Kougar?"

Maya pushed open the door and slowly walked in. She saw his cell phone on the night stand. She picked it up and saw all of her texts that were unopened. She walked into his bathroom and saw some items on the sink counter. She saw a contact case and opened it. Green contacts. She drew out the sink drawer and noticed the pale powder makeup and the can of spray-on brown hair color. She sighed, longing for Gaius. A crumpled shirt lay on the floor that she picked up. She could see the Super Vampire logo on the front and read the stenciled saying on the back: You Are Only One Bite Away From Immortality.

Her eyes moistened and she laid the shirt on the counter and headed out. She turned down the hallway and almost bumped into Kougar's mom, Maria.

"Oh!" they both said at the same time, startled.

"I'm so sorry, Mrs. Phelps," Maya began, embarrassed, "I know I shouldn't have walked into your house but I thought Kougar was here."

Maria was not alarmed as she noted Maya's formal politeness and her obvious innocence. She was overwhelmed by curiosity. Who was this beautiful, beautiful young girl and why was she looking for Kougar? Something about Maya's appearance made Maria stare at her as if she knew 'something' about her. Finally Maya broke the awkward silence between them.

"I'm sorry. I know it was totally wrong of me to just walk in here. I just wanted to see him. I'm Maya Virk."

"Maya... hmmm. So, how do you know my son?"

Maya flashed her winning smile. "We're in the same class together; in Mr. Grenfeld's AP Lit class. Kougar and I are friends."

Maria couldn't help the surprised shock that spread across her face and widened her eyes.

"Friends? You and my son?"

"Oh, yes," Maya replied cheerily. "We are good friends."

"Really?"

Maya again felt a surge of guilt pass through her and distress clouded her features. "Yes... very good friends. I—" and she paused as she thought it more appropriate to say something different. "I like him a lot. He's very different than anyone at school. But, we had a misunderstanding and it was my fault. I feel so bad about it. I just need to talk to him."

"Well, this certainly is a surprise. My son doesn't make friends… easily."

"That's for sure," Maya said as a small smile came to the sides of her mouth. "He's a little stubborn."

"Yes, he is," Maria nodded and she thought that Maya's sincerity was heart felt. Perhaps she could ask Maya a question about Kougar. She pursed her lips together and decided.

"Kougar, he is a different looking kid. Try as I might, I couldn't change his… ah, taste in clothes. I was never allowed to do anything with that mass of hair of his and I'm a hairdresser," Maria said through a low ironic soft laugh as an embarrassed smile broke across her features.

"I like his hair. It's unique," Maya said. "It's different. Different is good."

"Well, being different hasn't been good for my son. We've moved a lot because… because—"

"Because of the bullying," Maya finished Maria's thought.

Maria felt her interest quicken and her face showed surprise that Maya would know about it. "Kougar told me that he had been bullied at school. Do you know anything about it?"

Maya paused and looked away as she remembered the painful incident in the Commons, not what had happened between Hayden and Kougar. She turned back to look at Maria, sadness spreading across her face.

"Yeah, I was the bully… I need to see him. Do you know where he is?"

Maria studied Maya for a moment trying to absorb this whole improbable scenario where, somehow, her son and this beautiful girl… were friends. *Ah, a girl has finally come into his world—and not just any girl. What a beauty! No wonder he's troubled. This explains it.*

"I thought he was at school but when I pulled into the garage I noticed that his bike was gone. He must be out for a ride."

Maya nodded, determined. "I'll find him. I need to make it right. Sorry to come into your house like I did."

"I understand, Maya. When he comes back I'll let him know that you were looking for him."

"Thanks, Mrs. Phelps."

Maya turned to leave. As she got to the front door, Maria called after her.

"Maya."

Maya turned around and looked back at Maria who smiled.

"I'm very glad that you are my son's friend."

Maya responded with a guarded, tight smile. She had a lot of work to do. She closed the front door behind her and walked off, her strides quickening. She had an idea where Kougar might have gone. She looked up into the partly cloudy sky that looked more ambiguous than ever. *I can get there. I have to get there.*

Sanctuary's Price

Kougar pedaled up the logging road and stopped as he came upon the tree stump that had a rusty can on top of it. It had been a steady, gradual uphill climb the last thirty minutes. He wiped his sweaty forehead and let his breath return to normal. He felt he needed to get father away but his island, his sanctuary, would have to be far enough away for now. He looked around, surrounded by a thick forest green of tree trunks and intertwining pine-needled branches that seemed to undulate like an imperceptible tide of still but living things; other living things, none like him. He was ultimately a stranger here and that's the way he liked it. Here, engulfed in nature's raw green blanket, there was no fear, no flames, only the chance to forget, if for only a little while. Here he could fight the past. He often thought how, with the help of a rage compounded by his merciless history, he might die in an attempt to free himself. He didn't know how that might happen but he hoped he would not cower away if the opportunity arose to wipe the past away and extinguish the flames once and for all. Or, he could always solve things in a weary flash of deadly conviction; a final, vanquished riposte to being the cornered freak. Game over.

He got off his bike and walked it off the overgrown logging road that hadn't seen any traffic in thirty years. He laid his bike down and covered it with some dead branches that still sprouted rusty, dry needles. He moved into the thick forest and then came upon a narrow but visible elk trail and started up the rocky and uneven path.

He arrived at the base of a slight cliff that jutted up just off the trail. He walked along the base until he came to a rope than hung down the side of the cliff. He looked up and pulled hard on the thick static rope. It seemed secure. He remembered climbing up when there had been no rope. It had taken forty-five minutes of crisscrossing back and forth finding handholds to get up to the ledge. He started the long climb up making sure of his footing as he ascended.

246

Maya pedaled hard up Galveston. Her pedaling efficiency wasn't as good, she could tell, not being clipped-in. She had to change out her pedals so she could wear hiking boots. She wore thick riding tights and a grey Mt. Bachelor High sweatshirt. Her mind kept going over and over what she would say to Kougar when she got to him. She had to really tamp down the voice of reason and caution inside her that told her this was a very, very bad idea and so, so out of character for her. She agreed, but it didn't matter. *This isn't the time to be... me,* the 'me' who had hurt Kougar. She hated that 'me'. *I'm not that me—*

The screech of tires brought her out of her internal dialogue and she reflexively swerved away from the front end of an old, white, Dodge van in the roundabout at Galveston and Skyliner. Maya didn't even pause to put up her hand in apology but got up out of her seat and pedaled off picking up speed.

She passed under leafless maple trees their branches bare and white. The ubiquitous rabbitbrush had dried out, shrinking in upon itself, girding itself for the cold and snow. The whole landscape seemed to be waiting, holding its collective breath and limbs for the coming blast of winter. It certainly wasn't a day for riders to be out. The temperature was hovering around forty-five degrees and the trails were beginning to sprout wet spots that hadn't turned to thick mud yet, but one hard rain or snowfall would make the trails unrideable.

Maya passed Phil's Trailhead and there wasn't a car in the parking lot, and of course, she didn't look back to see the white van that was creeping down the turn off from Skyliner that led to the trail head. She sped down Phil's heading towards the Rock Garden and that junction where she would get off the trail and walk her bike to where the old logging road just emerged out from under the forest floor. As she rode father down the trail the forest got thicker and she didn't notice that the sky overhead was starting to grey up and a dark bunching of moody clouds started to gather in a line along the mountains from Mount Bachelor to Broken Top to the Three Sisters.

The Man could see through his small binoculars that Maya headed down Phil's Trail. Again, his trolling patience had paid off. When he was off work he often cruised around the west side of town, always hoping to get a glimpse of the girl that was *always* on his mind, hoping she would be alone and more amiable to what he had to offer. He had seen her other times but boy, she really attracted a crowd. Damn, she's too popular (he would sniff). But here she was... alone. Fortune favored him again. He knew of a fire road that intersected with Phil's Trail. He had jogged the fire roads as a teenager to get in shape for the track team. It was a guess, but he figured she would ride over the fire road that connected Phil's to Voodoo. A tight smile came to his lips, the kind that came to relentless lovers who knew that even as their love pedaled or ran away, they were always coming closer.

Maya went as fast as she could, pushing her skill level to the max. She felt for sure Kougar was at his tent site. All of her instinct told her so. If he wasn't then it was just part of the punishment she should endure for what she had done to him. *I have to try! We have to come back... together.*

> *I said: I liked you*
> *After I knew that I loved you....*

Her own words made her get up out of her seat and pump harder on her pedals. Her determination sharpened her focus and she flew along the trail holding off numerous skid-outs, shifting her weight properly as she jumped rocks and logs along the trail, the long minutes ticking off into an hour then an hour and a half.

She sprinted down a hill and then slammed on her brakes as she glimpsed what she was looking for. She stared off the trail into the forest. In the near distance she saw a smooth curve in the forest floor beyond the patches of bare Manzanita bushes. She got off her bike and navigated through the bushes until she walked onto the old logging road.

She felt her resolve waver as she looked down the seemingly endless road that led off into a part of the forest she had never been before and her father's Forest Ranger's words sounded in her head: *Never go into a part of the forest where you have never been, alone.* He would be furious with her. Furious.

She realized that in order to come here she had lied to her mom for the second time in the past few days. *I guess there's always a first time to get into trouble... big trouble.*

Second thoughts began to crowd her mind. While she pulled a long draw off her water tube, her eyes caught the indentation of mountain bike tire tracks off to her right. A single track!

Kougar!

She mounted her bike and sped off with renewed determination, the looming forest on both sides of her seemed impenetrable, wild, aware, and hostile to her presence. A slight rain began to fall as she pedaled on, following the bike tire track in front of her.

The Man watched through his binoculars as Maya had come to abrupt halt, then walked her bike off the trail and into the forest. She wasn't heading back to the trailhead that was for sure. Curiosity tempered his desire to pop up in front of her and say 'Hi'. And he knew the old logging road she was on. There weren't any bike trails that she was going to link up to from that road and, no other roads. It was a one-way road. She would have to come back this way. Patience was again on his side. Without hurry, he found a thick growth of scrub pine with a little opening and drove his van into the growth. It disappeared. He got out and covered his tire tracks. He put on his earplugs and scrolled through the menu and picked out U2's 'I Still Haven't Found What I'm Looking For'. He let the music move through his huge frame and felt the euphoria spread thru him. He did a little jig to the song, clapped his hands together a couple of times. He breathed deep, lifted his blunt face up to the sky to feel the drizzling rain land on his lumpy forehead. He felt... blessed. He then headed off in a quick jog through the thin brush his feet moving as effortlessly as the four hooves of a bull elk. He made sure not to run on the road. No need to leave shoe prints...

The apparently endless gradual climb up the road was sapping her strength. She plodded on as the soundless minutes turned into an hour.

Her breath came in a deep rhythm of the steady effort and she could hear her pounding heart. She pulled on her water tube and got nothing but gurgling air. She faintly registered that she was out of water.

Another twenty minutes of steady pedaling went by and she suddenly came out of her increasingly dazed awareness to realize that she couldn't find the tire track anymore. *It's gone!*

She took in a couple of panicked breaths and glanced around for the bare stump with the rusty can on top. Nothing... *I'm lost...*

"Kougar!... Kougar!" She shouted out and the dense forest seemed to muffle her shouts and toss them back at her. The cold wind started up in fitful gusts blowing in and out of the trees. She then took a slow, reality-inducing look around her. She was surrounded by an indifferent, green remoteness around her that was actually *watching* her. 'It' was watching her with a cold awareness. Watching... Waiting... The bruised sky then opened and the rain poured down.

With a growing sense of panic she started pedaling back down the road her speed growing quickly. It almost felt like the forest was... *after* her. Her long brown hair flew out from behind her helmet as she rocketed down the road. Suddenly, out of the corner of her eye she saw the tree stump with the rusty can on top. She skidded to a stop. In her daze, she had ridden past it. *There it is!*

The Man could see Maya through his binoculars about a half a mile away. He hummed to the tune in his ears and wondered where Maya was headed. The farther into the forest she went the better it was for both of them, The Man thought. Maya wasn't going anywhere. Even though she was headed *somewhere,* she was trapped already and didn't know it, but he did. He wasn't in any hurry. He was having fun. It was nice to get out for a jog and some fresh air.

Maya had to find the elk trail that led off into the woods and passed by the sharp cliff wall and the hanging rope that she could climb up to Kougar's tent. She then noticed that the slight rain had turned to a heavy downpour, drenching her. She laid her bike down and started wandering around, looking for the trail as the rain pelted her and her feeling of desperation increased. She looked and looked, walking off in this direction and that and realized she was going in a circle. Suddenly, she stumbled over something, a tree log she thought, but she saw an exposed mountain bike tire. She pulled the bike out from under the cover of dead branches.

Kougar's bike!

Hope surged within her. She looked off to her right and saw an opening in the scrub pine and instantly let go of the bike and headed off to the opening. She moved through it and ten more steps took her to a small, bare path of small rocks and overgrowth that led off into the forest. It was definitely a trail tamped down by elk and deer hooves. She started along it with quick steps. The continuing heavy downpour had soaked her sweatshirt and she could feel an insidious cold start to spread across her skin. Her face, hands and ears, were already numbing up from the gusting, freezing wind. And around her she sensed that the day was dying in the creeping gloom.

The Man decided that Maya was obviously lost. It was time to… *save her. That's it! I'll save her,* he thought to himself with a slow, asymmetrical grin that almost made him feel self-conscious.

If she sees that I'm rescuing her it might take the edge off our first meeting, he reasoned to himself. *Yeah, I don't want it to be messy and awkward. I don't 'do' awkward very well… Who does!?* He rolled that thought around in his head while he made an effort to grin again. He smoothed out his hair with his huge, thick fingers, like a grizzly running a paw through its fur and pulled on his facemask. At last, it was time to introduce himself to the beautiful and unique girl of his dreams… and sweet nightmares.

Stumbling along the rocky trail for fifteen endless minutes brought her to the start of a cliff wall of slate rock that rose up from the forest floor and wrapped along the curving trail. Then she came to it. Off to the right there was a ledge where the edge of the cliff stopped and rose straight up.

The rope!

She saw the rope swaying in the blowing wind. She walked over to the rope and looked up through the pouring rain as she pulled on it. The rope curved up and out of sight, but she could see the bottom of a ledge about a hundred and fifty feet straight up. She knew the cliff wall would be slippery. She just had to take her time and be sure of her footing. She took a deep breath, tightened her riding gloves, and started up. Pull, step, relax …Pull, step, and relax…

Kougar looked up from his moody reflection as he heard the heavy rain pepper his tent. Under the cover of a couple of huge Ponderosa Pine trees, his tent didn't feel the full impact of the pouring rain. His tent, set back about thirty yards from the ledge, backed up to the cliff that rounded off behind him. It was a two-person tent that he could almost stand up in and had a large covered opening that was staked into the ground. Over the summer he had stocked it with stuff: a couple of books, a small med-kit, a battery-powered light, extra bottles of water, and a small, folded, camping chair. He sat inside his tent, cross-legged, next to his rolled out sleeping bag.

Though not moving he felt like he had been running for miles. A bead of sweat started at his temple. All the events of the last few days, like a feverish memory, just kept bearing down on him. He couldn't slough off the claustrophobic feeling as if the tent was going to collapse right on him. He was happy for the storm, for how the storm suited his mood. Despite his best efforts, Maya's words and her exact tone came to him again:

Funny, I said: I liked you

After I knew that I loved you…

His anguished heart thumped in protest and he got up angrily, just like he had done in Grenfeld's class. He stripped off his light jacket down to his short-sleeved black turtleneck. He needed some fresh air and wanted to feel the cold wind of the storm. He stepped through the tent's opening. He stood under the tent's porch flap and stared out into the rain. He looked out over the ledge and the big Ponderosa that stood there like an ancient sentinel, its lightening scarred trunk impervious to the elements. Suddenly he heard a rubbing, friction-like sound and a movement caught his eye. His climbing rope that was anchored around the base of the tree was... moving! Incredulous, Kougar started toward the tree, picking up speed as he went. Sure enough, the rope *was* moving. Something was pulling on the rope. *No way,* Kougar thought as he walked over to the ledge to look down through the pouring, cold rain, the gusty wind blowing his wild, blond dreadlocks around.

WHAT THE HELL—his mouth formed the words soundlessly as his eyes widened with what he saw below him. There was no mistaking the long brown hair and the lithe figure hanging on the rope.

"MAYA!!!" Kougar shouted with shock and surprise, his call flowing down on the gusting wind.

Maya heard the call and her heart leaped as her footing slipped and she banged against the cliff face.

"Kougar!"

A caged joy burst out momentarily, but it didn't override Kougar's angry despair as he saw Maya dangling below him, but that anger soon turned to fear as he realized her precarious situation. She was about thirty feet up the rope. If she fell... *if she fell!!* He could see her feet slipping against the cliff face as she tried to get a foothold. *Jesus!*

"Go back down!" Kougar shouted above the wind. "It's too dangerous!"

Maya was breathing deeply with her effort. She could feel the rope was getting slippery and she tried again to get a foothold against the slick slate cliff face. She looked up at Kougar as the rain pelted her face and shook her head. The swirling gale took her voice up to him.

"No, I can make it!... I can make it!"

"Don't be stubborn! You can't come here! Go back down!"

Maya swayed precariously below him. He could feel panic spreading through him.

"Dammit, Maya! Don't be crazy! Go back down!"

Maya tried again, made a little progress and then slipped again almost losing her grip.

"And then what?!" she called up to him.

Kougar realized, even though it angered him, that she just couldn't stay there. It was getting dark, she was soaking wet. She couldn't ride back in this weather. She would get lost in the darkness and freeze. The whole bad scenario flashed through his mind. He had to act fast.

"Hold on, I'm going to pull you up!"

Kougar reached under the rope taut with Maya's weight and started to pull her up, his biceps bunched and his corded chest rose against his shirt. The wet ground under his feet started to give way. The wet rope was slick in his hands and slipped as he strained and pulled on it. The rope suddenly released in his hands. He heard Maya's surprised outcry as she banged against the cliff face and desperately re-gripped the rope just in time to keep herself from falling. Kougar remembered his riding gloves in the tent.

"Maya! You've got to hold on!" he shouted down to her. "I'll be right back! Can you do that?!"

Maya looked down below her and fear punched at her stomach. And for a quick moment she thought how mad her parents would be at her. Her father would be FURIOUS. She felt her arms weakening, her strength ebbing. Her shout came out weakly.

"I can do it!"

Kougar heard the fatigue in her voice and his face contorted with fear. He gave her a last look and sprinted back to his tent and dived into his backpack and fished out his riding gloves and put them on slapping the Velcro together. As he sprinted back to the tree through the driving rain, he heard Maya's muffled scream, the same scream he had heard that night in Drake Park... the one that sounded so much like Michaela's! He yelled out and ran frantically to the ledge.

"No!!!"

When Kougar looked over the ledge it had already happened...

"Maya!!!" Kougar could see Maya sprawled out on the bottom ledge below. She wasn't moving.

"Maya!" Kougar's frantic, grief-filled shout poured out of him and it was swallowed by the indifference of the storming elements around him.

He turned, grabbed the rope, and started to descend quickly, too quickly, slipping and sliding down. He lost his footing a couple of times and slammed against the cliff face. His mind reeled with all the horrible thoughts of how badly injured she was—or worse!

He dropped off the rope the last ten feet, trying to get to her as quickly as possible. He thudded onto the ground and moved over to Maya who had managed to get to her knees. The impact of the fall had knocked the breath out of her. She gasped for air. Kougar knelt next to her.

"Maya!" he said, relieved that she was moving. "Are you all right?" You said you were going to hold on! Are you all right?"

"I… think so," she finally managed as she recovered her breath and the shock of the fall.

Relieved that she was seemingly okay, Kougar's fear and panic turned angry as he helped her to her feet. Maya felt a tweak of pain as she put weight on her right leg.

"What the hell are you doing?" he accused, the wind blowing his words around.

"What are *you* doing?" Maya countered, her annoyed tone matching his. "You ditched Grenfeld's class. You keep doing that and you'll flunk out of that class."

Kougar frowned and rolled his eyes at the absurdity of Maya's comments. "Are you kidd—so what?!… Now, what are you doing here? Are you crazy?"

"Crazy," Maya barked a laugh through her rain-drenched lips, and then she looked softly at Kougar's incredulous face. "Crazy… yeah. I had to talk to you. I had to see you… I just came to talk."

Kougar's face twisted in anguish as he battled two opposite feelings. "Talk?!… Jeez, you can't be here. You've ruined everything by coming."

"I'm sorry."

"And, you almost killed yourself… You have to go back," he said without conviction.

"I'm… I'm in love with you."

The words were like a sweet lash on his skin, dampening his resolve. He looked away into a sharp gust of wind and stinging rain to hide his emotions.

"You have to… go back," he said weakly, still turned away from her, his voice betraying his words.

"I can't leave you. Don't you get it? I can't."

She saw Kougar's shoulders sag as he dropped his head down as if absorbing a blow. He turned back to her, his face a worn out mask of happy sadness. "Damn, you're stupid."

"Hey," she began in mock anger, "I have a 4.25 weighted GPA. I missed one question on my SATs."

Kougar grunted sarcastically. "Yeah, and look where you are right now… Stupid."

Maya smiled that warm beautiful smile of hers and locked eyes with Kougar.

"As a friend of yours said: I'm right where I'm supposed to be."

"Hummph," Kougar muttered under his breath as he looked around as the gusty wind blew his damp, blond dreadlocks all around his shoulders. The 'fun' forest that he had mountain biked in so many times suddenly showed him a new face, one that he now feared. "I guess you can't go back now."

"No… I'm getting cold. I'm soaked. It's getting dark. The rain's not letting up. What are we going to do?"

Kougar started assessing their mounting predicament as the rain pelted him. "No choice. We have to climb back to my tent. Let's go. You first. Take your time. I'll be right behind you… I don't have to tell you… we *have* to make it up. We can't stay here or go back. We have to make it."

Maya and Kougar shared a knowing look for a moment as both of them acknowledged the severity of their situation.

"I know," Maya nodded and said as she tightened her riding gloves.

"Okay, up you go," Kougar encouraged as he handed her the swaying rope.

Maya grabbed the rope and pulled up and onto the cliff face. She took a step and grunted out in pain and stopped. Kougar was ready to get up behind her.

"What's the matter?" he asked urgently through the blowing wind.

"Give me a second," Maya breathed out with pain.

"Are you going to be all right?" Kougar asked from below her.

Maya drew her mouth in determined line and took a few deep breaths, trying to ignore the stabbing pain radiating from her right knee.

"I'm okay."

Maya fought down the pain and started again, each step, a growing agony. Kougar moved up behind her.

"That's it," he said over the wind.

With each step her knee felt like a knife was jabbing into it. Her face twisted with effort and then contorted in pain. Finally a jolt of pain shot up and a sharp cry burst from her lips. She lost her footing and slid down into Kougar, who tried to hold her up, he strained for a moment, but then he slipped and they tumbled back to the ground. Maya grunted in pain while holding her knee. Kougar rolled back onto his feet.

"What happened?" Kougar said through a heavy breath. "I thought you were okay."

"My knee."

"What?"

"My knee. I think I twisted it when I fell. I can't put any weight on it... I'm sorry."

Kougar took a moment to absorb their worsening situation and tried to keep it out of his voice.

"It's all right."

"I tried," Maya anguished.

"I know… Come on, we still have to get up there. There's no other way."

"How?"

They both looked up the steep, one hundred and fifty foot tall cliff face through the pelting rain, and then looked to one another.

"I might be able to carry you," Kougar said as he rolled around the idea in his head.

"Could you?"

"I don't know," Kougar's voice wavered. "It's a long way to the top."

Maya read the uncertainty in his tone. "I wouldn't want you to try it if you didn't think you could make it."

"What's your suggestion then? Stay down here or try to walk out and freeze to death? I don't think you would get far on that knee."

"I guess our options are limited," Maya admitted.

"Doesn't matter if I want to or not. Come on, before it gets totally dark."

Kougar bent down and Maya grunted in pain and had to push off of her good leg to get up onto to his back.

"Hold on as tight as you can, especially if my footing slips."

"Kougar, I'm so sorry… for everything," she said into his ear and she laid her head against his. As the truth of her feeling moved through Kougar for a few moments, something in him relented and he let his head sag against hers. It was the deepest embrace he had ever felt.

"Don't worry. We can do this."

"Liar," she whispered softly, sweetly.

"So?" Kougar had to reply.

Maya shifted her head to Kougar's other shoulder and readied her grip. "If we fall… we fall together, right?"

"I guess you could say that."

"I'm good with that… you know I love you," Maya said into Kougar's other ear.

"Stop saying that. It makes me nervous."

"Sorry."

Kougar pulled on the rope and got onto the cliff face and started up through the lashing rain and cold gusting wind that blew down from the Cascades. After a few steps Kougar had to reshuffle Maya's position on his back.

"Jeez," he said through a deep breath, "you weigh a ton."

"That's not a nice thing to say to a girl in any situation," Maya said through a small smile.

Another couple of steps and Kougar could feel Maya's strong grasp was too far up around his throat. Her grip was blocking his air.

"Hey, you're choking me," he gasped. "Lower your grip a little bit."

"Oh, sorry."

Methodically, Kougar climbed, deliberately setting his feet to get solid purchase for each step. The wind howled down on them, its gusts buffeting them while the cold rain lashed their bodies. She could feel all the muscles of Kougar's tall frame bunching up with effort. His labored breath got deeper and deeper. She closed her eyes so not to see just how slow they were going and how… far they had to go.

Suddenly, Kougar's foot slipped and they banged against the hard rock shale face of the cliff. The pain of the impact on her knee blew open her eyes and she fought down the need to cry out. She didn't want Kougar to worry about her pain.

Kougar gasped: "Are you all right?"

Maya bit at her lip. "I'm fine," she managed to grunt out.

"Liar," Kougar shot back at her in-between deep breaths.

"All right, that hurt like hell. Please don't slip again."

A small gruff laugh let go of Kougar's mouth and Maya chuckled painfully in his ear.

"I have to stop a second," alarm came back into Kougar's voice, "catch my breath."

Kougar doubled the rope around his wrists to help hold their precarious position on the cliff face as he rested. He looked up through the rain and his face registered fear. The rain was lessening, and, as if a weather switch was flipped, big snowflakes started to fall and swirl in the wind. They were just over half way to the top. Maya looked up as well and saw what he did. Despite the cold, Kougar felt the sweat mixed with rain drip down into his eyes. A pang of despair rose up in him as he could feel his strength ebbing. He knew the feeling well as a weight lifter. The oxygen in his muscles was maxing out. He knew a few more reps and he would have to put the bar back on the rack. Maya could feel his discouragement.

"Hey, if we have to go back down, don't worry, I know you gave it your best try. We'll figure out something else. We're together. That's what counts," she said firmly into his ear.

Kougar shook his head. He wouldn't have the strength to try the climb again. And he knew that death waited for them in the freezing forest that night if they went back down. Maya could sense Kougar's growing desperation.

"I'm so sorry," she began sadly and finished in frustration, "I wish I could help."

Kougar re-gripped the rope and took a few deep breaths. "Talk to me," he whispered fiercely... "Distract me," he grunted as he started to climb again, his biceps popping with the strain.

Maya knew this was her chance to say the things to Kougar that she needed to and had always wanted to, because, *if we… fall, he might never know.* She felt joy surge within her as she realized that this was the most special moment of her life.

"When I saw you at the dance," she began into his ear. I—"

"When you saw *Gaius*," Kougar cut in through a couple of grunts.

"No, when I saw *you* …. You had your dreads all pulled back off your forehead in a neat ponytail, and you had on those cool, green contacts… and the Irish accent! You were totally stud'n it."

Kougar's jaw was set with effort but a tight smile pulled at the corner of his mouth. He then almost slipped but pulled up his other foot just in time, grunted loudly with the exertion of maintaining their balance. Maya looked up and she could see the ledge above them. *Twenty more feet!*

Kougar was struggling, gasping and grunting with each step. She could see that his riding gloves had worn through and a small trickle of blood seeped out from under his palms.

"You had that Super Vampire shirt on showing your buffed arms. Then you did that awesome dance! And, looking at me the whole time! Oh, my God, I really wanted you to bite my neck. That would have been sweet. I never wanted something so bad in my life."

The words flowed through Kougar's flagging muscles like an elixir enabling his heart to pump more blood; the sweet tone of her voice focused his mind like a laser, overriding all feelings of pain and fatigue. He couldn't let that voice... die.

One more step. Pull... One more step. PULL!

Maya put her lips on Kougar's ear as she continued to pour out her heart into his awareness, into his body... into his soul.

"In my life, I will never want anyone as much as I want you," she whispered with all the conviction of her being. She then knew exactly how her grandmother had felt. *I understand, Grandma Sania. I understand...*

Five more heaving pulls on the rope, and with a last deep grunt, Kougar yanked them over the top of the ledge. Kougar collapsed in utter exhaustion, with Maya falling on top of him. One side of Kougar's red face pushed into the muddy ground. He lay there gasping for breath, unable to cry out in victory.

We're safe! He shouted out in his mind.

Maya rolled off of Kougar's back onto the ground next to him and raised her arms full of relief and exhilaration.

"Yeah! Oh, yeah! I knew you could do it, KOUG!"

"I'll tell you what," Kougar said through steadying breaths, "I don't want to do that again anytime soon. I thought I was going to fall half way up. I—it was you... You did it."

"No way, buddy, it was all you. I didn't take one step. What you did was awesome."

Kougar turned over. They both looked up into the thick, swirling snow and gathering darkness, both searched for each other's hand and shared the solace of a firm grasp between survivors, now bonded through adversity. They were relieved to not have to face the freezing death that surely waited out there in the coming long night among the towering, old pines that, no doubt, had been witness to all kinds of deaths.

… The Man cursed lowly under his breath, without emotion, as he watched, from a dense ticket of scrub pine, the kid with the screwy blond hair, haul Maya up the cliff face on his back and finally over the top.

He had seen that kid before, the one with the goofy hair and funny accent. He cursed again, angry that he had not taken care of that idiot in the football field.

Now, he walked to the ledge, grabbed a hold of the rope and looked up into the swirling snow, the wind tugging at his listless tuffs of hair that stuck out from under his facemask. He pulled on the rope wondering if it would take his weight. Then it dawned on him as a dull light went off in his mind and his nose wrinkled in disgust as the *why* came to him.

It's a… lover's rendezvous… There must be a tent up at the top, a secret place for 'them'.

And to think that it was now a love triangle between himself, Maya and that stupid kid, hit him in the stomach like a blunt, iron poker. He envisioned all the faces that kid would make as he strangled him. A grin that went only half way across his mouth started. He needed to go back to his van and get a few more tools. His imagination ignited and lurid scenarios came to his mind. He put his earplugs back in and pulled out a headlight and strapped it around his head. In the darkening gloom, he headed off in an energetic jog, his headlight making him look like a weaving freight train moving through the brush and under the towering pines.

*

Kougar and Maya let their exhilaration run its course as they lay on the ledge. The adrenaline had worn off and they realized how soaked and cold they were.

"God, I'm freezing," Maya said through chattering teeth.

They slowly got to their feet. Kougar put his arm around Maya to support her and she leaned on him as she gingerly put weight on her knee as she stepped. They never saw the rope behind them go taut for a second.

"Come on," Kougar half shouted in the wind, "my tent is over there."

They made their way under a thick cover of pine trees where the snow didn't fall to Kougar's tent pitched against the back of the cliff wall. They walked under the tent's porch cover and Kougar pulled open the tent door flap, attached it to the Velcro patch, and they stepped inside. Kougar had to bend over slightly to keep his head from hitting the tent's ceiling. The battery-driven light threw a yellow-white light against the tent walls.

"Oh, it's so good to be out of that weather," Maya breathed out and wrapped her arms around herself.

"How's the knee?" Kougar asked.

"It hurts bad," she had to admit.

"I think I might have something that could help," he said as he dug around in his backpack that lay in the corner of the tent.

"We have to get warm. We have to dry our clothes. The temperature is just going to keep dropping. Do you have any dry, emergency wood for a fire?"

"Ah, no," Kougar said over his shoulder, "I ah, never light a fire."

Maya teased: "Geez, what kind of experienced camper are you? Besides, a fire is romantic."

"I've never thought about it that way," he said lowly. "Oh, here we go." Kougar lifted up the small med-kit in his hand. "There's some ibuprofen and an ace bandage in here."

"We *need* that fire," Maya said with emphasis. "There has to be some fairly dry scrub wood under the big pines."

"Okay. I'll go out and get some. In the meantime, my jacket is in the corner there. Put it on."

Maya took off her wet sweatshirt revealing her sports bra and put on Kougar's jacket. The relief was immediate.

"Ah, that's so much better. Hurry with the wood. Do you have any matches?"

He handed her the med-kit. "There's a pack in there. I'll be right back."

Kougar returned, his arms full of dead scraps of wood. He stood there under the tent porch. He looked sheepishly at Maya. She could tell he was a novice.

"Here, let me help," Maya said, and limped over to Kougar. "I've been camping since I was three. Get me some round rocks that can radiate heat and we'll set it just under the outside flap here, to keep the rain and snow off it."

Maya set the rocks that Kougar brought to her into a round pit. Kougar laid the wood inside the pit.

"Now, we need some kind of kindling. The wood is a little moist."

"I've got some papers, old notes from Grenfeld's class."

"That'll work fine."

Kougar handed the pages to Maya. She started to ball them up and stuff them between the twigs and branches crisscrossed in the fire pit. One written sentence caught her eye and she read it out loud: "Death should be an act of redemption, not the end."

"That's what Hamlet should have thought," Kougar said over her shoulder.

"I guess it wasn't meant to be for him," Maya said as she lit a match to the papers and the fire spiked up. Maya laid her wet, high school sweatshirt across the folding chair in front of the fire.

"Here, hold the jacket up for me."

Kougar held up his jacket as she turned her back to him and took off her wet sports bra. With her back still turned to him, she reached back for the jacket and put it on. She set her bra on the chair.

"Shirts first, then pants."

Kougar nodded.

"Give me your shirt and I'll lay it out. Hey—"she noticed his bloody palms. "Let me look at your hands... You cut them on the rope."

Kougar paused. "Ah, I'm all right," he managed in a mumble.

Maya pulled out a roll of gauze from the med kit. She removed Kougar's shredded riding gloves and wrapped his palms with the white gauze. "You should have said something. You have some bad rope burns."

"It's all right... I've had worse."

"And your shirt, take it off. It's soaked through. You must be freezing, Maya insisted. "Unzip your sleeping bag and drape it around you like a blanket."

"I'm really all right," Kougar said, his mumble now sounded nervous.

"Give it to me. Don't be stubborn... and don't be silly, I've seen guys' chests before."

"Turn around," he ordered.

Maya let go an exasperated sigh and pulled both hands through her long brown hair. She then crossed her arms and turned her back to Kougar.

"Don't... don't turn around," came Kougar's flat voice that had an edge, a warning edge to it.

Kougar paused, then started to take of his black turtleneck, ducking his head under the shirt to pull it free. Maya couldn't help but giggle.

This is stupid, she thought.

"Look, you don't have to be modest with me. Besides, I've already seen your scars. It doesn't matter to me."

She turned abruptly around and stopped herself from saying something else. Kougar, slightly hunched over, looked at her balefully, like a cornered cat, shirt balled up in one hand. The flickering firelight threw lights across Kougar's muscular chest and upper torso… The burn scars twisted and snarled across his stomach covering the whole right side of his chest. The marks of scorched flesh reached up and over his right shoulder and lashed out at the right side of his throat.

Kougar's jaw worked with tension, pulling on the scar beneath it. His voice came out tightly.

"I told you not to turn around… I know, it's ugly to look at."

Maya didn't answer him but slowly limped forward, her deep brown eyes locked softly onto Kougar's. His face was a tense waiting mask and his breath deepened. The storm had died down outside but a steady wind blew against the tent walls. She stopped in front of him and gently reached out with her hand and her fingers came to rest on the crisscrossing knife scars. Kougar's face winced as if his disfigurements were still open wounds. Maya's eyes told him not to fear… they told him that her touch was imbued with love and was a healing force. She looked down at the trauma under her fingers, trying to absorb the pain of those marks, to excise their origins; she wanted to take them on herself if she only could. Her hand moved onto his burn scars that twisted across his stomach, and then softly traced the path of scorching destruction up to the side of his neck. Kougar's hand reached up and stopped the movement of her hand with a tension that betrayed the battle inside of him. The moment was full of turning points; it swelled with a punishing history, and with a massing of emotional matter that was collapsing within Kougar. It could explode with the past… or, it could burst open a new horizon just beyond the flames that continually burned his flesh and the echoing screams of his little sister. Maya slowly looked back up at Kougar, her eyes gathering moisture that then dropped down her cheek.

"I understand," she whispered …"Everything."

Kougar's grip that stayed her hand remained conflicted. Emotion clutched at his throat and the word barely made it off his lips:

"Every… thing?"

"All of it," she whispered again right into Kougar's heart.

A new awareness began in Kougar's blue eyes, like the soft lights of a new, full moon. The crackling of the fire sounded behind him. His hand relaxed and gently pulled Maya's hand to his lips where all of his gratitude and trust passed through his kiss. He then looked down at Maya, and his moist eyes met hers: emotion for emotion. Their embrace closed and their seeking lips met in a mutual homecoming of innocent desire, of longing, and in the joy of having found each other, here, at this moment.

Maya's arms closed strongly around Kougar's hard, scarred chest, desperately clinging to the one who had opened her heart to such surging and raw feelings. Kougar's lips searched and searched every part of Maya's, seeking to lose his very being in the rescue of her full mouth.

Finally, they broke off their sweet kiss… Their foreheads touched together.

"Oh, Kougar," Maya breathed.

"Now we've done it," Kougar whispered through a smile.

Maya smiled back, their lips almost touching.

"I guess we have, God, how I've wanted this to happen. I am so much in love with you, and I so believe we were meant for each other. I *am* your kind. I always have been."

Kougar leaned his head back and a crooked smile stretched across his face. "Beauty and the Freak, eh?"

"Not in my eyes."

"Well, you're blind… and not very smart."

Maya's grin matched his. "That's something to be thankful for."

"So you say… for now."

"Now and forever, my sweet Hamlet."

"If you were my Ophelia, I would have never let you drown in the river. I would have stopped you because your life was, and is, more valuable than mine …" And Kougar looked intensely into Maya's eyes. "Like someone I knew, you are innocent, so innocent. You deserve… life."

"Yes," Maya whispered as she tightened her embrace, "a life with you… forever with you."

Reckoning

Kougar and Maya lay in each other's arms through the night, for love, for mutual warmth that kept the night's descending cold at bay. Secure in one another, they could finally talk… just talk. All doors were open between them except one whose molten hinges resisted the most loving attempt to pry loose. And they laughed… Kougar surprised Maya (and himself) with his dry, witty observations. Of course Maya did most of the talking which Kougar was fine with. He was intoxicated with the tiny sound of a song in her voice, her clothed body against his, the smell of her hair, her full moon eyes that glinted in the tent's darkness, and the way she softly, with patience, combed her fingers through his blond dreadlocks. The heavy, notched chains of his emotional resistance had loosened, allowing the feeling of *really* being touched and it resonated through him like a revelation.

Maya let the gathering understanding of what Kougar meant to her flood over her Merit Scholar's mind and her Indian heart, as the peace and passionate surrender of his embrace enfolded her. He *was* her life now. It was a simple admission whose emblazoned clarity informed all that she would do for the rest of her life. *It's simple…* The thought had glowed within her and she had suddenly stopped the words out of Kougar's mouth with a touch of her finger and smiled that beautiful smile that had so much of her grandmother in it.

Kougar's expression of 'what?' had shown on his face.

"You," Maya whispered.

Again Kougar's face had questioned.

"Just you," Maya whispered again and clutched tightly at Kougar and laid her head on his chest…

Dawn broke out over the wilderness and held onto the forested landscape with the first, cold lights of blue, then, with rosy fingers that heralded the slow rise of the sun. Last night's first snow of the season to reach down from the mountaintops, did not stick, but left a glistening moisture on the ground. Inside the tent Kougar and Maya were suddenly quiet with the growing reality of what existed outside their sanctuary as they prepared to leave. Kougar rolled up the sleeping bag and started putting the remaining water bottles and other items in his backpack. He zipped it up and the sound seemed to put a final period on their fairy tale night.

"You ready to go?" Kougar said half-heartedly.

"No," came Maya's subdued reply. "You?"

"No," Kougar sighed. "Leave this? Never."

A mourning silence passed between them. Kougar took a swig off a water bottle and finally said: "Your parents aren't going to be happy with you... If only it could have happened in a different way... you know—"

"You mean normally?" Maya smiled ruefully.

"I'm sorry about what happened in the Commons and over at your parents' house. I put on a freak show because I wanted you to reject me. I was afraid. I panicked. I had to stop it all."

"That's all over now." And Maya looked at Kougar, and her smiled broadened with resolve.

"I'm glad," Kougar said and his smile matched hers... "But still, the way your dad looked at me. I'm sure me being with you would be his worst nightmare."

"I'll work on him. I wish I had brought my cell phone with me. I bet they're both just freaking out.

"You won't get any reception out here."

"They'll notice I took my mountain bike out. I know my dad will be out looking for me. He knows this area like the back of his hand. And your parents?" Maya asked.

"Ah... they're kind of use to my... ah, strange behavior. They'll simply be glad I came back okay, and tell me not to do it again. I'm not really a good son to them. I want to be but ..." and he trailed off reviewing the past. "Maybe one day. I hope... Can you ride? I'm sure the trails will be muddy. It won't be easy pedaling."

270

Maya tested her knee with her weight. "Well, I really couldn't run for my life," she laughed a bit, "I would have to tape it up tight for that. But as long as I don't have to get up out of my seat that often, I think it'll be okay."

"Okay... I guess we're ready." And he drew both bandaged hands through his hair. The rope burns still stung.

They both looked at each other, Kougar's suddenly intense blue eyes bored into Maya's. They moved irresistibly towards each other and shared a deep embrace. They finally drew apart but held on to each other. Kougar's face radiated a fear... a fear of the future, of what lay beyond the tent, beyond the sleeping bag where they shared the joy and security of each other's arms. He knew what he was and what others thought of him. But he also knew that his feelings for Maya had created a new galvanizing reality within him, a reality of possibilities that he could never had imagined before.

Could there be another way of being... me? Has she saved me from... myself? It will all end out there... I know it. The thoughts tumbled through his mind like a deadly juggling game.

Maya easily read his fear and squeezed his hands. "We can do this... We can. We'll find a way. We will. I'll never leave you alone."

Kougar smiled slowly, hopefully. "Are we where we're supposed to be?"

Maya looked deeply into Kougar's sea blue eyes. "Yes," she said firmly with all the conviction in her heart. "Let's go."

Kougar finally nodded. "I'll make sure the fire's all out. Get your stuff ready."

Maya nodded back. Kougar stepped through the tent's door flap. He stirred through the ashes of last night's fire and poured some water from the bottle in his hand to extinguish all the wood coals that were still smoldering. And as he looked into the coals he thought he could see the same ones deep inside him. Did he see that the glowing embers were going... out?

A rubbing sound broke his deep reverie. He looked out towards the big pine at the edge of the ledge that secured his rope... *It was moving.*

His face wrinkled up in edgy surprise and something gnawed at his gut. He dropped the water bottle and started to walk towards the tree slowly as if the unconscious part of him didn't want to see what was making the rope *move;* it moved like some venomous snake, twisting, preparing to strike. He bent down to look over the cliff's edge and what he saw made him snap straight up and run the image through his mind again: something like a huge, silver-back gorilla in clothes was climbing up the rope: *The Man!*

PANIC flooded through Kougar's veins and his breath shortened. For a second that seemed like an eternity, he just froze. Then his paralysis broke like a rock shattering a mirror and he jumped out of his skin. He looked around frantically realizing he had no knife with him or in the tent to cut the rope. *I HAVE TO CUT THE ROPE!!!*

He dropped to the ground fishing around for a rock with a sharp edge. He finally found one and, on his knees, he started striking at the rope with the rock whose edge was more dull than sharp. Like a jackhammer, Kougar pounded down on the rope, his breath blowing in and out with panicked effort. The rope was fraying slowly... too slowly. Then, it snapped suddenly, and the rope went slack.

He jumped to his feet and ran to the edge and looked down... He saw The Man clinging to the cliff face and one of his big arms drew up and his hand wielded a big wall hammer, which he thrust into the cliff face securing his balance.

Kougar turned and sprinted back to the tent and flew through the opening, breathing hard. Maya looked up from securing her gear. She was getting ready to put on her riding helmet.

"What's the matter?" she almost cried out, shocked by Kougar's movement.

"We can't climb down," Kougar said, keeping the desperation out of his voice.

"What? Why?" I don't—"

"Someone is coming."

"Someone?! Who is—"?

"Someone bad. Very bad," Kougar said tightly. "That night in Drake Park... then, at the football field."

"You said that was you!" Maya shouted, panic now entering her voice.

"No, I just distracted him from—" and he stopped himself, but Maya finished for him:

"From me... He's after me! What does he want?!"

Kougar didn't answer but reached over and grabbed the med kit and took out a roll of athletic tape. He bent down in front of Maya and began to wrap her knee, the tape making lashing sounds as it rounded her knee in a tight spiral. Kougar tore off the end of the tape and stood up.

"You're going to have to run," he said intensely. "Come on!"

Kougar pulled Maya by the arm and they exited the tent and headed back around one side of the cliff. Maya grunted in pain trying to extend and flex her knee as she was running. She almost fell as her knee buckled.

"Oh, I can't!"

Kougar thrust his arm under hers to support her. "Come on!"

They hobbled around the side of the cliff moving as quickly as Maya's knee would allow. All the while, a thought kept pounding through Kougar's mind: *Nothing can happen to her. Nothing!* His fear began to sift through him until he had no fear for himself... only for Maya. It agonized him. *Not again!*

They came around to another ledge that separated the cliff from the forest beyond. It spanned twelve feet or so. They came to a stop at the edge and looked down into a drop of a hundred feet to the forest floor. Kougar looked at Maya, despair clouding his eyes.

"Can you jump it?"

Maya put her hands on her knees, breathing hard and shook her head. "I don't think so. It's too far the way my knee is." She then looked quickly up at Kougar. Resolve was in her eyes and voice. "You go."

"No! No way. I don't think I could jump it anyway. Sorry, I forgot this ledge was back here. I'm sorry. There's no other way to the other side," he said as he looked up the sheer cliff face next to them and then looked back behind them expecting to see The Man lumbering around the corner.

"Throw me!" Maya said suddenly, sharply.

"What?" Kougar gasped.

"Throw me. We'll get a running start. Grab a hold of my arm and put your hand under me. As we get to the edge, just throw me."

"No, no," Kougar said quickly. "If I don't throw you far enough you'll—"

Maya shuddered as she remembered how The Man's sickening grip had crushed against her shoulder that night in Drake Park. "Trust me," Maya began, desperately, "I don't want him to get a hold of me." Kougar shook his head. "No I can't."

Maya grabbed a hold of Kougar's face. "Kougar, please. It's the only way… You can do it!"

Maya glanced back behind them and saw The Man, his face masked, round the corner a hundred yards behind them. He walked deliberately with a horrible waiting aspect to him that flooded her with fear.

"COME ON!" Maya shouted into Kougar's ear.

Kougar and Maya backed up about twenty yards, they turned back and started to run. Kougar ran beside Maya. He had a hold of her left arm. Maya gasped as her knee sent shooting pains all up and down her leg. As they neared the ledge, Kougar reached behind and under Maya.

"Now, Kougar! NOW!" Maya shouted.

Kougar bunched up the muscle in his bicep, stomped on his front foot for leverage, grunted, and pushed with all his strength, a strength fortified by all the adrenaline that flashed through his body. He launched

Maya off the ledge and into naked space. Agonizingly, he watched her float through the air. She seemed to move in slow motion—then she fell out of the sky and slammed onto the edge of the ledge on the other side. Her arms grasped for a hold while her feet slipped underneath her. She tried to raise herself up and over the edge but kept slipping farther and farther. Kougar could see that she wasn't going to make it.

"Maya! Hold on!"

Kougar backed up, took a quick look over his shoulder and could see The Man advancing in his slow stalk. Kougar let out a bark of air and sprinted for the ledge. *She can't fall!*
He hit hard on his jumping foot and catapulted off the ledge. He sailed over Maya and tumbled into a landing. He scramble back to her.

"Kougar!" Maya shouted, as she knew her grasp was loosening.

Kougar reached down and snatched her falling hand. With one hand bracing him on the ledge, he pulled her up and over with a sudden infusion of unknown strength.

"Gotcha!"

"I knew you could do it. I knew it." Maya said as she clung to Kougar.

"Come on!" Kougar put his arm under Maya's and they moved off and were enveloped in the thick forest. Kougar looked over his shoulder, but couldn't see behind him. He knew The Man would still be coming, that he would jump the span easily.

They weaved in and around the old pines of the forest that thrust up from the ground like statues of cold, ribbed bark and offered no safe haven. Kougar pushed their pace as they half-ran, half-hobbled along. He knew Maya couldn't keep this speed up. He could sense her concentrating with determination, to will her knee to keep pumping. As he glanced down at her, her face was set, and she used all her runner's training to try and control her gasping breath to stay in the rhythm of her broken gait.

Now, every ten yards, Kougar had to carry more and more of her weight. *We need more time!* He shouted to himself in desperation. Maya's gasps now echoed with a mounting pain.

Kougar could feel that a hurtling reckoning was bearing down on them like a locomotive, a murderous locomotive. Despair clutched at his heart. Suddenly, a burnt curtain in his mind drew back and the face of his sister, Michaela, flooded his vision and a thought began to beat from the depths of his consciousness: *I... can go to her!* Michaela's sweet face then dissolved into her burning room and her flailing figure writhed as the flames consumed her child's body and her screams pierced through him as if she were right next to him. Then, a berserk-like *rage* started to gather within him under the sound of a throbbing base that drowned out his sister's screams. To think that another one, an innocent one, another one could have her life extinguished again... *no, no, no, NO!*

Kougar came to a sudden stop. Maya bent over and gasped out and with edgy fear in her voice"

"Why are we stopping?"

'You need to rest for a second," Kougar said evenly but with a guttural undertone.

Surprised by the strange tone in Kougar's voice, Maya looked up at him.

"Come on! We can make it!" came Maya's breathy, desperate shout, as she looked behind them into the dark, impenetrable forest, expecting The Man to burst through the trees. She pulled at Kougar but he didn't budge.

"No, *you* can make it," Kougar said again, his guttural tone getting deeper.

Maya grabbed a hold of Kougar's arms, looking up into his face and saw the dark roiling blood spreading under his smooth skin. It gave his face a strange dark cast to it, one she had never seen before. "We have to go together!... I can't leave you! I can't!"

"You can and you will," came the same voice. "Look, we can't outrun him. We have to split up. It's the only way... I have to distract him like Gai—like I did at the football field... He can't have you."

"But we—"

276

Kougar squeezed Maya's arms and his voice cut her off. His steely blue eyes held her with their intensity; she saw there was no fear in them, just a smoldering constancy that spoke of an ultimate decision.

"Look, there's no time. Head off to your right, keep going until you hear the sound of the river falls. Follow the sound until you get to the falls, then, make your way down alongside until you get to the bottom. There you'll see two huge rocks with an opening between them. Slide through the gap and you'll find a small cave. Wait for me there."

Maya tugged at Kougar's arms to get him to come with her.

"No, we have to go together. I can't leave you here."

"Don't worry, I'm right where I'm supposed to be. Go!" And he turned his back to her.

"No, Kougar, we have to—"

Kougar's rage was now bubbling up in him and his conscious mind went blank.

"Michaela! RUN!

Maya gave Kougar one last look as he stood in almost a crouch, like a predatory animal ready to spring, and she limped off as fast as her knee would let her.

Kougar felt all the flagellating years of merciless guilt, fear, and self-loathing pour into… rage; it worked through his face as he looked into the forest. He took off his jacket and let it fall next to him. His fists bunched together with the rage coursing through him. Before his vision, a line of flames sprung up. He had seen them before. They were always the same… He could hear the crackling and the loud, maniacal licking of the fire. He could feel the searing heat singe the hair on his arms. *He… Can't… Have her!*

He stepped through the flames and they dissolved before him, and as his vision cleared, he saw The Man come jogging through the trees and then slow to a deliberate walk towards him. Kougar raised his fists to a boxer's stance and shook his dreadlocked head like a bull with blood in its eyes. The Man stopped about twenty feet from Kougar and studied him, his face tilted to one side, his colorless eyes peering out of the pits in his facemask. He motioned with one thick arm for Kougar to step aside. Kougar just stood staring at The Man, his blue eyes animal intense beneath his white/blond brows, his weight moving to the balls of his feet. The Man gestured again, angrily. Kougar didn't move, his eyes locked onto the Man's in the oldest, atavistic connection of life and death.

The Man reached into his jacket and pull out a handgun. It seemed small in his huge hand, almost disappearing in his catcher's mitt-like palm. He pointed it at Kougar and cocked the trigger… Tense seconds passed and the night in the tent with Maya flashed before Kougar's mind: the way she smelled, her endless beauty, the way she had touched his twisted scars… and the way she said she loved him… *someone like… me.*

Every second meant Maya had more of a chance to get away. If The Man were to shoot him, so be it.

"This isn't the football field," the Man growled out, like the harsh cough of a grizzly, "you won't survive. You will die. Leave her to me. I can protect her. You can't."

Again The Man pointed the gun at Kougar whose unblinking stare remained …The Man then un-cocked the trigger on his gun and shoved the gun back into his pocket and zipped it closed. A grin twisted at the sides of his mouth.

Ah, he wants to fight… I guess I get to strangle this kid after all, the thought occurred to The Man like any routine notion. But he then dully remembered his disgust, the disgust at the thought that this punk with the stupid hair had *touched* his Maya.

The Man rubbed his hands together in a detached wonder at how it will feel when the kid spasms out his life under the unhurried vice-like squeeze of his mindless hands. But first, he had to feel *something* to get past his blunt interest.

The Man walked toward Kougar as if he were taking out the trash, deliberate, bored, his thick arms swinging at his side. He stopped ten feet in front of Kougar. He took no heed of the look in Kougar's enflamed blue eyes that revealed the rage—not fear—in his being, a rage that predicted only an End Game.

Suddenly, Gaius' Irish accent growled deeply within him: *When you are on borrowed time, who cares about death? Who cares about death when you have something to die for? Yes, for Maya... our Maya. I'm with you...*

The Man just stood there, arms down, waiting. His masked face lulled to one side as he looked at Kougar. Kougar bounced off the balls of his feet and moved in with his boxer's stance and his right hand snaked out, and with a grunt of full effort, he smacked The Man full in the face.

Kougar backed off to escape the sweep of The Man's arms that never came. The Man's head moved back with the impact of Kougar's blow. His mouth moved under his mask as if he was savoring something. He leaned forward and spat out some blood at Kougar's feet, his eyes looking dully at Kougar through the eye pits. He stood, waiting again. Kougar flashed forward and his hands blurred like buzz saws as he pummeled The Man's midsection. The Man staggered slowly back under the barrage of Kougar's fists. Kougar popped up and fired two quick blows striking The Man across the face.

That hurt, The Man finally thought.

Kougar loaded up a third blow and as he struck out, one of The Man's arms flicked up with blinding speed and caught Kougar's fist in his huge hand. They froze there for a couple of seconds. The Man slowly applied his giant's strength and began to push Kougar's fist down and pulled Kougar toward him. Kougar tried to punch futility at The Man's ribs with his left. With his other hand, The Man grabbed Kougar by the throat and lifted him up off the ground. He brought Kougar face to face with him. Kougar felt The Man's hot fetid breath blow across his face.

"Time to die," The Man growled thickly.

He dropped Kougar and swung his big arm and clubbed Kougar across the face knocking him sprawling backwards. Dazed, Kougar got to his knees, and The Man was on him. He grabbed a hold of Kougar's dreadlocks and pulled his head straight. He then raised his arm and then swung down with the point of his elbow, like a pile driver, right on top of Kougar's head.

Kougar's head exploded with bright lights... then... nothing but black emptiness. The Man pulled up Kougar's limp head that now sat on a rag doll's neck. He cocked back his fist to deliver the final blow—

"Please," came Maya desperate, loud, breathy call from the trees behind him, "don't hurt him anymore. I'll go with you."

Maya's half run, half hobble, slowed as she made her way toward The Man who still had a hold of the limp Kougar by the hair.

"Please... I'll...I'll go willingly... Don't hurt him anymore," Maya said lowly as tears streamed down her face. "I'll go."

The Man grunted and turned his masked head to one side as he studied Maya. He finally nodded his head and let go of Kougar who crumpled to the ground without a spark of consciousness, blood oozing from both ears, his nose, and down from the swollen side of his mouth. The Man kneeled down pulled out a couple pieces of twine rope out of his pocket and tied Kougar's hands and feet. He then got up and reached out his hand to Maya.

Maya walked passed The Man's hand and leaned down to Kougar and softly stroked his face and whispered:

"It's all right. It's going to be all right. I love you. I'm sorry he hurt you."

Maya got up and once more The Man offered his hand. Maya raised a struggling arm but couldn't quite reach for The Man's hand from hell. The Man quickly grabbed a hold of Maya's hand and they headed off.

Maya tried to steel herself for what was to come. Seeing Kougar's lifeless body was so terrible and gut wrenching that she had almost passed out, but she had to make the bargain... She had to. She looked up at the masked face and her lips quivered with fear and the mind-numbing question came to her.

"Why? Why are you doing this?"

The Man pulled her along to match his long stride. Finally, he looked down at her and his masked lips moved grossly before his words came out.

"You're too young to understand… I surrendered to my heart. Leave it at that," The Man's muffled tone rolled through her like a raven's croak that managed to mouthed words.

As they moved along through the cold, amoral forest, which would probably soon, throw her frantic, suffering cries back at her, Maya started to take an inventory of her body. She commanded each part to… not feel. Everything was to shut down… to die… She was willing her body to become an empty husk, long abandoned by hopes, dreams, feelings of love, the love for her parents—*oh, Mom, Dad, I'm so sorry for what you'll have to face*— and, the ache of never becoming… one with her sweet Kougar; to never share a life with him; a happy life that she had seen spread out before her mind's eye.

She was determined that in whatever way The Man would… do what he would do with her, her last thoughts would be with Kougar. She would latch onto the image of his young man's smile and detach herself from her useless, ownerless, body… *Why… Wh*—and she then choked off the last 'why' she felt she would ever utter.

*

The hammering inside of Kougar's head slowly opened his groggy eyes. As reality seeped into his consciousness, he rolled up onto his knees. "Maya!" he blurted out. He tried to get up and didn't realize his feet were tied together and he tumbled over onto the cold forest floor and felt the sharp prick of dead pine needles against his numbing face. He got back to his knees and looked around desperately for an object that might cut him free. He fished around on the ground looking for a sharp rock, his breathing rising with his panic. He had to get to her. He could only hope that she had the time to get down to the cave and that she was waiting for him. *Please. Please,* he cried to himself.

A thought occurred to him and he stopped his search. He looked down at the fresh, woven rope around his wrists. He tried to work his wrists together. The rope was tight and allowed no movement. He raised his wrists, balled his fists together, took a deep breath, closed his eyes and with a quick motion smacked himself in the nose… He open his eyes, gritted his teeth and gathered himself for a much harder blow. He grunted out as his self-administered blow crushed against his nose and knocked him over. He lay, stunned for a moment but he rolled back onto his knees as a fountain of hot blood poured out of his nose. He put his wrist under the spilling blood and started to work his hands as the rope became more and more moist with his blood.

Furiously he kept trying to slide his wrists against the rope that was slowly expanding. With a grunt, one hand slithered free, then the other. He reached down and gradually got his fingers under one loop in the rope and he leaned his head back and bunched all the muscles in his arms and back in a full effort to snap the rope. Three straining tugs on the rope and it snapped. He tumbled over onto his back. *Free!*

He stood up, blood still dripping from his nose. He tore off a piece of his shirt to stem the flow of blood from his nose. He then sprinted off into the forest in the direction he told Maya to go. He hoped with every part of his being that she was safe inside the cave and the bottom of the falls. *Please be there! Please!*

The sound of the gushing Big Cascade River and falls got louder in Maya's ears as she and The Man made their way into a clearing ledge that peered out over the falls. The falling water filled the sound around them. The Man stopped to look around. He had been to these falls a couple of times as a kid. They weren't easy to get to. He contemplated going up and around the falls. That was too far. They had to go down alongside. That wouldn't be easy either. It was steep and rocky. Maya looked over the pristine falls and past the river basin at the bottom, and then out beyond God's rolling forest up in to the glistening sun that continued to rise in the east unaware of life and death. The thought snaked through her mind of how… how such horrible things could happen amidst so much breath-taking beauty.

*

Raja Virk and his team had been searching for Maya starting late last night when he received a call. Raja was covering his zone moving through the trees, scanning the landscape with the binoculars around his chest. Intermittently, the radio squawked at his hip. He was feeling more and more desperate, along with more and more furious. It was not like his daughter to get lost or to go off riding by herself. She didn't. She went with someone… that freaky kid, that's who. The thought of his daughter with *that* weird looking boy filled him with such fear and loathing. *What was she thinking!* Now, she's in trouble and who knows what kind! His thoughts then went to his mother and what she did with the father he never knew. It was a family curse his Grandfather had told him: The family curse. It had broken his heart. Raja felt his chest tightening, knowing how much like his mother Maya was. *Damn!* The phone call had come from the kid's mother, Maria Phelps, who said that she had found Maya in her house when she came home. Maya had been looking for her son and that she seemed distraught but had an idea where he was. The mom then said that her son had a 'place' where he went sometimes, way out in the forest beyond the biking trails of Phil's.

Raja came to a stop as he came out upon a clearing half way up a heavily forested ridge. From here he could look down onto the Big Cascade River and the basin below. He took a swig off his hydro flask then lifted up his binoculars and scanned across his vision… THERE! Right below him, a hundred yards away, next to the falls, movement caught his eye. MAYA! She was standing next to—*Who's that?*

Some huge, masked man had a hold of his daughter's hand. It certainly wasn't the kid who had come to his front door yesterday. Raja dropped his binoculars back into its case on his belt and he sprinted down weaving through the trees, almost falling head over heels as his downhill speed almost tipped him over.

"Maya!" Raja shouted as he emerged from the trees.

"Daddy!" Maya cried out and tugged against the firm grasp of The Man.

Horrible scenarios flashed through Raja's mind as he ran up to confront the man with the mask on. *He's abducted her! Oh, my God! Has he hurt her?!*

The Man fished the gun out of his pocket and pointed it at the oncoming Raja, and his growl rumbled out:

"Stop right there."

Raja came to a skidding stop and put his arms out. "Okay… Okay, take it easy. Maya, are you all right?"

Maya just nodded her head.

"What are you doing with my daughter? Give her to me… Give her to me, and you can go. Please, just leave her with me. She's an innocent girl. She doesn't deserve this."

"Well, yes and no," The Man sniffed behind his mask. "Turn off your radio. Drop it on the ground and kick it away from you. Do it!"

Raja did as he was told and kicked his radio across the ground. "Please," and emotion clutched at Raja's throat, "I'm begging you. Let her go."

The Man sighed with reality. "I can't… ever do that. I'd like to be sorry but… it is what it is. It was going fine until you complicated things. Now, I can't let you go either."

The Man raised his gun. Maya started screaming and pulling uselessly on The Man's arm.

"MAYA!" came Kougar's guttural, primal shout. He had just caught sight of Maya standing with The Man and his heart boiled over with rage. He had only one imperative, one last act. *HE CAN'T HAVE HER!!!*

Raja, The Man, and Maya, turned to look as Kougar's hurtling shape burst through the trees. The Man flung Maya to the side and pointed his gun at the onrushing Kougar. The Man sighted and pulled the trigger.

"NO! Maya screamed.

"The bullet struck Kougar's shoulder, turning it back with the impact but Kougar's determined bull-rush plunged on and with six quick strides, he collided with a bone-crunching thud right into The Man's mid-section. The Man staggered backward and Kougar kept digging with his legs. With a sickening swiftness, Kougar drove The Man to the edge of the ledge and they then sprawled over, tumbling into empty space down into the falls.

Maya ran to the ledge's edge and screamed in anguish: "No!"

Maya backed up a step and started to jump off. Her father grabbed her arm just in time. She struggled against him for a second.

"Maya, no! That's not the way to help him. Look, come on, we'll head down to the bottom. There's a chance we can get to him in time."

"But Daddy," Maya's desperate voice was frantic, "he's hurt, he won't be able to swim. He'll drown!"

Raja put his arm around Maya and tried to soothe her. "Come on, we'll find him."

Maya let her father lead her off for a few steps and in her mind, her promise resounded: *I'll never leave you alone.* She let her body acquiesce and her father relaxed his grip. In one quick motion she broke away from her father and in three steps, she plunged off the ledge down into the falls.

"Maya no!" And her father's cry echoed down after her as she fell, swallowed by the roar of the falling water. He knew if he jumped in after her, he couldn't help if he died in the fall. He grabbed his radio, barked some urgent commands, and headed down to the bottom of the falls.

Maya hit the frigid gray water and the blow stopped her breath. Her whole body went numb and her mind crashed into blackness. Then, with a few hitching starts, her will kept sparking at the edge of the darkness that had enveloped her: *I can't die... Not yet. Kougar... Kougar.*

Her flowing body hit a rock in the rapids and the pain helped her grab a hold of her consciousness and she push up to the surface where she gasped out for air.

She let the rapids carry her as she scanned the river for Kougar. "Kougar! Kougar!"

Thirty yards down from her she saw what looked like a log bumping off a rock but the light gleamed off of exposed skin. One arm fished out weakly in an attempt to swim and stay afloat.

"Kougar!"

Maya leaned forward and started to swim towards Kougar whose head was below the roiling water. With a strong kick and the prevailing current sped up by the rapids, she made a beeline for Kougar who was starting to submerge under the swirling white water. Maya slammed into him pulling his head up by the back of his shirt as the rapids carried them off.

Kougar sputtered and coughed water as he heaved for air.

"Hang on to me!" Maya shouted above the roaring white water as she ducked under his arm. She looked downstream and saw a quiet pool of water cut off from the rapids by a line of boulders. If she timed it, she could steer them to a rock that lie just inside the churning water, just feet from the still water. She could use the rock as a launching pad, kicking off the rock with both legs to thrust them out of the rapids' current... *Right Now!*

Maya felt her legs bunch against the rock with the impact of their collision, and with a cry, she thrust out with all her strength, pushing them free of the rapids and into the quiescent water. Her right knee screamed in agony. Finally, her feet finally hit the bottom and she grunted as she took Kougar's weight onto her as they stumbled out of the water on the a small sandy bank.

Maya let Kougar down as softly as she could. He struggled with his breath but he was alive. *Alive!*

"Kougar. Kougar," Maya said insistently as she put an arm under his head to prop it up. With her other hand she brushed his wet dreads off his forehead.

"You're... here," Kougar managed in a whisper, his strength draining.

"I told you, I would never leave you," Maya said through a half smile that was full of concern as she caught sight of the bullet hole in Kougar's shoulder and the seeping blood.

"Maya! Maya!"

Maya heard her father's cries. "Over here. Hurry! Kougar's hurt!"

Raja burst onto the scene and knelt down next to Maya and saw what Maya was looking at. "We have to stop the bleeding."

Raja took a handkerchief out of his pocket and pressed it into the wound. "Help is coming. Try to keep him conscious."

"Stay with me Kougar, please," Maya pleaded as she put her face next to Kougar's. "You have to stay with me. Come on," her voice broke with emotion, "you can make it."

Kougar, with his last effort, pushed open his blue eyes as if he had awakened from a deep dream... *those brown eyes... it's a dream. It was always a dream,* the voice said from the blowing winds in his greying mind.

"You... are safe? Safe, now?" Kougar asked lowly, through blood dried lips now moist from the river's water.

"Yes. Safe. We are both safe," Maya said as much as her moist eyes did.

Kougar raised a weak hand up to touch Maya's face, feeling his life force drain away from him, but another force replaced it: joy. He summoned a failing but determined smile that momentarily lit his face with a glow. His arm then folded and dropped and his eyes fluttered closed. *Michaela... I can be with you now... and I want to tell you how happy I am... so happy...*

As if through a funnel of sound, Kougar heard the heavy swoosh, swoosh... like the sound of a giant angel's wings, along with Maya's anguished cries. He watched from the ground as his weightless body rose up into the embracing blue sky.

Michaela

Raja, Lisa, and Maya passed under the entrance into the ICU wing at St. Charles Hospital. Christmas decorations were haphazardly spread around the wing. The colored lights and decorations seemed forced and somber to Maya, not cheerful. She clutched at her mother's hand for comfort as they walked. Nurses crisscrossed in front of them as they made their way down the main hall. Maya glanced into the patients' rooms as she passed, with a slight limp, rooms that were full of machines with blinking and beeping lights, testimony to the fact that here, destiny was in the hands of machines, not in the administrations of humans. It filled her with a heavy foreboding... Would a machine save Kougar? Hospital settings were very familiar to her. Her mother was a nurse and she had volunteered many, many hours at the psychiatric hospital where her mom worked. She had acquired a 'practical distance' from the pain and suffering around her while she worked at the hospital but here, nothing looked familiar to her. Strange sounds, spoken words that came out unintelligible, trickled through her ears like nervous, white noise. Cascading waves of hopeless emotion and stark unrelenting pain filled the mental space around her, flooding over her 'practical distance,' making her want to cringe under the weight of it all.

Down the hall, Maya saw Mr. and Mrs. Phelps standing outside of a room talking with a white-jacketed doctor who had a caring hand on both Maria and Joe as he spoke to them, nodded, and then walked away. Maya dropped her mother's hand, quickened her pace into a hobbling jog, her fear rising with each broken stride. Maria and Joe turned as they heard Maya approaching. Their tightly set faces shared their concerns with her as Maya slowed for a second in front of them and said as she passed: "I have to see him."

Maria understood her husband's stare of... recognition. She had had it too when she first saw Maya. Joe started to reach out a hand to stop Maya but Maria's hand stayed his. Maya passed through the opened door and stopped in front of a curtain that blocked Kougar's bed from view, where she fought to compose herself.

"Hello," Raja began as he walked up, still in his Forest Service uniform. "I'm Raja Virk. I'm Maya's father. This is my wife Lisa." Raja reached out and warmly shook Joe, then Maria's hand. Lisa shook Raja's hand, and as the two mothers locked eyes with one another, they moved passed the handshake and embraced one another.

Raja cleared his throat that suddenly felt dry. "I can't tell you how sorry I am for Kougar's condition. Is... he—?"

"He's alive... right now," Joe said lowly, concern in his voice.

"I want to tell you how... brave your son was," Raja said, still feeling the wonder at what Kougar had done, his selfless sacrifice. *He saved my Maya!* "His courage saved my daughter's life... and mine. He's a remarkable boy."

"Thank you," Joe nodded and said.

"You probably don't know about this, but that I sincerely apologize for misjudging your son so hastily, in such a horribly wrong way. I'm so sorry."

"It's all right, Mr. Virk," Maria began with a slight, ironic smile, "our son has a way of making an unfavorable impression on people. He's... different."

"Well, if that being different is a part of what made him courageous, I'm grateful. My daughter is alive because of him... Can you tell me how he is?"

Maya gathered herself and parted the curtain. She drew in a trembling breath as she took in the sight of Kougar laying, seeming lifeless, between the upraised bars of his hospital bed. The beeping of a heart monitor signaled that he was alive. He sprouted tubes from his arms that snaked into machines, and one was attached to his chest. A ventilator kept him breathing. The top of his head and left shoulder was bandaged. A deep purple bruise ran across his right cheek. A piece of tape was strapped across the deeply colored bridge of his swollen nose.

Maya approached the bed and put a shaky hand to her mouth. "Oh, no… no," she managed in a shaky whisper. "Oh, Kougar… I'm so sorry."

Maya leaned over the bars and put her face next to his and tenderly stroked his cheek. Emotion rocked her low voice.

"Listen, you can't die. You have to live. You have to."

"My son would never let me show him affection," Maria said over Maya's shoulder… "Only now, with him lying there senseless am I able to give him a mother's touch. I can tell you've shared that with him and I'm grateful for that. It means so much to me."

Maria moved up behind Maya and put a hand on her shoulder.

Maya steeled herself, drawing in a supporting breath. "Tell me, what's his condition?"

Maria's voice started out with a tremble. "He was very badly injured. He …."

"Please tell me."

Maria steadied her words. "He has a collapsed lung. His nose is broken. He has a gunshot wound to the shoulder and suffered a severe concussion and head trauma. His jaw is deeply bruised but not broken. They had to induce a coma because of all the swelling in his brain. The doctors are using drugs to keep his temperature down. We are hoping that the hole in his lung will heal and we can take him off the ventilator. He's stable and unstable at the same time. There are no," and her voice faltered, "there are no guarantees. We can only… wait. These next few days will be crucial… dangerous."

Maya tried to take each injury in like a list to be analyzed in an attempt to rank them in terms of what was the most life threatening, but the totality overwhelmed her. She turned and flung herself into Maria's arms.

"We were just getting started," Maya began in anguish, eyes misting. "He's all I've ever wanted. We were made for each other. I know it. I know it. It's not fair. It's not… fair. How could this have happened?"

291

Maria clutched Maya tightly. "There's no 'why'… only now, what you have between each other. Think on that."

"I will. I will," Maya said. "I have to."

They pulled slowly away from their embrace but Maya still held onto Maria's arms. She took a moment to think it through and then asked: "Who is Michaela?"

Maria's eyes flooded with memories. She sighed and slowly moved away from Maya, turned her back and gathered herself. "Michaela," she breathed out. She then turned around to look at Maya.

"Michaela was Kougar's little sister. She was a beautiful, precious child… so much… like… you. We loved her deeply, especially Kougar. He adored her. They were bonded… like twins. She ah, there was an electrical fire… that swept through the house and got to Michaela so swiftly… Nothing could be done. We almost lost Kougar in that fire. He got burned very badly… Things changed after that… You try… you try to do what you can, but it's hard. Pushing aside love won't help… You have to believe in love, you have to accept its power. You have to. It's all there is."

Raja, Lisa, and Joe had entered Kougar's room and had watched the emotional scene before them. Joe and Maria shared a deep, emotional look, one that had been a long time coming… Joe moved over and embraced his wife; an embrace that begged forgiveness and promised a fealty of renewed love that would endure.

A nurse came in behind them. "I'm sorry folks, visiting time is up in ten minutes. Please know that we are watching him very, very closely."

As the nurse spoke, Maya had turned back to Kougar, took his hand in hers, and began whispering in his ear: "Kougar, it's me, Maya. I'm here… I'm here. I'm with you." Then, Kougar's monitoring heart beep quickened for about ten beats. Everyone turned to look at Kougar's heart monitoring display and saw the jump.

"He's knows I'm here," Maya said. "I'm not leaving." She then spoke directly to the nurse. " I'll be staying the night with him."

"Well," and the nurse looked at the cinnamon-skinned Maya with her Indian features, and then at Kougar's white/blond dreadlocks. "Are you a family member?"

"He's my family," Maya said firmly. "Please get the bed."

The nurse looked at Joe, Maria, and Raja. They nodded their heads and the nurse took one more look at Maya.

"Okay."

The nurse left the room and Maya looked at her parents and then to Maria and Joe.

"He needs me. I can help him... I won't have him die alone surrounded by machines."

*

Kougar's spirit flowed around weightless in an empty fog. It finally found an opening and drifted off down a long, grey, obscured hallway that was lined with weather-beaten doors.

He reached out a transparent hand and pushed on a door. It slowly swung open and his spirit glided through. All of a sudden he was lying in a golden meadow... Yes, that same meadow out behind the old house of his childhood that had burned to the ground. It was where he could come and get a look at Michaela and try to get to her but he could never bridge the gap between them.

A strong breeze blew through the tall grass around him and the sun bathed his face in warmth. The grass next to him parted and something moved over him. He couldn't see who it was because of the bright sun in his eyes.

"What are you doing here?" came a child's voice that he knew so well.

Michaela!

Michaela's six-year-old face came into view and blocked out the sun. Her long brown hair waved across the light brown complexion of her face, and her brown eyes looked down on Kougar with affection.

"Michaela" Kougar said weakly.

"Yep, that's me," Michaela smiled. "You know, nobody thought I was your sister."

"That's right," Kougar replied with a slight smile, remembering. "You were the Mexican in the family."

"Like mom said: I surprised everyone... Why are you lying there?"

"I'm here to see you; to be with you."

"Can you get up?"

Kougar tried to stir his body but couldn't gather himself. "I can't."

"Are you feeling pain?"

"No. I don't feel anything. I just can't move... I'm so sorry that you have to be here. It should have been me, not you. I know you are mad at me for not helping you. I'm so sorry. You shouldn't be in this place."

"You know, you were always kind of stupid," Michaela teased. "Look, it's all right ..." And she nodded. "I'm right where I'm supposed to be. You have to believe me," Michaela said with her child's lilt.

"No, no," Kougar said, grief in his voice. "No ..."

"Yes," and Michaela crouched down and stroked Kougar's forehead. "I was always... meant to be here. But you aren't. You have to stop looking for me. I'll see you one day but not now. Not now."

"But I'm ready," Kougar protested. "I'm all right with it... I'm happy."

"No," Michaela's voice turned angry... "Now look, I won't be able to do this again."

"What's that?" came Kougar's puzzled reply.

"I've brought someone for you." And Michaela stepped back into the flowing grass and then returned holding someone by the hand.

Kougar looked up but the glistening sun's prism blocked out the image. Michaela then pulled on the hand she held and the figure came out of the sun and looked down on Kougar.

Maya!

Maya smiled down on Kougar looking so much like—but a different version of a grown-up Michaela... She lowered her hand to Kougar.

"You have to reach for her," Michaela said. "You have to hold on to her. Promise?"

Kougar closed his eyes and his face tightened with pain, and his voice came out weakly: "I've walked on... I can't go... back."

Michaela crunched up her child's face and scowled down at Kougar. "Kougar, if you love me... do it... Do it, or the burning fires will never go out for me... or you."

The Bonding

The different beeps and clicks of the machines would startle Maya awake that first night as she stayed with Kougar. Soon she was able to distinguish which sounds 'meant' something and which ones didn't. But the sound of the ventilator held a special terror for her. She was horrified that the machine would just stop of its own volition, because its unknown mechanized awareness could live-and-let-die in a final gear-shifting decision. She would breathe in the rhythm of the rasping machine sound that blew dry mechanical air into Kougar's lungs. Every time the nurse would come in to administer something, Maya would get up and hold Kougar's hand and speak into his ear, telling him she was there, that she was with him and what they would do together when he woke up and was able to get around. *Together...* With Kougar, the future spread out before her vision in Technicolor possibilities, with all its 'first time' experiences that they would share and their bond would deepen into the only reality they realized: that they were two... yet only one.

After the third night, the nurse came in less and less. Maya's hope sparked. This was a good sign. Maya was happy that her and Kougar's parents had been having dinner every night together, taking comfort in each other's company. Maya stayed with Kougar the whole time. On the fourth day, Maya and Kougar's parents sat in a discussion with the Dr. Keyes who was in charge of Kougar's care. Dr. Keyes' full white beard was neatly trimmed and his blue eyes looked kindly and analytical all at the same time.

The discussion was about when they should try to 'wake' Kougar up and see how he does. The scary unknown was 'how' he would do. How would his memory be? Would there be any problems with his... motor skills?... His personality? There were... unknowns. Dr. Keyes said they had to wake him up, at least for an hour or so, so he could try breathing on his own.

"It's time to see where he is," Dr. Keyes finally said. "We'll do it this afternoon."

Joe and Maria nodded.

"Come on, Maya," Maria, began, "I'll take you home where you can get something to eat, take a nice shower, a change of clothes. I'll pick you back up when it's time to go."

Maya looked at Kougar, afraid to leave.

"He'll be fine," Dr. Keyes said.

"Okay," Maya said through a relenting sigh.

*

Maya stood in the shower, under the cascading warm water finding relief at first for a fleeting minute. Then the 'what ifs' started to work their way into her consciousness and she began to feel cold under the heated spray. She tried to fight off the misgivings. What if her Kougar doesn't return… right? The flood of water opened up her memory of the traumatic events in the forest… Her father said an exhaustive search found no trace of the criminal who had abducted her, and suspected that he was under the falls somewhere, drowned, and that they would eventually find his body.

The scenes and images floated through her mind like a slow, hesitating reel of film: Kougar's beating at the hands of The Man; the feeling as The Man clawed at her hand—and the fear-whipping scenario of what could have happened to her! Her gut wrenched as she saw and felt Kougar go lifeless as he lay on the riverbank, seeping blood from his wounds. She clasped her arms across her chest. A tremor at the corner of her lip started. Emotionally drained tears buffeted by the knowledge of so many life and death close calls, rolled down her weary face and merged with the flowing water. Her legs couldn't hold her anymore. She leaned her back against the shower wall and let herself slide down to the tiled floor where she drew up her knees. Under the water, she cried in a way that she had not allowed herself to. She couldn't hold that dam back anymore.

A merciful sleep of exhaustion came over Maya as she lay on her bed in her thick, white bathrobe. Her long brown hair sprawled out from under her head across the red pillowcase. Rays of sunlight passed through her bedroom window and spilled across her body like a benediction. She twitched a couple of times as if a fitful dream entered the peace of her slumber.

One more twitch... then another, and she sat up, her eyes opening. She sighed, relieved to be in her room. She passed a hand through her hair while the heavy pall of feeling alone... so alone, descended upon her.

Her cell phone then pinged. She started to reach for the phone and then slowed her hand, afraid of what the text might reveal. It was Maria Phelps:

> ... Maya! He's awake! He woke himself up,
> the doctor said. He's asking for you! I'll be
> there to pick you up in a minute! YAY! YAY!...

Maya flashed her thumbs over her Qwerty:

> ...That's wonderful! I'll be ready!..

Maya and Maria, hand in hand, moved quickly through the hospital hallway. Maya still limped, but she led, pulling on Maria's hand.

"Come on," Maya said excited, her face flushed with joy.

They arrived at Kougar's room and slowed down as they made their way, almost cautiously, to Kougar's bedside. Kougar was sitting up in his bed looking out the window. Maya and Maria gave each other looks of hesitation.

"Kougar?" Maya called out.

Kougar turned his head and his blue eyes looked through the lifting fog at them and a small smile began to move across his face.

"Maya. Mom." Kougar's raspy voice made its slow way through his dried lips. The alien sound of his voice froze them for a second. Maya then moved forward and grabbed Kougar's left hand.

"Ugh… Ah, not that one," Kougar rasped. And he offered his right, which Maya held onto tenderly with both of her hands.

"Oh, sorry!" Maya squeaked out.

Maria brushed aside Kougar's long bangs with her hand, caressing his forehead… *He let me…*

"Son, how are you feeling?"

"I feel great and crappy all at the same time," Kougar breathed out. "The nurse said my voice would come back soon. The ventilator dried it out. I still can't take a full breath." He tried and broke into a couple of coughs and said painfully: "coughing, not such a good idea."

"Your father is on his way. It's so great to see you awake."

Maya and Maria just looked at Kougar, their faces full of hope. They didn't know what to say. Should they ask more questions? Cautious, they waited for Kougar. He looked around at all the machines, then to Maya and Maria, then shook his head and sighed.

"How long was I out?"

"Four days," Maria replied.

Kougar looked at Maya and she smiled softly.

"You… you were here the whole time. I know you were."

"I was. I just left a few hours ago and was going to come back with your mom when she told me that you were awake."

Kougar drew a weak hand across his forehead under his matted, dreadlocked bangs. He squeezed his eyes shut for a second as if trying to erase the recent past that filled his mind like an unrelenting dream that kept pushing into reality.

"Man, so many dreams… And it seemed like just a few seconds ago I was lying next to the river and you were looking down on me… and then… here I am."

"Those four days were sooooo long," Maya said, still holding Kougar's hand that she caressed with her thumbs.

Kougar's blue eyes hooded for a moment and his throat worked convulsively until the words came out. "The... Man... What happened?"

Maya and Maria looked at one another.

Maria said: "We can talk about that later, son. It doesn't matter right now."

Kougar stirred in his bed. "I've got to get up. I have to walk."

"Son, I don't think you should. Relax for a while."

Kougar let go of Maya's hand and fished around and found the remote and beeped for the nurse.

A nurse came into the room, her face unconcerned. Routine.

"Demanding, aren't we? You want that steak you were asking for, don't ya?" It's not lunch time yet."

"I'm so starved. Can't wait." Kougar rasped. "But now I want out—I mean up. I want to walk. I need you to unhook me... Please."

The nurse pursed her lips together in mock thought. "Well, if you promise not to walk out of here. Just down the hall. I'll help you. We can't let you fall. You wouldn't be happy about that."

"No, I can do it," Maya interjected, "I got it."

"Yeah, she can do it," Kougar said. "But I am heavy."

"With what we've been through, I think I can manage," Maya replied through a smile as she shook her head and her beauty struck Kougar like a thunderbolt. He looked at her, disbelief in his eyes.

"You're... here ..."

"Of course I am."

The nurse finished taking Kougar off his monitoring equipment and unhooked him from the drip at his arm. She dropped the bars around his bed. The nurse smiled at him.

"The cage is now unlocked."

Kougar slid slowly off the bed putting a wavering foot on the floor. He put the other foot down and swayed, his balance unsure. Maria smoothed out Kougar's patient's gown. Kougar's blond dreads spilled out onto his shoulders. The low-necked robe revealed his burn scars that snaked up along the right side of his throat. His left arm hung in a sling. Maya ducked under his good arm and supported him.

"I gotcha."

They started to move and Kougar stopped and turned around to look at his mom, as the dream of Michaela moved through him like a soft afternoon. He internally watched it for a moment. Then a weary, but relieved smile came to him. He began to feel the slow, creeping release of the burning grasp and crushing weight of the past that had sat on his traumatize boy's psyche like an alien possession.

"Mom… Michaela… is doing all right. She's okay."

Maria nodded and a tiny smile of hope settled across her face. "I'm so glad, son."

Kougar and Maya made their way out of the room, through the open door, and headed down the ICU hallway that was decorated in Christmas ornaments. They walked along enjoying their half embrace. Maya still limped slightly. Kougar noticed and a half grin started across his lips.

"Geez, just look at us: you limping, me looking like I've been in a train wreck. People might think we're not good for each other."

"Too strange and dangerous eh?"

"You've got that right," Kougar rasped.

"Sounds like a perfect match to me," Maya smiled.

Kougar paused and glanced down at Maya who then looked up at him. They locked eyes: deep blue on deep brown. Kougar smiled: "Can I always quote you on that?"

"Yeah, any time."

The ICU wing spilled out into a waiting room with big windows that framed the sunlight that sparkled off the new snow that came with the first big storm of the season. Kougar steered the two of them towards the large window that looked out onto a snow-covered landscape of bare-limbed shrubs and small pine trees. Raising his head, Kougar could see, in the distance, the mountains blanketed in winter against the backdrop of a sharp blue sky. They stood, quiet for a time, the tightening of their half-embrace being the only words between them. Then:

"I remember …" Kougar began haltingly, his words just above a scratchy whisper, but the rest of the sentence went silent as a churning of disjointed images rolled through his mind.

Maya looked up at Kougar, her face and voice cautious. "What do you remember?"

Kougar's gaze probed out into the horizon as the damaged videotape of the traumatic scenes stopped and started up from his memory. But one scene kept finishing the others: the way Maya touched his burnt skin. Kougar turned to look down at Maya and their eyes reached out for each other.

"I remember… you… Just you."

Coming Out

Kougar's convalescence was slow and arduous. His parents had decided that it might be best to hold him out of school and just redo his junior year. But Maya convinced them that she would tutor him and make sure he stayed up with the classwork. He was going to be a senior with her next year, she had vowed.

"But there is a catch to all this help, she said one day with a mischievous grin on her beautiful face as they poured through their science books at Kougar's dining room table.

Unease clouded Kougar's eyes as he studied Maya. "Something tells me I'm not going to like the 'catch'."

"Prom," Maya said with simple conviction. "It's time for our first date."

Kougar's face tightened with fear and apprehension. He shook his dreadlocked head and sighed. Then:

"Prom?" his voice spat out with distaste. "Prom's not for a first date. It's... Its—"

"It's what we're supposed to do... dude," Maya interjected, stating the obvious, that mischievous grin still framing her lovely features.

"But... all those kids," Kougar protested, and got up from the table and paced the floor, his healing shoulder still holding his left arm close to his body for support.

"Yessss," she pronounced slowly, drawing it out.

"Looking at—"

"Yessss," Maya continued.

"I would feel bad for you ..."

"I think we'll be just fine," Maya had said as she moved to embrace Kougar, putting his left arm around her waist as if ready to start a slow dance.

"And... dancing?" Kougar had said weakly, beat down.

"That's what you do at prom, silly," Maya had said, lowly, sweetly.

"My arm is too weak, I won't be—"

"Your arm will be fine."

"But your parents? What are they going to think about... the Prom pictures? You can't do that to them," Kougar pleaded, grasping for any straw of an argument.

"They assumed we were going. Mom has already taken me to shop for a dress," Maya stated, "It's a *fait accompli,*" she tried, attempting her best French accent. "I learned that in my French class. It means: it's a done deal."

"Holy crap," Kougar moaned.

"It's settled then. We're going," Maya had clapped Kougar on the back to end the conversation.

"Well," Kougar had slowly replied in a warning sigh, "I am what I am. What you see is what you get."

"Perfect," Maya said through that lovely smile of hers.

*

Kougar's worst nightmare had come true. Both Maya and Hayden had been elected to be Prom Queen and King. It's not a big deal, Maya had said to him. And now the day had arrived. He sat on the side of the bed in his room, waiting to be 'sentenced,' filled with nervous dread and panicked thoughts. THE STARES!!! *If I don't show... she'll understand. She will. She knows me. All of her friends (hundreds of them) will be freaked out to see her with... me...* The panic wasn't lessening. His cell phone pinged. It was Maya:

> ...Hey handsome! R u all right? Thinking of u... On my way to the Prom Court walk thru. Hayden's been a real butt. See u soon. Can't wait...

He poised his thumbs over the Qwerty, but they froze. He set his phone back down on. *I can't go...*

All the other Court people had their dates with them for the walk thru and First Dance. Prom week had flashed by, so many things to do. Maya hadn't had a chance to see Kougar all week. She gave Kougar the option of coming for the short rehearsal or just to meet up on the floor when the First Dance was announced. She wasn't surprised when he managed to say in a wavering voice that he would, ah, see her on the floor. *What would he look like!* She wondered with anxiety and excitement. All those bushy dreads! She also had to prepare herself for the strong possibility that Kougar wouldn't show. He would probably text her that he was waiting outside in the car. *Yeah, that would totally be his style.*

The Prom was being held at the Tetherow Golf and Country Club on the southwest side of Bend, an exclusive club. The clubhouse looked out over its Links golf course. From its large balcony you could view beyond the course over to the beginning of the Deschutes National Forest. The view continued right over Phil's Trail and up into the mountains; it directly traced the path of the fear-drenched saga that Maya and Kougar had experienced in their battle with The Man.

The lowering sun still blazed in the sky above Mt. Bachelor as Maya walked through the parking lot. She passed a group of yellow-jacketed security personnel who were huddled together getting their instructions for the night. She made her way down the wood paneled hallway and walked into the club's Great Room through the two large doors. She glanced around at the decorations on the walls and the tables that illustrated 'The Night is Right' theme of Mt. Bachelor High's prom logo: a full moon with a rainbow pitching across the big yellow orb. She was pleased that she and her Student Council along with parent volunteers had done such a good job. *Not too gaudy or goofy. Just right.*

She was the last of the Royal Court to arrive. The couples were milling around, talking. Maya had not shown any of her friends the dress she had picked out, nor had she answered the barrage of questions about her date. They badgered her constantly: who was he? There was no mistaking Maddie's booming voice:

"Oh, my God, Maya! That's awesome!"

Maddie and Cheryl, the only other juniors in the Royal Court, hiked up their dresses and scurried over to Maya, their high heels clicking on the floor.

"Wow. Great dress, Maya," Cheryl gushed.

"Damn, girl," Maddie said in mock anger, "I almost picked that one out for me—but it wasn't me. IT"S YOU!"

The girls shared a good laugh.

"Step back, honey, let me take a good look," Maddie commanded.

Maya's long low-necked one shoulder-strapped, plush red formal gown flowed tightly down her athletic body, revealing her slender cinnamon-hued arms. She had a classy choker strand of gleaming white pearls around her neck with a matching pearl wrist bracelet. Her flowing brown hair was done up and two pearl studs glistened at her ear lobes. And from under the red felt hem of her gown, her black lace peep toe pumps peaked out.

"Yeah, girl," Maddie said lowly. "Definitely *hot.*"

"I like red," Maya smiled warmly and said with no pretentiousness through her full red lips.

"And red likes you," Maddie whistled.

"Who's the unlucky guy?" Hayden sneered through a smile playfully as he walked up in his black tux, black bow, black shirt, black cumber bun, and shiny black leather shoes. Maya detected the edge under his teasing tone.

"Hayden!" Maddie scolded.

"You'll find out soon enough," she said, trying to keep hope in her voice. "And he's not lucky. I am."

"Whoa. Well, he'd better rock it."

"He will," Maya said and flashed Hayden an angry glare.

"Hey, don't get defensive about your 'guy', whoever he is," Hayden, mocked, holding up his hands. "I'm just saying... I mean, after all, you're Maya Virk, the Prom Queen."

"Geez, my King," Maddie said quickly, "don't be such a meanie. Come on."

"All right people," Mr. Shultz, who was the Director of the music department at Mt. Bachelor High, called out, flaring up his arms with drama, his jowly cheeks quivering. "Let's get this quick walk thru down. Prom starts in twenty minutes."

Maya checked her phone before she and Hayden were to be introduced as Prom King and Queen. No reply from Kougar. She quickly texted:

…Hey there. I'm almost ready 4 u…☺

She could hear the excited and chirpy noise of the crowd as the students filed into the Great Room. The announcer/DJ was getting to their announcement:

"And now, for the first time in Mt. Bachelor High history, we have two juniors who have been elected Prom King and Queen. Give it up for Prom King Hayden Murphy and Prom Queen Maya Virk!"

The crowd cheered and clapped as they parted to let Maya and Hayden pass by, arm in arm. Maya saw her 'girls,' Carley, Amanda, and Breah, standing to one side applauding with their dates. Alex was there, too, with his date. He stood and nodded and pointed at Hayden, saying: 'you're the man.'

Maya and Hayden made their way up to the stage to sit in their royally draped chairs.

Maya heard Hayden's voice at her ear as he seated her in her chair.

"It should be you and me."

Maya had time for a quick look at Hayden when the announcer called everyone to the dance floor.

"It's now time for the King and Queen to preside over the first dance. Come on out! Let's get this party started!"

The students poured out onto the dance floor with their dates while the Royal Prom Court looked on.

"Shall I tell Maddie you said that?" Maya asked out of the side of her mouth as she glanced over the dance floor. She finally looked over at Hayden, her face annoyed.

Hayden shrugged, not returning her disapproving look. He just gazed outward, watching Alex and his date dance.

"So, did you go slumming at Bend High for your date, or did you find some cowboy at Mountain View? Or maybe you found some college frat boy who missed out on prom when he was in high school?"

"Dude," Maya said sharply, "what's your problem?"

"By the way, you look beautiful, very hot," Hayden said quickly, ignoring her question, turning his head sideways to give her a big, flirty smile. "Come on, permit me a little jealousy. This guy… Let me just say," and Hayden's face softened with a sincerity and wistful sadness that made Maya looked quickly away. "Let me say that I hope he understands what he has. I did."

Maya recovered to quickly say: "I think you and Maddie are cool together. She's right for you… I wasn't. I knew you would like her. She was more 'ready' than I was."

Hayden let out an ironic laugh. "We haven't done 'it', if that's what you're thinking."

"Doesn't matter what I'm thinking. Do what you want."

"I'm waiting… I know what we had—and you do, too. I know you do… Sure, Maddie's great. We have a lot of fun. Yeah, there are girls and girls, but there is only one Maya. I think you're are going to change your mind one day, and I'll be here for you. I'll wait."

"Well, you better get ready for disappointment. I've found someone… Someone for life."

"Now you sound like some movie," Hayden grunted, her words striking him in the gut. He regained his composure and barked a sarcastic laugh: "We're high school juniors, how can you 'know' something like that?"

Maya turned and smiled full in Hayden face. "It's in my genes."

The DJ called out from behind his media stand: "Okay, let's slow it down with a timeless love song and let the Royal Court come and join in the dance." The iconic sound of 'Unchained Melody' by the Righteous Brothers filled the room.

Maddie came for Hayden and with one piercing and longing look over his shoulder at Maya in her red gown, he disappeared into the crowd of slow dancing couples.

Suddenly, Maya felt apprehensive. She looked around; the growing realization that Kougar had become spooked and couldn't bring himself to come began to settle over her. She waded down onto the dance floor, her face beginning to shape with disappointment, while her friends all waved to her or said hi, curiously watching for who was to be her date. She glanced around through the milling couples that danced and turned around her. The haunting love song brought an ache to her heart. She had so much wanted to share this proud 'coming out' moment with Kougar in front of all her friends. She wanted to hold him in her arms, to press her body against his, to reaffirm their fateful bond that had been forged in the relentless need to be with each other, and in the crucible of the gasping, horrible struggle between life and death where they had 'found' each other. They had faced so much together. But ultimately, she knew Kougar. He wasn't coming. It was too much for him.

I was selfish. I shouldn't have put so much pressure on him. It was all about me... Sorry, Kougar... I love you so much...

Through the throng of dancers, she caught a glimpse of someone standing in the corner of the dance floor. His back was to her. Just the brief view told her it wasn't Kougar. The flow of dancers parted and she got a better look: silver suit that lightly glistened in the dance floor lights... tall like Kougar, but the hair... *No,* she said to herself, *not him.*

She looked around and then turned back to regard the grey-suited figure. She tilted her head and heard herself say Kougar's name, not calling it out, but just because it came to her lips.

"Kougar …"

The figure then turned around and Gaius' deep sea green eyes locked onto hers with a glowing intensity. A warm, seductive smile spread across his boy/man's face. The wild dreadlocks were gone. The blond-white hair was cut into a high fade, tight around the sides and back, with a wave of hair combed up and slightly to the side. Gaius wore a formal white shirt with a slim black tie that lay down under his suit coat. A burn scar reached up from beneath his collar and flared out over the right side of his neck.

Maya let out a quick sigh of joy and walked into Gaius' arms.

"I knew 'you' would come."

"I wouldn't miss it for the world," Gaius said through his smile, his Irish accent melodious. "I don't get out of the shadows that often... You know this is not his scene... But it is mine. And, I can dance, he can't."

Gaius enfolded Maya and they started to dance. Gaius moved deftly, smoothly. He led Maya easily, gracefully, with an old world poise. As Maya and Gaius danced, other couples craned their necks to get a look at them. None of them recognized Maya's date. Then, Breah, Carley, Alex, and their dates surrounded Maya and Gaius, gawking. Finally, Maddie and Hayden danced into the circle.

Maddie's grinning face drew close to Maya and Gaius. Maya noticed Hayden's competitive gaze as he stared at Gaius. Maddie nodded her approval.

"Nice snag, Maya. He's hot." She looked at Gaius taking him in with growing appreciation. "You're probably too good for her. I'm Maddie. This is Hayden."

Maya and Gaius looked at each other and a silent communication went between them. Maya turned to glance at Hayden and said:

"This is Kougar."

Hayden's eyes widened with surprise and he stopped something he was about to blurt out. He managed a puzzled, unbelieving question as he looked up at the tall figure in the sleek, hip suit... "You?"

Gaius said nothing but a slight smirk spread across his face and into his taunting green eyes. He shrugged knowingly. Maya smiled with pleasure: 'Coming out' had its rewards...

Gaius and Maya turned back to each other and again, silent words passed between them. Gaius tugged at Maya's waist and they danced off as the others looked after them.

For a moment they said nothing but enjoyed their closeness holding each other tightly. Gaius steered them off the dance floor and through a couple of double doors that led onto the balcony. The sound of the love song followed them through the outdoor speakers.

They continued to dance... The unrequited sunset was beginning to blink out in the ancient clarity of the high desert. The tie-dyed reds and yellows flaring off the weary sun irrevocably diminished as if eternity was shrugging off the moment... it always did, but always... promised another.

"The 'Night *is* Right', is it not?" Gaius purred out in his accent as he looked deeply into Maya's liquid brown eyes.

"With you, always," Maya breathed out lowly.

"Maya... you are too beautiful... a cinnamon rose. Your beauty is one for the ages and believe me," Gaius nodded, "I know a little bit about that."

Gaius then looked out over the flowing view off the balcony and sighed. He seemed to see his long life blowing in the wind like a lone, antique handkerchief hanging from a bare, ghost tree branch.

"How did you develop all that charm in the shadows," Maya said through a smile.

Gaius looked back at her his eyes full of testimony.

"All of the silent time, and enough longing to fill the deepest hole in any star above us, that's how... And now, it's all good."

311

Maya tightened her arms around Gaius and looked up into his eyes with a soft, but growing plea: "You know, you can do your vampire thing now if you want. I think I would like that very much. In fact, I am telling you to *do* it."

Gaius smiled softly and shook his head slowly, but not without some difficulty, and then sighed.

"No… no that would be a waste, but I will take that kiss that has been over a century in coming."

They tenderly leaned toward each other and their lips found what love had stored up for them, and their hearts began to write that voluminously intimate and indescribable narrative that sparked and flamed with new words, words that will never be read by anyone.

Softly, Gaius's lips retreated. He looked at her, a subtle cloud of sadness filling his green eyes.

"I came tonight… to say goodbye. It's time."

"No… no," Maya protested, shaking her beautiful head. "You can't. I understand you. I understand." And her eyes filled with a challenge. "Look, I am 'enough' for both of you. I can handle it."

"Whoa, now, that's quite a thing for a nice young woman to say, and one, I might add, who comes from a very respectable family."

"I'm a girl," Maya pouted.

"Not in my eyes."

"What do you see?"

"What *any* man would see …"

Below the balcony, on the golf course's driving range, a man… a big man, wearing a yellow jacket with 'SECURITY' in black letters across the back, cocked his head up and looked through his binoculars to catch Maya and Gaius in the lenses as they danced. The Man's mouth grew tight with determination and then turned slowly into a crooked grin. He broke off his view and started to slow dance with an invisible partner…

The End

ABOUT THE AUTHOR

Tim Mullane was born in Colorado into a military family. He spent his youth avoiding his Marine Corps Officer father, an experience that inspired his first novel, *Watching the Mudface*. He also authored *Down a Break,* and *The Fire Waits,* the companion novel to *The Piano Mirror's Power.* He attended UCLA where he managed to earn a Ph.D. in History. Tim is an inveterate dreamer, a sometime poet and a life-long writer. For years now he has worked as the Head Tennis Professional for a health club in Bend, Oregon, where he lives restlessly. There's a good chance you might find him on his mountain bike, deep in the Deschutes National Forest spouting off lines of narrative into a hand recorder.

Made in the USA
Charleston, SC
02 July 2016